# DAMNED

## Other Books in the Magnus Blackwell Series

Blackwell: The Prequel (A Magnus Blackwell Novel, Book 1)
Bound (A Magnus Blackwell Novel, Book 3)
Seize (A Magnus Blackwell Novel, Book 4)

## By Alexandrea Weis and Lucas Astor

Death by the River (A St. Benedict Novel, Book 1)

## By Alexandrea Weis

Realm

## Forthcoming from Vesuvian Books

### By Alexandrea Weis

The Secret Brokers

### By Alexandrea Weis with Lucas Astor

The Chimera Effect
4 for the Devil
A River of Secrets (A St. Benedict Novel, Book 2)

# DAMNED

## A Magnus Blackwell Novel: Book Two

Alexandrea Weis With Lucas Astor

Vesuvian Books

Damned
A Magnus Blackwell Novel, Book 1



Cover Credit: Original Illustration by Sam Shearon
www.mister-sam.com

Title Treatment and design layout by Michael J. Canales
www.MJCImageworks.com



ISBN: 978-1-944109-44-8

Vesuvian Books

Published by Vesuvian Books
www.vesuvianbooks.com

Printed in the United States

10 9 8 7 6 5 4 3 2 1

# Praise for the Magnus Blackwell Series

## Awards

**2018 American Fiction Awards**
Winner: Horror: Supernatural/Paranormal—Blackwell

**2018 Feathered Quill Book Awards**
Gold (1st Place) Winner—Mystery—Blackwell
Silver (2nd Place Winner—Adult Fiction—Blackwell

**2018 Readers' Favorite**
Finalist: Fiction—Paranormal—Damned

**2017 FOREWORD REVIEWS: Indies Book of the Year**
Bronze Winner: Horror—Blackwell

**2017 International Book Awards**
Finalist—Blackwell

**2017 Readers' Favorite**
Honorable Mention—Fiction—Supernatural—Blackwell

**2017 Best Book Awards**
Finalist: Horror—Damned

## Praise

"I love the storyline … The author throws fire on many pages through vibrant dialogue and fantastic scene writing … far from predictable, and so satisfying and rewarding."
**~*Feathered Quill Book Awards* Judges' Comments**

"A dark story of passion, revenge, and a Faustian pact ... a guilty-pleasure read that kept me captivated."
**~ Jessica DeBold, *New Orleans Magazine***

"... an intriguing, dark tale [that] seamlessly blends mystery, magic, and matters of the heart to create an enthralling read."
**~Melanie Bates, *RT Book Reviews***

"... the narrative is crisp and has a contemporary ease to it for a flawless reading. The vivid characters are one of the main strengths of this story … a provoking yet absorbing read about the dark, twisted and dangerous part of the human psyche"
***~Readers' Favorite***

"The first word I can think of is WOW ... it filled all the things I would want from a book ... I can't wait for more."
***~Paranormal Romance Guild***

"Damned is absolutely riveting, an absolute page turner. Just when you think the carnival ride is over you discover it's barely begun... If you only read one book, this should be it."
**~Tracy Riva, *Midwest Book Review***

"Damned is full of intricate characters, voodoo, and a luxurious setting that will steal your breath away. You'll want to follow Magnus and Lexie to Hell and back, and that's stunningly likely."
**~Mercedes B. Yardley, Bram Stoker Award-Winning Author of *Little Dead Red***

# Some Monsters Never Die

# Chapter One

## 2015

Small rocks knocked against the undercarriage of the red Volvo as it traveled along the bumpy gravel road. Boxes crammed the roof rack, the back seat overflowed with luggage, and the U-Haul trailer had a bungee cord across the doors to keep the contents from bursting out.

In the passenger seat, Lexie squinted to read the map on her cell phone.

"You must have passed it."

Will Bennett turned to her. "I know where I'm going, baby. This leads to the house."

Lexie scanned the dense brush at the side of the road. "What fucking house? We're in the middle of nowhere."

Will scowled. "Don't curse, Lexie."

"You curse, so why can't I?"

"Because it isn't ladylike. And I never drop f-bombs."

Lexie reached across the console and wrapped her arms around his neck. The first time she'd met him at a job site in Boston, his muscular build had been the first thing that attracted her. But as their friendship deepened, she realized the caring man beneath was a hell of a lot sexier than his tight ass and square jaw.

"Still want to marry me, Mr. Bennett?"

"You know I do."

Lexie kissed his lips and returned to her seat. "I'm glad you're free from that sadist, Jake Forrester. Forrester and Whitney were sucking you dry."

"But I sure liked the steady paycheck."

"Your clients are going to follow you." Lexie eyed the remote location beyond her car window. "If they can find you."

"There she is." Will leaned forward in his seat. "Altmover Manor."

Lexie searched the sky through the windshield until she spotted the two stone chimneys. She waited as the roofline came into view. Steeply sloped and covered with gray slate, the enormity of the structure hit her. A blend of Colonial and Greek Revival architectural styles, the stone structure's square facade had large Colonial windows with white shutters. Balconies jutted from the second and third floors while a porch extended along the front. Six Corinthian columns, in desperate need of a fresh coat of paint, added to the home's distorted presentation.

"Something, huh?" Will beamed.

Lexie forced a smile, the God-awful hodgepodge of styles was making her feel woozy. But Will looked so proud of himself she didn't have the heart to tell him his pride and joy was downright ugly. She took in a few gulps of air. "How did you find this place?"

Will maneuvered the car to a stop in front of the long steps. "A client, Bob Grenier, told me about the place. His bank has been quietly shopping for buyers."

Sunlight glistened on the leaded-glass front doors as Lexie inspected the porch. "How long has it been empty?"

"More than sixty years. The last person to live here was some old woman. Bob told me his bank has maintained the property for over a hundred years."

Lexie shifted in her seat. "Over a hundred years? Since when do banks maintain properties?"

Will switched off the engine. "One of the bank's owners, Miles Parker, had a daughter, Katherine, who married the man who owned this estate. Katherine and her husband died leaving no heirs, so her father inherited the house and all her husband's assets. His heirs made the bank hold the property until several years ago when they agreed to sell."

"What changed their mind?"

He unbuckled his seat belt. "For over a century, the Parkers had a trust set aside for maintenance of the home. When the money ran out, they auctioned most of the furniture to pay for the upkeep. The trust has kept up the general repairs, but the place needs updating. The wiring is old, so is the plumbing. Not to mention most of the interior design dates to the turn of the last century."

Across the gravel drive, Lexie spotted a ramshackle cottage with peeling yellow paint. "Does that belong to the estate?"

Will shifted around in his seat. "It's the caretaker's cottage. The bank hired a guy named Remi to stay on at the house when local teenagers started giving them problems."

"What kind of problems?"

Will reached for his door handle. "Break-ins. The kids on the island challenged each other to spend the night inside."

"Why? Is it haunted?"

After he shoved his car door open, Will glanced back at her. "Houses are never haunted. Ghosts aren't real; they're just fodder for Halloween decorations."

Lexie stood from the car. Something about the house set her teeth on edge.

An icy breeze enveloped her, and Lexie pulled her brown cardigan closer. In a second-floor window, a mist pressed against the glass, drawing Lexie's attention. The slightest hint of a figure formed.

"Hey, you ready to check out our new home?" Will nudged her.

Lexie flinched and narrowed her gaze on the second-floor window. The figure was gone. "How did they die?"

"How did who die?"

"Katherine and her husband."

Grabbing her hand, Will bounced up the steps, the twinkle in his eyes and smile on his face contagious, as he kissed her. "It was a long time ago."

Will wrestled keys from the front pocket of his jeans, bobbing his black eyebrows at her, making Lexie chuckle. He put a key in the lock, but the deadbolt groaned, refusing to cooperate.

Lexie sighed feigning impatience kicking at the accumulated leaves while Will struggled with the door.

After he put his shoulder into it, the front doors opened. Leaves fluttered and swirled around her, carried by a rush of air. Like a dust devil, the small cyclone swept from the porch into the home, depositing leaves in the center of the cold marble floor.

A jolt of electricity shot through Lexie. The hair rose on the back of her neck. She hesitated at the threshold. Something was wrong.

"Wait," shouted Will. "I need to carry you over the threshold." Before she had time to protest that they weren't in fact married yet he scooped her into his strong arms and strode into the house.

The piercing screech of an alarm echoed throughout the foyer. Will dropped her to her feet rushing to a console on the side of the front doors.

Lexie followed him in and checked out the alarm pad. "An alarm? Why do they have an alarm if they have a caretaker?"

Will punched in the numbers written on the key ring and the shrill alarm cut off. "The bank installed the alarm to deter the vandals. Remi told me it makes a lot of noise, but won't summon the local sheriff."

She stayed in the light coming through the open front doors. "I still don't understand how you got the place at such a cut-rate price."

"The bank was eager to sell. I made a lowball offer and they jumped on it. I was shocked, but this is the kind of house I've always wanted to own. I didn't want to pass it up."

Darkness shrouded the foyer, and a tingle ascended from Lexie's gut. Something small and dark dashed across the foyer floor.

*Holy shit! What was that?*

"Will, are you sure about this?"

He eased his arms around her. "I'll admit, we've got tons of hard work ahead of us, but it'll be worth it in the end." He kissed her forehead before seeking out the light switch.

"How many bedrooms?"

"Eight with six bathrooms. Two were updated in the eighties. So at least we'll have a decent bathroom to use." He flipped a switch, and several lotus-shaped sconces on the walls bathed the room in a warm light.

Lexie could not shake the sense of gloom lingering in the house. It was as if a great sadness filled the home and had seeped into every piece of peeling wallpaper and every broken light fixture.

Light played off the crystals overhead, causing shards of color to play along the walls, and she looked up.

Attached via a rusted chain to a medallion of interlocking rose vines, hung and enormous chandelier, there were a few missing crystals and appeared bent in sections, but it offered Lexie a glimpse of the home's bygone elegance.

"Where is the chandelier switch?"

Will's footfalls cut through the silence as he made his way across the foyer. He flipped several switches, but nothing happened. "Lights in several rooms, and an assortment of fixtures throughout the house, don't work."

She went to the wallpaper and ran her fingers along flowers of gold thread with leaves outlined in black. "This … this looks like Candace Wheeler's design."

"Most of the interior hasn't been updated since the Blackwells lived here. The place is filled with such nuggets."

"Will, do you know how rare it is to find an original design of hers nowadays?"

He took her hand, pulling her deeper into the home. "I knew you'd get excited once you saw the inside."

She explored the yellowed and chipped plaster ceiling. "Yeah, I'm getting there." She wasn't lying either the despite the uneasy feeling in her stomach the house was an interior designers dream, from the marble floors to the high ceilings her mind began to conjure endless possibilities.

Will wandered across the foyer. "The foundation is sound and the roof doesn't have any leaks. Until we get in these walls to start working on wiring and plumbing, we may not know the complete story, but there wasn't anything major on the inspection."

She frowned at the damaged ceiling. "Are you sure you didn't bite off more than you can chew?"

"We will be fine, baby. Stop worrying." Will led her to the black walnut staircase past the foyer. "Wait until you see this."

Carved into the banister's bottom newel post was the head of a dragon, its jagged teeth bared. The empty eye sockets glared into the foyer as if warning strangers to stay away. A railing with scales sculpted into the wood wound up the staircase, resembling a serpent's back.

Lexie paused, admiring the dragon's head. "Will, this is stunning."

"The house has dragons everywhere."

She dug her fingers into the empty eye sockets. "Was there anything here before?"

"I wondered the same thing."

The dragon's head suddenly moved beneath her hand. Lexie's heart rocketed to her throat, and she jumped back, staring at the decorative piece.

"What is it?" Will came up to her, putting his hand on her arm.

"The dragon moved."

"The wood might be rotted." Will tested the banister by shaking it, but the dragon's head never budged. "It seems sound."

Lexie wrung her hands. "I'm telling you it moved."

Will shrugged it off. "I'll check it later. I have a feeling a good bit of the wood will have to be replaced. It's a shame there aren't any old pictures of the house lying around. Might help us with the restoration."

Her line of sight ran up the marble inlaid staircase steps, made to look like piano keys. "What about the attic? Anything in there that could help?"

"I checked the attic during the inspection. There are a ton of boxes, trunks, damaged paintings, and some broken furniture, but someone has to go through it to see what we have. Some of the stuff goes all the way back to the early eighteen hundreds."

Lexie shuddered. "By someone, are you suggesting me?"

"I was hoping you would volunteer. I want this to be our project, baby. And when we finish, our home will mean so much more because we worked on it together."

Lexie didn't object as he put his arm around her and ushered her down the narrow hallway along the stairs. She wanted to, but she also didn't want to derail his excitement.

"Over here is the living room." Will dashed across the dusty hall floor, his footsteps reverberating around them. He eagerly pulled at the tarnished brass doorknob on a set of arched doors.

The creak of the doors opening carried throughout the empty first floor, heightening Lexie's unease.

Will turned an old-fashioned light switch and a crooked teardrop chandelier flickered before it came on.

Lexie's discomfort melted when she examined the oak-paneled walls with rosettes dotting the seams.

"Oh, wow. What a great room."

She toed a deep gouge in the parquet floor, pained to find such a beautiful design marred by neglect. More of the same interlocking rose vines from the foyer circled the border of the plaster ceiling, their detail eroded by time. Silence hung in the room as she turned toward the fireplace. Lexie's breath caught in her throat as her gaze swept up the mantle.

Centered above was a life-sized portrait of a man. He stood amidst the craggy land surrounding the home, a hazy fog enveloping the sky behind him. A black, fitted coat tapered from his broad shoulders to his narrow waist. A white ascot bulged beneath his chin, and a red vest added a splash of color. His squared jaw and cruel, thin lips rested beneath a long, aristocratic nose and gave the portrait a sinister feel.

"What a fascinating painting. Who is he?"

"Magnus Blackwell. He was Katherine Parker's husband. Altmover Manor was his family home."

Lexie wasn't certain whether it was the man's arrogant bearing or the cruelty in his green eyes, but something about the likeness unsettled her.

"There are portraits of him throughout the house. None as good as this one," Will said.

With high-cut black boots firmly dug into his land, Magnus Blackwell gripped a dragon's head fixed atop a long cane. Similar to the newel post in the foyer, the red eyes peered out as if cursing all those who dared approach the painting.

"Another dragon?" she commented, moving in closer to get a better look at the cane.

"Yeah, I noticed it, too."

"He's an angry man. The painting reeks of his attitude."

Will's rumbling laughter echoed throughout the room. "Not another one of your feelings. You know how uncomfortable I get when you talk about that stuff."

She turned toward him like an enraged lioness. "Who told you not to get on the flight to DC for your conference three months ago?"

He strolled up to her, grinning. "You mean *begged* me not to get on the flight."

"Your plane crashed, Will."

He wrapped her in his arms. "No, it ran off the runway, and the kitchen caught fire, but no one died."

"Why can't you admit my feelings are right?"

He kissed the tip of her nose. "Because I was raised to believe we live in a practical world where there's nothing mystical going on. I'll support you in anything you want to do, Lexie, but I have a hard time buying anything supernatural."

"What will you do if our kids are born like me? My

grandmother said the gift could get passed down. The same way I got it from her. How will you handle it if they have strange abilities?"

Will stepped back and held up his hands, calming her. "I will love our children no matter what. The same way I love you. Superpowers and all. So when are you going to give me those lottery numbers I need to win a fortune so we can redo this house in style, and," he held her left hand, "buy you an engagement ring?"

"I already told you, my ability doesn't work like that." She kissed his lips. "And I don't need a ring, just you."

"I'm still going to get you one … someday. If this place doesn't kill me first."

Lexie clasped his hand. "Show me the rest of the house."

The boyish enthusiasm returned to his bright brown eyes as he led her from the living room. "Wait until you see the view from the courtyard."

A wisp of smoke rose from the parquet floor at the edge of the living room. It swirled and twisted as it formed a shape. When the smoke settled, the light from the living room shone through the apparition of a man as he stood in the doorway. He tipped his head to the side, watching as the couple laughed and strolled down the hall. They dipped out of sight and the misty man's black boots and long black coat materialized. His dirty-blond hair and piercing green eyes were exactly like the portrait above the fireplace. Even his sneer was the same, displaying all the disdain Magnus Blackwell had frequently expressed in life.

He peered down at his empty hands and a low growl carried throughout the hall.

Magnus glimpsed his portrait over his shoulder, sighing as his eyes settled on the dragon cane.

"I feel naked without you, old friend."

A blur of gray shot across the living room doorway. Magnus turned and found a gray Maine Coon cat with a ruff of long hair sitting in the doorway. The animal hissed as it stared at him with its stormy green eyes.

"Don't push your luck, my friend," he said to the creature. "I tend to do terrible things when someone makes me angry."

# Chapter Two

Waves slammed into the rocky shore below as Lexie peered over the side of a sheer cliff to the sea. A spray of saltwater rose into the air as her stomach fluttered.

"You've got to be kidding me. The Atlantic Ocean is in our backyard."

Will raised his head to the rear of the home. "Yeah, gonna make this place a bitch to heat in winter."

"We can sleep in front of the big fireplace to stay warm." She put her hands on the rusty iron railing. "It will be cozy."

Will's snort carried around the courtyard. "Have you ever wintered in Maine?"

"No, but I'm sure—" The railing moved beneath her hands.

Will pulled her away from the edge and into his arms. "Are you okay?"

Her heart thumped against her chest as the furious beats reverberated in her ears. Things seemed to go from bad to almost catastrophic with the house. She put on a brave smile for Will.

"No harm done."

"From now on this courtyard is off-limits until I get the railing fixed." He ushered her toward the fountain at the center of the courtyard.

Lexie's curiosity forced her attention to return to the ledge. "Why on earth would anyone build a house near such a sheer drop?" The sharp twinge resurfaced in her stomach, making her tremble.

"You got me." Will scoured the glassed-in conservatory at the rear of the home. "This house is a puzzle. It's an odd blend of styles." He nodded to the green dragon mosaic on the courtyard floor. "You find courtyards mostly in French architecture, like in New Orleans. Not Colonial style houses in Maine." He patted the fountain's edge. "I found the original brass plate of the manufacturer under the pump housing at the bottom. It was made in New Orleans."

Lexie cringed at the sludge in the pond. "Seems like someone had a thing for New Orleans."

"And dragons," he reminded her.

"What are you getting at?" Will examined the exterior of the structure.

"Will, what is it?"

"I'm trying to find the theme. When you build or renovate a house, plans center around a theme, but this place has dragons, New Orleans, Greek Revival, and Colonial architectural styles."

Lexie surveyed the ornate fountain. Elegant and refined with its angry green dragon mosaic—the same green in that portrait's eyes. The house was like him, a juxtaposition of elegance and menace. "It isn't a theme so much as a person."

She recalled the man in the portrait over the mantel in the living room. The way his eyes cut through her, the anger in his stance—he made a statement with the painting. The house belonged to him.

"I bet that guy is the culprit. The one in the living room painting. The dragon cane he held meant something to him. Maybe the dragons came after he got the cane."

Will arched a dark eyebrow at her. "Is this another one of your feelings?"

Lexie wanted to share her suspicions with Will, but sensed he'd had enough of her "feelings."

"Nah," she lied, sounding upbeat. "He looked like the kind of asshole who expected the world to revolve around him."

Will chuckled. "He came from a different time when men were men and women knew their place in the world." Grinning at her scowl, he playfully smacked her backside. "Cut the guy some slack." He clasped her hand. "Let's check out the upstairs."

Will escorted her to the glass conservatory doors. As they reached the edge of the courtyard, the twinge in her gut progressed to a nagging burn. The sensation urged her to turn around. She glimpsed the fountain, and a cold breeze cut through her clothes. The green dragon in the mosaic seemed to wiggle. Lexie blinked, rubbing her eyes. The drive up here had really taken its toll. The creature continued to writhe rising from the courtyard, its massive head swung towards her, staring with ferocious red eyes. She stumbled to the side.

"Hey." Will caught her in his arms. "You okay?"

Her focus returned to the dragon mosaic. The creature was once again a portrait on the ground. She put her hand over her racing heart. "I think all these dragons are getting to me. I'd swear I'm seeing things."

Will held her to him. "Yeah, they creeped me out at first too."

Lexie doubted she would ever get used to the strange house and the weird vibes it gave off. Something wasn't right with Altmover Manor, but she had to keep silent for Will's sake. The house was his dream come true, and she wouldn't ruin it for him.

In the second-floor hallway, they passed broken sconces on the walls. The dingy burgundy carpet and cracked baseboards didn't fill Lexie with much hope for the rest of the house. Movement out of the corner of her eye, and she jumped. She caught a glimpse of gray fur and big green eyes.

*Is that a cat?*

At the end of the corridor, Will stopped before an ash-stained door.

"You're gonna love this."

"What, more dragons?"

"No." With a loud "Ta-Da," he shoved the door open.

Lexie stepped into the room, and Will flipped on the lights. Her dread retreated as the bright royal blue wallpaper and plaster ceiling with painted olive branches greeted her. Placed between the two Colonial windows on the far wall, a king-sized, four-poster mahogany bed beckoned. A shiny two-tiered brass chandelier hung from the ceiling and the dresser, night tables, and chest of drawers from their cramped apartment back in Boston had magically arrived.

"When did you do all this?"

Will smiled from the doorway. "I had the moving company collect our stuff while we took the leisurely drive up here. Why else would I want to stay overnight in Portland? To sightsee? I had to buy time so the furniture could arrive before we did." He joined

Lexie in the room.

"But that's not our bed."

"It was one of the pieces not auctioned off." Will pressed down on the new blue bedspread and winked at her. "The mattress is new." He strode across the room to a half-open door. "In here's the master bathroom with a new shower stall, double vanity, and an old-fashioned claw-footed bathtub. The hot water works, as do the electric heaters."

"How did you find time to do this?" The ceiling captured her attention. "And the decorations … this room is already renovated."

"Remi, the caretaker, and I did it the weekend I came for the closing. He set up the furniture yesterday so we would have a room to sleep in our first night here." Will rocked on his toes, proud of his accomplishment. "I, ah, asked him to stay on and help with the renovations."

Lexie's qualms about taking on the project intensified. "Will, can we afford that?"

"I offered to pay him a monthly salary, but he refused. So, we negotiated. He agreed to help with the renovations if we let him stay on in the caretaker's cottage rent free and cover his groceries and gas."

"What kind of person works for groceries and gas?"

"Who cares what he'll work for? He's handy and knows a lot about older homes. Parker and Mills Bank wouldn't have hired him to care for the house if he had a criminal history."

"I guess if he did all this for you … I can't believe you got so much done in such a short time."

He cozied up to her. "You weren't crazy about moving to Maine and taking on a project of this size. I want you to know I appreciate everything you're giving up so I can realize my dream."

Lexie wrapped her arms around his neck. "It's our dream. And so far, I like the house."

Will pulled away, rubbing his hand over his chin. "Yeah, well, you haven't seen the kitchen yet."

"It can't be that bad."

Will turned for the bedroom door. "Let's just say, I've saved the best for last."

"I'm gonna puke," tumbled out of her mouth before she walked into the room.

Last updated in the fifties, the kitchen had lime-green cabinets, white and beige-tiled countertops, and a white ceramic double sink wide enough to wash a golden retriever.

Will walked to the white refrigerator. "This is new, as is the stove."

Smirking, Lexie rested her hand on her hip. "What's the point? You hate my cooking."

"I don't hate it; I prefer we not eat it too often."

"Will, if I spend too much time in this kitchen I will end up killing someone." She noted the new appliances sitting on the counter. "At least you got a new coffeemaker."

"I know how much you love your coffee, baby."

Lexie pouted her lips and folded her arms. "You can't always bribe me with coffee."

He eased up to her, pulling her against him. "When the coffee runs out, there's always sex." He placed a soft kiss on her neck behind her ear making her tingle.

"Now you're talkin'."

"Hello?" A deep voice came from the hallway.

Will backed away from her, sighing. "Perfect timing." He ran his hands through his hair. "We'll be right there, Remi."

They hurried out the kitchen door and along the main hall. When they reached the foyer, a dark-skinned man holding a bottle of champagne waited beneath the giant chandelier, staring at it, grinning.

Lexie tracked his gaze, and another electrifying twinge jolted through her. Transfixed, she could not look away while the light fixture swayed as if moved by a passing breeze.

"Remi, this is my fiancée, Lexie Arden." Will poked her with his elbow.

Big enough to be a defensive end for any NFL team, the tall man before her had an intimidating presence. There was something else about the man. She sensed a strange darkness inside of him. *What is up with this guy?*

She held out her hand to him. "It's a pleasure to meet you, Remi …?"

"Glapion," he announced in a deep bass voice matched by his powerful handshake. "Welcome to Altmover Manor." Remi held up the bottle in his hand. "I went to West Tremont to pick up the champagne for you two."

She hadn't expected that. "Thank you."

Will took the champagne from him. "I'll put it in the fridge."

"What do you think of the house, Ms. Arden?"

"Please call me Lexie."

He cocked his head. "What does the Lexie stand for?"

She sized up the way his dark brown eyes contrasted against his bright-white smile. "My given name is Alexis."

He nodded. "Lexie, I like that. *Très jolie.*"

Impressed by his French, Lexie asked, "Where are you from?"

"New Orleans." He stuck his chest out with pride. "I relocated to Georgia after Katrina. The black water destroyed my home, so I had nothing to go back to. I worked construction jobs up the East Coast until I happened on the job with the bank taking care of this place."

"Will didn't tell me you were from New Orleans." Lexie raised her eyebrow as she glanced at her fiancé.

Remi pointed a long finger at Lexie. "I like her. She looks like the type that'll keep you on your toes. My Aunt Titu says, 'a good woman keeps a man on his toes, a bad one keeps him in bed.'"

Will regarded Remi with a playful gleam in his eyes. "Your aunt got it backward."

Remi winked at him. "I think so, too." His herculean laughter rocked the foyer.

Will took a step toward the open front doors. "I didn't see your truck out front when we pulled up."

"I hoped to be here to greet you, but you two arrived earlier than expected."

"Yes, Lexie was in a hurry to leave Portland this morning." Will placed his hand on her shoulder. "She's the reason we arrived ahead of time."

Leaves swept into the foyer settling on the marble floor. An eerie silence followed. The electric feeling dancing beneath Lexie's skin since first entering the house roared to life. She wanted to run through the open doors and put the foreboding sensations behind her, but she had to stay. She'd vowed to support Will.

"Remi, why don't you finish showing Lexie the house while I start unpacking the car?" Will's deep voice resonated throughout the foyer, comforting Lexie. "After, Lexie and I can head to West Tremont for supplies."

"You'd better get to town before dark," Remi counseled. "On the radio, they announced a storm's on the way."

"We have time. Anyway, you know more about this place than I do."

"Sounds good to me." Remi's turned to Lexie. "Have you seen the ballroom, yet?"

Lexie widened her eyes. "There's a ballroom?"

After Will dashed to the kitchen with the champagne, Remi escorted Lexie down the hallway toward the rear of the house.

"Will seems happy here. While doing some of the initial work after the closing, he talked about his plans."

She clasped her hands together, nervous to be alone with the peculiar man. What did she know about him? What did Will know about him? To Lexie, Remi felt off, like the house around them.

"Yes, he showed me our bedroom. You did a wonderful job. Thank you for offering to help Will. I was worried about him tackling this project on his own. It's a huge house."

"Yes, it is. But restoring old homes is a passion of mine. I grew up renovating them with my father. In this mansion, there are so many incredible details to preserve."

"Details or dragons?"

Remi's soulful laugh traveled the hallway. "Yes, there are a lot of dragons here. Did you know the dragon is sacred in voodoo?"

Lexie stopped in her tracks, disturbed by his question. "How do you know about voodoo?"

"In New Orleans, one can't help knowing about voodoo. It's part of the culture there influencing everything."

"You must have had an interesting childhood." Lexie moved along the hallway. "Is that what you did back in New Orleans? Restore old homes?"

"No, ma'am. I worked for the coroner's office as a lab technician. An interesting job, but not as depressing as what my brother does. Poor Emile works as a detective for the New Orleans Police. He's stationed right in the heart of the French Quarter."

"Your job sounds more disturbing than your brother's. I don't know how you dealt with all those bodies." She shivered and ran her hands over her arms.

"The dead have never bothered me."

She explored his face, for an instant, becoming spellbound by his long black lashes.

"I suspect you're comfortable with the dead as well."

"Me?" she croaked in surprise.

"You noticed the chandelier swinging in the foyer."

"You saw it too!"

He stopped before an arched doorway with a wide oak door. "I've seen many strange things in this house since I arrived. But I was born with the gift, as I suspect you were." He pushed the door open.

"What gift?"

He stepped in the doorway. "You sense things. Have strange feelings around people and places. And you've had an uncomfortable feeling building inside you since the moment you stood in front of this house."

"So there is something wrong with this house," she whispered. "It isn't just me."

Something ran past, heading deeper into the dark hallway. She caught a glimpse of gray fur and a tail.

"Remi, are there any cats in this house?"

"An abandoned building like this? It wouldn't surprise me."

He ventured into the dark room, a flash of light startled Lexie. Easing around the door, she gasped.

The light hardwood floors had fared better here than in the rest of the house. Copper-inlaid panels in the ceiling reflected the light from the three, eight-tired crystal chandeliers. The white and gold wallpaper had dulled outlines from where large frames had hung in the past.

"This is stunning." Painted white, the crown molding had small instruments stenciled in gold. "I can imagine the parties they had in here."

"Yes, I'm sure Magnus Blackwell had many lavish events."

Lexie could almost feel the laughter and gaiety the room had seen throughout the years. It wasn't at all dreary like the rest of the house. Was it because this had been the Blackwells' favorite room? Or was there something else going on?

"What happened to Magnus and his wife? How did they die?"

He placed his hands behind him and walked toward a set of tall windows. "Rumor has it they were found together on the cliffs below the courtyard."

"But how did they get there?"

"I'm not sure. It happened during the Blackwells' first wedding anniversary celebration." Remi fixed his gaze on the ocean view. "The morning after the party, they discovered Magnus and his wife at the base of the cliff. Must have taken them a while to find the couple after the ruckus."

"What ruckus?"

"The architect Magnus hired to renovate the house committed suicide during the party."

"Suicide?" The distaste of his disclosure rattled her. "Why did he kill himself?"

"It's a mystery." Remi stood back from the window. "He hanged himself from the chandelier you saw swinging."

The hairs on Lexie's arms stood up and a tingling rose up her spine. "How do you know all this?"

"Island gossip. People around the island have lots of stories about this old house. I'm not sure if any of them are true."

"There must be a way to find out. Newspaper articles, old records, something to shed light on what happened here. Perhaps the island's library has something."

"I'm sure they do, but no one cares anymore, except for the ghosts of course."

She paused, soaking in the confirmation of what she'd suspected all along. *See, I told you*, her inner voice chastised. *You need to listen to me more.*

"Does Will know the house is haunted?"

Remi furrowed his ridged brow. "He doesn't believe, Lexie. Ghosts to a nonbeliever are the ravings of an overactive imagination. Will wants to cover the scars on this house with a fresh coat of paint and move on. I would wager it won't be the first time you've dealt with spirits."

"What have you seen in this house besides the swinging chandelier in the foyer?"

"Nothing ever happened until today. The chandelier was the first hint I had of any presence. I've seen other things, but …" He shrugged. "They're fleeting."

Lexie got an uncomfortable vibe from Remi. His words came across as truthful, but the strange darkness within him confused her. "Why did something happen today?"

Moving away from the window, he grinned. "Perhaps the chandelier in the living room moved because someone wants to get your attention."

"You mean the ghost of the guy who hanged himself from the chandelier?" Her stomach dipped as she pursued him to the ballroom entrance. "But why me?"

Remi waited at the door. "I can't answer that. But I get the impression this house has been waiting for you."

"For me? I don't understand."

Remi tipped his head to the side as if listening. "Will is coming."

"Hey, come on you two. Enough sightseeing." Will shouted from the foyer. "We've got loads of unpacking to do."

# Chapter Three

Lexie, Will, and Remi stood in the driveway as a few gray clouds rolled in. Shades of pink, red, and orange streaked across the sky, in the distance thunder rumbled. Lexi shuddered at the sound, the coming storm reflected her mood. It was as if the hope she fought so hard to hold on to could not stand up to the dark forces closing in around her.

Remi sniffed the air. "You two better hurry and get to West Tremont if you plan on getting back before the storm."

"Do you need us to get you anything?" Lexie asked.

Remi backed toward the steps. "I'm fine. I've got enough in my pantry to last for a while."

A nudge of guilt ate at her. She should give the man a break and dispel her suspicious. "Then how about joining us for dinner. I could whip us up something to celebrate."

Remi's chuckle reverberated between the large home and the cottage. "No, I don't want to intrude. You two need to be alone for your first night in your new home. And Will has already warned me about your cooking."

Will snickered behind her. She turned and gave him a dirty scowl.

"I simply said your cooking could use some work, baby."

Grinning, Remi waved them to their car. "Get going. I've got some things I can do around here. I'll be gone by the time you return."

Will came around to her side and nudged her elbow. "When we get back, we'll celebrate."

He opened her door, before getting in the car, she glimpsed the second-floor window where she'd seen the misty presence. To her relief, nothing happened.

"What are you looking at?"

She faced Will, sporting a serene smile. "Not a thing."

Remi stood on the porch while the red Volvo turned off the driveway, heading to the main road. After the car had disappeared behind a clump of trees, the left side of his lips tugged upward in a baleful smile.

"You've been quiet."

A glittering beam of light shot up from the ground and a man emerged from it. Magnus Blackwell came into view. He was like his portrait in the living room, but without his dragon cane.

"You don't expect me to scare them to death, do you?" His form solidified into a human presence. "The living need to be gentled into the likes of me."

"Don't waste my time playing games." Remi folded his arms. "A few parlor tricks with dragons isn't going to scare the girl."

Magnus's chuckle wafted about the porch. "And what exactly are you playing at? You're not a handyman."

Remi glowered at the apparition. "Find the cane, Magnus. The girl has the gift. Use her to get me what I want, or I will make sure you're bound to this place forever."

Magnus floated around him. "I sense the black soul inside you, but why do you need her?"

"There are limits to what I can do to the living." Remi cast his eyes to the driveway. "However, this girl has a power like I've never encountered. I want to see what she can do, and I need you to motivate her."

"What if she can't get what you're after?"

Remi turned toward the open front doors. "Make sure she does, for both your sakes." He slipped inside.

Magnus took in the magnificent view of the surrounding land and shook his head. The gray Maine Coon cat slinked onto the porch taking a seat next to him. He stared at the lion-like creature.

"You do realize this is not how I planned to spend eternity."

The cat hissed at him.

Magnus chuckled. "My sentiments exactly."

After a short drive through the hilly terrain, Lexie and Will arrived in West Tremont. The quaint wooden cabins crammed along the main street had small porches and intriguing hand-carved signs, reminding Lexie of old photographs from the last century.

Due to the coming storm, many of the shops had closed early. Only Happy's General Store remained open. More like a small convenience mart with a quirky mix of food, household, and hardware, Happy's was the last place open. Thankfully, their little deli provided everything they needed.

With their salads and chicken lo mein loaded in their basket, they approached the checkout. The older gentleman waiting for them, behind a counter cluttered with candy and Powerball advertisements, had a grizzled face with pensive brown eyes.

Uncomfortable with his keen appraisal of her face and figure, she got the impression the cashier didn't like strangers.

"Don't get new faces around here in the cold months," he grumbled. "Where you folks from?"

Lexie and Will glanced at each other.

"Ah, we just moved here." Will set their basket on the counter. "The old Altmover Estate, you know it?"

The storekeeper cracked a bemused grin. "Sure do!" He held out his hand. "In that case, welcome to the island. The name's Ken Pritchard. Me and my wife, Lorie, own this store."

"Then who's Happy?" Will asked.

"The dog," Ken shrugged, glancing down at a very unhappy looking mutt.

Will laughed, shaking the store owner's hand.

"Tell me somthin'. Why would a nice couple, such as yourselves, want to live in that hell hole?"

Will's tight lips made Lexie cringe. His testy expression, as she called it, usually came right before an argument.

"Excuse me?" Will managed to say.

Ken reached for their coffee and turned to his register. "You two do know Altmover Manor is haunted. Or are you into that stuff? We get all kinds up here huntin' for ghosts."

She smelled an opportunity for information. She inched closer to the counter. "We heard some people died in the house. Do you recall anything about those deaths?"

Ken arched a single gray eyebrow. He bagged their coffee and stretched for the eggs. "Lots of people died in the house. The house has been bad news since the Blackwells lived there. Some say the land is cursed. Used to be sacred Indian land. Others say the family cursed it. Who knows? One thing everyone can agree on is the house is haunted."

Will bristled next to her. "I can't believe Altmover Manor has suffered such indignity. It's too beautiful to let crumble to the ground."

"Most people on the island would agree with you, but then there are some who would like the place taken away by the sea." Ken bagged their milk. "No one's lived there for over sixty years. Kids huntin' for ghosts is all that goes up to the house these days."

"But what about the caretaker?" Lexie pressed. "Surely you've seen him."

Ken shrugged, but his distrusting gaze never wavered. "Didn't know they had a caretaker. Surprised anyone wanted the job."

Will's reproachful scowl shut Lexie down. While Ken finished ringing up their groceries, she itched to question him more about Remi but didn't want to piss off Will.

Ken bagged the last of their items and checked the total on the register. "Fifty-six, seventy."

"His name is Remi Glapion. The caretaker at Altmover," Lexie blurted out. "You ever met him?"

Will's audible groan told Lexie the drive back to the house would be a long one. But she couldn't help herself; something didn't fit with the strange caretaker.

Ken took Will's credit card as he considered Lexie.

"Can't say I've ever met him. But I rarely work the register. My wife does. She'll know him. She knows everyone around here." He swiped the card through the machine. "I tend to stay in the back doing the books."

When Ken held out Will's credit card and the receipt, Lexie collected the grocery bags.

"Thanks for the help," Will muttered as he signed the credit card receipt.

After stuffing the receipt in his pocket, Will grabbed the grocery bags left on the counter and hurried Lexie out of the store.

Lexie wrestled with the plastic bags in her hand as she scurried next to Will.

"It's weird he's never met Remi."

"Lexie, you heard the guy: his wife's the one who handles the register. She knows everyone in town, not him."

"What do you know about Remi?"

Will fought to get the keys from his pocket, balancing the heavy bags in one hand. "He's what I need: a hard worker who won't break our bank account. The way our finances are, I'd hire the Devil himself if he agreed to Remi's wages. We can't afford anyone else and without extra help, I might never finish the house. Parker and Mills Bank believed in him; why can't you?"

"You should ask for references. Do a background check on him."

Will hit the keyless remote and the car's lights flashed. He opened the door to the back seat and dumped his grocery bags inside.

"This is Mount Desert Island, not the big city."

Lexie stood off to the side as Will opened her car door. "Look, I love that you're so concerned. It shows how much you care." He kissed her cheek before taking the grocery bags from her. "But I need this house. We both do."

While Will loaded her bags into the back seat, Lexie scoured the darkening sky. In the distance, thunder rumbled, and her stomach wound tight like a spring about to explode.

"I hope you're right, Will. But I've got a bad feeling about this house."

Fire crackled from the hearth as rain beat against their new home. Sitting on the floor in front of a mantel carved with dragons, they ate their salad and chicken lo mein sipping champagne. The wind howled, and Lexie listened as Will discussed his plans. She tipped the bottle over her glass, agreeing to everything he suggested for the house. Will spread out on his side, and she nestled up next to him. Buoyed by the champagne Lexie traced circles across his chest as her mind drifted to the subject eating at her.

"You knew about the people who died here, didn't you?" The weary sigh he uttered told her what she suspected. "You should have told me the truth."

"What truth? A couple of people died here over a hundred years ago. They're forgotten." He lifted his bulk and struggled to his feet.

She stood too. "Are you going to keep things from me in the future?"

He picked up his paper plate and sighed. "I'm sorry. I was scared if you knew about the house, you wouldn't come with me. I didn't want to blow my chance at owning this place, and I didn't want to be separated from you. Do you understand what a big decision this was for me? This is our future I'm gambling with. So please forgive me if I left out a few details."

"Your right. It's our future, but you're not the only one gambling here … I'm gambling too." She grabbed her plate and the champagne bottle. "And dead people aren't details. We should have discussed it before you bought the place."

He shook his head, turning to face her. "I didn't have time. The bank needed an answer right away. The deal they gave me was too good to pass up."

Lexie tucked the nearly empty champagne bottle under her arm. "This has got nothing to do with deals, or the Blackwells, or this house. It's about you and me. Don't keep things from me."

Will walked across the floor and took her paper plate. "I was wrong to hide the history of the Blackwells from you, but we've got a lot riding on this. I promise I'll do better." He pried the champagne bottle from her. "Let's finish this in bed."

He went to the dining room entrance, and Lexie was about to follow him when the dragons carved into the mantel moved. Pictured in a village with screaming victims clasped in their claws, their teeth glistened, and their tails whipped around them.

She wiped her hand over her damp brow. "No more champagne for me."

They climbed the stairs to their bedroom thunder shaking the house. Lexie cozied up to Will, distressed by the spooky atmosphere. For a second, the scales carved into the banister writhed beneath her hand. She shuddered, pulling away.

Will curled his arm around her shoulders. "It's just thunder, baby."

In their bedroom, Lexie wiggled out of her jeans. Lightning illuminated the room.

"Storm's getting closer."

"Ocean storms can be loud, especially when the ocean is in your backyard."

The brass lamp on the bedside table flickered.

"Will we lose the lights?"

Will reclined back on the bed, finishing the last of the bottle before setting it down with a decided thump. He drank in her figure. Lexie recognized the curl of his lip and the hunger in his eyes.

"You're drunk."

His black eyebrows bobbed. “And horny.”

She went to the bed. “You aren’t any good to me when you’re both.”

“Oh yeah?” Will threw his arms around Lexie and pulled her onto the bed. He kissed her lips and neck as thunder rolled.

Will kissed away her fright. Her fingertips drifted across his ripped abs and massaged into the hard muscles of his shoulders. The more she caressed his hot skin, breathed in his musky scent, the more she wanted him. Her fingers trailed the contours of his chest and lowered to fumble with the button on his jeans. He was already hard beneath the denim.

“I guess the champagne didn’t bother you as much as I thought it would.” She giggled into his chest.

He groaned. “I love your giggle.”

“Since when?”

He didn’t answer. He flipped Lexie onto her stomach. It was as if her laughter spurred on his desperation.

His fingers hooked her silk panties. While easing the frilly underwear over her ass, he whispered, “You have a beautiful ass, dear girl.”

Lexi frowned. “I thought you were a boob man.”

He bit down on her right butt cheek. “Not tonight.”

His hands caressed her backside, so the sharp slap that followed made her squeal.

“You’ve never done that before.”

He pulled her hips to his. “It’s my new game.”

Lexie could have sworn he sounded different.

Grinding her butt into his hips, she moaned. “Hurry.”

For several seconds, nothing happened.

“I don’t feel so good.” With a thud, Will fell onto the bed next to her.

“Hey.” She poked him hard. “Will?” But he was fast asleep.

Flustered, Lexie got up, removed her bra, and found her clothes packed away in a suitcase on the floor. She eased her nightshirt over her head, as the lamp flickered again. The instant she settled under the covers, the lamp went out. Nestled against Will, she shivered as rain pelted the house. Lightning lit the room; a man stood next to her bed. Heart racing, she froze, too scared to breathe. Another bright flash came in through the windows, revealing nothing, no one was there.

Will reached for her, his arms enveloping her. Her heartbeat slowed. *Calm down. It's all my imagination. Pull yourself together!*

With the restless storm beating against the windows, Lexie shut her eyes and concentrated on the patter of raindrops. Like a soothing lullaby, the tempest soon lulled her into a deep sleep.

A thin layer of mist covered the foyer floor as the lotus sconces glowed with an eerie light. Lexie wore a formal white gown, woven with lace and gold ribbons. The dress harkened back to a long-ago era. She didn't recall putting on the outfit or where she had gotten it.

She ran her hands ran over the smooth silk and played with the lace on her sleeves.

"This is weird."

The grand chandelier came to life, filling the foyer with its bright light. Ethereal music wafted through the house. Lexie swore she recognized the piece—a waltz. The music got louder; embedded in the notes was the distant murmur of conversation and glasses tinkling.

Lexie moved toward the sounds, stopping along the way to admire the home. The dull and drab foyer, once ravaged by time, blossomed before her as if magically restored. The golden wallpaper glistened in the candlelight, and the tears in the material came together as the dusty hardwood floors took on a dazzling shine. The chandelier appeared new, its chain covered with red velvet rope.

She made her way to the staircase where the red dragon's eyes at the base of the banister glowed. Her fingers caressed the colored glass, and she raised her head to the massive chandelier. The light fixture swayed.

Terrified, Lexie took off running down the hallway. Her flight halted as long, flowing, multi-colored gowns, intermingled with black tuxedos with long tails, sprung up around her. Couples caught up in the frenzy of the waltz kept time with the music, but these dancers had no hands and no heads. They were nothing more than costumes inhabited by ghosts.

"They've outdone themselves. Quite an event," a haughty man's voice came from the flurry of twirling clothes.

"Have you seen Katherine's dress?" a woman twittered. "He imported it from Paris for their anniversary."

Lexie carefully maneuvered through the swirling apparel, anxious not to disturb them.

"I never thought they'd last the year," another man said. "They're so ill-suited."

"Well, I've discovered the most scandalous things about Magnus Blackwell and the lurid things he likes to do with women," a woman remarked. "Do you think they're true?"

Eager to get away from the creepy dancing garments, Lexie ducked into the closest room. She slid inside a set of shiny double oak doors and closed them behind her. Resting her pounding head against the wood, she relaxed.

"This is a bad dream. Nothing more."

When she turned from the doors, Lexie somehow arrived in

the living room. But unlike before, the room had rich furniture, the polished paneling gleamed, and an oriental carpet with a green dragon graced the center of the parquet floor.

By the entrance, she toed the same spot where she'd found the deep gouge, but it wasn't there.

The bloom of a roaring fire in the hearth commanded her attention, drawing her gaze to Magnus Blackwell's portrait. Lexie stared at the painting. Something changed with the colors. They morphed and moved as if taking on a shape.

A voice emanated from inside the painting; a man's voice.

"I've been waiting for you, dear girl."

Startled awake from a sound sleep, Lexie gaped into the blackness of the strange bedroom. The storm had abated, and she detected the reassuring creaks and groans of the old house. A crack from the floorboards made her flinch. It came from Will's side of the bed. She reached out to shake him, but he didn't move.

"Will?"

She received a muffled grunt.

Another crack in the floor, but this time it happened right next to her side of the bed.

The dark scent of coffee lingered in the air.

A column of light glittering to her left made Lexie's mouth go dry. The oddity soon took on the shape of a man.

His strong frame, arms, and tapered hands came into view. Good-looking, despite the cruel curl of his lips, his chiseled features and engaging eyes made her insides tingle. As the cut of his old-fashioned red vest, long black coat, and white ascot tie took shape, Lexie understood this wasn't some hazy fantasy.

She clutched her bed sheet as a scream rose in her throat.

"Please, my dear, don't bore me with your petty shrieks," the figure said, his tone condescending.

Like a light bulb getting enough electricity to reach its wattage, his image brightened, bringing out the details. Lexie scrutinized the buttons on his coat, the fine craftsmanship of his high black boots, and grasped the identity of her visitor. A loud *pop* rang out, and he was gone. It happened so fast, Lexie questioned if it had happened at all.

"Welcome to Altmover Manor, Ms. Arden."

*Oh, God.* She recognized the voice of the apparition.

"I hope you enjoy your stay."

This time, Lexie did not hold back her scream.

# Chapter Four

"Lexie," a voice called from the darkness. "Wake up, baby."

Her eyes flew open. Will stood over her, already dressed.

"You need to get up." Sunlight streamed through the window. "It's past eight. We've got to get started."

Still groggy, she sat up in the bed. "I had an awful dream."

Will lifted a mug of coffee from her night table. "Yeah, so did I. Here, black Columbian."

"Thank you." She sipped the coffee. "What did you dream about?"

He tucked his shirt into the waistband of his jeans. "Being eaten alive by this house." He ran his hands through his damp hair. "I kept thinking of everything we have to do. Must have transferred over to my subconscious." Will sat on the bed and picked up a tennis shoe from the floor. "Why? What did you dream about?"

She lowered her gaze to the black coffee swirling in her mug. "The ghost of Magnus Blackwell."

Will snickered as he tied his shoe. "No more champagne for you."

She put her mug down on the night table. "I could say the same thing about you."

He reached for his other shoe. "What are you talking about?"

"Last night. You got me all turned on and then passed out."

He finished tying his shoe, wrinkling his thick brow at her. "Lexie, we were both so tipsy last night we barely got our clothes off before we made it into bed." He stood up. "You must have dreamt that, too."

"No, Will. You said you liked my giggle and then talked about my beautiful ass."

"Now I know you were dreaming. I hate it when you giggle." He grinned. "But you do have a beautiful ass." Will kissed her forehead. "Tonight, we'll christen the house, I promise." Enthused, Will bounded out the bedroom door.

Lexie tucked her feet under her as she recalled her dream. The part with Magnus Blackwell had to be a nightmare, but the other bit—where she and Will had gone at it in bed—seemed real. Maybe he was right. She'd downed plenty of champagne.

She tossed aside the covers vowing, "I'm never drinking again."

Lexie descended the grand staircase to find Will already waiting on the first floor. Remi was at his side, dressed in beige overalls with a leather tool belt on his hip, displaying screwdrivers, pliers, a hammer, and a flashlight. All Will had was his cell phone.

"What are you two up to?"

"We need to go into each room and do a survey. I'm going to take pictures and then download them into my laptop. I can make an inventory of what we'll need in the way of supplies."

"And what are you supposed to do, Remi?"

Remi chuckled. "That's up to Will."

To Lexie, they were two men setting out to kill a great white shark with a letter opener. "Yell if you need me."

Will approached the staircase, lowering his voice. "What I need you to do is hit the attic. See if you can find any old pictures of the house."

"You want me to go into the attic … alone?" She gulped.

"Yesterday we talked about this, remember?"

"Yeah, then I found out the living dead are creeping around our bedroom."

"Lexie, there are no ghosts in this house. There's nothing here but stone, mortar, and I hope only a little bit of dry rot."

"All right." She wrung her hands, avoiding his stare. She wanted to keep him happy, but she also wished to avoid the attic. "I'll head up there after I get some more coffee."

Will took the flashlight from Remi's tool belt, came up to her, and put it in her right hand. "I know you; one cup will lead to three. You need to go up there now and get it over with. You'll see there's nothing to be afraid of."

Lexie refrained from bashing him over the head with the flashlight. "What's up with you? You've been so bossy since we got here."

Will's mouth turned downward in a stunned frown. "Have I?"

"Yeah, and it's getting on my nerves."

He shook his head and ran his hand through his hair. "Sorry. I guess I'm more stressed than I thought. I've been on edge since we walked in the door."

She gripped the flashlight. "So, can I get my second cup of coffee?"

He smiled, touched his forehead to hers and stood back. "No. Get up there, bring down what we can use and put it in the living room. That'll be our command post."

She ascended the stairs, glaring back at him. "Command post? What is this D-Day?"

He waved her up the steps with a cocky smirk. "Get to it, Eisenhower."

Lexie's stomach curled into a knot as she flipped on the flashlight. "I'd prefer a bazooka to a flashlight." She skipped up a few steps. "First the weird shit in bed last night, then today he's barking orders at me like a barrack's commander. This is so not the Will Bennett I lived with in Boston."

On the second-floor landing, a gray Maine Coon cat stood waiting for her. With a fluffy coat, thick mane, and wide green eyes, the creature greeted Lexie with a friendly meow.

"Hello there." She stooped and rubbed the animals head. "Where did you come from?" Lexie glanced around the hall. "I bet you've been living in this place, huh?" She snickered. "What weird shit have you seen?"

The cat turned away and trotted down the hall. It disappeared into the shadows on the second-floor.

"Where are you going?" Lexie stood up. "At least you're not my imagination."

At the end of the long hall on the third floor, Lexie came to a short set of stairs. She examined the three short steps to the attic and shuddered.

Mustering her courage, she marched up to the attic door and turned the rusted knob. Nothing happened. She fought to turn the knob and still got resistance.

She set the flashlight down and used both hands on the knob. “Come on, you …”

Lexie had to put her shoulder into the door, but when it opened, she regarded her accomplishment with a touch of pride.

*Who needs men around to do the hard stuff? Ha!*

Ready to tackle anything—including some uppity ghost— she wiped her hands on her jeans and grabbed the flashlight.

She searched the entrance for a light switch. On her right, she found an old-fashioned knob. The entire attic became bathed in light. Secured to the high arched beam in the roof, three large light fixtures ran above the attic space. The immense area covered the length of the house.

Dusty boards with nicks and long scratches marred the floors. Boxes, trunks, old paintings, and furniture filled the attic.

“Wow,” she mumbled, no longer terrified but captivated.

A center aisle crammed with all the stuff people stored over the years yawned before her. At either end, two large, round windows allowed the bright daylight into the attic.

She wished she’d brought her phone as Will had done to catalog what she found.

Dust covered everything. After a quick perusal, she identified the newer items located closer to the entrance. Moving along the aisle represented a timeline of Altmover Manor’s history. The farther she went, the older the items and the thicker the dust.

At the back of the attic, she stumbled on paintings resting against the wall. After she rearranged several boxes, Lexie went to inspect the pieces, hoping to use them in the house.

There were a few landscapes and some ocean views. Lexie found the artistry impeccable, and although she didn’t recognize the signatures, she decided to take them back to the living room and check the Internet for any information.

It took her an hour to lug the heavy paintings to the attic door.

On her third trip, she discovered the portraits.

The first, of an older woman, had no nameplate at the bottom. She searched the floor and found a brass plate not far from the portrait.

*Emilia Hart Blackwell, wife of Reynolds Blackwell*

She studied the woman's blonde hair and sharp features, thinking them familiar.

"Dear old Mom?"

She set the portrait aside to bring downstairs and found another behind it. A small boy with blond curls posed resplendent in a blue-velvet costume with a white, ruffled collar. The nameplate at the bottom was intact.

*Edward Reynolds Blackwell*

She moved Edward Blackwell's picture to uncover another portrait behind it. An older version of Magnus Blackwell, the man's face, the fiendish twist of the lips, and intensity of his eyes mimicked the home's former owner.

"Reynolds Winston Blackwell," Lexie read from the nameplate. "Yeah, you must be Daddy. You look just like your son."

A man's chuckle floated through the air.

A cool breeze sailed past Lexie. Her first instinct, to drop everything and run, made her leg muscles quiver.

"Stay calm, Lexie." She put Reynolds Blackwell's picture to the side with the others. "Remember what your pain in the ass fiancé believes: ghosts don't exist."

A *thud* to her right brought on a brief bout of trembling. Lexie scanned the attic.

Was Will playing a trick on her?

Determined to find a logical explanation for the noises, she set out across the attic and then tripped over a collection of small frames. After a few curse words, she spied an odd-looking doll made of dried twigs and black ribbon hidden among them.

"Where did you come from?"

The moment Lexie touched the object that uncomfortable feeling in her gut surged to life. An impression of a dark abyss came over her. And in the darkness, a man's face—difficult to make out, but she swore they had a connection. Then the image faded and her uneasiness dissolved.

"This place must be getting to me."

About to set the doll to the side, Lexie spotted a grainy black and white photograph without a frame amid the debris at her feet. The two men in the picture stood before the manor house steps. Behind them, workmen and scaffolding surrounded one of the large Corinthian columns. She picked up the picture and squinted at the men. One had dark hair, a lean figure, and wore a frock coat and vest, but she had trouble making out his features. The other hid his face beneath a black hat, but in his hand, a dragon cane.

"Well, hello, Mr. Blackwell."

Outside the attic entrance, Magnus watched as Lexie patted the dust and cobwebs from her jeans while inspecting the portraits stacked on the small flight of steps.

She turned her back to the steps and stopped, sniffing the air. "Is that coffee? Up here?"

Magnus moved closer, smiling as he observed her. "You are an intriguing specimen, Lexie Arden."

She walked through his ghostly presence and away from the steps.

In the distance, a woman's faint, shrill cry carried throughout the hallway.

"What the hell was that?" Lexie took off in the direction of the stairs. "There's something seriously wrong with this house."

Magnus waited by the attic entrance as she dashed along the corridor. "You have no idea how right you are, Ms. Arden." He admired the way her blonde hair bounced while she descended the staircase. "So like Frances."

"Leave her alone, Magnus." The cold voice cut through the air.

Jacob O'Connor materialized next to him still wearing the tuxedo he died in. His sunken white face contained smudges of black along his chin and cheeks. His hands were also stained black and clenched into fists.

Magnus rolled his fiery green eyes as Jacob's form solidified. "Not a word for over a hundred years and today you speak to me. To what do I owe the pleasure, O'Connor?"

Jacob inched closer, the contempt swimming in his black orbs. "I have no wish to speak to you, but I can be silent no longer."

Magnus's rebellious snort circled in the air. "Staying silent was something you were rather good at as I remember."

"I despise you."

"Yes, I gathered as much the night you murdered me with my cane."

Jacob hovered in front of Magnus. "The girl has nothing to do with what happened between us."

Magnus frowned at his empty hand. He ached to hold his dragon cane and hum with its power. "The girl is the key, dear boy. We'll be damned for an eternity in this house without her."

"I will not allow you to include her in this charade."

"Not allow?" Magnus laughed at him. "This is not up to you or me. Another has the power. You are well aware of our precarious situation."

"I'm warning you. Do not hurt her."

Magnus stared him down. "'Let he who is without sin cast the first stone.' I'd say that puts us at a disadvantage."

"You're the one who chose this path. I wanted revenge; not eternity saddled with you."

Magnus flourished a hand in the air. "Yet here we are. We don't have to remain this way, O'Connor."

Jacob's ethereal image wavered. "I will not have anything to do with your games. The girl being here changes nothing between us."

Jacob faded.

Magnus let out a heavy sigh. "Always so dramatic. What Frances found appealing about you still eludes me."

He floated along the corridor until he came to the inlaid marble steps. Magnus peered over the railing to find Lexie rounding the landing and heading toward the first floor.

He gripped the banister, longing to feel the wood in his hands. "You're wrong, O'Connor. She will change everything for us."

Then Magnus Blackwell vanished.

Loud banging from the floor above the kitchen told Lexie where Remi and Will decided to concentrate their renovating skills. While plaster dust fell from the ceiling, she headed to the fridge.

Bent over and deciding between egg salad and chicken for lunch, she heard a disembodied man's voice.

"I approve."

Lexie stood from behind the fridge door. She listened to the whir of the appliances but detected nothing else.

"Either I'm going crazy, or that sounded like a man."

"What sounded like a man?" Will asked, bounding into the

kitchen. His jeans, T-shirt, and hair covered with dust.

After shutting the fridge, she moved toward him and wiped a smear of dust from his cheek. "I swore I heard someone whispering."

"I didn't hear anything," Will offered with a quirked eyebrow.

"In the attic earlier, a woman's scream scared the crap out of me. In here, a man's voice mumbled something. Doesn't that sound strange?"

"All the dust must be messing with your head." Will inspected her jeans and T-shirt. "You look worse than me."

Lexie picked a smattering of cobwebs from her jeans. "Gross."

Will brushed some dust from her shoulder. "You've got crap all over you. What were you doing in the attic?"

She stepped away and wet a paper towel in the sink. "The attic is a treasure trove." She wiped her face, and the white paper towel turned a light brown. "I found paintings of Magnus Blackwell's family and some cool landscapes."

"I'd like to see them." Will leaned against the counter. "Did you find any photographs?"

"One," Lexie reported. "I'm sure it's Magnus Blackwell."

"Such a poor photograph of me. Pity," a voice murmured in her ear.

She paused and explored the kitchen. "There it is again."

"Lexie?" Will snapped his fingers in front of her face. "Where's the picture? I'd like to see it."

Lexie shook her head, coming out of her momentary lapse. "Ah, I'll bring it down with the paintings I found. I want to photograph the artwork and search for the artists online. We could make some money selling them."

Will grimaced. "I'd like to keep as much of the original artwork as we can."

"Okay." She pitched the paper towel in the trash. "Where's

Remi?"

"He went back to his cottage to grab a bite to eat."

"He didn't want to eat with us?"

Will scurried to the fridge and opened the door. "I asked, but he said no."

"Doesn't he like us? Seems kind of strange to me."

He pulled out a loaf of bread and the chicken from the previous night. "The guy likes to eat alone. So what?"

"Aren't you going to wash your hands?"

Will held up his hands, inspecting them. "No, why?"

She refrained from snickering. "How's it going with Remi?"

"Great. He knows a ton about old houses. He learned a lot working on them in New Orleans."

"Did he mention any more family back in the city?"

Will plunked a mayonnaise jar on the counter. "No."

"What did you two talk about?" The alarm on the coffeemaker went off.

"We went through all the rooms on the second floor. We'll hit the third floor after lunch."

"That's what you did, not what you talked about."

He searched the cabinet above him. "Talk? Lexie, girls talk; men do stuff. Where are the plates?"

"Try the next cabinet to your right. They might be there." She poured coffee into two mugs set next to the coffeemaker. "But men also talk about stuff, right?"

"Well, we didn't." He found two plates and set them on the counter. "I swear this house is a museum to technological advances. Do you know there are still gas lines in all the walls from when the fixtures ran off the stuff?"

"That's fascinating." She put his coffee mug next to his plate. "Remi never mentioned anything else about the house?"

"Like what?"

She decided not to press the subject. “After lunch, can you guys help me lug those paintings I found down to the living room?”

Will slapped a chicken breast onto a mayonnaise-soaked slice of bread and then pressed the other slice on top. Lexie cringed as he lifted the sandwich to his mouth with his still dirty hands.

“You want me to make you a sandwich?” he asked while chewing.

She pushed him aside. “Thanks. I’ll make my own.”

“What’s wrong with my sandwich-making skills?”

“It’s a girl thing.”

# Chapter Five

Will and Remi carried the last of the paintings from the attic into the living room.

"Spread them out along the wall," Lexie instructed. "Standing up, if you don't mind. They'll be easier to photograph."

Once done, Will stood back, wiping his hands as he examined the paintings. "Is there anything else you want us to haul down from the attic?"

Lexie went to her camera bag set up next to her computer. "Not at the moment. When I get back up there and can go through more stuff, I'm sure I'll need your help again."

"You're going back up there? This morning you were dead set against it."

"No, the attic is growing on me." Lexie dug through her bag. "I'm like an archeologist uncovering the past."

Remi stepped over to Lexie's camera bag. He paused as he gaped at the small twig doll sitting on her computer.

"Where did you find this?"

She retrieved the doll and held it up to him. "In the attic. It was on the floor next to a bunch of broken frames. Why?"

Remi backed away from her. "Do you know what it is?"

Lexie shrugged as she examined the doll. "A child's toy?"

Remi's mouth dropped open. "Lexie, this is a voodoo doll. Fashioned by someone who's familiar with the art."

Will shook his head. "First, Lexie has some dream about a ghost, and now you want me to believe she's discovered a voodoo doll in our attic?"

Remi rushed right up to Lexie. "You dreamt of a ghost?"

Uncomfortable with his proximity and his question, she took a step back. "Yeah. Magnus Blackwell." She set the doll back on her laptop. "But I think the champagne you gave us yesterday was the reason for my dream."

A malicious smile spread across Remi's pursed lips. "You need to listen to your dreams, Lexie. He's reaching out to you."

"All right, that's enough. I don't want to hear any more of this." Will grabbed Remi by the shoulder and urged him to the living room doors. "We've got work to do."

She followed the men. "Will, we need to listen to what Remi has to say."

Will stopped at the doors and flexed his shoulders. "This is nothing but an old house with a tragic past, baby. There are no ghosts or magical happenings going on here. You know how uncomfortable I am with this nonsense."

Will pushed Remi out of the room.

Lexie listened to the men's heavy footsteps climbing the staircase. As their footfalls faded, she turned her attention to the twig doll on her computer. Sighing at her predicament, and the long afternoon ahead, she explored the paintings arranged in the living room. The lifelike eyes of the portraits sent shivers up her spine.

"I sure would love to prove you wrong, Will Bennett. I wish you would accept that ghosts are real and they're living in this house." Lexie went to her laptop and set the twig doll aside.

The computer warmed up, and Lexie prayed the promised Wi-Fi would work. When she connected to the Internet, she did a quick fist pump. The gods of technology were on her side.

She went to her camera bag next to her laptop and collected her digital camera. In the bright living room light, Lexie got a good look at the details in the paintings. The quality was good, and though she didn't profess to be an art historian, Lexie assumed the paintings might be worth something.

The portraits of Magnus Blackwell's family enchanted her the most. Especially the small boy. The details drew her in.

After taking her pictures, she hooked the camera up to the computer and downloaded the images. Waiting for the computer to finish, she stood and stretched her back. A nippy breeze entered the room. She went to check if someone had walked into the house. At the living room entrance, she peered down the hall leading to the foyer.

"Hello?" *Should I lock the front doors?*

The gray cat she'd met upstairs darted past.

She let out a huge breath. "It's the cat."

When she glanced down the hall to discover where the cat had gone, Lexie could not find it. "I should start leaving out food for the poor thing."

Back at her computer, Lexie pulled up the jpeg images. She blew up Edward's portrait first, anxious to make out the name on the bottom right corner. However, the scribbled signature was illegible.

"Damn. I hope the others are better."

Lexie returned to the paintings scattered about the room before turning her attention to Magnus Blackwell's life-sized portrait above the mantel.

The signature on the bottom right-hand corner was different than the young boy's picture. With a tilt of her head, she approached the fireplace, attempting to decipher the scribble.

The air in the room grew colder as she stood on her toes in front of the fireplace. Lexie almost turned back to the doorway when something brought her to a standstill.

Magnus's painting moved, or the image of Magnus moved, she wasn't sure. His figure floated above the surface of the canvas. Thinking she'd imbibed way too much coffee, Lexie blinked twice, but still, the illusion persisted.

As the temperature plunged, Lexie hugged herself and backed away from the mantel. Magnus Blackwell moved out from the portrait as if walking down an invisible flight of stairs. He wore the same coat and boots as in his portrait but lacked his dragon cane.

She attempted to scream, but nothing came out. She wanted to run, but her legs wouldn't move. Magnus came closer, and she discerned the smooth texture of his skin, made out the coarse fabric in his coat. Hell, she swore he even reeked of coffee.

The translucent man stopped before her. "Now, dear girl, perhaps you can help me find my cane?"

The scream stuck in the back of her throat finally erupted. Her shrill cry echoed throughout the house.

"What?" Will shouted as he and Remi ran into the living room. "What's wrong?"

Shaking like a leaf, she pointed at Magnus's portrait. Will took her hand.

"Lexie, what is it? Talk to me."

She couldn't form words.

Remi urged Will aside. "Allow me." He rested his hand against her forehead and cooed, "Breathe, Lexie. Look into my eyes and relax."

With every tremulous breath, Lexie calmed, and her reason returned.

"Good. Tell us what happened." Remi kept his voice steady.

"He … he came out of the painting. I was standing here, and he walked up to me."

"Who came out of the painting?" Will moved next to her.

Remi gave him a stern reproach with his eyes. "Will, please."

"Magnus," she got out. "Magnus Blackwell came down from his painting and spoke to me."

Will tossed up his hands. "Aw, for Pete's sake, Lexie, you can't believe—"

"What did he say?" Remi interrupted.

She ignored Will and concentrated on Remi. "He said, 'Now dear girl, perhaps you can help me find my cane.'"

"Lexie." Will pushed Remi out of the way. "You're tired. Your mind's playing tricks on you."

"Are my ears playing tricks on me, too, Will? I heard him."

"Let's all settle down." Remi's commanding voice rang out. "If she saw something, Will, we have to support her."

"I'll support her, but I won't believe she spoke to a ghost." The muscles in Will's clenched jaw quivered. "We have too much to do around here to get slowed down by this supernatural silliness."

"Damn it, Will, you sound like your mother. You're obsessed with fixing up this house." Lexie stomped her foot. "What's the matter with you lately?"

Remi got between the couple. "Will, why don't you go back upstairs. I'll stay with Lexie."

"I don't need a babysitter, Remi." She rubbed her hand across her face. Her head throbbed, and she felt drained. "Maybe I'm tired, like Will says."

Remi turned to Will. "Go on. I'll be there in a minute."

Still grumbling under his breath, Will strode out the doors.

While Will's pounding feet resonated on the marble floor in the foyer, Lexie gazed up at Remi. "Do you believe me?"

"Yes, ma'am," he drawled. "Where I come from ghosts are as real as you or me. Magnus Blackwell was reaching out to you for a specific reason."

"Which is what? To give me a heart attack?"

Remi studied the portrait. "That walking stick must have been important. He filled this house with dragons to show what it meant to him. Perhaps the cane had a special power. Remember what I told you about dragons and voodoo?"

"You can't be serious," Lexie said, staying far back from the portrait. "We have no idea if he added the dragons or if they were here when he inherited the manor. He could have had the stick made to represent the dragons already in the house."

"Magnus Blackwell added them, all right." Remi swept his large hand over the portrait. "Look at him. He's a man who made his impression on people and places. Not the other way around."

"So why reach out to me?" Lexie scratched her head, second-guessing her encounter. "If he did reach out to me."

"He told you why. He wants you to find his cane." Remi turned to her. "You have to do it, Lexie. Get Magnus Blackwell's cane back."

His insistence was so far from what she expected, Lexie stared at him, open-mouthed. "You're not serious?"

"If you don't, he may keep coming to visit you until you do find it."

She shook her head and went to her laptop on the floor. "This is crazy, I'm done in here. I'll move my research into the kitchen."

"Think about it, Lexie." Remi moved toward the doors. "You have the gift; use it."

She ran a thousand ways to word her refusal through her head, but never voiced it. Lexie hated to admit Remi's suggestion intrigued her.

"I'll head back up to join Will." Remi grinned at her. "Holler if you see any more ghosts."

When Remi left, Lexie gathered her laptop and camera bag. She went to the kitchen, relieved to be around the hum of modern appliances. She set up her laptop on the kitchen table and settled down to do more research, but Remi's words stayed with her.

*Where would I begin to find the cane?*

The clock on her computer read a little after five when a sweaty and dusty Will sauntered into the kitchen. He spotted her sitting at their small table, but moved over to the fridge. After grabbing a water bottle and taking a quick gulp, he let out a loud sigh.

"I'm sorry I jumped all over you earlier. If you saw a … ghost." He struggled to get the word out. "I believe you."

She sat back in her chair and admired the way his shirt clung to his muscular torso. "Did Remi tell you to say that?"

He came up to her, carrying his water bottle. "He told me I was an ass and I should keep my mouth shut from now on."

"I knew I liked the guy. Where is he?"

"He went back to his cottage. We're both beat. Been checking the wiring on the third floor."

"How bad is it?"

He shook his head. "I'm amazed the place hasn't burned to the ground yet." He set his water bottle next to her laptop. "What are you doing?"

She turned her laptop around to face him. "Research on the Blackwells."

He gleaned the page on the computer screen. "What did you find out?"

"They were into real estate, railroads, gold mines, and owned businesses from Boston to Maine. The entire family, including Magnus and his wife, are buried at Forest Hills Cemetery in Boston."

Will leaned against the table. "Can you tell me more about the house? I'm not interested in the people."

"Spoken like a true architect. You and Magnus Blackwell would have gotten along. He studied architecture at Harvard."

"Architecture?" Will perked up. "Did he redesign the façade of this house?"

"I'm not sure. Remi said Magnus Blackwell hired an architect to redesign this place. I found a picture in the attic of the house when they were putting in the columns and balconies. Magnus is standing with a man. He might be the same architect."

Will scrolled down the page on the computer. "Did you find anything on here with images of the house from before the renovations? Something we can use for the restoration?"

Her shoulders drooped. "The pictures I found dated after the thirties. Nothing sooner."

"What about the attic?"

"Will, the stuff in the attic goes on and on. It might take me months to find what you need."

He took another sip of water. "Why not try the archives at the local library? They might have pictures we can use."

She nodded, encouraged. "I want to spend more time in the attic before I head to the library. Who knows, maybe I'll find the family treasure."

"I hope so. We'll need the money to pay for the repairs." Will went to the refrigerator. "Is there any more chicken lo mein left?"

Lexie closed her computer. "I'll make us something for dinner."

"If you're going to start cooking, I'll have to hurry up and install those smoke detectors."

She went to the fridge and bumped him aside with her hip. "Very funny."

He patted her butt. "I thought so."

"Careful, Mr. Bennett, I'll make you pay for that comment later."

# Chapter Six

After dinner, Lexie and Will left the dishes for the morning and headed to the grand staircase. Before he escorted her up the stairs, Will guided her to the leaded-glass front doors.

He set the deadbolt, and Lexie viewed the yellow cottage through the glass. "We should invite Remi to stay in the house."

"Already did," Will said, urging her back to the staircase. "He says he's settled in the cottage. I think he wants to give us some privacy. You know, while we christen every room in the house."

She curled into his chest. "We haven't christened our bedroom yet."

Will grabbed her from behind and swung her over his shoulders. "I'm getting ready to rectify that situation."

He carried her up the marble-inlaid steps two at a time. Will reached the second-floor landing, and Lexie spied the magnificent crystal chandelier, rocking back and forth.

She wanted to tell Will, to show him something else lived in the house with them, but he slapped her bottom and her resolve evaporated.

Will shoved their bedroom door open with his foot, darted inside, and tossed her onto their big bed. Before Lexie sat up, he climbed on top of her, kissing her with such ferocity it took her breath away. Will hadn't been this passionate since the first time he'd coaxed her into bed over a year ago.

"I want you so much," he murmured against her cheek as he wrenched the T-shirt over her head.

"I can tell."

She helped him remove his dusty shirt. Lexie found the essence of a hard day's labor on his skin erotic, but she detected something else. *Coffee?* She shook off the perplexing odor and dropped her hands to the fly of his jeans.

Will flipped her over. "I want you this way."

She sat up. "Didn't we already do this last night?"

He pushed her back to the bed and tugged her jeans down her hips. "What are you talking about?"

"Last night. You flipped me over, made a comment about my ass, and then you passed out."

He finished getting her underwear down her thighs. "You must have dreamt that."

Lexie might have doubted the integrity of her dream, but the ghost she'd seen coming out of the painting in the living room had been real. She had no other explanation.

After throwing her jeans and underwear to the floor, Will bit her right butt cheek. "I want to fuck your ass."

"Whoa, what?" She flipped over and faced him. "What did you say?"

He stared at her like a deer in headlights. "What?"

"You said, 'I want to fuck your ass.'"

He arched over her, trapping her between his strong arms. "No, I didn't. I never use that word."

Lexie put her hand on his firm chest, holding him back. "Then what did you say?"

Will kissed the tip of her nose. "I don't remember." His lips teased her neck. "Come on, relax. You're so uptight."

"I'm not up—"

His deep kiss smothered her words. Lexie wanted to forget about the house, the strange occurrences, and about how much money they'd spent on Will's dream. She wrapped her arms around him, opened her mouth, and accepted his tongue.

His fingers dipped between her legs. She moaned as he drew circles around her clit. She arched her back when his fingers slipped into her. Will tantalized the spot that always made her scream.

She pumped against his hand, panting as waves of need rose and ebbed. So close to coming, Lexie tossed her head back as a wonderful groan traveled up from the back of her throat. Her guttural cry grew until it became an electrifying scream.

"That's what I like to hear," Will whispered in her ear. "My turn."

He tossed her over onto her stomach. The act shocked her. Will had never been one to play rough in bed. When he slapped her ass, hard, Lexie sat up.

"Hey, that hurt."

"I know." He sounded nothing like her Will.

He pulled her to her knees and before she protested, he pushed deep inside her. The unexpected force of his penetration made her gasp. She wanted to say something when he plunged deeper. Lexie moaned as the tendrils of excitement rose from her groin. He had never been this way before: brutal, hard, and hungry for her.

The pleasure he created urged her to keep quiet.

She vibrated as her orgasm crept upward. She clutched the

blue comforter as she rocked to and fro.

"Do you like this, Lexie?"

"Yes, you're so different tonight."

Will grazed his teeth down her back. "How about this?"

His fingers went between her butt cheeks. He moved a finger inside her ass, and Lexie's eyes shot open.

"Will, stop—"

A strong arm came around her middle, holding her to him. "Trust me, baby. I promise you'll find it better than anything we've done before."

He pounded into her, while his finger pressed deeper into her butt. Despite the strange sensation, her climax continued to intensify. Soon, she didn't care what Will did to her. She became too preoccupied with her pleasure to stop him.

She opened her mouth to scream, but her quivering muscles cut off her cry. Trapped in a whirlwind of indescribable intensity, Lexie's every fiber burned.

When she finally uttered an animal-like cry, she shocked herself.

*Oh, my God. I sound like one of those screaming monkeys at the zoo!*

The rhythm of heavy breathing filled the bedroom.

"I'm impressed." She rolled over and ran a hand across his broad chest.

"I wanted to christen the house in style." He patted her thigh.

"You've never done that before."

He raised his head. "Done what?"

"You know? What you did with your finger."

His brow furrowed. "What are you talking about?"

Fear tightened her stomach. She bolted upright in the bed and searched the room. This wasn't like Will. A very together man, he never forgot to get her flowers when she was sad, always showed up on time for their dates, returned her phone calls, and strived to be considerate in bed.

"Lexie, are you okay?"

She gave him a tepid smile and climbed from the bed. "I, ah, have to go to the bathroom."

Inside the master bathroom, she closed the door and switched on the light.

*What the hell is going on?*

At the vanity, she fought to find a rational explanation for the change in Will.

"He's worried about the money, and this house is zapping his energy. Get a grip, Lexie."

She flipped on the cold water, splashed her face, and reached for her toothbrush when a chill entered the room.

"Not again." She squeezed the toothbrush.

Her reflection clouded over as smoke obscured her bathroom mirror. She gasped as the smoke turned into the face of a man.

Lexie wanted to scream for Will, but the face changed. This wasn't Magnus Blackwell, but someone else. With black wavy hair, warm brown eyes, and a pleasing curve to his chin, he looked at Lexie and smiled.

"Hello, Frances."

Lexie dropped her toothbrush and ran from the bathroom.

"What's wrong?" Will asked as she entered the bedroom.

He'd changed into his blue pajama bottoms and thrown his jeans and briefs on the floor. Will seemed so normal, so calm, she didn't have the heart to upset him.

"I saw a big spider."

"Yeah, getting the exterminator out here to spray is on my to-do list." Will pulled back the covers on the bed. "I'll call him this week. Be careful rummaging around the attic. I don't want you to get bit by anything."

She jogged around to her side of the bed. "I'll keep an eye out."

Once settled under the covers, Lexie cuddled against him.

Will wrapped an arm around her. "You're shivering."

She nuzzled her head into his chest. "It was a really big spider."

"You want me to go in there and kill it for you?"

She sighed, calming down. "No, Will. This one may already be dead."

# Chapter Seven

The next morning, Lexie put on a brave face for Will but waited for Remi to walk through their leaded-glass doors. The more she kept from Will, the better for their relationship.

"Morning," Remi greeted when he strolled into the kitchen.

"Hey, Remi." Will picked up his plate of scrambled eggs and whole wheat toast on the counter. "You eat yet?"

Remi contemplated the toast. "I have room for a bite or two." He went to the counter and selected a slice waiting on a white plate. "You two sleep okay last night?"

Lexie appraised Remi. *Why he would ask such a question?*

Will slurped back some orange juice and wiped his hands on a napkin. "I'm heading up to the third floor and get started." He dumped his glass in the sink. "I want to check out the fuse box in the basement today. Might be why half the lights don't work in this place."

"Probably the cause." Remi took a bite of his unbuttered toast. "I bet the electrical panel hasn't been updated since the sixties."

Will shook his head. "I shudder to think how bad it will be." He kissed Lexie's cheek. "I'll see you later." He strutted out the door.

Lexie turned to Remi. "Something happened last night."

Remi eyed the doorway Will had walked through. "I can imagine. He seems happy."

She folded her arms, unamused. "I saw another ghost. A man. He called me Frances."

"Frances?" Remi took another bite of toast. "Who's Frances?"

"Who *was* Frances, you mean. If I tell Will about the ghost in the bathroom, he'll freak out."

He dropped his half-eaten toast onto the plate. "Will is the sort who likes to live in the daylight. A world of shadows and ghosts is too much for him." He pointed at her. "You and I, on the other hand, are tied to the shadow world. There, we are most comfortable."

"Well, I wasn't too comfortable last night. This house is creeping me out. With ghosts and dragons everywhere, and then the disappearing cat."

Remi frowned. "What cat?"

"I keep seeing a big gray cat around here." She shrugged. "It's friendly, but I have no idea where it lives."

"It's an old house with lots of mice. The cat has probably hunted here for years." Remi wiped his hands together. "As far as the ghosts go … you need to keep in mind there are two types of hauntings occurring in this house: the imprints from the past, and the spirits of actual ghosts."

"I have no idea what you're talking about."

Remi rested his hip against the counter. "Every event creates an impression. Murder, suicide, and unexpected death are intense experiences which can leave profound impressions on a place. Some things you may be experiencing are replays of the past. They're repeating impressions, like the scream you heard."

"Yeah, but unless Magnus Blackwell died on his painting, what I witnessed in the living room doesn't go along with your theory."

"No, Magnus Blackwell is haunting this house. He's here, and he's restless."

"Yeah, he wants his cane. But what does the other guy want?"

"Who knows? But you have an attic filled with answers waiting to be found. The cane might be up there, too."

Lexie picked up her coffee mug. "Why can't Magnus Blackwell just tell me 'go to this spot and find my cane'?"

"Ghosts are no different from people, Lexie. They need help like we do, and because their bodies are gone, they need help from someone connected to this world. If there are two men haunting this house, they're reaching out to you. You have to figure out how to help them."

"But why me?"

"Because you're here and you can see them." He raised his head to the ceiling. "I better get up there. He's wondering where I am."

"How can you tell?"

He tipped his head to the side. "To hear, one only has to listen. Remember that. It works on ghosts and people."

With a knowing grin, Remi sauntered out of the kitchen, humming an unfamiliar tune.

Remi was right. If she found the cane, and what the other guy wanted from her, then maybe the ghosts would leave. She could settle down to a normal life with Will in their new home and have peace.

"Please, God, help me figure this mess out."

An hour later, the cobwebs and thick dust in the attic enveloped her. This time, she'd brought her camera to document the contents. She worked her way down from the attic's opposite end—the oldest section—hoping to dig up more on the family who had once lived in the house.

She stopped to take pictures of the furnishings, framed paintings, and the numerous trunks scattered everywhere. When she leaned over to inspect a beautiful round mahogany table, she tripped on the corner of a steamer trunk. Lexie itched to open it.

After moving the round table and fragments of two ugly cement ravens to the side, she stood before the dark leather trunk. She ran her hand over the dusty top. Immediately, she spotted the initials MHB.

With a broken piece of wooden frame, Lexie jimmied the brass lock and lifted the lid. The inside didn't contain any hint of dust. The first thing to catch her attention, keepsakes from Harvard: a red sweater with *Harvard* in gold across the chest and a red banner, similar to the kind found on any college kid's wall today.

She pushed a green blanket beneath the mementos aside and uncovered a treasure trove of letters and books bound in leather. After reading a handful of titles, she paused when she found one she recognized: *The Picture of Dorian Gray.*

Lexie leafed through the pages until she found some handwriting on the title page. Her eyes stretched as wide as they could go.

"This is a first edition." Then she deciphered the signature. "No way? You were friends with Oscar Wilde?"

Unbeknownst to Lexie, Magnus stood over her and examined the book in her hands.

He smiled as he remembered his friend. The Irish storyteller had gone on to bigger and better things after leaving Altmover Manor but had stayed in touch through letters.

Amused by the way she hunched over, embarrassed by her loud outburst in the tomb-like attic, he perused the autograph in the book.

"We were friends once," he explained, hoping she reacted to his voice. "I liked Oscar. Better than I liked most people. He enjoyed life."

She replaced the book in the trunk and turned to the letters.

He sighed when she reached for a set done in a flowery script and tied with a red ribbon.

"Katherine Parker." Lexie untied the ribbon. "She was his wife."

The idea of a stranger reading his intimate correspondence with his darling Katie bothered Magnus. He spied another pile of letters tied with blue ribbon. Struck by an idea, he brushed his hand in front of the letters, sending the cold air surrounding him in their direction. The letters fell over, frightening Lexie.

Magnus chuckled when Lexie jumped back. But he knew her curiosity would outweigh her fright, and soon she was back, grabbing for the letters.

"Yes, read those." He smiled at her enthusiasm. "You will find them interesting."

While she read the masculine handwriting on the envelopes, Magnus admired the way the sunlight played in her hair. He'd forgotten how beautiful women could be. The perfume and softness of their skin, their curves, their graceful ways—it all came back to him. He knelt beside Lexie, captivated by her face.

"What I wouldn't give to touch a silky tendril of your hair."

"You kept private letters from Oscar Wilde," Lexie mumbled.

He waited as she counted the envelopes. There must have been over a dozen. He hoped the letters would be worth something. Enough to offset the couple's expenses. God knows, all the fiancé worried about was money. Magnus had spent enough time in his head to conclude they didn't have much of it. Magnus had to keep the girl at the house and didn't want finances to interfere. He had a job for her and couldn't afford distractions.

Lexie returned the letters to the trunk and was about to close it when something must have caught her eye. She worked a slip of paper from beneath some mementos. Magnus identified a program for a Boston Opera production of *The Mikado* dated, 1888.

The spot where his heart once resided, shuddered. Their night together came back to him in a series of tender pictures.

"Frances," he whispered.

Lexie tilted her head as if listening for something. He hoped she'd detected him, but like the teenagers, he enjoyed chasing from his home, she soon lost interest.

"I find it intriguing how the world has been able to continue with individuals who have the attention span of a gnat."

Something from underneath the program rolled to the side—a small perfume bottle with no name and a stopper shaped like a flower. Lexie lifted the stopper and placed the bottle under her nose.

"Smells like honeysuckle."

Magnus closed his eyes and remembered Frances's favorite perfume. The bottle had been among the things Jacob had left behind after departing Altmover Manor. Magnus ached to hold it once more.

She placed the perfume bottle and program back in the trunk. The loud thud of the lid closing brought Magnus back from his memories.

"There's no cane here, Mr. Blackwell. Now what?"

Magnus studied her profile as she scanned the attic. He found her curiosity endearing. She wondered if his cane hid in another trunk. But then, he would have pointed her in the right direction and appeased Remi.

"It's not here," he said to her.

Lexie spun around, a hint of fear in her eyes. She rubbed her arms. "I need to get out of this attic."

She patted the trunk while staring at the attic entrance. Magnus assumed she debated how to get the large chest out of the attic.

"You're going to need some help, dear girl."

Lexie stood and nodded. "Yeah, I've gotta get some help."

She strolled toward the entrance, and Magnus grinned, pleased with his progress. With a little manipulation, Lexie should find his cane and help free him from of his bond to his home. He still wasn't sure how to accomplish such a feat, but sooner or later Magnus had to find his cane. If he didn't, chaos would rain down on Altmover Manor and destroy everything he held dear.

# Chapter Eight

Will and Remi carried the large trunk down the staircase. "You think the signatures are authentic?" Will asked Lexie.

"I'm no expert, but I can check online to see if they match. We'll have to get someone to authenticate them if we want to put them up for sale. But if they are genuine, they might be worth a fortune."

"I watched a television program about a guy who found a copy of the *Declaration of Independence* in his attic," Remi added. "He made millions."

"I'd settle for enough to pay an electrician to rewire this entire house," Will said.

"Where do you want this, Lexie?" Remi questioned when they reached the first floor.

"In the living room."

Both men stopped in the foyer and confronted her with their downturned faces.

"Are you sure?" Will's voice dripped with skepticism. "What if Magnus makes another appearance."

Lexie held back the smartass return she wished to give him. "I've come up with a solution," she said instead. "I'm going to take his painting down and have it face the wall."

Will chuckled as the men moved toward the living room. "Yeah, that'll show him."

After setting the trunk on the floor by her computer, Will and Remi removed Magnus's painting, insisting the piece was too big for her to handle alone.

Once Magnus faced the wall, Lexie's trepidation eased. It helped not having the man's menacing gaze overseeing everything she did.

Will clapped his hands together. "Anything else you need us to do to keep ole Magnus away?"

She noted his sarcastic grin. "No, thank you."

"Good." Will walked up to Remi. "Let's grab some lunch."

Alone in the living room, Lexie opened the leather trunk. She removed the voodoo doll from the top of her computer and put it on the floor. Then she pulled out Oscar Wilde's letters and went to a search engine to find his signature.

It didn't take long for her to discover the letters seemed genuine, at least to her untrained eye. Eager to see what Magnus Blackwell and Oscar Wilde had in common, she opened the first letter.

Entranced by the letter, she jumped when a furry head butted against her hand. The gray cat insisted on her attention.

"Hey, where have you been?" She scratched under its chin. "Are you hungry?"

The cat stopped as if listening, and then slipped out of the room.

"Guess you're not hungry." Lexie went back to her letter.

When Remi and Will passed by the living room after their lunch. Lexie sat on the floor, still reading the letters.

"I saved you some tuna salad," Will said from the living room doorway.

She didn't look up from the letter in her hand. "Perfect. I'll have to save some for the cat."

"What cat?" Will asked.

"Lexie keeps seeing a stray cat around the house," Remi explained.

"Wonderful. Now we have a cat." Will entered the room with Remi on his heels. "What's so interesting?"

Lexie finally peered up at him. "Oscar Wilde based his character, Dorian Gray, on Magnus Blackwell."

Will shrugged. "You mean the film about the guy who never ages but his painting does?"

Remi nodded. "Yeah, I remember that movie."

"It's based on a book," Lexie pronounced in a flat tone. She held up *The Picture of Dorian Gray*. "This book. This is a first edition copy signed by Oscar Wilde to Magnus."

"Is it worth more than the letters?" Will's brow rose.

"Would you stop thinking about money and consider what this means? Our Magnus Blackwell is the basis for the most well-known literary character in modern times. Didn't either of you ever read the book?"

Remi and Will exchanged glances. "No," they said in unison.

Lexie stood from the floor, holding the book to her chest. "The character of Dorian Gray is cruel, conniving, sinful, and his horrible deeds are taken on by his portrait while he remains forever young and unsullied by his sins."

Will snapped his fingers. "The black cat did it." He smiled, acting pleased with himself. "I remember that part." He turned to Remi. "Which version did you see?"

"I liked the black and white one best."

"Guys, forget the movie." She held out the book to them. "If Magnus exhibited half the maniacal tendencies Wilde wrote about in his book, he must have been a diabolical asshole."

"So what? He's a dead diabolical asshole," Will argued.

She inhaled a calm breath, relaxing her tense shoulders. "I'm saying Magnus had some secrets. His restless spirit might be seeking us out to share those secrets."

"I knew it." Will threw up his hands. "The ghosts again."

"One minute, you're supportive; the next, you're attacking me." Lexie glared at him. "What's your problem?"

"I'm not attacking you," Will countered. "Can't I be a little freaked out when you keep talking about ghosts?"

Remi went to the voodoo doll on the floor. "Why is the doll still here?"

"Thought I would keep it as a good luck charm," Lexie told him.

Remi approached the doll but did not touch it. "That's not a good luck charm. It's bad gris-gris."

"What's gris-gris?" Lexie questioned.

"An amulet or talisman meant to protect a person from evil. But this doll is cursed with black magic. Whoever's tied to it still suffers."

"Aw, for the love of God." Will spun around to the door. "I'm going back upstairs."

Remi waited until Will left the room before he spoke. "Lexie, you don't want to keep anything associated with black magic around."

"Then why is it in this house?"

Remi shook his head and backed away. "I have no idea. You have to get rid of the doll. Burn it."

"I'll throw it out with the trash on Monday."

"No!" His voice rose, sounding panicked. "The only way to release a curse is to burn the object associated with it." Without another word, he walked out the doors.

Put off by his abruptness, Lexie chalked up his reaction to more superstition than sense. No matter what Remi believed, Lexie suspected the doll held an important clue to the strange occurrences happening around her. She wasn't about to get rid of it. Not just yet.

Exhausted, Lexie changed into her white nightshirt and climbed into bed next to Will. He had his laptop open, going over his plans for the restoration. Lexie reached for the Oscar Wilde letters she'd left on her night table.

While the tapping of Will's fingers on the computer keys disturbed the silence in the room, she devoured the correspondence between Magnus and Oscar Wilde.

"These two men met in New Orleans. Oscar makes several references in his letters to the time they spent there."

Will didn't look away from his laptop.

"Maybe the doll I found came from there," Lexie went on. "Magnus might have brought the voodoo doll home from his trip."

Will rolled his finger around on the mouse, rotating the house on the screen. "Most people bring home hurricane glasses as souvenirs. Our guy brought home a voodoo doll. Imagine that."

With the letter in hand, Lexie sat up in the bed. "Listen to this. *I implore you to stay away from O'Connor and his bride. I know your innermost feelings, my friend, and I fear what you may do.* What do you think that means? I wonder who O'Connor was."

"I have no idea," he mumbled, sounding bored. "Maybe the guy pissed him off. Or this O'Connor owed him money."

"Or he might be our architect." Lexie slouched, remembering the grainy photograph she'd found in the attic. "But these letters are dated before the changes to the house in 1890, so it can't be him."

He pushed his laptop aside. "How do you know when the changes were made?"

"I found a picture in the attic made during the renovations and dated 1890."

"Where's this picture?" His voice dropped, a sure sign of his frustration.

She put down her letter. "The living room. I put it with a collection of old paintings I found."

"Why don't you get the picture for me?"

"But …" Lexie hesitated. She feared going into the living room alone at night.

"Lexie, you'd better not say anything about ghosts."

"I know, Will. I'm not sure I can …"

He took a flashlight from his night table. "Then please get the picture. It might help with my notes."

She didn't want to argue. Lexie would rather face a boatload of Magnus Blackwells than have a confrontation with Will. She snatched the flashlight from him and climbed from the bed. After pulling on her fuzzy robe and finding her slippers, she looked at him.

"If I don't return …" She yanked the door open.

In the hallway, she flipped the switch for the sconces lining the walls. The pale light comforted her but faded as she approached the black staircase. Lexie turned on the flashlight and pointed the beam down the stairs.

She made her way down the white marble-inlaid steps, but as the darkness from the first floor closed in around her, Lexie picked up her pace. When her slippers hit the marble floor, she ran to the light switch controlling the foyer's lotus sconces. Jogging through the hallway toward the living room, Lexie fought to keep her dread from getting the better of her.

Once the lights in the living room came on, she let out a relieved sigh. The room was the same as she had left it. Paintings sat arranged against the walls, and Magnus Blackwell's portrait remained where Will and Remi had left it. Eager to retrieve the picture, Lexie went to the pieces she'd brought down from the attic and sifted through them.

The desired photograph in hand, she darted for the light switch, and an odd sensation came over her. She froze. Something wasn't right. She stifled a cry when she discovered Magnus's painting back above the mantel.

His condescending grin taunted her as if saying, "You can't get rid of me so easily."

She ran out of the living room without bothering to turn off the lights. In the hallway, she slapped the foyer light switch and rushed to the stairs.

Lexie trembled as the scales of the dragon undulated. She yanked her hand away from the banister and bounded up the last steps, eager to escape her nightmare.

Magnus's jubilant laughter carried throughout the downstairs as Lexie rounded the second-floor landing. The banister stopped moving and once again became a lifeless piece of wood.

When Lexie had noticed his painting hanging above the fireplace, he had found her fear adorable. He had a difficult time remembering when a human had sparked his interest as well as his amusement.

"She's so much like Frances."

"How dare you speak her name." The malevolent voice circled the foyer.

Jacob soon showed himself on the second-floor landing, not far from the chandelier. The fixture's gentle rocking warned of his former friend's distress.

"Must you go upsetting my home with another of your temper tantrums, O'Connor?"

Jacob descended the steps to confront Magnus.

"I'm not the one bringing the dragons to life with my anger. I told you to leave the girl alone. You've been hovering around her like a jealous lover."

"Me a jealous lover?" Magnus's cold snicker rose between the two men. "That's a role better suited to you, dear boy."

"How dare you say such a thing!" Jacob sneered, and the chandelier's sway accelerated. "Frances was my wife, not yours. You still hate me for marrying her, don't you?"

"Hate?" Magnus clenched his fists. The dragon head at the base of the staircase rose up, baring its sharp teeth. "A strong word for the dead to use. Hate belongs to the living."

"Our hate keeps us here, Magnus." His face soured. "The girl can't help you."

Magnus took a step back. "You're a fool, O'Connor. The

girl is going to find my cane and get me out of here."

"You think that charlatan is telling you the truth? He offered you a deal to find the cane, but he won't stick to it. He has no intention of freeing you from this house."

"I'm not going to spend eternity trapped here with you. If I must sacrifice my cane to buy my freedom, then so be it." Magnus dimmed, wanting to vanish.

"You're still obsessed with it, aren't you?" Jacob asked, stopping him. "You made this house a shrine to that damned cane, and still you want to possess it. You're dead. A ghost doesn't need a cane."

"What about its power?" Magnus snapped as his apparition revived. "You felt it. When you held the cane in your hands as a man, you became invigorated by its energy. We may be dead, but there is another who wants to possess the cane's power. Remi Glapion may be a liar and not what he seems, but if he can get me out of this house, then I'm prepared to do whatever it takes to get him the dragon cane."

Jacob turned to the stairs, and the chandelier's rocking eased. "Your damned cane has brought us nothing but grief."

The dragon's head in the banister shrank to its original size. "Only in life. In death, the cane will bring us salvation."

Jacob coasted up the steps. "I will stop you in any way I can from hurting the girl. You've destroyed enough lives. If you continue to haunt her, I will intercede."

Magnus chuckled as Jacob ascended the staircase. The banister writhed next to him. "I'd like to see you try, old friend."

At the top of the steps, Jacob glared down at him. "I'm not your friend. I never was." He walked off the landing and into the massive chandelier, evaporating from view.

Magnus sported a devilish half-smile. "Keep burying your

head in the sand, O'Connor. One day, I'm going to chop it off."

Not until she arrived at her bedroom door did Lexie regain her composure. She couldn't let Will get wind of her distress. Lexie went to the bed and flung the photograph at him.

"Here you go."

"You made it back in one piece. Amazing." He picked up the picture.

She wrung her hands, anxious to ask him a question. "Did you put Magnus's portrait back above the mantel?"

He studied the photograph. "What do you mean?"

"The one you and Remi took down for me today. I'd swore it was still on the floor when I entered the living room, but when I went to leave it was back up on the wall. Care to explain?"

Will turned the photo over, examining the back. "There's no paranormal activity going on in the living room, Lexie. Everything can be explained."

Lexie sensed pursuing the issue would make tension worse between them. Biting her tongue, she wrestled out of her robe, kicked off her slippers, and crawled back into bed. Lexie decided to forget about the incident downstairs and lose herself in Oscar Wilde's flowing penmanship.

Several minutes passed before she came across another interesting passage.

"Wow! Magnus and Oscar Wilde went to a voodoo ceremony at Bayou St. John. He writes how they visited several voodoo sites in New Orleans."

"No wonder you're freaked out. Ghosts, haunted pictures, and voodoo rituals. You need to stop reading this crap. Give me the letters."

She held the letter against her chest. "But I'm doing research."

"All you're doing is giving yourself nightmares." Will took the letter from her, plus the bundle on her lap, and set them on his night table. "Why not get out tomorrow? I can give you a list for the hardware store. You can do a little shopping while you're in town. How does that sound?"

Lexie entertained spending some time away from the house. She could use the opportunity to expand her search. "While I'm out, I'll stop by the library and check out their archives like you suggested. See if they have pictures of the house."

He shifted his attention back to his computer. "Great idea. You need to stay out of the attic for a while. You reek of the place."

She sniffed her nightshirt. "What are you talking about?"

"You smell like some old perfume." He moved something around on his computer screen.

"What perfume?"

"Honeysuckle. It's everywhere on you."

She remembered the perfume bottle in Magnus's trunk. But she hadn't touched the contents.

Lexie settled back into bed, perplexed by the situation. "You're right, Will. I need to get out of this house for a while before I lose my mind."

# Chapter Nine

The next morning, Lexie took the keys to the Volvo and headed to West Tremont. The smaller the rooftop of Altmover Manor got in her rearview mirror, the more she relaxed; her spirits lifted. People in cars reassured her the world beyond the manor was still there. Pulling into a spot in front of the local Ace Hardware, she removed Will's long list from her leather purse.

*This might take a while.*

Thirty minutes later, a muscle-bound teenager named Kyle helped Lexie carry the bags stuffed with Will's supplies to the car. After getting everything crammed into the trunk, Lexie turned to the young man.

"Any idea where I can find a grocery store?"

"Um, well." Kyle cleared his throat. "Happy's is our general store. They have a good selection, but if you want something bigger, Southwest Harbor has got a Walmart."

"A Walmart? How do I get there?"

Kyle turned to the street behind them. "Follow the main road till you see the sign for Bass Harbor Road. That will turn into 102."

"102, got it. And where is the library?"

Kyle scratched his head. "Ah, they got a small one in Bass Harbor. The big one is over in Northeast Harbor. It's on the other side of the island. The busy side." He stared at her for a moment, crinkling his brow. "You ain't from around here, are you?"

"No, I moved here a couple of days ago. I'm staying at Altmover Manor."

The boy's hooded eyelids popped open. "The haunted manor up on the cliff?"

Lexie cringed. *Thank God Will's not here.* "What do you know about the house?"

"I heard all kinds of scary shit goes on there. The rich guy who owned it and his wife were murdered by some wacko, and—"

The twinge reawakened in Lexie's gut. "Did you say murdered?"

"Yeah. They got pushed off the cliff and found together." Kyle shrugged. "Then a crazy old lady lived there for years until they found her dead."

"What crazy old lady?"

Kyle scrunched up his face. "I don't know; some lady. Me and a few guys used to go and hang out there in middle school. Sort of like the thing to do at the time. Check out the ghosts and all."

Lexie glimpsed the keys in her hand. "Ever see any?"

He shook his head. "Nah. My friend, Gerry, went there one night with his brother and they swore they heard a woman scream." He scrutinized her with his blue eyes. "You ever see anything?"

"There are no such things as ghosts, Kyle. Altmover is nothing more than an old house with a sad past."

Lexie left the bewildered boy behind and set out on the road out of town.

Navigating the island turned out to be easier than she imagined. With a handful of main roads, everything had been set to return to them. In Somesville, she followed the signs to the main public library in Northeast Harbor.

Built on a hill, the gray stone structure resembled a house more than a public building. The library's modern presentation appealed to Lexie. She hoped the inside didn't disappoint. Etched in the glass door was the familiar lighthouse logo found all over the island.

At a dark wood desk with stacked bookshelves behind it, a lone red-haired librarian squinted at her computer monitor through her reading glasses.

"Excuse me." Lexie lowered her voice. "Can you help me find some information on a local landmark?"

"No need to whisper, dearie." The older woman's tight blue jeans and black ZZ Top T-shirt clashed with the silver-beaded necklace attached to her reading glasses. "No one is in here so you can talk as loud as you like." She winked at Lexie. "I'm Mabel, chief librarian. How can I help you?"

Lexie leaned over the check-in desk. "Hi, Mable, I'm Lexie. I need information on Magnus Blackwell and Altmover Manor near West Tremont."

"Oh, the haunted manor." Mabel stood from the desk. "We've got lots on the manor and Mr. Blackwell." She looked Lexie over. "What's your interest, if you don't mind my asking?"

"My fiancé recently purchased the manor. We're renovating the inside and need pictures of the interior to help with the restorations."

"You're Will Bennett's fiancée?"

Lexie's gut twisted tighter. "How do you know Will?"

Mabel waved off the question with a wicked grin. "Never met the man. You can't piss in the ocean without half the island hearing about it." She came around the desk. "All everyone's been talking about is Altmover Manor getting bought by a private owner. People 'round here been screaming for years for the property to be saved, but no one ever had the balls to set foot in the place. It's haunted, don't you know?"

Lexie smiled, shaking her head. "Yes, I've been told."

Mabel's chuckle was as flirty as her grin. "I'll bet. The records are this way." She set out at a brisk pace. "We keep all the archives for the Mount Desert Islander Newspaper in this library, so we've got everything on the Magnus Blackwell murders stored here."

"Who murdered Mr. and Mrs. Blackwell?"

"Jacob O'Connor, the architect hired to do renovations on Altmover Manor. He pushed them over the cliff behind the home."

*O'Connor!* Lexie stumbled forward, filled with questions, but Mabel was too fast for her. Lexie took off after the librarian's black shirt as Mabel turned left into an open room with skylights.

"Is Jacob O'Connor the one who hanged himself from the foyer chandelier? Because he killed the Blackwells?"

Mabel abruptly halted and turned to Lexie. "How did you know he hanged himself?"

Lexie took in Mabel's bright pink running shoes. "Island gossip. But that doesn't tell me the real story about the murders."

"No, I 'spect not. Anything you hear about the house deals with the night Magnus died. After his murder, the estate came under the management of the Parker and Mills Bank. They hired a caretaker to oversee the place, but no one's ever made up any sensational stories about her."

"Is she the woman who lived in the house until she died? Do you have any information on her?"

Mabel took another sharp right at a pair of glass doors. "Let's find out." She opened the doors, and the bracing air conditioning hit Lexie's skin. "We never got enough funding to update the archives to computers, so you'll have to go through the original newspaper articles in here. We keep this place at a cooler temp and lower humidity than the rest of the library, hence the AC."

Inside the glass room, several metal shelves boasted numerous large leather-bound books. Mabel raised her glasses and perused the bindings.

"The murders happened in November, 1894." She removed a volume from the shelf. "Been a while since I hunted through any of this stuff."

"Has anyone else been searching for information on the house?"

Mabel's hazel eyes analyzed Lexie through her thick lenses. "Not that I know of. Why?"

"Anyone named Remi. Remi Glapion. He's the last caretaker the bank hired to oversee the manor. We've kept him on to help with the renovations."

Mabel carried the book to a wooden table. "I was under the impression the bank did away with caretakers when they put in the alarm system a while back."

Lexie stayed close on her heels. "But I heard they had problems with the local teenagers and kept on a caretaker to keep an eye on things."

Mabel set the book on the table. "By then, the place had been empty for years, but the local sheriff always checked on it for the bank. When they found the house broken into, the bank put in the alarm. I never knew they got another caretaker."

"Maybe Remi kept a low profile. He's a big black man from New Orleans and would stand out around here."

Mabel chuckled and opened the book. "Everyone on the island would have spread the word about him. I can assure you, I'd remember such a man coming into this library."

"Is it possible he went to the library in West Harbor?"

Mabel scanned the pages. "Doubt it. Only archives on the island are here." She stopped in the middle of a page. "Here you go. This is where the Blackwell murders start."

Lexie reviewed the yellowed newspaper headline. "*Murder at the Manor*. How original."

"Yeah, we didn't have any Pulitzer Prize winners working at the paper back then, or now, for that matter," Mabel admitted with a curt snort.

Lexie analyzed the grainy photograph of the house on the front page. "This is after the renovations."

"Yes, the ones done by Jacob O'Connor," Mabel confirmed. "Magnus's architect."

Lexie skimmed the other photos in the articles. "Do you have any pictures of the manor before the renovations? Perhaps of the interior?"

While Mabel deliberated the question, the crease between her eyebrows deepened. "Years back, Jenny Driscoll did a senior paper on Altmover Manor. I remember the library had a book with older photos of the home." She patted Lexie's shoulder. "I'll go find it."

Mabel rushed out the glass doors and back into the library.

Lexie settled down to read the sensational story of Magnus and his wife's murder.

> *Magnus Blackwell and his society wife, Katherine Blackwell née Parker, were brutally murdered last Saturday night at the Blackwell estate, Altmover Manor. The couple had been celebrating their first wedding anniversary with a hundred close friends and family when the heinous crimes occurred. The local sheriff has told this reporter the couple was thrown over a railing in the back of the home to*

*the craggy rocks that line so much of the island. The culprit: the architect Mr. Blackwell hired to do the wonderful new renovations on the manor, making it an architectural masterpiece.*

*Jacob O'Connor, formerly of Boston, was blamed for the deaths. By chance, the dastardly Mr. O'Connor hanged himself from the massive chandelier in the foyer shortly after authorities believe he committed the crimes.*

*Many guests left the grand soiree without knowing the atrocity committed under their noses. The broken and battered couple were not found until the morning after the party.*

*Funeral arrangements for the Blackwells are pending and …*

Lexie turned the page. "Enough of that."

The next article she found pertained to Jacob O'Connor and his apparent motive for the crime.

*Incensed by the loss of his wife to suicide three years before at the same spot behind the manor house, Mr. O'Connor blamed Magnus Blackwell for his wife's demise. Friends of the late Mr. O'Connor tell this reporter he was not a stable man. After his wife's death, he worked for B&M Railroad in Boston and returned to Altmover Manor after an injury disabled him.*

Below the article, a picture of Magnus, Katherine, and a man identified as Jacob O'Connor, stood before the steps of the home.

This image of Jacob O'Connor resembled the same man Lexie had seen in her bathroom. What she found troubling was Magnus Blackwell's dragon cane in his hands. The same cane Magnus had asked her to find.

"Here it is," Mabel announced, returning to the room. "The picture you want is in *Famous Houses of Maine.*"

Lexie could not tear herself away from Jacob O'Connor's image. "Any idea when this was taken?"

Mabel clasped the book to her chest and raised her glasses to inspect the grainy photo. "Oh, the night of the party, right before they died. Creepy, huh?"

"What did they do with Jacob O'Connor's body and his things?"

"Keep going. There's a brief article on his funeral."

Lexie turned the fragile, oversized pages.

"There." Mabel pointed to a small byline.

> *The funeral for Jacob O'Connor, murderer of Magnus and Katherine Blackwell, was held today at Forest Hills Cemetery in Boston. With aid from an unidentified source, he was laid to rest near his late wife, Frances O'Connor née McGee. Orphaned at the age of eight, Mr. O'Connor is survived by no family.*

The bitter air in the room seeped into Lexie's heart as the name bounced around her head. "Frances. His wife's name was Frances."

"You okay, dearie?"

Lexie shook off her stupor. "If he had no family, who got his stuff?" She turned back the pages to the picture of Magnus, Katherine, and Jacob. "Like this cane? Where did it go?"

Mabel removed her glasses. "I couldn't tell you. They buried people during those times with precious objects but was his cane precious to him? I have no idea."

"No, but the cane is precious to someone else." Lexie tapped on the book Mabel set in front of her. "What's in here?"

Mabel jumped to attention and flipped through the pages. She stopped on an image of a gloomy stone house. "I found a picture of Altmover Manor before Magnus Blackwell changed it. Magnus's grandfather bought the land—we call that section of the island the 'quiet side'—and built the house. Says here he named the estate Altmover after an ancestral home in Ireland."

Lexie read the brief caption. "Can I take this with me?"

"You can check it out at the desk after you sign up for a library card," Mabel said. "The book will be due back in two weeks."

"Is there anywhere else on the island with information on the Blackwells?"

"You might try the Mount Desert Historical Society. They're back up in Somesville, right off 102. You can't miss it."

She closed the cover on *Famous Houses of Maine*. "Can you tell me anything else about Magnus Blackwell or the house?"

Mabel's lips came together in a grim line as she sat down next to Lexie. "What you learn about these small islands doesn't come from books, but from its people. I've lived here all my life, and I've heard lots of stories about Altmover Manor and Magnus Blackwell." She placed her hand on the old newspaper articles. "What they don't say in here is the bad reputation the man had. For years, people feared going to the house. Young women especially. Rumor has it he did unspeakable things to his maids and then paid them off to hold their tongues."

"'Unspeakable things'? In this day and age, that can mean anything."

"Reports vary from orgies to devil worship, but who knows the truth. Gossip is rooted in fact most times. Unfortunately, by the time the gossip takes hold, the facts are forgotten." She smiled at Lexie. "There's another book you can read to learn more about Magnus: *The Picture of Dorian Gray.* He was the model for the main character, and Oscar Wilde's friend."

"I've read it." Lexie kept up her cheery demeanor to hide her frustration from Mabel as she closed the tome filled with old newspapers.

"I'm afraid this is about as close as you will get to Magnus Blackwell, Lexie. Unless you can travel back in time or speak to his ghost, his life will remain a mystery."

An excited tingle ripped through Lexie. If Magnus Blackwell walked out of a painting to talk to her, maybe she could turn the tables on him. One conversation with the man had the potential to put to rest years of mystery.

"Thank you for everything, Mabel." Lexie stood, grasping the book, *Famous Houses of Maine,* in her hands.

Mabel rose from her chair. "Let's get you set up with a library card."

# Chapter Ten

Lexie raced through the Walmart in Southwest Harbor at record speed. With Will's Volvo packed to capacity, she took the main road back toward West Tremont.

The sun dipped below the horizon when she sighted the manor's rooftop. Lexie should have dreaded her return to the house, but instead, she anticipated the intrigue to come. What did she have to fear? Magnus lived as a person, like her, suffering through sorrows and keeping secrets. Shouldn't his spiritual being communicate in the same logical and communicative manner as his physical being had once done?

"This is going to be the stupidest thing I've done since sleeping with Barrett Kelsey."

When she entered the front doors, Lexie called out for Will and Remi to help unload the car. After dumping the grocery bags on the kitchen counter, Will stuck his head in the door.

"Did you get everything on my list?"

She frowned at the dust and grime on his T-shirt. "Yep, it's in the car. Where's Remi?"

"He went back to his cottage. Said he had a headache."

Lexie walked up to him. "Does he need anything?"

Will dug through the bags on the counter. "If he does, he'll come over."

Lexie frowned as she rested her hand on her hip. "I wanted to ask him something."

"About what?"

She brushed some dirt off his shirt. "Nothing important. Come on; you can help me unload the car."

After doing an inventory of his hardware supplies, Will searched the fridge for dinner.

"It's already in the microwave," Lexie told him.

"What is?"

"Lasagna. I got a frozen one for us, and ..." She lifted a bottle of Chianti from the counter. "I went all out at Walmart."

"Is that possible?" he joked, taking the wine from her.

"You'd be amazed." Lexie retrieved the two wine glasses set aside on the counter. "I spent over five hundred dollars today on food and supplies. Any idea how long our savings will last?"

He twisted the tin cap off the bottle. "My calculations say three months. Then we'll need to start lining up jobs."

"Unless we sell some stuff in the attic."

He poured the red wine into a glass. "Let's hope you find the family jewels up there then."

"I got an exterior picture of the old house today at the library, but nothing from the inside. Did read some badly written articles about the Blackwells' murder though. Sensational stuff."

His mouth fell open. "They were murdered?"

"Yep. The newspaper articles I read said Jacob O'Connor, the architect hired by Magnus Blackwell to renovate the house, pushed him and his wife off the cliffs outside."

"Probably pissed with his boss for making so many changes to the house. I can relate." Will cocked an eyebrow while filling another glass. "Digging up sensational stories wasn't the reason for your trip to the library. I need architecture, not drama."

"Yeah, but the sensational stuff is a lot more interesting." Lexie selected a wineglass. "I spoke to the librarian there who had some dirt on Magnus. Things not in the books."

Will put the bottle on the counter and lifted his glass. "Only you can go to a library and find the island gossip."

"Mabel, the librarian I met, said she's never seen Remi in the library there."

"So? He doesn't like libraries." Will went to the microwave door. "Is the lasagna done yet?"

Lexie thumped her drink on the counter. "She said no one on the island has mentioned anything about a black man staying at Altmover Manor. We should get him checked out."

"Lexie, the guy knows more about renovating old houses than me." He took a sip from his wineglass. "He's not a thief or a con artist. Remi wants to work on old houses and nothing more."

"Why doesn't he come over for dinner?" The microwave beeper went off.

"Maybe the guy can cook."

"Oh, ha, ha." She removed the bubbling lasagna from the microwave, then tossed her oven mitts to the side. "At least call the bank and check him out."

"If you drop the subject for the rest of the evening, I'll consider calling the bank."

"Stop fighting me on this, Will. Why do you have so much confidence in Remi?"

Will went up to her and tugged her into his arms. "For this place to work, I need Remi. I can't risk losing him because of background checks or too many personal questions. Let's not look a gift horse in the mouth. Okay?" He kissed her forehead. "Time to eat."

While Will scrounged around in the cabinet for dinner plates, Lexie considered his explanation. It didn't make sense to her. The Will Bennett she'd spent the last year with would never have allowed a stranger like Remi into their lives without a thorough vetting.

After dinner, and a good bit of wine, a tipsy Will encouraged Lexie to bed. "Let's go up before I fall asleep downstairs."

"You go on. I'll finish in here and be on up in a sec."

With a loud yawn, Will shuffled out the kitchen door. At the sink, Lexie pretended to wipe the counter down for the third time, but on the inside, she was as jumpy as a Chihuahua on meth.

Movement from the floor above assured her Will had made it to their bedroom. After throwing the paper towel in her hand into the garbage, she snapped up the Chianti from the counter and shot back a hefty swig. If she went ahead with her crazy plan to talk to a dead man, Lexie needed all the encouragement she could get.

"Consider it surgery. Nasty, painful, but it has to be done."

At the entrance to the living room, she spotted the large gray cat hissing at something.

"Hey, kitty."

The cat gave her an indifferent glance and sauntered away. .

"Damn. Where did it go?"

The cat forgotten, Lexie ventured to the living room entrance, her stomach a ball of jumbled nerves.

*Maybe I should leave the lights off—don't spirits prefer the dark?*

Once in the center of the living room, Lexie struggled to recall the séances she'd seen in the movies. She didn't have any candles, didn't own a spirit board, and had no experience with summoning the dead. Lexie would have to take a more practical approach.

With a *thud*, she had a seat on the floor. The wine must have been kicking in because the room wobbled. She relaxed her shoulders and concentrated on Magnus's portrait. She envisioned the haughty man in the painting as he had been in life.

"I'm here Mr. Blackwell. I'm ready to listen to anything you have to say. Well, almost anything. Don't ask me about your cane. If you ask someone to get you something, a hint about where to find it would help." She paused, tilting her head. "And by the way, you've got a hell of a reputation on this island. I don't know what you did, but you sure—"

"You talk too much."

The man's voice came from behind her. The heady aroma of coffee wafted past her nose. Lexie's heart skipped a beat as an icy breeze enveloped her. She squeezed her eyes shut, summoned her courage and swiveled around on the floor.

After a deep breath, Lexie opened her eyes. Magnus Blackwell glowed before her as if standing inside a brightly lit doorway. He presented as he did in his portrait, but with some changes: he didn't have his dragon cane, his coat had tears in the lapel, and his tie came across as more gray than white. His fingers, no longer pale and smooth, resembled the black digits of someone infected with gangrene. Magnus's sneaky grin remained intact, but the scar on his right cheek had not been there before.

"I never let myself be bothered by what others said about me when I was alive, dear girl. Why should that change when I'm dead?"

He hovered off to the side, near where she'd left her computer and the voodoo doll.

"I must be drunker than I thought," Lexie mumbled.

Magnus chuckled, sounding more amused than malevolent. "Obviously, not drunk enough." He tapped his foot on the floor. "Where's my cane?"

She struggled to stand. "Why do you want your cane?"

"I don't, but someone else in this house does. Be careful of him."

"Him, who? A man? Another ghost? Jacob's ghost?"

He rolled his eyes. "O'Connor is a thorn in my side."

Lexie leaned in closer. "He killed you."

"Yes, I'm well aware of how I died."

The cool air in the room tickled her skin. "Is he here?"

The scowl on his face softened. "Everything is not as it seems in your world, Lexie. Trust what's inside you."

"Wait, what about—?"

"Find my cane and be quick about it. There isn't much time." Then he disappeared.

Lexie gaped about the empty room. "You can't go. I need more information." She waited for a response, but he never returned. Stamping her foot on the floor, she shouted, "Shit!"

"What are you doing?"

She spun around. Will had his shoulder propped against the doorway. The faint light from the room bathed his face, but his half-naked body remained hidden in the shadows, giving Lexie the impression of a floating head.

"Will, you scared me."

His scowl reminded her of Magnus. For an instant, the two men blurred into one.

The floorboards moaned as he entered the room. "Didn't think I'd find you in here. Last night you were terrified of coming into this room alone."

"I got over it."

Will strolled up to her. "Why were you cursing?"

"I was searching for that cat. It ran in here."

He slipped his arm around her waist. "You can hunt for the cat tomorrow. Come to bed."

She let him guide her to the entrance. "Aren't you tired?"

His hand dropped to her ass. "Not anymore …" He squeezed her butt.

After turning off the lights, Will nuzzled her neck and urged her up the staircase. As she twisted in his arms, she remembered Magnus's ghost. Was he watching them?

"Take off those clothes," Will murmured, pulling her inside their bedroom. "I want you beneath me."

Lexie wrestled her T-shirt over her head. "What brought this on?"

He reached around to undo her bra. "I was lying in bed, ready to fall asleep, and then I pictured your fine ass and all the things I'd like to do to it."

"This doesn't sound like you."

He lowered the zipper on her jeans. "You haunt my dreams, dear girl."

She arched from him. "What did you say?"

Without answering, he lifted her in his arms and took her to the bed. Will set her on the bedspread, removed her jeans, and bent over her like a predator about to go in for the kill.

Lexie cupped his face and studied the strange way his eyes changed color in the light—from brown to green, and back to brown.

Will kissed her with such ferocity Lexie forgot about the phenomenon. She wanted him, more than any time before.

She wrapped her legs around his waist, she begged for him to hurry. He wrestled his pants over his hips, and when his erection rubbed against her thigh, she guided him into her.

Will moved in and out, his thrusts relentless. Never had their love making been so overpowering.

Her muscles tensed as the rising crescendo of pleasure took over her senses. She clawed at his back, desperate to come when the all-consuming wave overtook her. Calling his name, she bucked beneath him.

He tightened his grip on her. Lexie anticipated his release. Then, without warning, he stopped.

"What is it?"

Will grabbed her butt, squeezing her tighter around his cock. "I'm not done with you."

She gasped as he rammed into her, sending a jolt through her system. He carried her to a swift second orgasm. He paused while she caught her breath, before once again, slamming into her until she screamed.

When he finally came, Will collapsed on top of her with a loud grunt.

Spent, her body humming with satisfaction, Lexie reflected on Will's unusual behavior.

"What's gotten into you?"

He kissed her forehead and then rolled off her. "I have no idea."

Within seconds, he fell asleep, leaving Lexie perplexed.

She checked his breathing, tiptoed into the bathroom and closed the door. In front of her vanity mirror, she pondered Magnus's warning.

"Where do I go next to find this cane?"

The lights in the bathroom flickered, and the mirror clouded over. A few days ago, the idea of speaking to ghosts would have sent Lexie screaming from the house, but her curiosity had replaced her fear. To get answers, Lexie understood her only option was to embrace her newfound ability.

Jacob O'Connor, with his curly black hair and kind brown eyes, manifested in the smoke. This time, a discoloration presented around his chin—a blackness Lexie had not seen before.

"Hello, Ms. Arden."

It took a second for his greeting to sink in, but then Lexie's lips stretched into a gaping grin. "You know my name?"

"You remind me of my Frances. She too was a woman with gumption."

A comforting pride permeated her limbs. "Mr. O'Connor, you can call me Lexie."

The ghost nodded. "Be careful, Lexie. All is not what it seems in this house. You are in danger."

The lights flickered again, and the smoke in the mirror vanished, and Jacob O'Connor with it.

"Wait! What do you mean, I'm in danger?"

Lexie rubbed her hand across the mirror and then knocked against the glass, hoping the ghost would return. But nothing happened.

She shook her head and turned on the tap. "Good thing I'm already crazy because living here would drive a sane person over the edge."

# Chapter Eleven

A woman's scream roused Lexie from a deep sleep. When she sat up in the bed, Will wasn't beside her.

"You okay?"

Still in his blue pajama bottoms, he stood in the bathroom doorway brushing his teeth.

Lexie flopped back on her pillow and slapped her hand over her forehead. "No. The Chianti from last night is killing me."

"No more Chianti for either of us. I had bad dreams all night long." He went back into the bathroom.

With a groan, Lexie climbed from the bed. She shuffled into the bathroom and nestled behind him, resting her head against his back.

"I had this weird dream of a woman screaming."

He reached for a hand towel. "Must be the house getting to

us. I kept seeing Magnus Blackwell in my dreams."

Lexie pushed away from Will, troubled by the mention of the ghost. "What did he say?"

"Nothing." Will shrugged as he wiped his face. "He kept smirking at me."

She relaxed and gave him a flirty grin. "Maybe he's proud of your performance last night."

Will tossed the towel onto the vanity counter. "What performance?"

"What do you mean 'what performance'? Last night you were like a bull. You've never held off so long during sex. I screamed so loud, I'm sure they heard me in West Tremont."

His eyebrows knitted. "I'd sworn I dreamt that."

Alarm bells went off inside Lexie's head. "You don't remember?"

Will rested his hip against the counter. "I had this strange dream I went to get you in the living room and brought you up here and … Well, you know the rest. Guess it wasn't a dream after all." He pulled her into his arms. "Probably the damn wine. You know how I get with wine. The stuff messes me up."

Not wanting to fan the flames of her unease, she cuddled against his chest, eager to accept his explanation. "Yeah, you're a lightweight. I did have a good time though."

"I aim to please, Ms. Arden."

Will's cell phone rang with its jazzy ringtone from his night table. He jogged back into the bedroom, while Lexie waited at the bathroom door.

"Hello?" Will grimaced. "Yes, Mr. Lawrence. Yes, sir, I realize the end of the month is this weekend. We still have several boxes left in—" Will stopped talking, and his mouth turned down at the edges. "Yes, Mr. Lawrence. I can have Lexie drop the keys off to you. Ah, she will be heading back there soon to clear out our stuff and then you can show it to the new renters." Will scratched his head. "Yes, sir, we enjoyed renting there. Will do." He hung up the phone. "Guess who?"

Lexie sagged against the doorway. "We don't live there anymore and he's still hounding us."

"He wants the keys and our stuff out of the apartment so he can show it to the new renters this weekend."

She pouted her lips at Will. "Why do I have to go to Boston? Why can't you go?"

He put his phone on the night table and ambled up to her. "Because I have to work on the house with Remi. I need to spend every second I have here. You can leave for Boston today, stay the night at your mom's, and come back tomorrow."

She stomped on the floor. "Since when did you start giving me orders like a servant?"

Will chuckled at her outburst while rubbing his hand along the stubble on his chin. "Did I sound too harsh?"

"A little." She playfully slapped his chest. "Besides, I wanted to do some more hunting in the attic today since I spent yesterday running errands. I can go tomorrow."

He kissed her cheek. "Fine. Go tomorrow. You can appease old man Lawrence and have a nice long visit with your mom."

"Are you being funny?" She turned back to the bathroom. "She's going to hound me while I'm there."

"Would you like me to call and tell her for the hundredth time I have every intention of marrying you?" Will relaxed against the doorframe. "I haven't given you a ring or set the date, but I can give her a note written in blood if she prefers."

"Like that would help. After Cindy's perfect wedding, she'll want me to do the same thing. The big guest list, the lavish reception, the ridiculously poufy dress … ugh."

"Then tell her you're not like your sister. You're not marrying a pilot. You're marrying an architect. We're more grounded."

"Cute." She picked up her toothbrush.

He came up behind her. "Why not tell her we set the date. Let her know we're getting married here, in this house, next year—in the fall. October? By then we should have the place presentable for a wedding."

Lexie studied him through the vanity mirror and put down her toothbrush. "You never wanted to set the date before."

Will massaged her shoulders. "Things are different. We have a venue, and your mother will find the guests. All we need is the cake and a band. We can dance the night away in our ballroom, and you can toss the bouquet from the top of our fancy staircase."

She spun around to face him. "All right. I'll tell my mother next year." She slid her arms around his neck. "Is there anything you want me to get while I'm in Boston?"

He kissed her chin. "Yeah, some special chicory blend from the coffee store down from our old place. I have a feeling we're going to need it."

"A feeling?" she said as he stepped alongside her at the vanity. "But you don't like coffee."

Will plugged in his electric razor. "I know, but I've got a craving for it."

She picked up her toothbrush. Between the strange dreams, newfound lust, and hankering for coffee, she debated whether the house had gotten under his skin.

---

Lexie wiped the dust from her hands as she stood in the living room evaluating the treasures she'd brought down from the attic. Her morning hunt through boxes and broken furniture had been fruitful, but one piece called to her. A small trunk—not well made—stood out from the others in the attic. She knelt before it, hoping something valuable lurked inside.

The lock fell apart in her hands, having rusted all the way through. She flipped open the lid, a pungent aroma of mold hit her. A tattered black tuxedo lay on top of a man's black leather shoes. Tucked against the shoes were some books on architecture, which had fared better than the clothes. A gold pocket watch peeked out from between the books and letters tied with red ribbon. Wedged against the trunk's side was a well-preserved wedding photograph in a tarnished silver frame.

The groom she recognized as the ghost in her bathroom mirror, Jacob O'Connor. His bride bore a striking resemblance to Katherine Blackwell, and to Lexie.

She turned to Magnus Blackwell's portrait. "You and Jacob had the same taste in women, eh, Magnus? Interesting."

"It's dangerous to talk to the dead," Remi commented, strutting into the room. "They see it as an invitation back into this world."

"I'm guessing that doesn't apply to our two ghosts."

Remi's ceaseless grin wavered. "Has something happened?"

"Other than I have two dead men haunting me, a fiancé who is acting strange, and a house sucking the lifeblood out of me? No, everything is great."

"No one said possessing such a gift is easy." Remi made his way to her side. "Have the ghosts harmed you or Will?"

"Harmed, no. Bothered, yes." She went to the trunk and pulled out the framed picture. "This guy showed up last night." She held out the picture. "Jacob O'Connor, the architect who killed Magnus Blackwell and his wife."

Remi shifted his focus from the photo to Lexie. "You look like her."

"Both ghosts called me by name, and they speak in full sentences. Weirdly cryptic sentences, but full ones, nonetheless. Can you explain why?"

"Magnus spoke to you again?"

"Last night. I came in here after Will went to bed and talked to his picture, encouraging him to communicate with me."

"You mean you summoned him." Remi folded his thick arms, his lips twisted in a disapproving frown. "And?"

"He showed up, but he was different." She replaced the picture in the trunk, uncomfortable with his sullen stare. "When he first walked out of his portrait, he came across as bright and shiny. But last night, he had dingy clothes, a scar on his right cheek, and black fingers. I might have been drunk, but he didn't resemble the other Magnus Blackwell I met."

"My aunt used to talk about stains on the soul. When we die, what we did in life can mark the spirit. All the evil we do can stain us on the inside. Our souls can blacken, have spots, scars, or tears. This time you may have encountered his true soul."

"The ghost I faced in the mirror last night looked different, too. He had a blackness around his chin."

"The stain on his soul for his crimes, no doubt," Remi said.

The wheels turned in Lexie's head. *There's a pattern here.* "Sounds like what Oscar Wilde did in *The Picture of Dorian Gray,* but instead of a stained soul, it's a stained portrait."

Remi placed his hands behind his back as he towered over Lexie. "What else did Magnus's ghost say to you?"

Intimidated by his disturbing presence, Lexie fought to recall the brief encounter. "Something about someone else in the house wanting his cane. He didn't give me any specifics."

"He must mean the other ghost. Jacob O'Connor wants the cane." Remi's wintry gaze shifted to the painting. "You need to be careful. Both men are using you to fight their battle. They want to sway you to their cause."

"You think so?"

Remi ventured closer to the fireplace. "What they competed for in life, they're competing for in death: the love of a woman."

"I think you've stumbled onto something, Remi. They were both in love with the same woman." She snapped her fingers. "It must have been Frances. Magnus wanted her, but Jacob got her?"

"And Magnus married Katherine Parker because she reminded him of Frances." He turned to her. "And you remind both men of her. It's the reason they're reaching out to you."

"Is that why Frances threw herself over the cliff? Because she was torn between both men?"

"Who knows what goes on in a woman's mind? She could have loved Magnus or argued with her husband." He tilted toward her, grinning. "Or someone pushed her."

A coldness stabbed into Lexie's chest. She hated to think of Frances's soul suffering through such tragedy. "How can you suspect such a thing?"

"I'm a man, Lexie. You're chasing the romance; I'm hunting for a motive."

She wanted to make a snarky comment about not having to think with her balls but held her tongue. How men could be practical when speaking about such atrocities confounded her. She saw the same characteristic in Will. She would fall apart during a sappy commercial, and he would gawk at her as if she'd sprouted wings. Lexie decided to brush off Remi's comment and redirect their conversation to a more pressing matter—for her, anyway.

"Did Will tell you I went to the library in Southeast Harbor yesterday?"

"And you asked the librarian about me, yes." He nodded. "He already warned me you would have a thousand questions about why no one has reported seeing me. The answer is simple, Lexie.

Because I am a big black man, I've kept to myself while on the island. I'm smart enough not to go asking for trouble."

Suddenly feeling foolish, she blushed. "I'm sorry. I didn't think …"

"Not to worry. You haven't walked in my shoes." He made his way back to the doorway and then halted. "Oh, any leads in the attic for Magnus's cane?"

She shook her head, sighing. "No, and tomorrow I have to go to Boston, so I won't be able to get back into the attic for another day or so."

"You'll be in Magnus's old stomping ground. You could do some digging while you're there. Might help to narrow the search."

"Thanks for the tip."

Remi motioned to Magnus's portrait. "And don't talk to any more paintings around here, Lexie. You've got about all the ghosts you can handle."

Frustrated with the girl, Remi walked out the living room doors and went to the foyer. Before he reached the staircase, Magnus materialized.

"I want you to follow her to Boston," Remi commanded under his breath as he inspected the dragon's head at the base of the stairs. "I'd like to keep an eye on her."

"I can't leave this house." Magnus hovered over the bottom step, insinuating his displeasure with his unyielding glower. "Unless you'd like to unbind me. You have the ability."

"An ability I will not use until I get what I want." Remi approached the step, determined to show the ghost who was boss. "I wish you'd make yourself useful. Encouraging the girl is one thing, but I need her motivated."

"Should I have another go at the fiancé? Occupying his skin helps pass the time."

"Keep your bedroom antics from interfering. When she returns, I want you to double your efforts."

To remind the ghost of his position, Remi passed through Magnus's image and trotted up the steps.

"You should take care how you talk to me," Magnus warned.

Remi stopped and sneered down at the ghost. "Remember your place, Magnus. I'm the one with the power here. If you don't work with me, I'll leave you to rot in this house."

"And what is the girl?" Magnus shot back. "She has more power than you."

Remi drummed his fingers on the banister, unhappy with the reminder. "The girl is a threat to what I am, and her gift will be dealt with eventually. For the time being, I want to see what she can do."

"Remi? Where are you?" Will called from the second floor.

Man and ghost peered up the steps.

"He sounds more like you every day," Remi said.

"I'm working my magic on him." Magnus faded. "Better run along to your day job."

After Magnus dissolved completely, Remi gripped the banister. "When the time comes, I'll find something to drive Lexie Arden and her oblivious fiancé out of my life for good."

# Chapter Twelve

The next morning, while driving to Boston, Lexie mulled over her time at Altmover. Between the stress of the move, the money, the ghosts, and the change in Will, she questioned if seeing her mother was a good idea. An evening with Angela would drive anyone to hari-kari.

A familiar churning plagued Lexie's stomach—the same discomfort she got whenever she dealt with her mother. After a lifetime of deliberation, Lexie had convinced herself the root of her anxiety was her over-controlling mother. After all, she had already driven one man to an early grave, and Lexie suspected her stepfather, Kevin, would be kicking the bucket sometime soon.

Parked outside her old apartment building in West Roxbury, she assessed the rather plain ten-story structure comparing it to the architectural wonder of Altmover Manor. She didn't miss her former home; she just wished her new one wasn't so haunted.

Once her elevator reached the eighth floor, she hurried to their former apartment. The door hung crooked from its hinges, and it took a swift kick to open—she wouldn't miss that.

In the living room, boxes they hadn't been able to pack into the U-Haul sat piled in a corner. She lifted one of the boxes, and a small ornament fell on to the gray carpet.

Made from blue and white yarn, it was woven to resemble a spider's web. Fondling the dangling white feathers, she remembered how her grandmother had made the dreamcatcher for her to hang over her bed. When she'd moved in with Will, Lexie had brought the memento with her to remember the grandmother who had taught her so much about listening to her inner voice.

She turned the charm over in her hands, yearning to talk to her grandmother again. If anyone could decipher the supernatural, it was her Nana.

"You need to figure this out, Lexie." She tucked the dreamcatcher in her purse. "There's got to be some way to get rid of these ghosts before they destroy everything."

Two hours later, she gave their pesky landlord, Mr. Lawrence, his keys. Lexie drove away, leaving West Roxbury behind her. While on the road, she noticed a sign she'd passed a thousand times before.

*Forest Hills Cemetery Next Right.*

Wait. Wasn't that where Magnus and O'Connor were buried?

Lexie took a hard right off the road and ended up in the small neighborhood of Jamaica Plain. She'd never visited the historic cemetery in the past—she'd been too busy with work to take in the sights. Today, she felt compelled.

Parking her car next to the Gothic stone gate marking the boundary of the cemetery lands, she took a moment to relish the quiet. After days of peace at Altmover Manor, the cacophony of the city had grated on her nerves.

"Welcome to Forest Hills, can I help you?" a freckled receptionist asked inside the administrative offices.

"Yes, I'm searching for some graves. Ah, long lost family."

The bubbly strawberry blonde tapped the keys on her computer. "No problem. All I need are names and dates around the time of burial."

"Ah, the first is Blackwell, Magnus, and Katherine. They died in 1894."

The young woman entered the information into the computer. "Here they are. The Blackwell crypt is located in plot E. Go through the gate and follow the signs. There's parking in that area of the cemetery. Their crypt is a short walk down the path. You can't miss it. Big ole' gray thing with two ravens on top."

"Ravens?"

The receptionist shrugged. "People pick the craziest things to put on their graves. We had one guy who wanted a smiley face on the top of his headstone. Go figure; a smiley face in a cemetery."

Lexie feigned an interested smile. "There's another name. Jacob O'Connor. He died the same year, 1894."

The receptionist typed the name and then frowned. "Do you have any other information? He's not showing up in my system."

"He was buried with his wife, Frances O'Connor."

She typed something else. "I have a Frances McGee O'Connor?"

Lexie nodded. "Sounds like her."

"She's with the McGee family also in plot E. You should run into their grave site about a hundred yards before the Blackwell tomb. It's in a section where most prominent families of the time were buried."

Several minutes later, Lexie drove along the narrow lane leading deep into the cemetery. She admired the tombstones and crypts rising against the landscape. When she spotted the sign pointing the way to plot E, a nervous tickle caught in her stomach.

"I should have my head examined."

Lexie left her car in the appointed lot and made the trek down the path leading to the older section of the cemetery. She didn't have to go far before she spotted an elongated headstone around a plot enclosed with a cement wall. Carved in bold letters into the headstone were the names and dates of the McGee family members interred there.

*Frances McGee O'Connor Born 1865 Died 1891*

Lexie read through the names twice but found no mention of Jacob O'Connor. She wasn't surprised he hadn't been buried with his in-laws. In a time when social standing meant everything, Lexie suspected the McGee family had refused Jacob's remains. After all, the man had murdered two people and then committed suicide.

She moved up a grassy hill, leaving the McGee plot behind, taking in the changing leaves as songbirds filled the air with music. The peace amid the weathered tombstones provided a welcomed distraction from the bustling metropolis, but the lack of any other visitors in the cemetery creeped her out.

Lexie had not been walking for long when she arrived at the round, gray tomb dedicated to the Blackwell family. A breeze kicked up as she viewed the domed roof supporting a ring of smooth stone Doric columns with *Blackwell* carved deep into the lintel above the crypt. On the black iron doors to the burial chamber, brass plaques heralded the names of every Blackwell entombed there. Two ghoulish ravens, their heads bowed and carved out of the same gray stone, guarded the doors. Below their talons, scratch marks marred the cement.

The wind died down around her, and the chatter of the birds ceased while Lexie perused the list of names. She paused and looked around, a little spooked by the sudden stillness. Returning to the names, she smiled when she finally came to the last two.

*Katherine Parker Blackwell Born 1874 Died 1894*

*Magnus Harrison Blackwell Born 1864 Died 1894*

But what of their murderer?

She unearthed no sign for Jacob O'Connor at the Blackwell tomb or in his wife's family plot. Lexie concluded it might take hours to find his grave and she didn't want to spend her afternoon alone in a deserted cemetery. Besides, she still had her mother to contend with.

Unnerved by the continued silence around her, she backed down the last short step from the Blackwell's tomb. The instant the soft grass greeted Lexie's feet, the frenzied chirping of birds filled the air. She released a breath she hadn't realized she'd been holding and glanced back at Blackwell's resting place. Her brief detour had given her no new insights into the man who had consumed so much of her thoughts.

Content her search had come to an end, Lexie moved away from the gray memorial. Her mind preoccupied, she took a step back and almost toppled over when she tripped. At first glance, she shrugged off the blame for her misstep on a rock, but on closer inspection, she discovered a small headstone.

Positioned right outside the entrance to the Blackwell family tomb, the location of the grave puzzled her. A funny tingle in her belly took hold.

She stared at the collection of leaves covering the nameplate and was about to reach out and remove the debris when the wind whipped around her.

The clutter magically swept away, and the name became

legible.

*Jacob O'Connor Died 1894*

"Oh, my God." Lexie stumbled back.

They'd buried him right in front of the Blackwells' final resting place. He forever faced the couple he murdered. Lexie considered it a harsh penance for his crime. Life in prison was one thing; eternity was something different. Who had footed the bill for such an act? The proximity to the grave implied the Blackwells' had a hand in the design, but Magnus and Katherine had been the last family members.

Lexie hurried away from the tomb, anxious to return to the land of the living. Whatever drama occurred between the two men still played out in her home. Their grudges continued long after they had shed their mortal bonds, making her doubt the eternal peace promised by many religions. Did Heaven exist, or was it another empty fairy tale? One day, she would know the answer, until then she had the ambiguous ramblings of two ghosts and one baffling fiancé to decipher.

# Chapter Thirteen

The sun had already set below the horizon when Lexie parked in front of her mother's Beacon Hill home. She collected her purse and said a silent prayer of deliverance. Lexie asked God for an extinction level event to wipe out 1535 Cambridge Street and spare her from an evening of hell.

With a brief shudder, she took in the three-story, Federal-style house. Her stepfather, Kevin Lafferty, had inherited the home from his father—a US Senator who'd served three terms in office. His son had followed in his political footsteps by becoming a state senator, but Lexie's mother harbored hopes for Kevin to take up his father's old post in the US Senate. Angela Bartlett Arden Lafferty had always longed to be among the Washington elite.

Her mother never went anywhere with a hair out of place, a wrinkle in her designer dress, or a scuff mark on her Manolo

Blahniks. All her life, Lexie never measured up to her sister Cindy—Angela's lookalike daughter and most ardent fan. Lexie's saving grace—her father, Ray. He had died in a car accident when Lexie was thirteen. Life with her mother became unbearable after losing her father. The pampered, perfect, former Miss Idaho, social climbing, Martha Stewart wannabe was the woman Lexie fought all her life not to be.

She retrieved her battered black overnight bag from the backseat and shoved the straps over her shoulder along with her purse. She imagined her mother screaming at her for her ratty luggage.

*This is going to suck!*

"Darling," a resplendent voice called as the front door opened.

In a white Chanel pantsuit and black heels, her mother appeared camera ready for some posh political event. Her makeup hid any hint of her fifty-eight years.

"Oh God, Alexis, you didn't park that piece of shit in front of our house, did you?" Her mother examined Will's car. "Can't your man buy something better?"

She pressed her overnight bag against her chest like a security blanket and climbed the bricked steps to the front door. "Will doesn't want to spend money on a new car right now."

Angela's gaze swept down her long-sleeved T-shirt and jeans.

"What is it, Mother? Do you want to fumigate me before I come inside?"

Angela rolled her blue eyes. "Get in here, Alexis, before the neighbors see you." She waited until Lexie's tennis shoes squeaked on her polished parquet floors. "Kevin, Alexis is here," her mother shouted with the volume of a motor cross sports announcer.

Her stepfather sauntered into the entrance hall. Attired in jeans and a knit shirt, he made her comfortable around her impossible mother.

"Hey there, sweetie." Kevin kissed her cheek. "How's the house?"

"It's going to be a long work in progress."

Angela frowned. "Will's crazy to sink everything he has into such a monstrosity."

"It's early, Angela. Can we save the interrogation for after dinner?" Kevin took off down the hallway.

Her mother strutted up to her. "Why didn't you answer my texts and phone calls?"

"I had things to do." Lexie dumped her purse and the bag of coffee she had gotten for Will on the bench inside the door.

"What things?" her mother grilled.

"What's your problem, Mother?"

"You're late!" Angela lowered her voice. "You know how I hate tardiness."

"I'm sorry if I didn't abide by your ironclad rules."

Angela put a manicured hand on her hip. "Go upstairs to your old room and change. You look a fright."

Lexie curtailed the expletives she wished to scream and headed to the stairs.

In her old bedroom, Lexie tossed her bag and purse on her bed. She wanted to talk to Will. He could soothe her anger.

She pictured him next to her, laptop open, working away on some new project or his plans for Altmover Manor. Images of the intimate moments they'd shared rushed across her mind. While staring at the white canopy above her bed, she recalled his touch, his kiss, and the way his—

A knock on the door scattered her visions.

"Lexie?"

"Yeah, Mom, you can come in." She unzipped her purse.

"I wanted to talk to you." Her mother sat on the bed.

Lexie readied for another fight. Whenever Angela wanted to "talk," it ended badly. "What is it?"

Her mother's ramrod posture made Lexie wary. When the former beauty queen squared her shoulders, the news was never good.

"Lately I've had uncomfortable feelings about you and your house."

"What do you mean?"

"You know what I'm talking about. They're the same feelings my mother taught you to control."

Lexie removed the dreamcatcher from her purse and placed it on the bed. "You said Nana was crazy for believing in her ability."

Angela snickered. "She was crazy, but at times she did sense things. People coming over, death, or lost souls. Your grandmother spoke with many spirits."

"She never mentioned any spirits to me."

Angela patted her daughter's knee. "Because I insisted she not scare you or your sister. From a young age, you exhibited the same ability as your grandmother. You used to tell me about people in your bedroom at night when you were small."

"When was this?"

"You were four when I told my mother to make sure the spirits stopped bothering you. So she made a special charm to hang on your bed to keep the spirits away." Angela fingered the blue and white dreamcatcher. "Native American mothers and grandmothers would weave those magical webs for their children. The dreamcatchers are meant to filter out bad spirits bringing nightmares and allow good thoughts to enter their minds. But I get the impression yours isn't working anymore."

Lexie longed to tell her mother about the house and the strange occurrences, but distrust nudged at her.

"I'm fine, Mother. There are no bad spirits haunting me."

Angela stood from the bed. "If you ever do want to talk, I'm here for you." Her mother slipped from the room.

Lexie caressed her dreamcatcher and traced the spider web pattern with her finger. She hoped the charm still had some magic left in it because spending the rest of her life in Altmover Manor with all those restless spirits was beyond comprehension. If she didn't do something to get rid of Magnus and his friend, Lexie feared the future she'd planned with Will would soon go up in smoke.

# Chapter Fourteen

Early the next morning, Lexie packed her overnight bag, anxious to get on the road. She had one more stop to make before tackling the five-hour drive back to Mount Desert Island.

As she slinked down the stairs, she discovered her stepfather on the sofa in the living room. The news blared from their big screen TV while he nursed a mug in his hands. His bare feet rested on Angela's prized coffee table.

"She'll have you flogged for that."

Kevin juggled his coffee mug in his hands, spilling a little on his robe. "You scared the shit out of me."

"Why are you up so early?"

He inspected her T-shirt and jeans. "Are you sneaking out without saying goodbye to your mother?"

Lexie rolled her eyes. "She doesn't come down until after ten.

I can't wait around until then."

Kevin sipped his coffee. "She's worried about you, Lex."

"I'm worried about me," she mumbled.

Kevin put down his mug. "She hates the house you moved into. She's been digging up everything she can find on it. Your mother thinks something bad is going to happen to you."

"It's nothing but an old house. There's nothing sinister going on there." She walked into the kitchen.

"Promise me if things get hairy, you'll come back here," he insisted. "You and Will. I'd rather know you two are safe under my roof than staying in some dangerous house far away from anyone who can help."

At the coffeemaker, Lexie selected a blue mug set out next to the machine. "I promise to call you if we get in trouble." She lifted the mug. "Do you mind if I take this with me?"

He stood from the sofa. "Don't tell your mother. She'll have a fit." Kevin came into the kitchen. "Sure you can't stick around for a little longer?"

Lexie filled her mug with coffee. "I have to go to the bank."

Kevin rested his hip against the counter. "Anything wrong?"

"No. I want to get a peek at their paperwork on the house see if they have any old pictures we can use."

Kevin kissed her cheek. "Call when you get back to Maine."

Her stepfather returned to his comfy sofa. Lexie wanted to stay with him. Kevin had brought stability to her life. He'd never been a replacement for her father but had become a good friend.

"You take care, Kevin," she called while hurrying to the front door.

"You too, sweetie."

In the car, Lexie blew out a long breath. She'd survived another encounter with Angela. Would her mother mellow with age? Lexie laughed out loud. Some people acted impervious to change.

Heavy downtown traffic moved at a snail's pace, by the time she maneuvered the car into the Parker and Mills Bank garage, it was well past nine.

A bright lobby, done in alternating shades of gray and silver, already teemed with customers. Right before Lexie came to the line for the tellers, she veered toward the cubicles belonging to the bank managers. An elfish-looking receptionist with lovely green eyes showed Lexie to the desk of Bob Grenier.

They soon arrived at the desk of a paunchy man with a pasty face. His snug black tie forced the skin around his neck to cascade over his shirt collar.

"Mr. Grenier, I'm Lexie Arden. You worked with my fiancé, Will Bennett."

"Oh, yes, Will." His face changed from businesslike to cheery as he stood up. "How is the house working out for you two?"

She took the black vinyl chair he offered. "That's why I'm here. Will and I wondered if the bank has any more information on the house."

Bob got comfortable behind his desk. "What kind of information do you need?"

Lexie shifted her purse from her shoulder to her lap while searching for a way to be diplomatic. "Do you have any pictures of the property from when the bank first acquired it? Interior pictures would help us with the restoration."

"Let's take a look." Bob typed something on his keyboard.

"Also, do you have any information about the former owners? For something we're putting together for the historical society on the island."

"I can check." He shifted in his chair. "Afraid I'm not the one who handled the closing, so I will have to track down the file. May take me a little while. Do you have time?"

"I'm in no rush," Lexie sat back.

He typed something, and the screen changed. "Okay. I have to go upstairs for your file."

She waited at the desk while Bob hurried across the bank to the elevators. She craved a sip of her coffee still sitting in her car. The caffeine jolt would help chase away the cobwebs and prepare her for the long drive home.

The cell phone in her purse vibrated. Her heart sped up when Will's name popped up.

"Hey, is everything all right?"

"Everything's fine." His dulcet voice soothed her rattled nerves. "I wanted to ask how it went with Angela."

"She made the family sit down to a compulsory dinner. Even dragged Paul and Cindy over to listen to her BS."

"Did you tell her about the wedding?"

Lexie sighed. "I mentioned we set a date."

"She's still insisting you need a ring, huh?"

"Kevin was excited," she added.

Will's rumble of laughter warmed her heart. "Where are you? I hear people moving about."

"I'm at the bank," she admitted, wincing. "I wanted to find out if they had any pictures of the house. Something missed at the closing."

"Great idea." He sounded enthused. "Are you working with Bob Grenier or someone else?"

"No, I found Bob. He's getting the file for me."

"Call me with what you find out."

"I will." She clutched the phone tighter. "Is everything okay? At the house, I mean. Any sightings of my cat?"

"Nope. The food you left out for it is still there. But the ghosts have been busy while you were away."

Her stomach dropped. "What makes you say that?"

Will remained quiet for a moment. "Magnus came out of his painting again and asked for you. He wants you to pick up some burgers on the way home."

She shook her head and smiled at his joke. "I'll be back soon."

He chuckled, sounding like his old self. "Call me along the way to let me know where you are. I'll worry until you're back here." His voice dropped. "I love you, baby." Will hung up as Bob returned to his desk.

"Okay, got it. The file was in the storage area. I had to do a little digging." He plopped a thick manila folder in front of her.

Lexie rubber her forehead. The file had to be at least three inches thick.

He opened the folder and read through the papers on top. "All the newer information on the house is in our computer system, but this file contains the records before 1970, which never got added."

He flipped through some papers. "This has mostly annual property summaries, bills, and updates." He read from a sheet in front of him. "This is from 1964 and says the house continues to be overseen by the bank and the amount of funds available in the trust set up for the estate's upkeep."

"What can you tell me about the trust?"

Bob went to his computer. He typed in the name *Altmover Estate Trust* and waited.

"Here we go," he said when the account page came up. "Set up by Miles Parker, the trust was based on the assets he inherited from his daughter and son-in-law's estate. At the time their estate settled, the account was worth ten and a half million dollars."

Lexie's jaw dropped. "Ten and a half million dollars?"

"Yep. In 1894 that was a lot of money."

"In 2014, it's a lot of money, Bob." Lexie contemplated the folder. "I don't understand. Where did the money go?"

Bob shuffled through more papers. "The records of all the accounting should be in here." He lifted a yellow slip from the pile. "Here's a bill for a new roof from 1969. Also plumbing repairs in the same year. Then there's the annual property tax bill and insurance coverage." Bob held up a pink piece of paper. "This one's from 1970 for fifteen thousand dollars." He found another handful. "Here is a bill for a kitchen overhaul in 1961. And an older one from 1904, changing all the fixtures in the house from candlelight to gas. And then another attached from 1920, changing everything from gas to electric." He dropped the papers back into the folder. "You get the idea. The house needed work, the taxes had to be paid, insurance covered, and the salaries of the caretakers through the years also had to be deducted. But with no further income generated by the estate, the trust eventually got eaten up."

"What about the caretakers? Do you have any names?"

Bob went back to his computer. "That will be in this system. The bank handled caretakers as employees of the trust and kept their files in our HR department." He read the page on the screen. "Since 1956, there have been more than two dozen different caretakers. Each one lasted a few years."

"What happened before 1956? Who took care of the house then?"

Bob scrolled to the bottom of the page. "One caretaker is on the books from the time the bank was made the property manager in 1894 until 1956. A Miss Emily Mann. The trust gave her charge of the day-to-day operations of the house and property."

"She was Magnus Blackwell's secretary," Lexie mumbled. "What happened to her?"

Bob read on. "She died in 1956."

"Did she die at the house?"

Bob shook his head. "Doesn't say." He paused while reading the page on his computer. "The Altmover Estate Trust paid for her funeral, and her will bequeathed her worldly goods to the Mount Desert Island Historical Society. Says here, the transfer date of her property was July 18th, 1956. There's a receipt from the Mount Desert Historical Society." He motioned to the folder. "It'll be in there somewhere."

Lexie rested her hand on the thick folder. "Will this tell us where she's buried?"

Bob arched his eyebrows, furrowing his brow. "Is that relevant?"

Lexie scrambled for an excuse. *Make it sound good, Lex.* "She was a long-time resident. I'd like to add her story to the history of the house. I know where the Blackwells are buried and I want to find out if she's buried with them."

Appeased, Bob went back to his computer screen. "Afraid I don't have that information on here, but if the trust paid for it, the location would be in our folder."

Lexie considered the mound of paperwork and questioned how hungry she was for the information. Without it, her search for the cane would turn cold.

*Yeah, it's important.*

They divided the file and went through their sections while sitting at Bob's desk. Lexie went through receipt after receipt for repairs and got a good idea of what the behemoth house had cost throughout the years. She worried if the trust had gone through ten million, how long would she and Will last with their limited savings.

"I found something," Bob declared. He displayed a pink slip in his hands. "From Forest Hills Cemetery dated 1904. It's a renewal for the upkeep of the Blackwell tomb and, 'one grave located adjacent to the family crypt.' Must be our lady."

Lexie took the slip from him and read the contents. "I was there yesterday and checked out this grave. It belongs to Jacob O'Connor."

"Who?" Bob asked.

"The man who killed Magnus Blackwell and his wife, Katherine Parker."

Bob sat still for a moment with his head cocked to the side. "But why would he be buried there?"

"Someone with the trust must have buried him there."

Bob snorted. "The guy killed the bank owner's daughter and then the trust paid to bury him next to her. As a father, I'd see that as the final insult to my daughter's memory. Someone else must have made the call."

Lexie knew Bob was right, but how had Jacob ended up buried so close to his victims? The act reeked of revenge as if someone wanted Jacob to spend eternity suffering for his crime. "Maybe someone else did make the call." Lexie sat forward in her chair, grinning like a contented cat. "How much control would Emily Mann, the original caretaker, have had over the dispensation of funds from the trust?"

Bob chuckled and held out the pink receipt to her. "Here's the bill from the cemetery. Check out the approval signature at the bottom."

Lexie read the name written at the bottom of the page. *Emily Mann*

"So if she arranged for Jacob O'Connor to be buried at the cemetery, the trust would have paid it?"

"Appears that way." Bob returned the receipt to the folder. "All the bills I've seen from before her death were approved by her. Miles Parker must have given her some control over the trust funds. I don't find any evidence the bills she generated ever got questioned by the trust."

"She put Jacob O'Connor there, for what?" Lexie mumbled. "As revenge for killing her boss?"

Bob shook his head. "I don't follow."

"It doesn't matter." Lexie leafed through the receipts in front of her. "I'm afraid what we're looking for isn't here. I've wasted enough of your time."

"I wish I could have done more. The file has only bills for the trust, no pictures and nothing about the people who lived at Altmover Manor."

"Maybe the historical society will have more information on Ms. Mann." She dumped her receipts back into the pile.

"I hope so." Bob straightened the papers before closing the folder. "A shame the lives of all those people, all their hopes and tragedies, ends up as nothing more than a bunch of receipts in a bank file."

Lexie reached for her purse. "I haven't given up yet. I'll get their story." She stood and extended her hand. "Thank you for everything."

He gave her hand a gentle squeeze. "Give my best to Will. I wish you two nothing but good luck with the house. Call me if I can be of any further assistance." He reached for a card on his desk.

Lexie tucked the card in her hand. She was about to turn away when she stopped. "Oh, I do have one more question about the caretakers. Do you have any information on the last one the bank hired? A Remi Glapion?"

Bob sat back in his chair and scrolled up the page on his computer screen. "Nothing shows up here, but he might have been hired and not added to the system before the account closed. Our HR is known for their lag time on inputting."

"When was the last caretaker hired?"

He scanned the screen. "Ah, 2004. Says here they installed the alarm system at that time. I don't see any more after that, or HR never bothered to update the file."

"Can such a thing happen?"

Bob eyed the thick folder on his desk. "Sure can. Especially when you're dealing with such an old account."

Lexie hoped he was right, but her gut told her something was amiss with Bob's explanation. Remi's absence from the caretakers' list in the computer worried her. She hated to believe Remi wasn't who he claimed, but then again, why would the man work for nothing and stick around? It didn't make sense.

Exiting the bank garage, Lexie debated why Emily Mann had received such a prominent role in running the estate after Magnus's death. His devoted secretary until the end, she could have arranged Jacob O'Connor's burial as a last insult to the man who had killed her boss. Or, she hated Magnus so much, she arranged for him to peer out at his killer for the duration of his eternal rest.

Her trip to Boston had created more questions than answers. How did she proceed with her quest for the cane? Short of a miracle or some divine intervention, Magnus's mysterious dragon cane would remain lost.

The sun rose to its zenith as the old Volvo hit cruising speed on the interstate. In a couple of hours, Lexie would be home. Back in the arms of the man she loved—and once again surrounded by ghosts.

# Chapter Fifteen

Thunder rumbled and her apprehension resurfaced. Even though the light from the giant lamps on either side of the leaded-glass doors gave a welcoming impression, Lexie knew better. The house didn't want visits from the living; it only embraced the dead.

While a light rain tapped against the car, she gathered Will's coffee, her purse, and the bags from a fast food restaurant where she'd stopped to pick up a late-night dinner. About to open her car door, Lexie jumped when someone did it for her.

"He's been chomping at the bit for you all day," Remi confided as he helped her from the car.

Her unease intensified as he escorted her up the steps and out of the rain. Rain droplets left marks on his dusty beige overalls. The image of holy water sprinkled on the damned dashed across her mind.

"What have you two been doing?"

"Attacking the damaged plaster in the bedrooms and checking for pipe leaks." He brushed a bit of dust from his shoulder. "Luckily, there aren't any."

She held out a white paper bag to him. "I got dinner. A burger and fries for you."

Remi pushed the bag back to her. "Thank you, but no. I don't eat any animal flesh."

"You're a vegetarian? Will didn't tell me."

"I follow a strict diet—for health reasons. No animal protein and no saturated fats." He stopped outside the glass doors. "I can only eat fruit, vegetables, whole grains, and nuts. Food of the earth, it's called. Does wonders for longevity."

She held the fast food bag against her chest, scheming how to get the man to eat with them. "Come inside and let me cook you some fresh vegetables."

His laughter bounced between the manor house and the cottage. "You know Will's warned me about your culinary skills."

"You can't believe a word he says, Remi."

He rested his hand on his hip and curiously tipped his head. The gesture struck Lexi as odd for a hulking man like Remi.

"I can believe one thing: Will loves you, Lexie. My Aunt Titu once told me, 'love is the most powerful magic there is, because true love knows no bounds, and can never be broken even by the most potent of spells.'"

"Are we talking magical spells?"

"Voodoo spells. Voodoo is the only true magic there is." Remi turned toward the last vestiges of the setting sun. "Go inside. He's waiting for you." He strolled down the front steps and into the rain.

As she shut the heavy glass doors, a familiar voice called,

"There you are."

Before she faced him, Will kissed her neck and wrapped his arms tightly around her.

"I'm starved." He took the bags and turned for the foyer.

He walked away, and Lexie smiled admiring the curve of his firm ass. "It's good to be home."

She strolled through the foyer, and the slight sway of the massive chandelier made her stomach shrink. "Then again …"

Will gave a detailed account of all the problems found in the house over dinner. Lexie's appetite waned as she worried about the mounting costs. Will, on the other hand, seemed excited.

"Remi and I might be able to do all the plaster work ourselves. I tell you, Lexie, the guy has been a lifesaver." He reached for his coffee mug.

"When I was at the bank, I asked Bob Grenier about Remi. He isn't listed in their computer. His records showed the last caretaker to work here was in 2004 when they put in the alarm system."

Will didn't bat an eye. "So?"

"They had records on every caretaker. There've been over two dozen caretakers for this place from 1956 through 2004."

"What about before 1956?"

Lexie ran her finger around the rim of her coffee mug. "They had only one. Magnus Blackwell's secretary, Emily Mann, took care of the house until she died in 1956."

Will sat back in his chair. "Wow. She must have been devoted to him."

"Yeah, a little too devoted."

Will arched an eyebrow. "Meaning?"

"I went to Forest Hill Cemetery to find the Blackwell family tomb where Magnus and his wife are buried. While I was backing away, I tripped over something. I thought it was a stone. Turned out to be the nameplate on Jacob O'Connor's grave. They put the guy facing the Blackwell tomb."

Will snatched up one of her fries. "Are you gonna eat these?"

She banged her mug on the kitchen table. "Emily Mann is the one who buried Jacob O'Connor. She had control over the trust money and wanted revenge for what happened to Magnus, her boss. Don't you find this weird?"

He swiped the rest of her fries off her plate. "What difference does it make? These people have been dead for over a hundred years. So what if the secretary stuck it to the guy who murdered her boss. Maybe she liked her job. Makes sense to me."

"But why? Why bury Jacob in such a manner and then live in Magnus's house for another sixty years?"

"Sixty-two years," he corrected.

"Whatever." She tossed up her hand. "I suspect she was in love with her boss."

Will snorted. "Hunting for the reason why this woman did what she did is futile."

"Yeah, well, I found out she left her things to the local historical society. I'm going to go there tomorrow to see what I can find."

"While you're there, you can check if they have any pictures of the house." He stood and went to the coffeepot. "Since you're going out, you can pick up some more supplies."

"Will, you've had enough coffee."

He filled his mug halfway. "I want a little more." He came back to his chair and then scrutinized her chicken sandwich. "Are you going to finish that?"

She shoved her plate across the table to him. "Haven't you eaten since I left?"

He snapped up her sandwich. "I've got to enjoy the good stuff while I can."

Once he'd secured the house for the night, Will joined her in the bedroom. He came up as she unpacked her overnight bag and put his arms around her waist. He crept his hands around her hips, squeezing her ass.

Lexie angled away from him. "You reek of coffee, Will."

"Does it turn you on?"

She retrieved the blue and white dreamcatcher from her bag. "Not at all."

Will eased away from her. "If I brush my teeth, will you get in the mood then?"

Lexie took the dreamcatcher to a corner of the bed.

"Why does that look familiar?" Will asked.

"I had it in our old bedroom, remember?" Lexie tied it to the post on her side of the king-sized bed. "My grandmother made it for me and—"

"I don't feel so good." Will sat down hard on their blue bedspread.

Lexie moved to his side and touched his brow. "You're flushed."

"I got dizzy for a moment."

Her fingers combed through his hair. "You want me to get you something."

"No, I'm okay. I've been pushing too hard with the house."

"This is more than the house. I'm worried about you. Perhaps you should take it easy for a while."

"I'm fine, love. Just a little tired. Since when does thirty-two feel so old?" He stood up again and wrestled his T-shirt over his head.

She stayed next to him, caressing his chest. "No one would ever consider you old." Her hands went to his ass. "Especially when you're walking away from them." She leaned in and nipped his chin.

He pushed her hands away. "I'm beat, baby."

The brush off flustered Lexie. How could Will blow hot one minute and then cold the next? He'd never done that before. The mounting changes in her fiancé confused her. Should she blame the house, the stress of their situation, or was there another culprit?

Will stepped out of his jeans and slipped on his blue pajama bottoms, avoiding Lexie's pensive gaze.

He yanked back the covers. "You coming to bed?"

Lexie shook off her worry. "Yeah, let me brush my teeth and change."

In the bathroom, she went to the vanity and ran the water in the sink. She reached for her toothbrush, and when she raised her head, smoke clouded her reflection in the mirror.

She trembled, readying herself for another ghostly interaction. After her encounters with Magnus, speaking with the dead should have felt less terrifying—but it didn't. Her skin prickled and her common sense urged her to run. Was this going to be the rest of her life in the house? Would she remain torn between this world and the next while fighting not to act scared out of her wits?

Lexie waited for Jacob O'Connor to arrive, but nothing happened. The smoke dissipated and her face stared back at her in the mirror.

"What is going on around here?"

Bewildered, she climbed into bed and discovered Will already in a deep sleep.

"Three cups of coffee and he's out like a light."

Lexie got comfortable in the bed, but sleep eluded her. Wide awake, she listened to every groan and creak the house made, waiting for a ghost to take shape. After a while, the first nudge of sleep weighed down her eyelids. Before she closed them for good, Lexie caught a glimpse of her dreamcatcher.

Maybe her grandmother's gift still had some magic left in it after all.

# Chapter Sixteen

The next morning, she awoke from a sound night's sleep. No ghosts had plagued her dreams, and no shrieks had scared her awake. She'd enjoyed her first peaceful night since moving into the haunted manor.

She stretched, turning to find Will still sleeping—another first. She sat up and played with a lock of his dark brown hair, curling it around his ear.

He batted at his ear while keeping his eyes closed. When she tickled his ear again, he groaned.

"I hate when you do that."

"I have to go into town." She kissed his cheek. "And you need to get up and work on this house."

"What time is it?" He yawned next to her.

Lexie checked her cell phone on the night table. "Almost

seven." She patted his chest. "Hey, where's Mr. Energy? You've been up before me every morning since we moved here."

His arms went around her. "Today I'm tired."

She snuggled against him. "Let's sleep in."

Will snickered and shoved his erection into her thigh. "I have another idea."

His slow and sexy kiss felt familiar. The way he eased her nightshirt over her head and tempted her with kisses brought back memories of the way it had been between them before arriving at Altmover Manor. His frenzied love making seemed replaced by the gentle ways of the man he'd been before coming to Maine.

His kisses became more urgent. His fingers crept between her legs. When his thumb rubbed over her clit, Lexie sighed. Will did all the things to her he'd always done: kissing her neck in that certain spot, and pinching her left nipple hard enough to make her moan.

Excited, he shoved back the covers. He moved his thumb faster, making her toes curl. When he kicked off his pajama bottoms, Lexie was happy to have her old Will back. But when he reached for the night table and grabbed the condom box, an icy stab tweaked her gut.

"Did you use condoms the other times?"

He ripped the package open with his teeth. "What are you talking about?"

She sat up on her elbows. "The past two times we had sex. Did you use a condom?"

He worked the condom over his erection. "I'm always careful, Lexie. We can't afford a baby."

Will pushed her back on the bed and lifted her hips. He eased into her, and Lexie became acutely aware of how different Will had been during the past several days. He moved in and out, and when she wrapped her arms around him, the dreamcatcher caught her eye.

Maybe her imagination had played tricks on her, but the man she loved no longer acted like a stranger.

"I love you, Lexie," Will murmured against her cheek.

She held him close and prayed for their happiness to begin.

The Mount Desert Historical Society, located in Somesville, was a short drive from the manor. The enchanting gardens greeting Lexie offered a bouquet of sweet aromas. For a tantalizing moment, she forgot her troubles.

From the parking lot, she passed a small white cottage with a ticket window and signs pointing to paths leading to the museum gardens. Lexie followed the sign directing her to the main museum.

After crossing a quaint white picket bridge over a rushing brook, she stood before the double doors of a charming schoolhouse museum. When Lexie tugged at the doors, they didn't budge.

"Can I help you?" A woman wearing a floppy sun hat and blue overalls dirtied around the knees surfaced from a path on the other side of the bridge.

Lexie went back to the bridge. "Ah, yes. I'm looking for some information for a house on the island."

The woman approached the bridge. "Which house?"

"Altmover Manor."

She removed her gardening gloves. "What kind of information do you need?"

Lexie crossed the bridge, and the woman's sharp green eyes came into focus. "My fiancé, Will Bennett, purchased the house. We've recently moved in."

The stranger shoved her gardening gloves into her overalls side pocket. "You're the new owners."

"Yes, I've been told news travels fast on this island." Lexie made a mental note to never underestimate the speed of gossip. "A former caretaker of the house, a Miss Emily Mann, donated some personal items to the historical society. I was wondering if I could see them … for research purposes."

The restrained smile crossing the woman's lips told Lexie she had said the right thing. "Come with me."

She turned and headed back down the path toward the gardens. Lexie hurried to catch up, second-guessing if her trip had been a good idea. She longed to get back in her car and drive away from the island, forget about Magnus Blackwell, Emily Mann and the damned dragon cane. But like an addict seeking their next fix, she needed to know how the story of the cane ended.

*And if this is another dead end? What then?*

Lexie shoved the ugly questions back into the depths of her mind. She didn't want to deal with what ifs until she had to.

"We shut down the museum when the weather starts getting cold," the museum worker said. "I tend to the gardens before we get our first frost. We have two gardens open to the public during the warmer months." They passed a sign directing the way to the Heirloom Garden. "The Heirloom Garden has plants that have flourished on the island from the late eighteenth century all the way up to today. We like to teach people how the native plants were used by the early island settlers."

They came to a white picket fence around a cultivated area with colorful flowers, shrubbery, and trees. A black-shingled roof rose from behind the garden. The brown and red leaves of the trees contrasted against the white wood boards on the rectangular building.

"This is our storage facility," the woman told her. "It's where we keep the pieces not on exhibition."

The metal doors creaked open. Above, fluorescent lights sparked to life, illuminating rows of wooden shelves crowding the cement floor.

In the entrance, two wooden work tables took up most of the space. The woman went to the first table and then turned back to Lexie.

"What's your name?"

"Lexie Arden."

She held out a hand. "I'm Virginia, Virginia Ward, executive director here." Virginia tossed her gardening gloves onto the work table. "I hope you know what you're getting into with that house."

"I'm not sure what you mean."

"When Emily Mann died, she bequeathed her worldly possessions to our society on one condition: when the manor was sold, we were to give her possessions to the new owner."

Lexie gaped at her. "Excuse me?"

"Altmover Manor has a nasty reputation, but when Emily Mann left us her things, her letter stated that her possessions had to go to the new owners. She wrote, and I quote, 'They're going to need them.'"

"Are you saying Emily Mann expected someone to come looking for her things?"

Virginia shrugged. "I didn't believe it until you showed up. For years, I've kept the contents of Emily's letter to myself. When I got wind that Altmover Manor had been sold, I had a feeling you would make your way here."

Lexie's palms itched at the notion of getting close to unlocking another piece of the puzzle. "What did she leave behind?"

"Wait here. I have to dig out the box from the back." She disappeared into the vast rows of storage shelves.

She set her purse on the table and rubbed her hands together.

*This gets stranger and stranger.*

When Virginia returned, she had a long box secured with string clutched in her arms.

"She bequeathed these items to us in her will." She struggled to set the box on the table. "I have no idea why she chose to leave this with the historical society, but what's in here has fascinated the hell out of me."

Virginia untied the string, lifted the lid, and removed a long object completely swathed in red silk. She gingerly put the item on the table, then Virginia removed the bag to reveal a wooden cane.

The intricately carved dragon's head handle caught the creature in a silent roar. With black onyx stones in the eyes, it appeared ready to breathe fire. The handle sat atop a slightly crooked shaft of marbled colored wood, which had been carved to represent the dragon's body. Scales fashioned into the cane appeared so lifelike, they seemed to undulate on the table.

Her audible gasp received a concerned glance from Virginia. "You recognize this?"

Lexie caressed the wood along the shaft as she examined the detail in the handle. "Magnus Blackwell is painted with a cane much like this, but the eyes are red in the painting, not black."

Virginia moved the box closer to Lexie. "What about these?"

There were several leather-bound books in pristine condition. She reached for the book closest to her.

As she scanned the spine, Virginia said, "Voodoo. All the books in the box are about voodoo."

Lexie hurried to put the book back as if discovering it carried some strange disease. "Voodoo?"

Virginia fingered the books in the box. "Every book is rare and considered a bible in the voodoo world. I've spent the past couple of years appraising each one, and I've come to find out this collection is worth a fortune."

"I don't understand. Why did Emily Mann have a collection of expensive books on voodoo?"

"I'd hoped you might enlighten me, Ms. Arden." Virginia lifted a book out of the box. "Whatever she was doing, I wouldn't call it collecting. Passages have been underlined in these books, lots of them. Some were underlined in pencil, some in ink." She patted the book in her hand. "When you collect expensive books, you don't deface them. I got the impression Emily Mann was searching for something."

At a complete loss, Lexie blew out a long breath. "And here I believed she was just Magnus Blackwell's secretary. Perhaps a bit infatuated with her boss, but I never dreamt she would end up a practitioner of witchcraft."

"Not witchcraft. Voodoo," Virginia corrected. "There's a difference. Voodoo is a distinct religion, not unlike Wicca. Whereas witchcraft is the practice of magic."

"But don't they both cast spells, hex people, and do evil?"

"Witchcraft and voodoo aren't about evil but belief." Virginia set her book back in the box. "Voodoo revolves around rituals and is usually more aggressive than witchcraft. Although spells are cast by individuals, most rituals for this religion are performed in groups, which makes the magic very powerful. These ceremonies can involve anything from animal sacrifice to spiritual possession."

She recalled what Remi had told her of voodoo, and the things she'd found in the attic. One particular item jumped out at her.

"What about voodoo dolls? Are they used in a ritual?"

"Yes, sometimes." Virginia nodded. "Voodoo dolls are effigies of a person someone wishes to harm, usually by sticking pins into them, but they can bind spells and curses to them as well. They may be called voodoo dolls, but in reality, the practice of making effigies for a spell comes from European folklore, not African."

Lexie put her book back with the others. "You must know a

lot about voodoo."

"I used to know very little about voodoo." Virginia hovered her hand over the cane. "That was until I found this piece. I've spent several years studying it. I've become rather obsessed with this cane, I'm afraid."

She examined the cane, searching for the reason behind its allure. Magnus Blackwell's ghost had demanded it—so had some other mysterious person—and Virginia Ward admitted to her obsession with the piece. As far as Lexie could tell, there was nothing extraordinary about the cane. It was a little longer than most walking sticks, and the wood was an intriguing blend of light and dark swirls, but other than the carved dragon's head and the black stones in the eyes, she didn't get the fascination.

"Ms. Ward, what is so special about this cane?"

Virginia smiled as her hand lingered over the cane.

"It's called a *baton juju* in voodoo lore."

"A baton …?"

"Juju," Virginia enunciated. "It's a ceremonial staff held by a voodoo priest or priestess in a ritual. Although most practitioners of this art are women in the South."

"So, why did Magnus Blackwell have a voodoo ceremonial staff in Maine?"

"Good question. Emily Mann might have been wondering the same thing." Virginia pressed her lips together as she browsed the book collection. "Whatever she learned, I got the impression she was afraid. Why else would she have devoted so much time to the study of voodoo?"

"But voodoo's a crazy religion, right? It can't hurt anyone."

Virginia stood back from the table as if spooked by the books. She crossed her slender arms over the bib of her overalls. "Voodoo itself doesn't have power; no magic does. It's the belief behind it that matters. Whether religion, ritual, or magic, belief provides the power to create change."

"You sound like you've had some experience with this stuff."

She dropped her head, hiding her face. "I worked for a museum in New York before I came here. I've recorded many strange stories attached to artifacts: curses, hauntings, what have you. I never believed in any of it until something happened to me."

Lexie arched closer to the table. "What happened?"

Virginia curled her shoulders inward and hugged herself. "I was alone one night in the artifact room doing research, and I witnessed an event I couldn't explain. I never mentioned the incident to my colleagues because I didn't want to be laughed out of the building. It's one of the reasons why I took a position at this museum. No ghosts." Her hand settled over the cane. "That was until I discovered this in our inventory." She returned the cane to the red bag. "I must warn you to be careful with the information in these books. Magic is seductive when you don't know what you're doing. You can't allow yourself to be tempted. Otherwise, you might end up in a dangerous place."

Lexie promised to be careful, but she had no interest in the books. All she cared about was the cane.

Virginia helped carry the box to the car. After they slid it into the back seat, Lexie shut the back door, glad her search had ended. She hoped this meant Magnus and Jacob would leave her and Will in peace. But in the back of her mind, she doubted getting rid of Magnus Blackwell would be an easy task.

"I do have one more question." Lexie scanned the peaceful surroundings. "Where was Emily Mann buried? I found the family tomb for the Blackwells, but I couldn't uncover anything about her resting place."

"Emily Mann wasn't buried," Virginia affirmed. "In her will, she requested to be cremated. Her ashes were spread around the grounds of Altmover Manor."

She shook her head, befuddled. "Living so many years in that house would have driven me mad, but she wanted to stay. I don't get it."

Virginia shrugged her hands into the front pockets of her overalls. "Altmover was the only home she ever knew. When she died, there was no mention of family in her will. No one came searching for her effects. I get the impression she had no one."

"Makes you appreciate what you have, doesn't it?"

"Yes, it does." Virginia held out her hand. "Good luck to you, Ms. Arden. I hope you and your fiancé can finally bring some happiness to Altmover Manor. Lord knows, the place deserves it."

After thanking Virginia for her help, Lexie got into her car. She viewed the box through her rearview mirror.

"What the hell are you up to, Magnus Blackwell?"

Lexie drove through the winding roads of Mount Desert Island, putting pieces together. Why a ghost would need a cane eluded her, but knowing the prized artifact's history linked it to voodoo explained why so many sought to possess it. Was that why Magnus haunted Altmover Manor, because of his cane? And what about Jacob? Had the cane tied him to the house as well? Lexie doubted she would ever figure out the mystery.

One thing she knew for certain, life at Altmover Manor was about to get a lot more interesting.

# Chapter Seventeen

The afternoon sun covered the long porch steps when Lexie arrived at Altmover Manor. Still reeling with excitement, she wanted to hurry and get the mysterious dragon cane inside to gauge everyone's reaction—ghosts and humans.

She entered the foyer and a cacophony of banging assaulted her ears. Lexie left the bags from the hardware store at the bottom of the staircase. When she returned to the front doors, a familiar face waited. The gray cat stood in the shadows, out of reach from the sunshine sneaking inside.

"Where have you been?" She scratched behind the cat's ears and received a soft *meow*. "Why haven't you eaten the food I left out?"

She left the cat and proceeded down the wide steps to the car. Lexie lugged the heavy box inside the house as Will breezed up to her, a hammer in his hand.

"What's that?"

"It's real heavy."

He hurried to take the box out of her arms. "Why didn't you let me carry it in from the car?"

"Because I couldn't wait to show it to you." She searched the foyer. "Where did it run off to?"

"What are you talking about?" Will grunted as he struggled with the box.

"The cat. I just saw it."

"What's in here?"

"I got it at the historical society. Emily Mann left it to us." The who-in-the-hell-is-Emily-Mann stare he gave her made Lexie chuckle. "Emily Mann? Magnus's secretary and the first caretaker of this house? She left this in her will to the new owners of Altmover Manor."

"Please tell me it's the family fortune."

Lexie guided him toward the living room. "Put it in there, and I'll show you what's inside."

Will carried the box into the living room. He set it on the floor next to Lexie's laptop.

She knelt down and lifted the lid. Will leaned over the box, his dark eyes coming together as Lexie retrieved the red fabric bag. He waited as she placed the bag on the floor and removed the cane. Once Lexie placed it on the floor, he stood by as if waiting for the cane to float in the air or perform a trick.

Lexie sighed and waved at the portrait of Magnus. "It's his cane. The one in the painting."

"What? Am I supposed to get excited?" Will knelt to get a closer. "Is it worth any money?"

"I have no idea."

Remi entered the room. "Will, where do you want—?"

He came to a grinding halt when he spotted the cane on the floor. His mouth fell open, and his eyes gleamed. Lexie wasn't sure if he was happy or angry about her discovery.

"You found it," Remi whispered.

"The historical society on the island had the cane all along," she said. "Emily Mann willed it to the new owners of Altmover Manor."

"Why? To make sure it stayed with the house?" Will reached to pick up the cane.

"No," Remi shouted, stopping him. "Don't touch it."

Will jumped back. "Why on earth not?"

Remi cautiously approached the cane. "Do you know the power it contains?"

"Power?" Will snickered. "It's a stick, Remi."

"It's a baton juju," Lexie declared.

Will stood from the floor. "A what?"

"A ceremonial baton or stick used during voodoo rituals," Remi explained.

"How do either of you know about this?" Will demanded.

Remi's odd grin roused her distrust. "The lady at the historical society told me. She's done a good bit of research on the cane."

Will swerved to the fireplace, scrutinizing the painting. "There's no voodoo in Maine, so why did Magnus have it?"

"Good question." She observed how Remi practically drooled over the cane. "How did you know?"

He arched over the box, inspecting the contents. "I'm from New Orleans. I grew up with voodoo. Even had a priestess or two in my family." Remi carefully circumvented the cane and selected a brown leather book from the box. "The baton juju carries prestige in voodoo, especially if it belonged to someone powerful. You don't want to touch it and have all their power transferred to you."

"It's just a stick, Remi," Will argued.

"We need to learn more before we mess with it." Remi held up the book. "I suspect someone else was trying to do the same thing."

"*Famous Voodoo Queens, Priestesses, and Practitioners* by H.E. Llamos," Lexie read out loud. "Do you think Emily Mann searched for the original owner of the cane?"

Remi ran his hand over the book's soft leather cover. "Perhaps she knew where Magnus got it and wanted to return it to the original owner."

"Okay, you two have completely lost me." Will marched toward the doors. "Remi, we have a house to repair." He stormed out of the room.

Remi put the book back in the box. "Let's hope Magnus will rest easier knowing his cane is back under this roof."

"There's one thing I'd still like explained." Lexie faced the hearth. "In the portrait, the dragon's eyes are red." She turned to the cane on the floor. "Here, they're black."

Remi knelt to get a closer look. "You're right. Someone must have replaced the red stones with black ones at some point."

"Or these books can help me figure it out. The woman at the historical society said Emily Mann underlined passages in them. Something has got to be there to explain this."

"Stay out of those books, Lexie. Voodoo is dangerous. You're not strong enough to handle it."

His challenge agitated her "I'm a lot tougher than I look."

With a shrug, Remi held up his hands, acquiescing. "Be careful. Magic at first blush can be appealing, but soon it can turn ugly."

Remi strode out of the room. Lexie reached for the book he had set back in the box.

She shifted her focus to the portrait over the mantel. "I hope you're happy."

Silence.

"Just like a man. You bug a woman until you get what you want, and once you've got it, you hit the road."

Comfortable on the floor, Lexie flipped through the book. She came to a chapter on famous voodoo priestesses and read the list of names. One stood out—Simone Glapion.

*Another Glapion? What are the odds?*

A draft brushed a wisp of hair across her cheek as a chill settled in the room. Lexie shoved the lock behind her ear and turned the page, entranced by the story of the voodoo priestess from New Orleans.

Lexie paused and sniffed the air. "Is Will brewing more coffee?"

The cold in the room seeped beneath her skin, making Lexie shiver. She wanted to continue reading, but a nagging thought entered her mind. She wasn't alone in the room.

When she raised her head, Magnus stood in front of her, grinning.

The book flew out of her hands and across the room. She jumped to her feet, about to scream and then remembered Will and Remi. Her hand over her chest, begging her hammering heart to calm, she sucked in gasps of air.

"Holy shit!" Her fright turned to anger. "Don't just appear out of nowhere like that! You scared the piss out of me!"

"What would you suggest? Knock before I enter a room?" He floated toward the box. "I see you found my cane."

His wrinkled clothes gave the impression of fading in and out in the light, but the black on his hands stood out and had spread to his wrists. Dark circles rimmed his eyes, adding a touch of gloom.

"Well done, my dear. Now I'm afraid you must go."

"Go? I'm not going anywhere. I have questions. For one,

why—?"

"You and your fiancé will not be safe if you remain. I cannot protect you if you stay in this house. He wants you gone."

"Jacob? Is he the one who wants us—?"

Magnus's spirit evaporated as Remi entered the living room.

"Lexie, who are you talking to?"

The cold around her did not leave with Magnus. Instead, the room hummed with an oppressive heaviness. She hugged the book to her chest, not sure how to behave. A cautious inkling stirred in her. "I, ah, was reading out loud."

An insidious twinkle flickered in Remi's eyes. "You expect me to buy that?"

His threatening vibe disturbed her. With every passing day, Remi's easygoing charm seemed to retreat behind a caustic essence that added to Lexie's distrust.

She opened her mouth to plead her sincerity when another idea popped into her head. She eased her grip on the book as her determination took over. "I read something interesting in this book. About a woman from New Orleans: a powerful priestess named Simone Glapion. Ever heard of her?"

He crossed his arms, accentuating his bulging biceps. "It rings a bell."

She met his gaze, damned if she'd let the man intimidate her. "She ran an establishment called the Mahogany House in the red-light district of New Orleans. Many of the city's rich and powerful were her clients. She died there in a mysterious fire. It's funny you two share the same last name."

"Glapion is a common name in New Orleans." He stepped into the room, drawing closer. "Glapion was also Marie Laveau's married name. The Voodoo Queen and Madam Simone were related by marriage."

Lexie didn't budge from her spot on the floor. "The question is, are you related to them?"

"Everyone in New Orleans wants to be related to Marie Laveau. She did have fourteen children, and I could have her blood in my veins, but who knows?" He came right up to her, a sly grin on his lips. "Who was in here with you?"

The agitation in his voice set off an uneasy ripple in her. Lexie couldn't understand why her impressions turned darker around Remi, but she had to trust her instincts. Her grandmother taught her to listen to her body. It would always tell her the truth.

"Like I said, I was reading out loud."

Remi turned away. She caught the angry sneer he gave Magnus's portrait.

When he left, Lexie explored the room. "Magnus?"

No whispers called to her, no artic breezes crossed her path.

"Son of a bitch." She stomped her foot.

She returned the book in her hands to the box and spied the voodoo doll still sitting next to her computer. Would another book in the collection shed some light on the curiosity? Lexie sorted through several books, gleaning the titles.

One title intrigued her: *Voodoo Magic, Spells, Rituals, and Ceremonies.*

She wrestled the heavy book out from under the others, and then the cane caught her eye. Still laying on the floor, the stick looked so ordinary. Lexie couldn't understand why it commanded such fascination and fear. It was a walking stick and hardly capable of possessing any evil. Her inquisitive nature getting the better of her, Lexie set the large book in her hand to the side and scooted closer to the cane.

At that moment, the gray cat trotted into the room and up to Lexie. She nearly jumped out of her skin when it took up position between her and the cane.

"What? You don't think I should touch it, either?"

To her amazement, the cat moved behind the cane.

"Whose side are you on?"

Wary of the cat, Lexie tapped the cane with her index finger. Nothing happened. No gates of Hell opened and the ground did not rumble beneath her feet.

"This is silly."

She picked up the cane by the handle. When her hand gripped the wood, a strange tingling rose up her arm.

Like a snake wiggling its way through her, the sensation permeated muscle, bone, and nerve fibers. Euphoria overtook her senses. It was as if she hung over the edge of a sheer cliff, seconds away from letting go. The fears she once harbored ebbed, and her confidence skyrocketed.

Lexie rationalized away the exhilaration. But as the tingling intensified, an unrelenting burst of strength seized her. It was as if she'd downed a half dozen espressos in one shot.

She rubbed her fingers along the scales on the cane's shaft. "Why does everyone think you're so bad? You're miraculous."

The cane vibrated in her hand.

Lexie peered around the room, searching for a cause for the shaking, but everything appeared normal. Spooked, she dropped the cane. It smacked against the floor. The black eyes flickered.

The air in the room thickened, and a fine mist came out of nowhere. It circled her, and Lexie detected the faint sound of drums.

Scared out of her wits, she attempted to back away from the cane, but the mist held her in place. The drums grew louder, or was that her heart beating?

The scales on the shaft writhed as if the cane were awakening from a long sleep. The dragon yawned, its bejeweled orbs changed from black to a lovely shade of rose. The creature turned to Lexie. It studied her for a moment and then dipped its head.

The mist disappeared, the drums faded, and the cane returned to being a lifeless piece of wood.

Lexie scurried back from the cane. "What the fuck?"

The cat came up to her and rubbed against her hand. The creature's touch calmed her. Lexie didn't know what to make of the act. Before she could pet its thick scruff, the cat ran from the room.

Her attention returned to the cane as she wiped the beads of sweat from her upper lip. To Lexie's horror, the rose color of the stones did not change back.

"You touched it, and it changed to this color?" Will glimpsed the handle of the cane. "What do you think it means?"

Lexie sat on the bed with several voodoo books scattered around her. "I have no idea." She peered down at the open book in her lap. "I've been going through these books all afternoon to find an explanation. Nobody mentions anything about weird canes or stones changing color."

Will rested the cane against the foot of the bed. "Why are you getting upset about this? It's our cane, right?"

"You don't get it, Will. Holding it made me feel weird. Like I'd done something wrong. I must have broken it."

"Lexie, it's a cane. Remi can profess all the scary stories about voodoo he wants, but we're in Maine. Voodoo doesn't work up here. Too cold."

Lexie smirked. "That's the stupidest thing I've ever heard."

He moved close to her on the bed. "Trust me, when February rolls around, you will understand."

She patted the open book in her lap. "The stuff I've been

reading about is scary. Emily Mann did ample research on voodoo." Lexie reached for a book to her left. "In this one, she underlined a paragraph about a ritual for burying a murderer. The book says, 'You take the murderer's coffin to the grave of his victim, bury them within ten paces of each other and make the murderer face his victim's grave, thereby binding them together for eternity.' Emily did the exact thing to Jacob."

"Creepy, but I guess she did have an incentive. The guy killed her boss."

"And this one." Lexie snatched up another book. "This has all kinds of spells. Like the voodoo doll I found. Some voodoo priestesses would use them to bind a soul. All they needed was a person's hair, blood, or saliva. After they placed the object on the voodoo doll, they bound it with ribbon. The color of the ribbon determined the type of binding. And black was for when a person died, their soul belonged to whoever had requested the spell."

"The doll you found is a souvenir, Lexie, not some soul-binding torture instrument. You're getting carried away with this stuff."

"Am I?" She held up the book to him. "In the same book, I found a ritual for possessing another person's body. The priestess must choose the person she wishes to be, drink their blood, and the possessed body must live on a diet of fruit, vegetables, and whole grains. 'Food of the earth,' they call it. And the spell only works from sunup to sundown. At night, the possessed host falls into a deep sleep and must slumber in the earth so as not to be disturbed. Does that sound like anyone we know?"

He took the book from her and set it with the others on the bed. "It sounds like what the American Heart Association advocates. Or it's a plot to take over our planet, like in *Invasion of the Body Snatchers*, but they're using voodoo instead."

"Will, I'm serious. It's Remi's exact diet. And he's always in such a rush to get out of here before sunset."

His laughter rocked the bed. "Remi? You can't believe such nonsense?"

She waved her hand over the books gathered around her feet. "People all over the world believe in voodoo. It's still an active religion in Haiti and—"

"Enough, Lexie. I want to be supportive of your interests, but this is going too far." He collected the books on the bed and brought them to the closet. He opened the door and tossed them inside. The thud of the books hitting the floor reverberated around the room.

"Taking away my reference material isn't going to stop what's happening here, Will."

He came back to the bed. "Nothing is happening. There are no voodoo conspiracies, ghosts, vengeful secretaries, demons, boogeymen, or healthy-eating men being used as a bodysuit by wacked out witches."

"Voodoo priestesses," she corrected.

"Lexie, you're stressed and grasping for something to blame for what you're feeling."

She hunched down on the bed. "What am I feeling?"

He put his arm around her shoulders. "Homesick. You went back to Boston, and you missed it." He hugged her. "Give this place some time. You'll learn to love it as I do."

"And if I don't?" she murmured against his chest.

"Then I will sell the house and move anywhere you want."

She sat back from him. "You would do that for me?"

He rubbed his thumb over her bottom lip. "I would do anything for you, baby. I love you."

All her discontent brought on by Magnus, voodoo tales, and suspicions about Remi quieted when he spoke those words.

Will inched forward and kissed her chin. "Were there any

magic words in those books a guy could use on a girl to get her to do his bidding?" His lips slid down her neck.

"There might have been. Why?"

His teeth nipped her skin. "I'd like to get you to take off your clothes and make mad, passionate love to me."

Lexie nuzzled his cheek. "You already found the perfect words, Will."

"I did?"

She touched her forehead to his. "Yeah, I love you."

Out of the corner of her eye, she swore she saw the rose-colored dragon's eyes illuminate with a fiery glow.

She sat up to get a better look, and the upsetting scene in the living room came back to her.

The mysteries surrounding the cane, the house, Magnus, and even Remi's strange behavior weighed on her mind. Like quicksand, her troubles enveloped her and shattered all reason. How was she going to discover the truth? And what if all she had witnessed had been her imagination like Will professed?

*No, it was real. I'm certain of it.*

"Hey?" Will moved closer. "You're a million miles away."

"Sorry." She kissed his lips. "I've just got a lot on my mind."

"We can't have that now, can we?" He coaxed her beneath him with a long kiss.

Lexie lost herself in him. She forced the strange events in the house out of her head. For one brief moment, she wanted to forget about uppity ghosts, dancing dragon canes, and the dark corridors of Altmover Manor. She needed to return to a time when all that plagued her thoughts were her demanding clients and sharing the night in the arms of the man she loved.

# Chapter Eighteen

The early morning sun crept into their bedroom. Yearning for more time to snuggle, Lexie spooned against Will and buried her head in his back, blocking out the light.

"We have to get up."

She groaned. "Give me five more minutes. You wore me out last night."

"That's what you get for being so insatiable, baby." Will reached around and patted her thigh. "You do the coffee while I grab a shower. Remi will be here in half an hour." He sat up and tossed back the covers. "Do you think you might skip going into the attic today?"

"Why? I thought you wanted me to hunt for pictures of the house?"

He sat on the edge of the bed. "I do, but I'd feel better if you stayed out of there for a while. Suddenly, the idea of you up there all alone makes me nervous."

"What changed your mind?"

Will shook his head. "I have no idea."

Lexie hid her smile, encouraged by the change in his demeanor. "What would you like me to do instead?"

He rubbed his chin. "Why don't you run some computer searches for me? The fixtures in this house have to be changed. You could find matches for them online so we can keep the aesthetic, but still bring the place up to code. How does that sound?"

Lexie sat up and wiggled against his back. "How many fixtures do you have to change?"

He held the hand she'd hooked around his chest. "All of them. I've got a breakdown on my laptop. I've cataloged the pictures I took by floor."

She glimpsed his computer on the bedside table. "Anything else?"

He stood from the bed. "Isn't that enough? It should keep you out of the attic for a few days."

A pot of coffee and chicory filled the kitchen with a heady aroma. Lexie spooned some scrambled eggs onto Will's plate. He walked into the kitchen, his dark brown hair still damp, as she set his plate on the kitchen counter.

"Coffee smells good."

The sight of Will in his snug jeans and fresh white T-shirt made her want him all over again.

He poured a cup of coffee and smiled at her. "You look cute."

She motioned down the front of her fluffy blue robe. "In this?"

"Makes me want to take you right back upstairs."

Lexie blushed and tucked a stray blonde hair behind her ear. "I was thinking the same thing. I can't remember the last time we acted like this."

His arms slid around her waist. "Yeah. It's like we're under some kind of spell, huh?"

*A spell?* Lexie's passion cooled as she pictured the cane leaning against their bed throughout the night. She remembered how the eyes glowed during their love making but had passed it off as a trick of the light.

"Will, do you think—?"

He let her go and raised his nose in the air. "Do you smell that?"

"All I smell is coffee."

"Smoke," he shouted and ran out the kitchen.

Will stood like a statue at the base of the wide staircase, transfixed by the chandelier. When Lexie caught up to him, the sway of the light fixture alarmed her. Did he see it? Would he believe in the hauntings faced with such evidence?

A streak of smoke rose from a spot in the ceiling above the chandelier.

"Go get Remi!" Will dashed up the stairs.

Gripped with panic, Lexie bolted for the front doors. She bounded outside, running down the slick steps in her slippers and across the gravel drive, calling for Remi.

Lexie made it to the yellow cottage and rapped on the window pane built into the front door. She strained to see inside, but all she detected was darkness.

The nagging twinge of her intuition flared in her stomach, putting her fear about the fire aside. She needed to get a peek inside the cottage.

Lexie wiped away the thick layer of dirt covering the window.

She put her nose up to the glass. It took her eyes a few seconds to adjust, but she didn't see one stick of furniture.

*The place looks deserted.*

A brisk breeze blew by, and she tugged at her robe. For a second, her reflection distorted in the glass. A woman in a high lace collar and upswept honey-blonde hair smiled back at her. The hairs rose on the back of her neck.

"Lexie."

She spun around, stifling a scream.

Remi clasped her arms, his eyes burned into her. "What are you doing here?"

"Fire," she got out despite the quivering of her lips. "There's a fire in the house."

Remi sprinted toward the house.

"Upstairs above the chandelier," she called behind him.

After a wary glance back at the cottage, Lexie set out for the house.

She entered the open front doors and heard Will and Remi's booming voices echoing throughout the foyer.

Their frantic shouts spurred her to hurry up the staircase. Right before she reached the second-floor landing, the banister wiggled under her hand.

She jumped back and clung to the wall. She watched in horror as the scales on the banister bucked and rolled.

An icy embrace enveloped her. Condensation from her breath appeared, and goose bumps rose on her skin. The yelling from the men obscured her cries for help while the banister's snake-like movements robbed her of the ability to flee.

"Get out, Lexie. This is a warning."

At the top of the staircase, Magnus floated like mist above a still lake. His green eyes teemed with hostility.

The banister ceased its wriggling, and she moved away from

the wall. "Did you start the fire, Magnus?"

"No. I would never destroy my home, but he will." He rushed down the steps to her as if carried on a wave of wind. "You found the cane, and he wants to scare you out so he can steal it away. He wants no questions and no suspicions of his crime."

She recoiled as his ghostly presence drew near. "Who is it, Magnus? You must tell me."

"Leave while you still can, my dear."

Magnus dissolved into a thin line of light and vanished. Remi and Will's voices grew louder. Following their shouts, she found them in a bedroom off to the right.

She stood in the doorway as the men pulled at the floorboards with their bare hands, smoke billowing around them.

"Call the fire department!" Will bellowed.

Remi raised his head to her. "No, wait!" He reached in below the floor and grabbed at some wiring, the smoke coming from the wires snaked around his hand like the stream from a cigarette.

"I found it."

Remi twisted the wires together, and the smoke ceased.

"That was close." Will sat back on his heels. "We need to go through the wiring in the entire place. We'll shut off the electricity until we're positive it's safe."

"Might take us weeks to check all the wiring," Remi countered. "Are you sure you want to live without heat and light?"

"I don't care." Will stood up. "Better than the house burning to the ground."

"We should call an electrician," Lexie suggested.

"We can handle it," Will told her.

"I'm not living in this house for weeks without electricity."

His brow lowered. "What do you want me to do?"

"Let's everyone calm down," Remi edged in. "Will, before you cut the electricity we can go to the basement and check the electrical box for a short. Then we can test the circuits on this line. See if we need to cut some of the load."

Will contemplated the exposed wires in the floor. "The big chandelier is on this line. I already checked."

"Then let's take it off the line," Remi proposed in an upbeat manner. "We've got a short somewhere going into the chandelier. I'll wager that monster's the cause of our problem."

Will wiped his hand across his forehead. "Fine, but if any more fires like this occur, I'm shutting off the power."

"I agree." Remi went to the door. "I'll get my tools, and we can get started."

"Thank you, Remi," Lexie whispered when he came to the doorway.

He patted her shoulder with his thick hand. "No problem."

Will nodded to Lexie. "Go around the house and unplug as many things as you can. Appliances, phone chargers, lights, anything sucking electricity. Let's lighten the load on the wiring."

"Will, what if the fire was deliberate?"

He squinted at her. "What are you talking about? Who would do such a thing?"

"Someone who wants us to leave."

He waved off her comment. "Don't be ridiculous. It's a short in the wiring. No one snuck up here and started a fire. We were in the house and would have heard them."

Lexie wanted to argue that perhaps a person didn't start the fire, but a ghost. However, the angry glint in his eyes told her not to push the point. Will wasn't ready for the truth.

*Would he ever be?*

"You're right." She turned for the hallway. "After breakfast, I'll disconnect everything in the kitchen."

He held her arm, giving her an affectionate grin. "Make sure to leave the coffeepot plugged in. We're gonna need it."

After the morning's excitement had died away, Lexie returned with Will's laptop to the living room and searched the Internet for the new light fixtures.

On the floor, with a fresh mug of coffee at her side, Lexie scrolled through the long list of various antique fixtures. She reached for her coffee knocking over the voodoo doll next to her computer. When she rescued the mysterious object, Lexie scrutinized the way the black ribbon weaved in and out of the twigs. If it hadn't represented something so devilish, she would have considered the doll pretty.

When she placed the keepsake aside, a chill entered the room. Preparing for another ghostly visit she got to her feet, but instead an overwhelming sense of grief pressed down on her.

The cat appeared at the entrance, standing on its toes and hissing.

"What's wrong, kitty?"

In the corner, a black mist rose from the floorboards, swirling like a dust cloud. But this time it wasn't Magnus.

With muscular shoulders, a wide chest, and handsome features, Jacob O'Connor was better looking than the man she'd encountered in her bathroom mirror. His tuxedo, however, reminded her of Magnus's clothes: dusty, torn, and wrinkled. She also detected a hint of blackness around his fingertips.

"He's deceiving you, Ms. Arden. He deceives every woman."

"Who, Jacob? Magnus? Is he deceiving me?"

"Don't trust anything Magnus says. He's the evil in this home."

"O'Connor," a voice thundered from the other side of the

room.

Lexie trembled, and the sorrow in her heart turned to anger. Jacob's ghost floated closer, and suddenly she was afraid—something she'd never experienced before with his visits. What was different about him?

She backed away in time to witness another tornado of black dust rising from the floor. Magnus materialized, and Jacob faced him.

The tension between the two entities sucked the air out of the room. Lexie was about to call for Will when a woman's shrill scream came from outside.

"Frances!" Jacob cried and instantly compressed into a flash of light.

Lexie blinked, and the room was empty—even the cat had vanished. The weight in her chest dissipated, her anger paled, and everything was calm.

*What the hell happened?*

"My God, Lexie, what's wrong?" Partially bent over in the doorway, Will gasped for breath.

"What are you talking about, Will?"

"You screamed."

Remi ran up beside him and stopped. He too was out of breath. "You okay?"

"I didn't scream," she insisted.

Will slumped against the doorframe. "Lexie, we heard you."

"I'm telling you it wasn't me."

"You're the only woman in the house."

Aggravated with the back and forth, she put her hands on her hips. "I'm the only living woman in the house. Perhaps you came across one of the dead ones."

Will's snicker reeked of frustration. "Not this again."

"The scream came from outside, not inside this house." Lexie appealed to Remi for support. "Tell him, Remi."

"It's true." Remi nodded as he faced Will. "The house is haunted. I've experienced many strange things since I moved into the cottage."

"Now you're on her side?" Will combed his hand through his thick hair and glared at Lexie. "You're spooked from the fire this morning. Admit it!"

"Will, this house is haunted," she declared. "Why can't you accept the fact? The ghosts may be trying to tell us something. The fire was a warning!"

"Just please stop!" Will's voice rang out like a hammer hitting an anvil. "I've tried to understand this ghost business, I really have. But I can't listen to this anymore. I'm not going to run out of here like a kid afraid of monsters in his room. This is our home, so deal with it. Or you can pack up and go."

He spun away from the door, his harsh words echoing in her head.

"Now, now." Remi moved toward her. "He didn't mean that. He's upset."

She stepped away, unnerved by his approach. "This house is tearing us apart."

Remi's smile encouraged, but his hollow eyes lacked any warmth. His face reminded her of a lifeless doll.

"Lexie, it's not like that. The man was terrified something happened to you."

"Something did happen to me. I saw—" She slammed her lips together, giving into her distrust for the man.

"Go on." His tone was impatient. "What did you see?"

"Shadows," she offered instead of the truth. "The room filled with shadows. Then the scream happened, and they disappeared."

Remi's features fell faster than rain. "Are you sure that's all it was?"

"I'm sure. There were ghostly shadows without any shape or faces." She rubbed her arms, daunted by his arctic stare. "It feels like things are getting out of hand. I'd hoped finding the cane would quiet the spirits in this house, but they're more active than ever."

"Have you put the cane in a safe place?" Remi's voice sounded off.

"What difference does that make?"

Remi arched over the box on the floor, his movements stiff and awkward. "Where did you put the cane, Lexie?"

The sharp lilt in his voice gave Lexie pause. She carefully considered her answer.

"The cane is fine."

He stood and marched up to her, his nostrils flaring. "Did you touch it?"

The apprehensive twinge in her gut morphed into a steady burn. "Ah, no. You said not to."

He blew out a long breath. "Good. If you had touched the baton juju, things would have gotten much worse."

"Worse? We have ghosts, spontaneous fires, screaming women, and voodoo canes to contend with. How much worse can it get?"

Remi hooked his thumbs under the straps of his beige overalls, acting as if he were mulling over her question. "We're dealing with voodoo, Lexie. It can always get worse, but we have to avoid becoming part of the negativity going on in this house. We can't get sucked in. Distance and calm heads are warranted. The cane is the epicenter of everything. If you touch it, the negative energy might transfer to you."

Lexie recalled holding the cane and the power flowing through her. But what she'd sensed from the cane wasn't bad. She suspected the rush of energy had led to her amorous night with Will.

"How do we distance ourselves from everything going on?"

"You and Will should get away for a while and forget about the house. I can watch over things and do some work on the wiring while you're gone."

Lexie snorted, balking at the suggestion. "Like Will would go for that. Guess again." She shook her head. "No, we have to do something else. I can call a priest and have the house blessed. Or have someone perform an exorcism."

"There's one way to cleanse a house. The voodoo way … with fire."

"That's not an option, Remi!"

He gave her a pensive half-smile. "Then we will have to come up with another solution."

When Remi sauntered out of the room, the tic in her gut grew louder. The longer she spent with the man, the more convinced she became he hid a terrible secret. Lexie had no idea how to uncover the real Remi Glapion. And if she did, she feared things would soon spiral out of control.

At the front doors, Magnus waited while Remi strutted up to him. He hated the man's cocky arrogance hidden beneath the friendly exterior. At least people knew what they got when Magnus walked into a room—or had known when he'd thrived among the living.

"You started the fire. Tell me why, Glapion."

Remi stopped and faced the ghost. "Motivation. You used money to get people to do your bidding. I use fear."

"What good would come from destroying my home?"

Remi opened the front doors and breathed in the air. "I need the cane's loss to look like an accident. A little fire would make sure there's no evidence left pointing to me."

"Leave the couple their future. Don't destroy their dreams."

Remi snickered at him. "Since when do you give a damn about anyone?"

"Despite what you may think of me, I don't want to see the innocent hurt. I'm not the man I was. I've destroyed enough lives for one eternity."

"This is a new side of you, Magnus." Remi tilted his head, studying the ghost. "Fine, whatever damage I do, I'll make sure the couple is compensated, but you have to find the cane. Check their bedroom. I've searched the other rooms in the house."

Magnus hated the way the man ordered him about. "I can't go in their bedroom anymore."

Remi sneered at him. "You spent enough time toying with them before. What's changed?"

"There's something stopping me. Perhaps a spell. I'm not sure." Magnus waved to the staircase. "You will have to search the bedroom."

"She's suspicious of me. I can't chance it. Not yet."

"Uncertainty, from you?" Magnus's low *cluck* hung in the air. "You once professed the cane meant everything to you."

"There's something more I require. The girl has a tremendous ability. I can use her."

The ghost detested what he identified in the man's eyes.

"Leave Lexie to her future husband. She means nothing to you."

"You're wrong." Remi's harsh cackle rattled Magnus. "I'd like to test her abilities. See what she's capable of before I return to New Orleans."

"How would you accomplish that?" Magnus inquired, hiding the anger in his voice.

"Never you mind. Get my cane, Magnus. I'm growing

impatient."

Magnus displayed an unperturbed grin. "Get it yourself."

"Don't push me." Remi walked through the open doors. "Anger me, and I will destroy this house and you."

Magnus waited in the shadows of the entrance as Remi jogged down the massive steps.

"You've made a deal with the devil, Magnus," Jacob's ethereal voice admonished.

Magnus raised his head and chuckled into the air. "The devil has got nothing on me."

# Chapter Nineteen

A horrible nightmare woke Lexie before dawn. Her heart thudded, and her damp nightshirt clung to her back. Will remained in a peaceful slumber next to her.

When she swung her legs over the side of the bed, the dream came back to her. In the living room of the house, two men—mere shadows—had been out to destroy each other. She attempted to stop them, but couldn't. Lexie reasoned the dream resulted from the previous day's events.

Not wanting to go back to sleep, she stood and reached for her fuzzy robe. She craved coffee to clear her head and a few minutes of peace.

Lexie snuck down the staircase, hoping it too early in the morning for any ghostly visits. She wasn't in the mood for any more of Magnus's antics.

In the kitchen, she loaded the coffeemaker and waited for the muddy liquid to fill the pot. The first rays of sunlight crept over the floor, and she ran her fingers through the beams. She watched through the window as the sun rose over the horizon. Lexie smiled. It was a shame the house had endured such misery. It was a beautiful place to live. Coffee in hand, she had a seat at the kitchen table and put her feet up on a chair.

"You're up," Will said from behind her.

"Couldn't sleep." She spoke without turning around.

He filled a mug with coffee. "You okay?"

"Yeah. I'm good."

"Wanna talk about it?"

"I told you I was okay."

Still in his blue pajama bottoms, he lifted her feet from the chair placing them in his lap as he sat.

"You never get up this early unless something's bothering you." He took a sip from his mug. "When you're sad, you eat ice cream. When your mother pisses you off, you drink. And when something is really bothering you, you don't sleep."

"You know me pretty well, don't you?"

"I know you, baby." His hand rubbed along her calf. "I'm sorry I was such an ass yesterday. This house must be getting to me. I shouldn't have said the things I did."

"It's fine. I understand. We've both been under a lot of stress lately. And you're right, this house is getting to us."

"So if you're not mad at me, what's wrong?"

She put her coffee mug on the table. "This house is haunted, Will." She bit her thumbnail while she waited, anxious for his reply.

"Okay. Why do you think this house is haunted?" he asked, remaining calm.

"I've spoken to Magnus Blackwell's ghost, and I've seen Jacob

O'Connor. They're here, trapped in this house. Something is about to happen."

"What is about to happen?"

She shook her head. "I wish I knew."

"I'll admit you do have a gift. You can sense things I can't begin to grasp. I'm trying to understand it, but this is new territory for me. I know I've been rash and not wanted to speak about it before, but if it bothers you this much, I want to help. Tell me how to help you."

She eased closer to him. "Stay open minded for me. If I have to appease you and a house filled with discontented ghosts, I may have to leave."

He put his coffee down and pulled her into his lap. "Don't ever leave, Lexie. I'd die without you."

Her tears blurred her vision as his arms held her close. "I never want to leave you."

"From now on, I swear I will listen to your ghost stories and not get angry. And if you can talk to ghosts," he nuzzled her neck, "ask them where the family treasure is buried."

Relieved, Lexie laughed and wiped her eyes. "You got it."

"I need this house to work, baby. It's a once in a lifetime opportunity for us. I'll do whatever necessary to keep it."

In the distance, a rumble of thunder shook the house.

"Storm's coming."

"Yeah," Lexie agreed. "Sounds like a bad one."

He kissed her cheek. "I'd better get upstairs and change. I need to secure the shutters before it arrives."

A thick wall of black clouds gathered in the distance to the east, consuming the rays of light in its path. The energy in the air changed, and an edginess seeped into her. Wanting to view Mother Nature in all her fury, she headed for the conservatory. The brisk storm's winds blew onshore as a mass of black clouds rolled in off the ocean. She stepped outside into the courtyard, and the leaves whipped around her. Lightning flashes danced as she headed toward the fountain. The static electricity in the air enlivened her senses.

A movement at the railing by the cliff's edge drew her gaze. A woman's shape formed gradually emerged. She wore a pink and white gown with a bustle and lace skirt. Her frenzied movements insinuated a bitter quarrel was in progress. The back of a long tuxedo jacket materialized. Silhouetting against the foreboding sky.

The woman, graceful in her movements, was like a dancer gliding across the stage. The man fought with her. As he crept closer, she stepped back and almost fell over the cliff. The old iron railing remained, but the figures moved around, ignoring it. The woman's panicked face became clear. Lexie recognized Frances, Jacob O' Connor's bride.

The gentleman grabbed her, keeping her from falling to the rocks below. Relief swept over Frances's face. Their eyes met, locked in a loving gaze.

"This doesn't look like a suicide to me," Lexie mumbled.

The man reached for Frances, pulling her into his arms and demanding a kiss. A horrified Frances struggled with everything she had. The man's hands eased around her throat. She dangled precariously close to the courtyard's edge. Her feet slipped as her head turned to the rocks below.

Without hesitation, her cruel assailant pushed Frances over. Her ear-piercing scream carried until the thud of her impact resonated around Lexie. The scream was the same Lexie had heard again and again since coming to Altmover Manor.

When the killer in the tuxedo turned, Lexie got a good look at his face.

"You bastard!"

"Lexie?" Remi moved from inside the conservatory doors.

"What are you doing out here? Will sent me to find you."

Lexie scrambled to explain what she'd observed. "The cliff . . ."

Remi came up to her. He gripped her shoulders. "What about it?"

"Magnus," she finally got out. "He killed Frances O'Connor. I watched him push her over the cliff."

He let her go. "Then the rumors aren't true. The woman didn't kill herself."

"Jacob O'Connor must have figured it out. To get revenge, he killed Magnus Blackwell and his wife. He hanged himself when he got what he was after."

Remi raised his head to the heavens. "The storm." Thunder echoed as black clouds arrived over the manor. "A storm's power can give life to the past. The electricity in the air feeds the impressions left behind. You had a vision, Lexie. Jacob O'Connor is showing you the reason for his vengeance."

"Did you see it?" she demanded.

"No, but I suspect it's a warning. You and Will need to leave this place."

She gawked at Remi, unhinged by the suggestion. "I can't and Will certainly won't. He's convinced he can save this—"

"Leave the cane and go," Remi interrupted.

"The cane?" Filled with trepidation, she backed away from Remi. "If I were to leave, why would I leave it behind?"

"The cane's the reason why things are intensifying. You can feel the change in the air."

She waved to the cloud bank over them. "You said it's the storm, Remi."

"The storm brought the past back to life, but what's coming is justice. All the wrongs committed in this house are finally coming due."

As fat raindrops fell, leaving wet spots on the green dragon in the courtyard floor, Remi ushered her to the safety of the conservatory.

They stopped inside the glass doors as rain pummeled the courtyard. The drops on the glass roof sounded like the tapping of a thousand fingers.

"Please, consider what I'm proposing," Remi begged. "You have the gift. Listen to it."

She contemplated the puddles forming in the courtyard. "I'm not sure about anything, anymore."

He tugged at her robe lapel. "Go upstairs and change. After some breakfast and a strong cup of coffee, you'll put these visions behind you." A howling wind blew across the courtyard. "Storm or no storm, we have work to do today."

Lexie left Remi in the conservatory. Rehashing what she'd witnessed in the courtyard. All along, she'd understood Magnus to be the one wronged by Jacob O'Connor. With the truth revealed, Lexie had to deem everything he'd told her to be a lie, a manipulation to get her to do his bidding. The one thing she still couldn't fathom—where did the cane fit in?

On the staircase, Lexie trembled while the violent storm lashed against the house. The lights flickered, and claps of thunder made her flinch. When she reached the second-floor landing, the grand chandelier swayed. Another thunderous rumble rang out, and for an instant, the chandelier lights flickered.

"Hey, where's Remi?" Will came from the third floor.

"He's in the conservatory. Hey," she reached for his shirt sleeve as he passed by. "Did you cut the power to the chandelier?"

He frowned. "Yeah. Why?"

Should she mention the chandelier? After everything in the courtyard, sputtering lights were the least of their problems.

"It's nothing." She let go of his sleeve. "Not sleeping last night is getting to me."

Will kissed her cheek. "Get some more coffee and get dressed, baby. We've got lots to do." He continued down the stairs. "Some storm, eh?"

He strode away, a happy spring in his step. She chastised her hankering to tell him of her vision. Lexie couldn't screw up his dream. There had to be a way to make the house work for both the ghosts and the humans. But how? Was it possible for two worlds to work together for a common cause?

"I'm gonna need years of therapy after this."

Once in her bedroom, fatigue hit her. Lexie stood before her unmade bed and ached to rest her head. A *thud* on the floor stopped her from crawling into bed. The long cane with the dragon's head had fallen at her feet. Lexie picked it up and inspected the rose-colored eyes.

"Why are you so special?"

A knock from inside the closet frightened her. What was going on? Was Remi right? Had the activity in the house ratcheted up a notch or were her nerves making it seem that way?

Lexie weighed the closet door. What if she opened it and something bad happened?

*It's not like you haven't seen a ghost before.*

"Magnus, are you in there?" She took a step closer to the door. "I've got some choice words for your murdering ass."

Not a peep came from the closet. After further deliberation, Lexie imagined a giant rat hiding in her wardrobe and brandished the cane like a weapon.

"Where's that damned cat when I need it?"

With one swift movement, she kicked the door open, but nothing was inside. Their clothes and the books Will had dumped on the floor remained untouched.

A book sitting open atop the pile caught her attention. Lexie picked it up and perused the pages. An old black and white photograph of a woman stared back at her. Frustrated with the weak light in the closet, Lexie put the cane to the side, snapped up the book, and carried it to the lamp by the bed.

On closer inspection, the picture turned out to be a painting. The attractive woman portrayed had a regal bearing, dark hair, and intense, catlike eyes. Her beaded white gown hinted at another era, but the object in her hand floored Lexie. The same dragon cane was in the painting. She quickly read the caption.

*A portrait of the renowned voodoo priestess, Madam Simone Glapion. Photographed in 1917.*

With outrage coursing through her veins, Lexie slammed the book closed. "Magnus Blackwell, what have you done?"

# Chapter Twenty

After a full day and night of stormy weather, and a brief power outage, Lexie was glad to see the sun shining through the leaded-glass in the front doors when she came down the staircase the next morning.

Clutching a coffee mug, Will rushed up to meet her on the steps. "I made cheese omelets. They're in the pan on the stove."

She admired his ass as he took the stairs two at a time. "How can anyone over the age of ten be hyper in the morning?"

Before heading to the kitchen, Lexie stopped in the living room. She cringed at Magnus's portrait, remembering the events in the courtyard the day before.

"You must have been a real piece of work. No wonder you haunt this house."

Lexie waited for the ghost to form, to make a noise, something.

But the living room was as silent as the grave. *Typical.* She rolled her eyes, and her gaze stopped on a black spot on the ceiling. *Where did that come from?*

She squinted at the spot. The eighteen-foot ceiling made it impossible to identify. Lexie feared a burn mark from faulty wiring in the floor above might be the cause. She had to get closer. Lexie found one of Will's ladders in the office behind the stairs. With several grunts and a curse word or two, she lugged the tall ladder into the room. She set it right below the spot and made sure the ladder's legs spread out evenly on the floor. She stuck her tongue out at Magnus's portrait on the way up the ladder, thinking the smirk on his lips was meant for her.

Lexie honed in on the discoloration in the ceiling. "Please don't be a plumbing leak."

Something moved in the corner of the room. The overwhelming rush of grief came over her again. The episode hurt so much, she feared not being able to climb down the ladder.

In the haze of her discomfort, shadows rose from the floorboards. Like waterspouts on a lake, the shadows danced around the room and came precariously close to her ladder.

Terrified as the shadows bobbed and weaved around her, making the ladder shake, she was about to call out for Will when the men's shouting enveloped her. Lexie recognized one of the voices—Magnus Blackwell.

"I'm trying to help her, Jacob."

"I warned you, Magnus. Leave her be."

Convinced the ladder might topple over, Lexie willed her body to move. She was halfway down the ladder when the metal frame shuddered as the shadows below twirled faster around its base.

She screamed as the ladder tipped over. The hardwood floor came up to meet her. She put out her arm, bracing for the fall. Then everything went black.

"Lexie?"

She opened her eyes. Will hovered over her.

"Are you okay?"

He helped her up. She touched the spot where a shooting pain flared from her forehead.

"What happened?"

Her hand was wet. "The ladder fell over." She peered down at her fingers. "Is that blood?"

Will lifted her into his arms. "Yeah, it's blood."

She clung to him to quell the dizziness. "What are you doing?"

"Putting you in the car and taking you to the emergency room."

Will's strong arms felt so good around her, but she fought against him. "I had the weirdest dream … I don't want to go to the emergency room. They have needles there."

He hurried to the front doors. "They have doctors, too. You need one."

"No doctors. Put me down." The bright morning sunlight made Lexie wince as he carried her out to the porch. "Oh, this is worse. Take me back inside."

"Lexie, you're hurt. You have to see a doctor." His voice sounded strained.

Remi appeared out of nowhere. "What happened?"

"She fell off the ladder in the living room." Will trotted down the front steps. "Get the car door for me, Remi. I'm taking her to the emergency room."

"No emergency room," Lexie insisted, louder than before.

Will set her in the front passenger seat. "Stop fighting me on this. You've hit your head, you're bleeding, and you're not making any sense."

Remi leaned into the car. "She's making sense to me."

Will reached for her seatbelt. "You're not helping."

She shoved Will away as he buckled her in. "Stop it." She pressed her hand against the tender spot on her forehead. "All I need is an aspirin, and some coffee. Then I'm good to go."

Will sat back on his heels. "You might have a concussion or a bleed in your brain. You know how fast one of those things can kill a—"

"Will, you're getting carried away," Remi inserted.

She stretched for the car door and attempted to stand. Determined not to show any weakness, she rose to her feet and held on to the car door to steady herself.

Will sagged forward. "Tell me what happened. How did the ladder fall over? What were you doing on it in the first place?"

Remi stood behind Will, waiting for her response. She couldn't tell Will the truth—not with Remi listening.

"There's a black spot on the ceiling in the living room. I went to check it out when I got dizzy. I climbed down, but the ladder toppled over before I got to the floor."

The scowl on Remi's face told her he wasn't buying any of it.

"You're sure you're all right?" Will ran his finger across her jaw.

To ease the spinning in her head, Lexie concentrated on the open front doors. "I need to get back to work."

Will took her arm. "You're working in bed for the rest of the day." He guided her up the steps to the porch. "If you won't go to the ER, then you should at least take it easy."

She circled her gaze back to Remi. "Help me."

Remi chuckled as he came up the steps behind them. "I agree with Will. You need to spend the day safely tucked away in your bed. It's the one place to make sure you stay out of harm's way."

Confined to her bed, Lexie kept busy searching the Internet for light fixtures. After she got bored, she explored the bedroom for another distraction. She set her sights on the voodoo doll next to her on the night table. She'd brought it up to her room, along with her laptop, when Will insisted she spend the day in bed. While fingering the doll's black ribbon, she remembered the books on the closet floor.

Later in the afternoon, Will stopped by with more aspirin and a soda. He recognized the books on the bed, and his face reddened.

"You need to rest, Lexie." He put the can of soda and bottle of aspirin on the night table. "I swear you're becoming obsessed."

Lexie sat back on her pillows, fed up with his nagging. "Your obsession with this house is no different, Will Bennett, so don't bitch at me."

The color in his face eased, and he sat on the bed. "You've been talking about ghosts, voodoo, and whatever supernatural nonsense there is since we arrived on the doorstep. You can't go on like this."

"Will, are you ever going to accept the supernatural nonsense happening in this house is real?"

"I'm trying, baby. But it's hard when I can't see what you see." He touched the Band-Aid on her forehead. "You could have been seriously hurt today."

"It was an accident. I'm fine. I'm ready to get back to work."

His sigh lingered between them, adding to Lexie's guilt. "Tomorrow, you can help Remi and me around the house. We'll need a third person to assist us."

"Doing what?"

He stood and picked up the aspirin bottle. "I have to get this house up and running as soon as possible so there are no more accidents. I've decided tomorrow we're going to get as many lights working as we can on the first floor. Remi and I have been running new wiring through the house, but we need someone to tell us if a light fixture is working or not working when we test the new line from the electrical box in the basement. That's where you come in." He poured two aspirin tablets onto his hand. "You can be our lookout while we're in the basement."

"Sounds boring."

He held out the aspirin to her. "No, it sounds safe. At least you won't be off climbing ladders or getting attacked by God knows what in the attic."

Lexie frowned and snatched up the aspirin. "I never got attacked by anything in the attic."

He handed her the soda can. "You'll be staying out of there until I have an exterminator go through the place."

"What am I supposed to do until then? There's some valuable stuff up there. I need to catalog everything." She washed back the pills with soda.

"Well, Indiana Jones, I guess you'll have to work as my assistant until the attic is fumigated."

She slapped the can on the night table. "I'm not a child. I don't need to be supervised."

"That's exactly what you are." He gathered up the books in his arms. "And these are to go back to the historical society along with the cane."

"No!" She sat up in the bed. "The cane goes along with the house. It's tied to its history."

He arched over her, his withering expression challenging her. "I don't give a damn about this house's history. I'm more concerned with its future, and ours. I'm serious. No more ghosts, voodoo, murder mysteries, and no more ladders for you. I would like for you to be in one piece for our wedding." Will carried the books to the door. "I'll bring you up some dinner in a short while."

When he shut the door, Lexie sank into the bed. "Shit, shit, shit!"

She spied the cane resting against the wall, grateful he'd missed it. But without the information contained within the rare books, her search for the cane's past would be difficult at best.

"Listen to me. I sound as crazy as Emily Mann. Will's right. I have to think about our future."

Lexie had almost convinced herself to give up her fascination with the cane when the cat jumped on her bed.

"How did you get in here?"

The cat purred, rubbing against her leg.

She glimpsed the closed bedroom door and figured it must have snuck in when Will had left.

"Doesn't matter. I'm glad for the company." She picked up the cat and set it in her lap.

Lexie went back to her laptop and the hunt for Will's light fixtures. Deep into her search for brass sconces shaped like lotus flowers, she didn't notice when the cat left her bed.

*Thud.*

She looked up from her computer. The cat stood next to the cane now laying on the floor.

"What did you do?"

She got out of bed and retrieved the cane. "Did you knock it over?"

The cat rubbed against her leg, purring.

The cane pulsated. Its power surged through her once again. Her obsession with Magnus, Jacob, and Altmover Manor resurfaced stronger than before. Lexie didn't understand why the events of the past resonated more than a future with the man she loved. It was as if the house, the ghosts, and the damned cane had awakened something. But what?

She settled on the floor. “If I learn the truth, then I’ll walk away for good.” She stroked the cat’s head, and it meowed at her. “Yeah, I don’t believe me either.”

# Chapter Twenty-One

Ready to tackle the house's lighting problems, Will positioned Lexie in the foyer. Up first, the lotus-shaped sconces along the walls. Lexie discovered from her internet searches, the exquisite fixtures had been hand-blown in Florence and were irreplaceable.

She waited for Will to shout from the basement door underneath the staircase. Lexie prayed all the priceless fixtures would work with the new wiring.

"Lexie!" Will's thunderous voice rattled around the foyer. "What have you got?"

She counted the fixtures on the wall. "All working."

Seconds later, footfalls dashed across the marble floors.

"Get to the base of the stairs," Will said. "We're going to try the chandelier next."

Fear caught in Lexie's throat. "Are you sure? What about the fire?"

"We've rewired everything up to the connection in the ceiling. If there's a problem, it's in the fixture, and that's going to be a bitch to fix."

Lexie looked at the enormous chandelier. "Why is it so difficult?"

"Because then someone is going to have to go through each bulb socket to find the short. There's got to be close to a hundred lights up there."

"You should check the sockets first instead of lighting it."

"Why on earth would you want me to risk my neck?" Will held up his hand. "Never mind. If you tell me you're having another one of your feelings, I might lose it."

Will hurried back to the basement door while Lexie took up her spot at the bottom of the staircase.

She stood by the dragon's head carved into the newel post and waited for his signal. An ice-cold wind swept through the foyer. Lexie crossed her arms, her shoulders curling inward. The dragon's head slowly turned to her.

Her cry remained trapped in the back of her throat. She wanted to flee from the foyer but could not budge. The empty eye sockets of the dragon glowered at her as the foul creature snarled.

A thin veil of smoke floated up in front of the dragon and crept along the foyer floor. It gathered around Lexie's feet, and the dragon backed away, shrinking back into the decorative post at the bottom of the staircase.

Seconds later, voices echoed throughout the foyer. The voices grew louder until she discerned two men, shouting at each other.

"What are you talking about?" Magnus sounded panicked. "Where is my wife?"

"She's with my wife, now." Jacob's deep voice rang out.

The sconces on the walls flickered.

"Lexie? Let me know what happens?" Will sounded so far away.

Two men gripped in a bitter battle danced in and out of the smoke. Jacob O'Connor had his hands cinched around Magnus Blackwell's throat. Magnus gagged, clawed, and fought to get his breath while Jacob's eyes bulged with rage. A flash of light blinded Lexie, the scene in front of her changing.

The men were on the edge of the courtyard, positioned close to the iron railing; they struggled as the lights of the house shone down on them.

"You killed Frances," Jacob shouted at a terrified Magnus. "You pushed her over this cliff and took her away from me."

Lexie cried out as he bent Magnus over the iron railing.

"I have been waiting for this day, Magnus. How does it feel to lose the only thing you ever loved?"

Magnus struggled to pry Jacob's hands off his neck as he gasped air. He punched Jacob, but the man's hold on him never let up. Magnus twisted his shoulder up and into Jacob's grip, and finally broke free.

Unable to turn away, Lexie witnessed Magnus's retreat from the railing. He attempted to flee when Jacob picked up the dragon cane from the ground. Magnus cried out as the handle came crashing down on his head.

Dazed, Magnus stumbled backward, but Jacob went after him, whacking him over the head once more. Magnus fell to his knees, protecting his head.

Lexie covered her mouth as Jacob beat Magnus with the cane. Every time Jacob raised the cane to strike, Lexie noticed how the green eyes in the dragon glowed brighter.

*When had the stones turned green?*

By the time Jacob finished, Magnus's face was unrecognizable. Panting, Jacob dropped the blood-covered cane to the ground.

"An eye for an eye, my friend," Jacob said to Magnus.

"Lexie? What's going on?"

Will sounded insistent.

In the cloud of smoke before her, Jacob tossed Magnus's body over the courtyard railing. Then he picked up the cane and hobbled toward the conservatory.

Inside the glass room, Jacob cleaned the cane with scraps of cloth. All around him, green plants and shelves overflowed with herbs and blooming flowers. He then scurried into the house.

A party captivated Lexie's senses. Women in colorful gowns laughed with men in long-tailed tuxedos. The strains of a waltz drifted down the hallway. There was furniture in the rooms, lit candles in the lotus sconces, and familiar paintings on the walls.

She followed Jacob as he climbed the polished staircase to the second floor.

"Lexie?" Will grabbed her, but her attention stayed on the stairs.

The partygoers ignored Jacob O'Connor as he stepped out on the second-floor landing holding a rope fashioned out of linen in his hands. He set the dragon cane against the banister and watched the revelers below.

He spoke words Lexie could not hear over the din of the party. While he tied the rope to the end of the chandelier, Jacob's serene smile puzzled her. How could he appear so accepting of his death?

Without hesitation, Jacob pushed the grand fixture out over the crowd and leapt over the black banister.

Numerous screams and the sound of crashing glass reverberated throughout the foyer. Silence descended over the room as Jacob O'Connor's convulsing body swung from the crystal chandelier. In the last throes before his demise, the cane he had left resting against the banister toppled over.

"Lexie, say something!"

Will's shouting snapped her back.

The chandelier above her rocked, but Jacob O'Connor didn't hang from it. She gaped around. The house was empty again. The wallpaper faded, the sconces broken and lifeless.

"Are you all right?" Will squeezed her upper arms. "You were like a statue."

A loud *pop* filled the room. The chandelier came to life and illuminated the foyer. The brilliant light accentuated the shabbiness of the floors and wallpaper. Then another *pop* rang out. A lightbulb in the chandelier blew, and a small fire broke out.

Will took off for the door beneath the stairs. "Remi, shut it down! Shut it down!"

Another bulb blew in the chandelier and then another. Small fires broke out on the fixture. Lexie's vision clouded over again, and the chandelier was as it had been with Jacob O'Connor's lifeless body hanging from it. The apparition of a woman formed on the landing. She had bucked-teeth, glasses, mousy brown hair, and wore a green gown gathered at the shoulder in a big bow.

She picked up something from the floor. Lexie gasped when she spotted the cane. The stones in the dragon head shone black as the woman carried it down the stairs.

*They were green before. When did it change?*

Before the misty figure reached Lexie, she grinned.

"I'll show you, Jacob O'Connor."

The ghost cackled, and the startling noise sent Lexie backward into the foyer. The laughter was everywhere, spreading into every room.

Lexie placed her hands over her ears, not wanting to listen to any more of the evil sound. She wanted to block the visions and stop the nightmare.

Hands gripped her arms. Lexie became paralyzed with fear when she beheld Magnus's blackened fingers squeezing her flesh.

"Get out, Lexie!"

The moment the words left his lips, a menacing shadow blossomed behind him.

"This isn't finished, Magnus," a voice inside the shadow roared.

Jacob's ghost formed in the blackness. His dark essence enveloped Magnus. Forced to let her go, Magnus confronted his foe.

He dove into the shadow. Magnus's head or red vest would briefly surface as he struggled with the black depths of Jacob's soul. The two ghosts thrashed around in dizzying circles. A blast of frigid air released from their battle knocked Lexie to the ground.

From the floor, she looked on as Magnus and Jacob thrashed about the foyer, bumping into walls. The lotus-shaped sconces above them exploded in flames.

Lexie trembled as fires broke out around her. All the light fixtures in the foyer went up. Loud popping sounds erupted all over the house. Fire engulfed the chandelier, quickly spreading to the banister.

"Will!" she screamed.

Will and Remi came barreling out from beneath the staircase, panic distorting their faces. Will ran to help her from the floor. The ghosts of Magnus and Jacob continued fighting in the foyer.

"Who are they?" Will asked, his gaze riveted on the ghosts.

"Magnus Blackwell and Jacob O'Connor."

"Holy shit!"

"You two have to get out of here," Remi yelled. "This place is going up."

"No." Will faced him. "We have to shut off the power."

More popping ignited around them.

"No, Will." Remi pushed them toward the front doors. "We have to get out."

Will retrieved his cell phone from the back pocket of his jeans. "I'll call 911."

When they were all safely on the front porch, Will shouted into his cell phone for the fire department. Lexie watched the foyer fill with smoke. The gray cat ran through the smoke into the living room.

*Oh no!*

Hands spun around, and she came face-to-face with Remi. "Where is the cane?" he demanded in a frantic tone.

"What?" Lexie didn't know how he could worry about the cane at such a time.

"The cane, Lexie? Where is it?"

"Upstairs, in our bedroom. Why?"

He pushed her against Will. "You two need to get away from here. Wait down the drive for the fire department."

He was about to rush back inside when she reached for his arm. "Remi, no. It's too dangerous."

The nasty sneer curling his lips was alien to Lexie. She'd never seen such a dastardly expression before. Hate radiated from his black eyes. His skin turned to ice, and she yanked her hand away. Lexie swore it wasn't Remi glaring down at her, but someone she'd never met.

"Don't you fret, sweetie. Nothing's gonna happen to me." He darted into the smoke-filled foyer.

"Where the hell is he going?" Will hollered.

Lexie pulled him away from the front doors. "Will, we need to go."

"Not without, Remi!"

She held his arm. "You can't go in there." Lexie yanked him back to the steps.

An explosion rocked the first floor. Will covered her with his body, turning her away from the doors. Hot air gushed from inside the house.

Will scooped her into his arms and jogged down the steps to the gravel driveway. He wrestled the car keys out of his jeans front pocket as they rushed to the car.

"Get in." He ran around to the driver's side door.

Lexie opened the passenger door and jumped into the car. "What are you doing?"

The engine turned over, and after putting the car in reverse, Will stomped on the accelerator. "We have to get clear before the fire hits those gas lines."

Gravel spewed from the tires as Will maneuvered the car down the driveway and out to the main road. Over the tops of the trees, smoke billowed from the gray slate roof.

"Oh, God, Will. No. It's your dream."

"It doesn't matter, baby." The car spun around when he came to the main road. "We made it out alive. That's all I care about."

His overalls untouched by the flames, Remi emerged from the front doors of Altmover Manor. Smoke poured out of the house as he strolled down the front steps, twirling the dragon cane in his hand.

Remi made his way along the driveway, admiring the cane as he went. He stopped watching as the ugly, orange flames consuming the house. The earth-shattering sound of glass windows bursting and timber crashing swelled around him.

He sauntered away, unfazed by the destruction, dragon cane in hand. The stones changed from rose to an angry shade of red.

Remi rocked his head back and opened his mouth. But what came from his lips, wasn't a fit of gravelly laughter—it was the high-pitched, resonating cackle of a woman.

# Chapter Twenty-Two

Altmover Manor was a pile of ash and charred beams. Remnants of the grand staircase were all that was left standing, but its beautiful carvings did not survive. The newel post was reduced to a lump of unrecognizable burnt wood. The tops of the Corinthian columns had cleaved off when the roof collapsed during the blaze. Soot covered what remained. Water still trickled from inside the home and down the porch steps to the driveway. Across from the destroyed manor, the yellow cottage had escaped unscathed.

Wisps of smoke rose from the black rubble as several firemen in protective yellow attire sifted through the debris. Two fire trucks remained parked next to the house while Will and Lexie stood off to the side, talking to a man from the sheriff's department.

The chunky officer's snug gun belt and ill-fitting gray shirt stretched across his belly. Pad in hand, he read from his notes as she struggled to pay attention.

"There's no record of Remi Glapion ever working for the bank," the officer said. "After they installed the alarm in the house years ago, they eliminated the caretaker position. We checked the caretaker's cottage. It's been empty for years." The officer pushed his black hat back on his head. "I don't know if you folks got swindled or robbed by this Remi Glapion, but we can't find any trace of the man."

"Thank you, Lieutenant Hartwell," Will said, still holding tight to Lexie's hand. "I appreciate you checking for us."

"I can have the department run his name with the police in New Orleans. See if they have something on the guy," Lieutenant Hartwell added.

"No, that won't be necessary." Will let go of Lexie's hand and put his arm around her shoulders. "He didn't steal anything from us. The fire was an accident."

Lieutenant Hartwell shifted his attention to the mansion's remains. "The fire chief agrees with you. It was an electrical fire."

Will nodded, surveying the destruction. "The wiring was so frayed and worn in places I'm surprised it hadn't burned down sooner. I'd hoped to fix everything, but ..."

The officer put his notepad back in his shirt pocket. "Any idea where you folks are going to stay?"

"We got a room at a B&B in Somesville for the next three nights," Will said. "Then we'll be returning to Boston."

Lieutenant Hartwell tipped his hat. "We have your cell numbers. We'll be in touch if we find anything more. I'm very sorry, Mr. Bennett, Ms. Arden. This old house is part of the folklore on the island. People are gonna miss it."

Will scrubbed his face with his hand as the officer returned to his black and white cruiser. "I feel like I'm walking around in a nightmare. Was any of it real? Was Remi a ghost like Magnus?"

She studied his profile. "Remi's real. The question I want answered is *who* is he, not what."

As the police car headed down the gravel drive, Will turned to her. "How do you explain it? How do you deal with it?"

"There's no explaining why ghosts exist, they just do. You either choose to believe, or you don't. I believe. How about you?"

"I'm still trying to get my head around what happened. I know I saw something. Believing it though … well, that's something else entirely." His voice gentled as he grazed his thumb across her cheekbone. "But I do believe in you. I was an idiot for doubting you, and I'm sorry I didn't listen before, baby. I truly am."

All the heartache brought on by his disbelief faded like a shooting star across the horizon. "Thank you. Just to hear you say that almost makes the hell we suffered through worthwhile." She slipped her arm around his waist. "What do we do now?"

He scanned the area around the home and sighed. "I guess we can sell off the land. And after you add in the insurance money, I might recoup some of what I shelled out for the manor."

"I wish I knew if the cat made it out."

"I'm sure it's fine. Probably hightailed it back to the woods."

She could only imagine the disappointment weighing him down. She wanted to ease the loss of the home he had dreamed of, but how?

Will inspected the ruins. "I still can't believe every last trace of Altmover Manor is gone. The story of such a magnificent house ends here."

A cool breeze brushed Lexie's face, carrying the essence of coffee with it. In the smoldering debris, she found them. Two faint images stood out against the charred wood. Magnus Blackwell rested his shoulder against what remained of the leaded-glass front doors. Jacob O'Connor waited farther back, next to the destroyed staircase.

"This may not be the end of the story."

"What are you talking about?"

"Magnus and Jacob are not at rest."

Will scrutinized the house. "Can you still see them?"

Magnus dipped his head, taunting Lexie. Jacob O'Connor's forlorn features appealed to her as if pleading for direction.

"Yep. They're still here," Lexie said. "The house may be gone, but they're sticking close to me. I've got a feeling they're not going to leave me alone."

"A feeling?" Will ran a hand through his hair. "I'm attempting to be open-minded about this Lexie, but I'm not ready to share you with two dead men."

Lexie considered the ghosts for a moment; she smiled. "I have an idea."

"I can't believe you talked me into this," Will said, standing next to the open grave. He tugged at his black tie. "Is all this necessary?"

"Yes. We're paying our respects." Lexie waved to the two cemetery workers waiting to lower the shiny new oak casket into the ground. "Go ahead."

A priest at the head of the grave recited the 23rd Psalm.

"Did you have to buy him a new casket, too?" Will whispered. "It's not even been a month since we lost the house. We need every penny we have to start over."

"How do you think I got the Forest Hills Cemetery people to go along with this?" Lexie shot him a sly side-glance. "They wanted a court order to dig him up. That usually takes months."

The cemetery workers waited as the electric winch set up

above the grave lowered the casket into the ground.

"You never did tell me what you said to them." Will kept his voice low.

"I told them the truth. He's a restless spirit buried according to a voodoo spell to make him roam the earth to pay for his crimes."

"And they believed you?"

Lexie clasped her hands in front of her dark blue dress. "I did mention I'm engaged to the renowned local architect, Will Bennett, who would be more than happy to design the new wing they are considering for their administration offices."

"You didn't."

"You're the one who's been bugging me to get rid of them. Living with two ghosts and you while under my mother's roof has been sheer hell."

Will hid his grin behind his hand. "I guess donating my time and coming up with some plans is better than having your ghosts haunting us forever."

The casket came to rest at the bottom of the grave. "They're not haunting. It's more like hanging around."

Will adjusted his jacket sleeve. "Well, whatever they're doing, I'm not comfortable with it. It's like we're being watched all the time. I'm even getting paranoid in the shower."

"They're not perverts, Will. And they're not around all the time. Since the house burned down, they've been sticking close to me. They want me to help them, although I'm not sure how."

The priest closed the Bible in his hands. "Do you have any last words, Ms. Arden?"

A twinkling column of light sprouted up from the grass, catching Lexie off guard. Jacob O'Connor stepped from the light and stood next to the grave. His tuxedo coat whipped around in an invisible breeze. He set his hands behind his back and bowed to

Lexie.

"I hope this will do, Jacob."

A ray of ethereal light shone behind Jacob adding a luminescent quality to his skin. Lexie stared in wonderment as the black patches on his face and hands faded.

"I want to apologize, Ms. Arden, for the incident with the ladder. I thought Magnus was out to hurt you. I was wrong. He's here to help you."

"Help me?" Lexie snickered. "He's got a funny way of showing it."

A thin beam of light popped up next to Jacob. The light twisted and turned until it took on a woman's shape. As the figure came into focus, her honey-blonde hair, delicate features, and pink dress sparked a memory for Lexie.

It was the same woman she'd seen in the wedding picture in Jacob's trunk. Her beautiful face had been the one staring back at her from the window of the cottage.

"Frances?" Jacob's features softened as he gaped in amazement at his wife. The light behind him stretched out like the tentacles of an octopus wrapping around his waist.

"Hello, Jacob." Frances's entire being pulsed, emitting a warm glow enveloping everything around her. "I've missed you, my love."

"I can't believe you're here."

Frances took his hand, and the light around her changed from a light shade of yellow to a warm rose color. "Where have you been? I've been waiting and waiting for you."

Jacob turned to Lexie, the tendrils of light hugged him, wrapping around his body like a mother's arms. "I've been stuck for a while."

The last of the blackness on Jacob's chin disappeared. He was perfect again; cleansed of his darkness.

Lexie's insides tingled, but this wasn't a warning of danger or malice; it told her it was time to send Jacob on his way.

She picked up a handful of dirt from the mound off to the side and held her hand over the open grave. She smiled, dropping the dirt on Jacob's new casket.

"You're free, Jacob O'Connor. Rest well."

"Thank you, Ms. Arden. From both of us."

Jacob O'Connor reached out and held his Frances in his arms. The woman's giggle flooded the cemetery. The light around them burned brighter until it blotted out every trace of the couple.

Lexie shielded her eyes, and the light dissolved, taking Jacob and Frances with it.

A stiff breeze rose around them. Within seconds it dispersed, like a door opening and closing.

Lexie sighed, heartened by the event. Her cheer quickly disintegrated when she spotted Magnus Blackwell, leaning against a nearby tree, his ever-present grin grated on her nerves.

"One down, one to go."

"Is that it?" said Will oblivious to the miracle she'd witnessed. "Is he happy in his new resting place?"

Lexie wiped the dirt from her hands. "I think he's gone for good."

"You think?"

"Hey, I'm new at this. I have no idea what to expect."

"I'll have to take your word for it." Will grasped her hand and led her from the grave site as the workers covered the casket with dirt.

"I'm still not sure why you had to use the last dregs of our money on this funeral," Will admitted as they walked along the shady path toward the parking lot. "I wanted to buy you an engagement ring."

"Making sure Jacob O'Connor is at rest is more important.

You can buy me a ring another day."

"What about Magnus?" Will stopped walking and let go of her hand. "Is he still with us?"

She sighted the ghost off to her left. "For some reason, he didn't leave with Jacob."

"I am not going anywhere, dear girl," Magnus said to her in his haughty manner. "It's going to take more than a bit of dirt to send me on my way."

Lexie rolled her eyes at the ghost's comment.

Will crossed his arms, frowning. "It's going to get crowded with three of us in our new apartment."

"I promise, sooner or later, I'll find a way to send him to the other side."

"I hope it's sooner." Will reached for her hand. "A lot sooner for both our sakes."

They strolled back toward the parking lot, with Magnus following close behind.

# Chapter Twenty-Three

Three weeks later, Will and Lexie settled into a modest apartment not far from Angela and Kevin's trendy Beacon Hill neighborhood. They had returned to their former jobs and put the events at Altmover Manor behind them.

"I have a late meeting this evening," Will told her before shoving a slice of toast in his mouth.

"That was fast. It's not even your third day back." She adjusted his crooked tie. "Don't let Forrester and Whitney work you to death like they did last time."

"I don't have much choice, do I? We need the money." The insurance company was dragging its feet with the settlement, and the new apartment and furnishings had cleaned out what savings they had left. His eyes devoured her snug green dress. "You got another client meeting today?"

"Yep." She went to the coffeemaker.

Will lifted his mug to his lips. "Fifth one this week, right?"

"Kevin has been referring new people to me. Every time Mother says I told you so about the house, Kevin sends another lawyer, housewife, or golf buddy my way. I think he's making up for Angela's hounding."

"She'll never let us forget about it, I'm sure." He held his cup out to her and scowled. "What is this?"

"The coffee and chicory you wanted."

"Don't buy me this stuff anymore. It's too strong."

"No problem." Lexie grinned while lifting her coffee to her lips.

He took his mug to the sink. "Why are you smirking?"

She put her drink down. "When we lived at Altmover Manor, you changed. You got a sudden love of coffee, were saying some strange things, and a few times in bed, you …"

His lips smashed together, and redness tinged his cheeks. "What?"

Should she tell him her suspicions? "You were playful … in the bedroom. Maybe it was the house."

"I have no idea what you're talking about," Will said, his voice peppered with irritation. "I didn't change. I'm always playful in bed."

Magnus dropped in, wearing his usual red vest, long black coat, and ascot tie. "You still haven't told him it was me? Lexie, you should be honest with your future husband."

She glared at Magnus. "I guess I'm still coming to terms with everything we went through."

"That makes two of us." Will turned away from the sink.

Magnus motioned to the hallway. "Someone is at the front door."

A light chirping sound rolled around the kitchen.

"Who's that at this hour?" Will checked the microwave clock. "It's not even eight."

"I'll get it." Lexie rushed to the kitchen door. "You eat your breakfast."

"You burnt the eggs again," Will called as she exited the kitchen.

Lexie hurried past the sparse furniture and bare white walls in the living room, cringing at the reminder of all they had lost in the fire.

She opened the front door, a tall gentleman holding a black chauffeur's hat under his right arm greeted her. His short gray-tipped hair added a coldness to his face. The bulge of his black suit accentuated his thick, muscular body.

"Lexie Arden?"

Lexie put her hand on the door. "Yes?"

The man held out a white envelope. "A gift from a friend."

Will arrived in time to see the chauffeur replace the black hat on his head.

"Who's that?"

The man in the doorway smiled, and then briskly walked away.

She held up the envelope. "He left this."

Will took the envelope and ripped it open. He pulled out a piece of paper, read it, and dashed into the outer hallway, searching for the stranger.

"What is it?" Lexie asked, following him into the hallway.

Will handed her a cashier's check as he marched back in the front door.

She gasped when she read the amount. "Will!" Lexie ran after him. "This is the exact amount you spent on Altmover Manor."

Lexie found Will standing at the bay window in the living room. She joined him at the window and held out the check.

"Who did this?"

Magnus's voice filled her head. "If you question this gift, Lexie, it will lead you down a dangerous path."

She paused, considering his comment. *What dangerous path?*

"What did the guy say to you?" Will demanded.

Lexie followed Will's gaze to a limousine parked on the street outside their window. "He said it was from a friend."

The man in black exited the building and went to the driver's side door of the limousine. In the back, through an open window, Lexie caught sight of the dragon's head of a cane. The red stones in the eyes flashed back at her. The pale, diamond-clad hand of a woman gripped the handle.

"Will, tell me you saw that."

"I saw it," Will muttered. "It can't be the same cane, can it?"

She turned from the window to Magnus. "What does it mean?"

"It's not over, Lexie," Magnus whispered.

Will sighed. "I have no idea what it means. We should be grateful we got our money back and not question anything."

She locked on Magnus's eyes. "Do you think so?"

A sly grin slid across Magnus's lips. "I have a feeling."

Will put his arm around her waist. "Let's forget this happened, deposit the check, and put everything behind us."

"Is that what you want to do, dear girl?" Magnus pressed.

After Will had coaxed Lexie back into the kitchen, he got excited about the money. Between mouthfuls of scrambled eggs, he spoke of his plans for the extra funds and the wedding they would have. While he prattled on, a funny twinge flared in Lexie's gut.

*Oh, no. This isn't good.*

Whenever she got that certain feeling, things happened—very bad things.

# Chapter Twenty-Four

"Why are you so quiet?" Will shrugged on his gray suit jacket. "Come on, out with it."

She stood from the breakfast table, her happiness marred by her escalating apprehension. "Aren't you the least bit curious? It's an awful lot of money."

"Lexie, I don't want to be curious. And I'm thrilled it's a lot of money," he said, sounding upbeat. "We need it. My savings are wiped out, and we barely make enough to pay for this apartment and cover our bills. If you ask me, it means our luck is finally turning around."

"It's not like we set up an internet account asking for donations. Someone took the time to find out where we live and sent a chauffeur to our door with a cashier's check. Aren't you the slightest bit creeped out?"

Will laughed, shaking his head. "Baby, I'm not the one who sees Magnus Blackwell walking around our living room."

"At least I got him to agree to stick to the kitchen and living room."

"Only after you threatened to have him exorcised. We've been living with the man, or ghost, for a couple of weeks and he's already getting on my nerves."

Magnus materialized next to their fridge. "You can tell him the feeling is mutual, my dear. I preferred my manor home to this hovel."

"Thank God your burial stunt got rid of Jacob O'Connor. Can you imagine if we had both of them living with us?"

"Yes," Magnus agreed. "O'Connor is probably playing a harp on some fluffy white cloud with Frances, thanks to you, Lexie. Meanwhile, I am still here."

Lexie held up her hand, demanding silence. "Look, I don't know why Magnus is still attached to me, but I promise we'll figure it out. I'm as anxious as you are to get rid of him."

Magnus dramatically slapped his hand over his heart. "I'm crushed."

Will adjusted the knot in his tie. "At least we've got my savings back. We can afford to get married and pay a witch doctor or priest or whoever to get rid of our unwelcome guest."

Something was wrong. Lexie sensed it. Her time at Altmover Manor had taught her to listen to her intuition. Suddenly, it screamed at her to pay attention.

"There's something we're missing. One element that ties this mystery together. Don't you see? Remi Glapion came from New Orleans. The cane made its way to Maine from New Orleans. And Magnus renovated his house after a trip to New Orleans. Whatever is going on, the answer has to be in New Orleans."

Magnus rested his hip against the kitchen counter, his trademark grin spread across his face. "Oh, I like where this is going."

"Remi Glapion might have been from Cleveland, for all we know," Will argued. "He's a hustler who planned to rob us."

"You liked him." Lexie raised her voice. "You're the one who hired him. You kept telling me I was overreacting whenever I asked you to check him out."

Magnus chuckled. "She has a point."

"What are you saying? We should go to New Orleans?" Will tossed up his hands. "Forrester and Whitney just hired me back. Jake Forrester isn't going let me take time off to go ghost hunting in New Orleans."

"I can go," she countered. "I'll see what I can find out about Remi Glapion. And if I can track down our dragon cane."

"The cane? You're not serious? Why on earth do you want to go after the cane? All our troubles started when Magnus asked you to find his cane and things only got worse when you found it. Why would you possibly want to find the cane?"

Tapping his black finger on the kitchen counter, Magnus studied Will. "Tell him you might learn a way to get rid of me in New Orleans."

She gaped at the ghost and then tentatively eyed her fiancé, formulating a plan. Lexie inched closer to Will. "I might find a way to get rid of Magnus. If I can locate Remi Glapion and get the cane back, Magnus can cross over. The dragon cane has a strange power. When I touched it, I felt ..."

"Invincible," Magnus fit in.

"What about our wedding?" Will put his hands on her shoulders. "Your mother is already at Def Con One with the wedding plans. We need to set a date and start booking caterers."

"I'll take one short trip to New Orleans. We can start making plans as soon as I get back."

Will shifted his attention to the clock on the microwave. "I've got to go. We'll talk about this tonight."

He kissed her nose before bolting out the door. Lexie slouched against the counter.

"He will give in," Magnus asserted. "He can never say no to you."

She pushed away from the counter. "You're not helping."

"As a once married man, I can assure you I am."

"Magnus, you know nothing about staying together in this world. You didn't even pay income tax back in your day."

"You pay income tax?"

Lexie rolled her eyes and left him in the kitchen. She retrieved her laptop, and settled into the sofa's soft cushions.

Magnus floated into the room. "What are you doing?"

"I liked it better when you spoke in cryptic messages."

Magnus stopped at the edge of the sofa. "I was bound to the voodoo doll then. Manifestation and communication required tremendous effort. Since I've been attached to you, everything is easier."

She tapped on the keyboard. "Who did I piss off in my last life to get stuck with you in this one?"

Magnus took a seat on the arm of the sofa. "Most people might consider this a gift and not a curse."

*A gift?* Lexie wanted to shriek at the suggestion. His face and toned body appealed to her at times, but then he would smile or curl his lips into his cruel grin, and her stomach would turn with the memory of what he had done to Frances O'Connor.

"You are a liar, a cheat, and a murderer, Magnus. You killed Frances without a hint of remorse. What makes you think anyone would want a ghost with a past like yours around them?"

Her remark cut right to his heart, or where his heart should have been. Such comments, when he was alive, would have slid off him like water on well-oiled skin, but somehow, she penetrated what was once impervious.

"My sins I wear like a mantle in this afterlife." He held up his black hands, sickened by the sight of them. "I do not profess to have been a good man, Lexie, but I hope to be a better ghost if you will let me."

The lines around her mouth softened. Her curiosity about him had overcome her anger. It was a good sign. Maybe there was a chance for him after all—his last chance at making amends.

She sat back on the sofa, a hint of incredulity lingered in her features. "Why should I trust a tainted soul like you?"

He summoned every ounce of sincerity he possessed. "Because I am the only one who can help you figure out who you are."

The doubt in her eyes told him his words had hit home. Ever since the first day she'd stood on the steps of Altmover Manor, he'd sensed her abilities. She yearned to find out more and discover what she could do.

"What happened to you in New Orleans?"

The question took him by surprise. So many things had happened to him there, but he wasn't ready to divulge his secrets. He would have to find another way to get the answers they both needed.

"Let's go there together, and I will show you."

She returned to her machine. After a second or two, she typed something.

Pictures changed on the strange instrument—a computer,

she'd called it. The concept of why so much information was necessary eluded him.

"What are you doing?"

She continued typing. "Finding a hotel in New Orleans."

A sweet ribbon of victory wound through him. She had taken the bait. Now, to guide her in the right direction. Magnus had no doubt their destiny awaited in New Orleans. But what compelled him to take her to such a city? He had no clue.

She scrolled through a selection of different hotels in the city. None meant anything until a familiar name jumped out at him. He touched the screen and proclaimed, "This one."

Lexie squinted at his choice. "Hotel Monteleone?"

He did find her most delightful at times, when she wasn't glowering at him or chiding his behavior. Lexie would have been a woman he would have pursued when alive. But the Magnus Blackwell he had been would have driven her away.

While she read from the page on the computer, he smiled, admiring the delicate curve of her chin.

"Did you stay here?"

Magnus nodded, remembering his good friend. "Yes. I recall it being a nice hotel in the heart of the French Quarter." He tapped the picture on the computer. "We must stay there."

The shock on her face confounded him. "It's a hundred and fifty dollars a night, Magnus."

"Good Lord. That was the annual wage for many people in my time."

Lexie circled her finger on a square pad of her computer. "Things have gone up a lot since then."

He became fascinated as she filled out a form. "Well, your fiancé is a wealthy man, and we deserve the best."

Her eyebrows went up. "We?"

"Where you go, I go, dear girl."

"I still don't understand why you aren't privy to the ways of the universe. Aren't ghosts all knowing?"

"Unfortunately, being dead doesn't make us any different from you. I guess other ghosts can offer enlightenment or predict the future. I, however, cannot."

"Do you talk to other ghosts?"

"My abilities are tied to you, Lexie. I can only perceive what you do."

"I wish someone would explain this relationship to me."

He chuckled. *That makes two of us.*

From the day his beloved Altmover Manor had burned to the ground, he'd felt attached to Lexie. He'd attempted to leave her many times, but the tether joining them was too powerful.

"My wagon is hitched to yours, and instead of grumbling, we must make do."

She raised her head and searched the living room. "Where did I leave my purse? I need my credit card."

An image of the object came into his mind. "In the bedroom, on the chair by the door."

"Any chance you can get it for me?"

He shook his head. "I do not have a body. Therefore, I cannot move what I cannot lift."

"Why don't I believe you?" She put the computer aside and stood. "What about that stunt you pulled at the manor house with Will? When you possessed his body?"

"I was having a bit of fun," Magnus said. "He, unlike you, is susceptible to such things, but all those who cannot fathom my realm are that way. I can whisper things to them, put images in their heads, possess them, and make them perform my will. Sort of like marionettes on a string."

She strode out the living room and into the hall. "You damn near got me pregnant," she called out.

He snickered as he remembered his fun with Lexie and the impressionable Will during those first nights in his home. "Would a child have been such a bad thing? I was under the impression women wanted children."

Wallet in hand, she returned. "Things are different, Magnus. A woman is no longer defined by motherhood or marriage. She can have a career, wealth, a future, and doesn't need a man."

Magnus clapped. "Oh, bravo. You almost had me convinced."

"Did anyone ever call you an asshole, Magnus?" She sat down on the sofa and picked up her computer.

"Not to my face."

She filled out another form on the computer. Her fingers flew across the keyboard.

"And this communicates to the hotel? This Internet?" He still had a hard time picturing such an invisible realm.

"Yep," Lexie replied. "I can talk to anyone in the world."

"Has it solved all the world's problems like disease, hunger, atrocity, and poverty?"

Lexie waited for something on her computer while ignoring his probing gaze. "I'm afraid technology has done nothing more than cut us off from our humanity, not improve it."

"Then why have such a device?"

"Because we hope one day it will." A number flashed on the computer. "Okay, we have a hotel room. Now to book airfare."

Magnus crinkled his brow. "What is airfare?"

# Chapter Twenty-Five

Curled up in their king-sized bed, Lexie worked on her computer when Will returned from work later that evening.

"You're still up." Will shut the bedroom door.

"I wanted to wait up for you. Running late, huh?"

He pulled at the knot in his tie. "The new clients are the yappy kind. They had more ideas for my designs."

She shut her laptop. "Did they leave happy?"

He dropped his tie on the chair by the door. "I give it a week, and they'll be calling me with changes."

She pulled her legs up and hugged them. "You hungry? I got pizza."

Will eased his gray suit jacket from around his shoulders. "We ordered in at the office." He went to the closet door across the room. "How'd the meeting go with your clients?"

She shrugged. "The usual. A housewife who lives down the street from Mother wants her house to look like Downton Abbey. The other is a lawyer friend of Kevin's wanting to update his offices."

"Are you going to take them on?" Will kicked off his black loafers.

"Not sure yet." Lexie reclined on her pillows as she waited for him to remove his shirt. "I'll decide after I get back from New Orleans."

He pivoted around to her. "Are we going to talk about this?"

"I have to go, Will. If I stay here and don't pursue this … You know me."

He sat down on the bed. "For how long?"

She scooted across to him. "A week, tops."

"What am I supposed to do without you for a week?"

She admired his rugged face and caressed the dark stubble on his cheek. "You'll be too busy with work to notice I'm gone."

Will put his arms around her. "What about him?"

She cuddled against him. "Where I go, he goes."

Will kissed her neck. "I don't like the sound of that."

"I can't do anything about him."

He arched back from her. "Knowing he's going to be with you will drive me crazy."

"He's an asshole, Will. And a ghost. There's no reason to be jealous."

"Not jealous, baby." He stood and unzipped his trousers. "Worried. I don't trust him."

She scurried behind him as he walked into their bathroom. "Well, if it's any consolation, I don't trust him, either."

Will tugged off his trousers and briefs. "Then why is he with you?"

"I've been racking my brain to figure out why we have this connection and I get nothing. He's right. In New Orleans, we might find the answer."

Will ran the shower and tested the water with his hand. "You'd better find a way to get rid of him."

"What's up? You usually take your shower in the morning."

He came up to her and gripped the hem of her nightshirt. "We're not taking a shower."

She put her hands on his muscular chest after he yanked the flimsy nightshirt over her head. "What do you mean, *we*?"

He pushed her toward the shower stall. "I've been doing some reading on ghosts." He went to the vanity a picked up one of the packets of condoms he had left there. "Did you know ghosts hate water?"

"They do?" She stepped into the shower, and the water sprayed her body.

"Yes, ma'am." He cozied up to her. "It's the one place I can make love to you without an audience."

She grabbed his perfectly formed ass. "If I go to New Orleans and get rid of him, we'll be able to do it everywhere in the apartment."

He bit her earlobe. "Go then." He leaned back from her. "But you have to call me every day. I want you to promise you will stay out of trouble."

She nodded. "I promise."

Will wiped the water from his chin. "When we're married, this has to stop. I want a normal life. No ghosts, no voodoo, and no more feelings."

"I'm going to New Orleans so we can be normal." She tilted her head. "Will you still love me if I'm a normal wife?"

"I'll love you no matter what."

He kissed her and Lexie handed herself over to him. He lifted her onto his hips. She held on to him as he pressed her back into the tile. Lexie reached for his erection, eager to have him inside her. Will curled into her as she stroked his shaft.

"You're killing me," he whispered.

Lexie took the condom package from his hand, ripped the foil pouch open with her teeth and rolled it over his cock. He dropped his hands to her butt, positioning her right in front of his hips. As she guided him into her, Lexie rocked her head back.

She locked her ankles behind his back. He thrust hard, going deep, creating a burning tingle that rose up her back. She panted into his neck when the first tremors of her climax stirred. Will slammed into her, sending her over the edge. He groaned, biting the nape of her neck. Holding him to her, Lexie trembled as he came.

"We need to do it in the shower more often," Will said, catching his breath.

"When I get back from New Orleans, I promise it's the first thing we're going to do."

He sighed and tightened his arms around her. "When will you go?"

"My flight leaves tomorrow afternoon."

Will laughed into her cheek. "Why am I not surprised?"

# Chapter Twenty-Six

A cab arrived outside the opulent white façade of the Hotel Monteleone on Royal Street late in the evening. Lexie stepped from the car, and the essence of New Orleans hit her.

The street vibrated with a jazzy tune from a nearby bar, the clip-clop of a horse-drawn carriage, the laughter of tourists, rumbling traffic, and in the air, the smell of heavy Cajun spices blended with a certain *je ne sais quoi*. Lexie understood why everyone succumbed to the city's delights; New Orleans intoxicated the soul.

"Welcome to the Hotel Monteleone, ma'am. Checking in?"

Lexie nodded at the doorman as the cab driver popped the trunk to retrieve her suitcase. She scoured the sidewalk beneath the white canopy for Magnus. He'd not showed himself since leaving Boston earlier in the afternoon. She wasn't sure if the travel, the noise, or the crowds had made him withdraw, but she'd enjoyed the break from her disconcerting spirit.

She wandered through the all-white lobby, taking in the trey ceilings decorated with stained-glass. For a moment, she was back at Altmover Manor. Her heart tugged with regret at its demise. The house had deserved to be a showplace.

After checking in, she caught the elevator to her room on the twelfth floor. It took two swipes before she got her hotel key card to work.

Once inside, she put her bags on the king-sized bed, scrutinized the gold-striped wallpaper and large gold-framed mirror, before heading out onto the balcony overlooking the French Quarter. The view offered a glimpse back in time. The tightly packed Creole cottages and jagged roof lines reminded her of a European city, not an American town. The modern, high-rise hotels along Canal Street dwarfed the old-world buildings, creating a stark boundary line between the present and the past.

"It's not like I remember," Magnus admitted, materializing next to her.

Startled, she raised a hand to her chest. "Where have you been?"

He leaned over the railing. "The airplane was too much to bear. What happened to trains and traveling in style?"

"We don't have time for them nowadays. People want to get places faster."

"I don't understand this obsession with time. You spend an inordinate amount of energy accruing it, but never enjoy the time you save. Tell me, when did attempting to cram so much into your life make you forget how to live it?"

She breathed in the heavy, humid air. "We live, Magnus. You only had your home and your city to take in. In this digital age, we have the entire world at our fingertips. Life is global."

"The world is still the same size, Lexie, but how much of this added knowledge do you savor?" He turned toward the French Quarter. "I was raised to believe a gentleman takes the time to relish what he has acquired."

She rested her hip against the railing. "Who taught you that? Your father?"

"I would advise you not to lean so on that railing. I've already been credited with letting one woman fall to her death; I do not wish to be accused of another."

Lexie jumped back and glared at Magnus. "There's something I'd like to know."

He adjusted the sleeve of his coat. "You never do run out of questions, dear girl."

"Why did you kill Frances?"

"That is a topic for another time." Magnus floated to the balcony door. "Will is hailing you on your … what is the device called again?"

Lexie went inside, and her catchy ringtone carried from her purse. "A cell phone." She sat on the bed as she took the call. "Will?"

"You all checked in?" His deep voice sent a trickle of contentment through her. "How's the room?"

"A nice single."

"What did you-know-who say?"

Magnus strolled in from the balcony. "Thank him for asking about me."

"He didn't travel with me," she told Will. "He cropped up once I got to my room."

"Remind him of his promise."

Magnus went to a chair in the corner. "I have no interest in seeing you naked." He had a seat. "You can assure him I will honor my word."

"He knows." She went to the television set on a high dresser and picked up the remote. "The city has changed a lot from when he was last here."

"What did he expect?" Will's voice grew impatient. "Enough about him. What are you going to do for the rest of the evening?"

"I guess get a bite to eat and then go to bed." She switched on the television and Magnus perked up. "I want to get an early start tomorrow."

"Any idea where you'll begin?"

Magnus eyed the television. "I know where to start."

She leaned against the headboard. "He said he has a plan. I guess I'm in his hands."

"If anything happens to you I will find his ass on the other side and kill him all over again," Will asserted.

Magnus snorted with protest. "I have no intention of letting anything happen to you. You're the reason I'm here."

"He understands." Lexie got up from the bed and went to the open balcony doors. The music rose from the streets below. "Wish you were here."

Will's heavy sigh came through the speaker. "I had to do a lot of ass-kissing to get my old job back. I couldn't ask Jake Forrester for a vacation."

"One day you'll have Bennett Architects. I know it."

"You feel it, you mean."

A sense of certainty rose in her chest. "When you least expect the opportunity, it will find you."

"I'll hold you to that, baby. Be careful down there, and call me with updates." Will paused. "Is he still there?"

She nodded and turned back to the balcony. "Watching television."

"You should go into the bathroom and turn on the shower."

"I'll keep that in mind."

"Call me before you go to bed. I'll be waiting." Will hung up.

Magnus was at her side. "What he read about water keeping ghosts away doesn't work."

Lexie stomped to the bed and dropped her cell phone next to her purse. "You're an ass."

She snatched up her suitcase and unzipped it.

*This is going to be a long week.*

# Chapter Twenty-Seven

At the painted glass entrance to the Criollo Restaurant, Lexie took one look at the prices listed on the menu displayed and kept on walking.

Lexie ended up purchasing a bag of pretzels from the hotel gift shop. She had a seat at one of the several white couches located throughout the lobby. A translucent figure formed on the couch next to her.

"What in God's name are you eating?"

She admired a giant red floral arrangement, intent on ignoring his behavior. "They're called pretzels."

"I'm well aware of what they are. I also know you need to eat proper food."

"Proper food in this hotel is too expensive. I'm on a budget." She stuffed another pretzel in her mouth.

An older couple turned her way, curiosity written all over their faces. Lexie lowered her head and munched her snack until they moved on.

Magnus stood from the couch, tutting with disapproval. "Put those foul things away. You're attracting attention, and we will get nowhere if the authorities are called."

She shoved the pretzels into her purse while muttering a few expletives.

"What do you have in mind?"

"Come with me." He floated in the direction of the restaurant.

At a podium inside the entrance, a lovely woman in a long black dress greeted her. "A table for how many?"

"Ah, one."

Round glass globes hung from the ceiling of the intimate art deco dining room, and white-granite tables covered the black floor. When she was shown to a table with sparkling crystal, white china, and silver utensils, dread rose in Lexie's throat.

*This is a mistake!*

She took her seat as Magnus settled in the bench across from her.

"This is too expensive," she said, lowering her voice so as not to draw the attention of the other diners.

Magnus glanced at the gold menu resting on her plate. "Tell me what you want."

Lexie refrained from picking up the menu. "The house salad is fine."

He leveled a scowl at her. "Pick up the menu and tell me what you would want if money were no object."

She snapped up the menu, gleaned the mouth-watering selection, and wanted to kill Magnus … again. "It all looks so good. I don't know."

"Before the next millennia would be nice."

"Fine. The baked stuffed Creole redfish." She slapped her menu on the table. "Happy?"

A waiter scurried up to her. The short round man with a tight black cummerbund around his hefty waist set a glass of water next to Lexie's plate. "Are we dining alone this evening, Miss?"

A bundle of nervous energy, Lexie cleared her throat and put her menu to the side. "Ah, yes."

"My name is Harry. I will be your server tonight." Harry removed the other place setting from in front of Magnus. "An appetizer to start?"

Magnus nodded to her menu. "Tell the man what you would like."

She glared at him. *Asshole!* "I'm not sure."

"It will not cost you a penny, trust me."

"The shrimp, blue crab, and avocado stack?" she requested, cringing.

Magnus laughed at her. "Bring her a glass of your best house white wine."

The waiter dipped his bald head. "The shrimp, blue crab, and avocado stack along with a glass of our house wine. Anything else, Miss?"

"The lady will have the baked stuffed Creole redfish for dinner," Magnus stated.

"And the Creole redfish dinner." Harry flashed a hint of a smile. "My personal favorite, Miss."

After Harry left, Lexie leaned across to Magnus. "How did you do that?"

He reclined on the bench and set his black hand on the table. "I told you. Those who cannot see my world are susceptible to the power of suggestion. Like your Will."

The pompous way he spat out Will's name concerned her. "You don't like him, do you?"

Magnus ran his fingers over the smooth white table. “Quite the opposite, my dear girl. I admire him. He’s one of the things I aspired to be: an architect. A much better one than I would have ever been. Your Will has talent. I’ve seen it in the drawings he’s brought back to your apartment.”

“Did you have a chance to pursue architecture after finishing Harvard?”

He tapped his finger on the table. “I never finished my degree at Harvard. I left before my senior year.”

She rested her arms on the table, charmed by his tale. “Why did you quit?”

“My father died, and I was forced to take over the family business.”

“What about your family? I found their portraits in the attic.”

Magnus folded his hands. “I am well aware of your activities in my attic.”

“So that was you laughing. I knew I’d heard someone up there.”

Harry returned, carrying a glass of wine. “Don’t mean to disturb you, Miss.” He set the wineglass in front of her. “You’re talking to someone on your phone, right? Do you have the new invisible Blue Tooth?”

Lexie touched her ear, playing along. “Yes, hold on, Mom.”

Harry gave her the thumbs up as he backed away. “Cool. You can’t even see it.”

She placed her napkin in her lap. “I guess technology can be good for something.”

“Blue Tooth?” Magnus asked.

“A small cell phone device. It fits in your ear. Everyone will assume, like our waiter, I’m talking on the phone and not to you.”

“So conversing with a ghost can appear normal.” Magnus chuckled. “So much has changed, but the predictable nature of people remains the same."

"Exactly." Lexie picked up her wine glass. "What was your time like? I've seen pictures and dreamt of the elegance, but you lived it."

"I remember the peace of my world the most. We had much less noise. Simple pleasures were more important."

Lexie sipped her wine. "What simple pleasures?"

"Eating, for one. Food was meant to be enjoyed. Meals took hours and menus were deliberated over for a lot longer than you gave yours. We talked more, as well. Conversations are too short in this time. Everyone is too busy with those cell phones."

She found herself agreeing with him. Conversation had become an endangered species. If something could not be said in a hundred and forty characters or less, many people chose to say nothing at all.

"It's as if all the time you are hurrying to save, you spend on yourselves rather than with each other," he said. "Which defeats the point of saving time."

"Does it? I don't agree. Sometimes people can take you away from what you want. Artists and writers are renowned loners, and look what they accomplish."

He browsed the other diners in the restaurant, smiling. "When you get to my side of the looking glass, dear girl, what you share with another far outweighs any single achievement."

"What about you? From what I learned about your life, you seemed to be a man with few friends."

"Most people bored me." His smile lifted his sullen features. "Except for Oscar. What became of him? Do you know?"

"Oscar Wilde?" Lexie picked up her wine. "He's considered a literary giant. One of the true masters."

"That would have pleased him immensely. He loved writing above all things." A wicked grin crossed his lips. "Well, not all things."

"What things are you referring to?" She took another sip of wine.

Magnus waved her off. "It's not something a gentleman discusses."

"You're dead, Magnus. And you murdered a woman, so how can you be considered a gentleman anymore?"

"You have an aggravating habit of speaking your mind, Lexie Arden."

She set the glass on the table. "What else did Oscar Wilde love?"

Magnus hesitated, avoiding her stare. "He found good company with others of his kind, is the best way to put it."

Lexie shrugged. "You mean, he liked men."

"It's improper to discuss such matters with a woman."

She snickered at his reaction. "You don't strike me as a man who shied away from the topic of sex."

The hint of aristocratic nonchalance returned to his features. "Sex is a tool, Lexie. I was a man who took what I wanted from women and had no regrets."

"Did those women freely give themselves to you? Or did you take them without their consent?"

He remained silent and turned away. Lexie studied his shadowy profile, knowing his answer. "Is that why Oscar Wilde used you as the basis for his character, Dorian Gray? Because of the life you lived?"

"In life, I was a cruel and selfish man. And my sins …" He held up his hands. "They have pursued me. Oscar attempted to show me the error of my ways, but I didn't listen."

"Are you still cruel and selfish?"

He tipped his head to the side, a half-smile gracing his lips. "I'm learning not to be with you."

When Harry left the bill on the table, perspiration gathered on Lexie's brow. The way she stared in horror at the black billfold, Magnus expected her to run shrieking from the restaurant.

He couldn't understand her concern over money. At Altmover Manor, the couple often discussed their tight finances, and her worry had touched him. Never before had he connected to any living creature in such a way. It was as if she haunted him as much as he had haunted her.

"I told you I would take care of this," Magnus declared.

"With what? Your Visa card?"

He found Harry across the room and said, "Come here, my good man."

The waiter's mind presented like a smooth pond to him. All he had to do was blow on the surface, and the happy-go-lucky man would do his bidding. Lexie, however, did not bend to his will. Her mind remained an impenetrable wall. He read her emotions, but never influenced her thoughts.

Harry dashed from the customers he was with and returned to her table.

"Yes, Miss?"

"You can bill the meal to my room 1407," Magnus told him.

Harry took the billfold away. "1407. Yes, Miss."

"Add a generous tip for you," Magnus added.

"Thank you, ma'am. Come back and see me again." Harry returned to his other customers.

The heat rose on Lexie's cheeks. "That's stealing."

"It will be considered a clerical error."

"What if someone is in room 1407?" she whispered, glancing

at the tables around them.

"There is no room 1407. I checked with the front desk."

"When did you do that? You've been by my side since I got here."

"I may be sitting here with you, but my consciousness can be in many different places at once. One benefit of being out of the body."

She clasped her coffee cup. "It's still wrong."

"Would you have preferred to dine on those inedible monstrosities you still have squirreled away in your purse? If we're going to find a way to be free of each other, I need you attentive, healthy, and not fretting over how to afford your next meal." He stood from his bench. "Time to go."

"I haven't finished my coffee yet."

He went around to her chair. "Will is wondering why you haven't contacted him. I will escort you back to your room so you can use your cell phone."

She reached for her purse. "Your consciousness isn't limited by distance? How does that work?"

He guided her across the black floor to the entrance. "Will is connected to you. Hence, he is connected to me. Don't ask me to explain it. I cannot. All I can do is heed the urge."

"Must bug the hell out of you, having to give in to such urges."

Magnus floated next to her, scowling. "You have no idea."

He kept Lexie entertained as they walked across the lobby by divulging tidbits of information filling his head from other hotel guests. One couple they passed seemed to be very much in love, but Magnus tapped into their concerns for the spouses they had left at home while pursuing their affair. The night manager who greeted them behind the check-in desk considered how to have his way with his pretty, and much younger, assistant manager. An older lady waiting next to the elevators reflected on the two husbands she'd poisoned to afford her trip to the city.

Once the elevator doors closed, Lexie said, "I didn't realize ghosts could do such things."

"I have no idea if they can, either." Magnus floated next to her. "You're the first person, dead or living, I've spoken to since my demise."

"What about Jacob O'Connor? Didn't you two speak?"

He concentrated on his black boots hovering above the dull gray carpet in the elevator. "We communicated, but when in each other's presence things … well, you saw what happened the day you fell from the ladder. We never meant to hurt you."

"And the fire?"

"The fire wasn't our doing. There had never been a fire at Altmover Manor until you and Will arrived."

"What are you saying?"

The car stopped on her floor. "The cane was the reason for the fire, dear girl."

When the elevator doors opened, Lexie hesitated. "But the fire inspector said old wiring started the blaze."

"Lexie, you've seen what I can do in the restaurant. What do you think a much more powerful spirit could execute? There is a darker force at work here."

Magnus strode from the elevator. He could sense her mulling over what he'd told her.

"What about the money? Who sent it?" she pestered when they reached her room door.

He touched his hand to the automatic lock on the door, the light flashed green, and the door popped open. "I'm convinced the money was either meant as an incentive to keep you out of New Orleans or to lure you here."

"Lure me? Why?" She walked into her room.

Magnus stayed in the doorway. "We shall begin answering

your questions in the morning. Good night, my dear." With that, he vanished.

He could still see her, although she did not perceive him. He waited as she shut the door and when the safety latch clicked in place, Magnus moved away.

The time had come for him to dissolve into the world somewhere between the living and the dead. Magnus equated the misty place to slumber without the benefit of dreams. He could still sense her in his empty realm, could still detect her voice in case she needed him. More than ever, she did need him. His purpose was to guide her toward something, but he wasn't sure what. The direction came from inside him, but he had no control of it—he could only obey.

Letting the mist envelop him, Magnus questioned if Lexie would be safer with Will in Boston.

"No," he whispered as the mist seeped into his soul. "I need to keep him in the dark a while longer. At least until I figure out what's going on."

# Chapter Twenty-Eight

"Are you ready to begin, my dear?"

She slipped her room key in her purse as Magnus showed up in the hotel corridor. "Any idea where to start? It's a big city."

"We will go to the places I visited when I was here."

She examined his tattered black coat and shabby high-cut black boots. "Why do you always wear those clothes?"

He tugged at his tie. "This is how I wish to be seen."

"Don't you want to wear something else?"

"Would you prefer me naked?"

She held up her hands. "No. I might lose it completely if you were naked."

Outside the hotel, Lexie peered up and down Royal Street. The early morning sun stretched over the rooftops. "Which way?"

Magnus floated to her right. "This way."

After she caught up to his long stride, Lexie studied the Creole townhouses and romantic balconies. The first floors of the buildings housed businesses—art, jewelry, and antique stores operated on either side of the narrow street. They progressed down Royal Street, and the stores changed to tourist-driven boutiques offering a wide array of T-shirts, souvenirs, and anything with NOLA printed on it.

"Is it much different from when you were here last?"

"Yes. These were private homes back then." He stopped and viewed the crowded sidewalks. "The streets were not as congested. Vendors, men with carts, would be out delivering food, ice, and assorted goods to the residents." A passing cab chugged out fumes next to them. "These things—"

"Cars," Lexie cut in.

"I prefer the hoof beats of a horse on a stone-paved street to that rumbling." A street performer on the corner broke out in song. "There were no peddlers cluttering the walkway and lamps flickered with gaslight, not …" He gestured to a flashing neon sign.

"I agree. The modern-day trappings mar the beauty of these old buildings."

"Ah, you're a romantic, Lexie Arden. I would never have guessed."

She spied a couple holding hands as they walked by. "All people in love are romantics. Weren't you when you met your wife?"

Magnus's mouth turned downward at the mention of his wife.

"Did I say something wrong?"

He lifted his head and listened to a blaring trumpet solo coming from an open bar door.

"What is this music?" he asked, halting. "I've noticed it since we arrived."

"Jazz. It began here. Around the time you visited."

He closed his eyes and listened to the steady beat. "There's an African influence in the drums."

"The African influence is everywhere in the country. Carries all the way to the White House."

"I don't understand."

"The current President of the United States is black."

He smiled. "Things have truly changed then."

At Jackson Square, Lexie explored the tall spires of St. Louis Cathedral, the gray stone of the Cabildo and Presbyter Museums, and the black fence around the square's perimeter.

Street performers distracted with their juggling, music, and dancing. The artworks displayed on the iron fence were as colorful and diverse as the city's inhabitants.

On Decatur Street, he spotted a row of horse-drawn carriages. "We must take one of those." He took off in their direction.

"Those are for tours, Magnus." She chased after him. "They're not meant for transportation."

When she caught up to him, he stood next to an open white carriage at the rear of the line. The horse hitched to the carriage sniffed his clothes, and Magnus rubbed the animal's shiny dapple gray coat.

"Can he see you?" Lexie approached the horse with caution.

"Yes. All animals can recognize us. And he is a she."

Atop the carriage, a man in black had his feet kicked out in front, and his cap lowered over his eyes.

Magnus went up to him. "We need you to take us around the city."

The carriage driver jumped to attention and untied the reins secured to his bench. He said nothing as Lexie and Magnus climbed into his carriage.

"What did you do to him?" Lexie asked.

"He's asleep. We are ghosts in his dream."

"Is that safe?" She considered the cars, tourist buses, and other buggies clogging the street.

"Curtis will act as if he's awake. Not to worry."

"His name is Curtis?"

Magnus lifted the edges of his mouth into a rascally grin. "It is now."

When the horse merged into the traffic, Lexie's stomach fluttered.

"We should get a cab."

"Nonsense." Magnus leaned toward their driver. "Take us to St. Louis Number One Cemetery, my good man."

"What's there?" Lexie took in the decorative swirls in the wrought iron balconies overhead.

"The Voodoo Queen's tomb and the start of our journey."

The heavy traffic on Decatur Street faded as the carriage turned down a quiet side street. The clip-clop of the horse's hooves echoed between the old cottages helping to settle Lexie's edginess. She noticed the ghost next to her soaking in the architecture.

"Why did you come here that first time?"

He kept his gaze on the buildings. "To run away."

"From what?"

"A broken heart." He turned to her, his face bereft of emotion. "The woman I loved had married another, and I thought by going to the city she loved, I would find solace."

"Who was she?"

His ethereal light dimmed. "You already know."

She recalled the tokens she'd found in his trunk in the attic and the vision of Frances O'Connor's horrible death.

"How did you and Frances meet?"

"She was Frances McGee when I met her. Fiery, determined, and studying at Radcliffe. Every man wanted her, but I got her."

Magnus shifted in his seat, seeming uncomfortable with the topic. "You remind me of her in some ways."

Lexie noted how his slight smile softened his features. "Can I ask what happened?"

His chest expanded as if taking in a breath. "I was arrogant, self-assured, and convinced I would remain impervious to the influence of a woman. When I found my every waking moment consumed by her, I …"

"Got scared?" Lexie inserted.

His expression hardened. "In any case, she found O'Connor."

"Until you took her away from him," slipped out before she could stop it.

"I'm aware of what I did and make no excuses for my actions. I had hoped she would see the error of her ways with O'Connor and come back to me, but I got angry."

Lexie wanted to press him about the murder but reconsidered. Perhaps working with him would prove more productive than attacking what he was.

"Did your wife know about your feelings for Frances?"

"Katie?" The affection in his voice erased his icy demeanor. "No. She never knew. Katie was so much fun. She brought me a great deal of happiness for a time."

Captivated, Lexie asked, "Did you love her?"

He browsed the passing cottages. "Despite the monster you think me to be, I was once capable of love. That has to count for something."

"I'm sure somewhere it does."

The carriage arrived at the high white plaster walls of St. Louis Number One Cemetery. Located on a busy street, the cemetery epitomized everything unique about New Orleans—a place where the old and new coexisted.

When the carriage came to a stop at the square white pillars marking the gated entrance, Lexie looked at the driver. He sat motionless on his bench, staring ahead as if hypnotized.

"Is he all right?"

Magnus went to open their carriage door. "He'll be fine." He tilted toward the man in black. "Wait here until we return, Curtis."

Their driver reclined on his bench, acting as if he was ready to resume his nap. He shifted his cap on his head and crossed his arms over his chest.

She climbed down the steps making a mental note to ask her ghost exactly how he did that. She waited as he went to the gray dapple horse and spoke to the animal.

*Can he manipulate animals, too?*

Several tour buses and local cabs waited next to the cemetery wall. A peek over the top of the walls hinted at the statuary and crosses adorning the mini-mausoleums. Tourists in colorful T-shirts and shorts snapped pictures of the brass plaque at the entrance identifying the cemetery as the oldest in the city.

"Blend in with the others." Magnus stepped up to her. "That way you'll get a tour guide to take you around the cemetery."

"I don't like this."

Magnus encouraged her toward the crowd filing through the black gate at the entrance. "It's research. We're learning about voodoo, and perhaps we'll uncover who stole my cane."

"In a cemetery?"

The right side of his mouth twitched into an insolent smirk. "Where do you suggest we start?"

"At the police station!" Lexie lowered her voice as more people gathered around her.

"What we're dealing with is not of this earth, my dear."

A round woman with a black pack across her stomach and khaki shorts blended with Magnus's image.

Acutely aware of the other tourists, Lexie whispered, "Remi is real."

"So am I, but yet they cannot see me."

The crowd entered the gate, and flashes from cameras and cell phones blocked out the sights. When the photo frenzy died down, the monuments took shape.

Houses of the dead in various states of disrepair lined a narrow street. Some had fared better than others, but most had lost sections of their plaster covering, allowing the red brick underneath to show through.

A tall woman in a black cap and T-shirt reading *Cemetery Tour Guide* clapped her hands, to gain the group's attention.

"Ladies and gentlemen, before we begin our journey, let me start by telling you a little about the cemetery. It is one of three named St. Louis in New Orleans. Established in 1789, it was built to replace the city's older St. Peter Cemetery, which is no longer in existence."

Lexie tuned out the tour guide and searched for Magnus. Ahead, he waited next to a white pyramid tomb that clashed with the other square vaults in the cemetery. As she turned to leave the group, he raised his hand, and she stilled.

"If you come this way, we will visit the tomb of the first mayor of New Orleans, Etienne de Boré." The tour guide disappeared down a narrow walkway.

Lexie fell back to the rear of the group, hoping Magnus would join her.

"Someone else sent Remi to my home," he said, manifesting in front of her.

"How do you know?"

A few in the group stared at Lexie.

"Take out your phone and keep your voice down," Magnus suggested.

Lexie dug out her phone and placed it against her ear. "What are you talking about?"

"Remi, not O'Connor, was the one I warned you not to trust. From the moment Remi entered my home, power pulsated from him. Someone sent him, and whoever it is lives in this city."

Her grip on her cell phone tightened. "Why didn't you say anything before?"

"I couldn't. He threatened to destroy me unless I helped him find the cane."

"But after the fire, you should have told me what you knew."

"I knew nothing about him except for what I sensed." His image faded in and out as they walked along a gravel path. "Would you have listened to me before the mysterious check arrived?"

"We're going to see one of the most famous tombs in the city." The tour guide's voice boomed over the group. "That of Marie Laveau."

Magnus motioned for her to follow. "She's the reason we're here."

Unsure what he meant, Lexie kept to the rear of the pack.

Mold and decay hung heavy in the air, turning her stomach. "Aren't you uncomfortable here?"

"No. There's nothing here for me or any other spirit."

"Then where has everyone who is buried in this cemetery gone?"

"Marie Laveau has often been called the Voodoo Queen of New Orleans," their guide broke in as she patted a freshly painted white rectangular tomb. "Marie Catherine Laveau was a mix of African, Indian, and Caucasian blood, known as a Quadroon. A hairdresser by trade, she had access to the richest and most powerful women in the city. She collected family secrets, stories of affairs, and tales of family histories reinvented to delete references to questionable ancestry. If knowledge is power, Marie Laveau became a queen."

Magnus whispered, "Get closer. You need to remember this."

Lexie maneuvered her way to the front of the huddle. *Why did she have to remember this?*

"By 1930, Marie Laveau was considered the undisputed Queen of Voodoo in New Orleans," the guide went on. "A born showman, Laveau added mysticism and sensuality into voodoo ceremonies, gaining a wide following in the city. She borrowed heavily from the Catholic tradition and was a devout Catholic who attended mass daily. She included ritualistic elements such as incense, holy water, and prayer in her ceremonies. Her rituals on the banks of Bayou St. John became legendary. She would also practice her rituals in her St. Ann Street home. Many people don't know Laveau was an activist and voice for the poor blacks in the city. She would provide funds for the defense of many wrongly accused and used her influence to help save criminals from public execution, a practice she considered inhumane. She's also known for her healing skills and cared for the sick and dying during the yellow fever epidemic in 1853."

Lexie shifted her attention from the tour guide to the tomb. She'd always considered Marie Laveau a practitioner of witchcraft, but the woman who had risen from nothing and used her influence to help others had been far from evil. Marie Laveau had used voodoo to do good.

"Married at twenty-five to a carpenter named Jacques Paris, he abandoned her a short time later." The tour guide's voice edged into Lexie's thoughts. "Marie's lifelong affair with a Christophe de Glapion resulted in fourteen children, but the two never legally married. She's buried here in the Glapion family tomb along with her famous daughter, also named Marie Laveau."

*Glapion.* A shiver ran through Lexie. Was this what Magnus wanted her to remember?

Several individuals moved forward to photograph the tomb as

Lexie eased back.

"Why are the beads and candles around the tomb?" one woman asked with a Texas drawl.

"Visitors leave tokens for Marie Laveau to ask favors," the guide explained. "She's said to hear the thoughts of those who visit her and will grant their wishes if deemed worthy." Their guide waved her hand, summoning the group. "We're going to move on to the tomb of Ms. Marie's relative."

Lexie's mind reeled. She recalled Remi mentioning how common the Glapion name was in the city, but after visiting the Voodoo Queen's tomb, and hearing Magnus speak of Remi's strange power, she suspected Remi had kept a great deal from her about his past.

The leggy tour guide herded them along a grassy path to a corner of the cemetery. She stopped beside a square mini-mausoleum rising off the ground and surrounded by a decorative black iron fence. High grass poked out between cracks in the masonry, and though not in the dilapidated state as some of the other burial sites, the tomb still came across as shabby.

"This is the resting place of Madam Simone Glapion," the guide said.

Lexie remembered the name. She was the original owner of the dragon cane.

She searched around the tomb for Magnus, but he was nowhere in sight.

Magnus didn't want to be near Madam Simone's grave and faded from view.

"Madam Simone ran an establishment of ill-repute in

Storyville called Mahogany House," the guide said. "Sister of Christophe de Glapion, and aunt to the Marie Laveau's children, she's rumored to be the person who replaced the voodoo queen as head priestess in the city. She possessed a famous dragon cane—a gift from Marie Laveau—and believed by many to be the source of her power. She died in a fire in her beloved Mahogany House in the summer of 1889."

"What happened to her cane?" a man called from the back of the group.

The guide shrugged. "No one knows. It hasn't been seen since her death."

While the tour moved away from the tomb, dread enveloped Magnus. Though baffled as to why Lexie's opinion mattered to him, he couldn't abide losing her trust.

He willed his image back into her dimension. He found Lexie not far from the iron fence.

"I didn't know she'd been placed here," Magnus said next to her.

"Ever since I saw the photo of her painting, I suspected you knew her." Lexie waited as several members of the group brushed past her. "How did you meet?"

"I was a client."

"I don't understand how you ended up with Simone Glapion's cane."

He went around her and tapped the iron fence surrounding the tomb, contemplating his answer.

"She gave it to me the night she died. For safe keeping."

Lexie inched closer. "You've felt its power then. What can it do?"

"Help a person attain what they crave most."

"I don't get it." Lexie shook her head. "If the cane is a voodoo relic and has such power, why did she give it to you and not pass it on to another priestess?"

Magnus had to admit, she was a sharp little vixen. "I have no idea." He glided away from the grave, hoping to end the conversation.

"Did you start the fire?"

He stopped on the grassy path and faced her. "No, my dear." He needed to distract her from the ugly topic. "We should move on. Clarisse is waiting."

"Who's Clarisse?"

Magnus's grin returned. "Clarisse is our carriage horse."

"Did you just make that up?"

The tension between them abated. "Would I ever lie to you, dear Lexie?"

As he took the path to the entrance, Lexie muttered behind him.

Magnus hated to admit it, but she was growing on him.

# Chapter Twenty-Nine

Curtis drove their carriage to St. Ann Street and halted Clarisse in front of a one-story Creole cottage with a gabled roof, yellow plaster, and two white french doors.

Lexie read the sign hanging from the balcony. "The Marie Laveau Shop?"

Magnus waited as she stepped to the curb. "No, the home of Marie Laveau. The cottage was a gift from a wealthy patron. I came here when her daughter used it as a shop."

Lexie wheeled around to him. "You met her daughter?"

"The voodoo doll you found in my attic was fashioned by her." Magnus focused on the still transfixed Curtis. "Stay here."

The man slumped down in his seat and tilted his black cap over his eyes. Clarisse turned her head and observed Magnus descending from the open white carriage.

"She can see you?" Lexie asked.

"All animals can see us." Magnus floated ahead to the cottage door. "When we step inside, stay attuned to your feelings."

"My feelings? Are you sure?"

"Information can be gleaned through questions, but also through other methods. Keep your mind open."

Lexie opened the french door. "This should be fun."

The cottage was not a museum to the late Voodoo Queen, but a gift shop. Voodoo tokens of drums, bells, cloth voodoo dolls, and candles lined the walls. Racks of T-shirts promoting voodoo and Marie Laveau cluttered a corner. A glass case against the far wall housed a jewelry selection. A woman with coffee-colored skin and a bright red turban stood behind it. Her long nose and high cheekbones appeared carved by a master sculptor. She gave Lexie a cordial smile, but when her gaze went to the spot where Magnus stood, her black eyes filled with fear.

Lexie crossed the floor, hoping someone else detected her ghost. "Good morning."

The beautiful woman collected herself. "Welcome to the Marie Laveau Shop. How can I help you today?"

Perplexed at how to approach the subject, Lexie scanned the empty shop to make sure they were alone. She then tapped above a silver necklace with assorted charms in the jewelry case.

"I adore those little charms."

"You're not serious. Those hideous baubles?" Magnus snickered.

The woman scrambled to open the back of the glass case. The way she trembled as she handed Lexie the necklace confirmed her suspicions.

"I promise you, he's real." Lexie winked as she took the necklace.

Magnus leaned against the case. "She can see me?"

The shopkeeper crossed herself and muttered prayers.

"Does that answer your question?" Lexie quipped.

"The spirit, he's with you?" the woman whispered in a tremulous voice.

"Yes, he's a friendly spirit." Lexie put the necklace on the counter. "He won't hurt you."

"This is not a good idea." Magnus took a step back from the counter. "We shouldn't be announcing my presence to strangers."

"Why not?" Lexie's demeanor reflected her excitement at meeting someone who shared her gift. "How long have you had your ability?"

The attendant inhaled deeply, and her shaking eased. "Ever since I was a little girl, I've had visions of spirits. Most are fleeting, but yours isn't going away."

Magnus honed in on the sales clerk's face. "She can see me, but can she hear me?"

Lexie turned back to the woman. "Can you hear what my ghost is saying?"

"I can only see them." She twisted her hands, her shiny rings drawing Lexie's attention. "I've never communicated with any because I was too afraid. But the gift runs in my family. I carry the blood of Marie Laveau. My family can trace their line back to her firstborn daughter, Marie Christine. That's how I inherited this house. It's been passed down to the firstborn daughter every generation."

"We haven't been introduced." Lexie held out her hand. "I'm Lexie Arden, from Boston."

"Aimee Henry." Her smile accented her exquisite cheekbones.

"Ask her what happened to Marie Laveau's daughter," Magnus demanded.

Lexie gave Magnus a stern scowl before confronting Aimee. "We're searching for information on Marie Laveau's daughter. Can you help us?"

Aimee stayed mindful of Magnus as he floated around her shop. "Marie Laveau the second, as she was called, carried on her mother's work. Unfortunately, she never became as famous as her mother."

Magnus rushed up to Aimee. "When I was last here, she fashioned a voodoo doll for me. I want to find out what she did to it—did to me. Why was I tied to the doll?"

Lexie relayed his question.

With a faraway look, Aimee tapped her finger against her lip. "When she made the doll, did she ask you to do anything to it?"

Magnus recalled the creation of the doll. "She molded it out of dried herbs and told me to spit on it. Then I was to name it after the person I wanted to be cursed."

Lexie repeated his words for Aimee.

Aimee paled and stepped back from the counter. "You can't be angry with me, spirit, for what my ancestor did."

Lexie arched closer to her. "What did she do?"

"The doll …" Aimee's lower lip quivered. "If you spit on the doll, it took on your essence. You were cursed, not the one you named."

Lexie spun to Magnus. "Why would Marie Laveau's daughter curse you?"

"I have no idea. I'd never met the woman before I set foot in this shop." He pointed to Aimee. "Ask her why?"

Lexie held up her hands, assuaging Aimee's distress. "He's not mad at you. We need to understand why Marie Laveau's daughter cursed him."

Aimee's frightened gaze went back and forth between Lexie and Magnus. "Marie Laveau the second was nothing like her mother. Considered a cruel mistress by many, she used her voodoo for intimidation and to assert her power over the city. However, one high priestess challenged her: her aunt, Simone Glapion."

Lexie's breath caught in her throat. "Magnus was acquainted with Simone Glapion."

"If Marie the second suspected he was Simone Glapion's friend, it may be the reason why she cursed him." Aimee paused and shook her head. "My grandmother told me stories about how much the two women hated each other. They fought over a ceremonial staff, called a baton juju. A symbol of voodoo power and shaped like a dragon, Marie Laveau passed the baton juju on to Simone Glapion and not her daughter. She didn't trust her daughter to keep the peace in the city. When Simone Glapion died in a mysterious fire, everyone suspected her niece of the crime."

"I was cursed because of her aunt?" Magnus tossed up his hand. "That makes no sense."

"Would there have been another reason to curse Magnus?" Lexie pressed. "Something he missed at the time?"

"Who knows?" Aimee shrugged. "Marie the second dealt with the dark side of voodoo. When she took over the town after Simone's death, the city was thrown into chaos. The spirits were not happy because the right high priestess had died, and the wrong one had ascended. Many insist the bad gris-gris resulted from Simone Glapion's death and continues to this day."

"How has it continued?"

Aimee scurried to a collection of books at the end of the counter. She selected one and opened it to a specifics section. "There have been several high priestesses from the time of Simone Glapion who've ruled over the city. All brought misery to New Orleans, and enslaved the followers of voodoo." She tracked her finger down the page. "This is a timeline of all the high priestesses of New Orleans since Marie Laveau's death in 1881. At the bottom, you will see the current high priestess, Bloody Mary."

Lexie skimmed the list, and when she came to the name

Bloody Mary, she noted an asterisk and another name.

"Who's Helen Shaver?"

"A white woman from Nebraska. She arrived in New Orleans many years ago. She can't see or speak to the dead, cannot prophesize the future, or heal the sick, but she has a powerful network of associates who bully, intimidate, and kill to keep her in power." Aimee turned the pages for Lexie. "That's her picture. She has a vast knowledge of voodoo and can cast spells many priestesses dare not attempt. But her wealth comes from the drugs."

"She's a drug dealer?" Lexie's voice rose in disbelief.

Aimee nodded. "She uses voodoo ceremonies as a means to distribute her drugs. Many say the reason for her rule goes back to the death of Simone Glapion."

The revelation weighed Magnus's soul down like a boulder around his neck. He had killed Simone Glapion, and her death had set in motion a chain of events that continued until modern times. But discovering the ramifications of what his crime had done to change the course of a city was overpowering.

*Can the actions of one man cause so much damage?*

"What do you think, Magnus?"

Lexie's voice brought him back.

"The rituals on Bayou St. John this Bloody Mary has, should we attend one?"

"You need to be very careful around Bloody Mary," Aimee warned. "If she gets word of anyone powerful enough to challenge her authority, she destroys them. She fears an *haute défi*."

Lexie's nose crinkled. "A what?"

"A high challenge," Magnus replied. "When two voodoo

priestesses battle over control of a territory."

Lexie rested her elbow on the counter, giving him a once-over. "How do you know about this?"

"Aimee's ancestor told me. She said it was feared by many because of the chaos it would bring."

Lexie shifted her focus to Aimee. "Why would I be a challenger to Bloody Mary's authority?"

Aimee gestured to Magnus. "You walk with a spirit guide and have the sight. To someone like Bloody Mary, who has no power over spirits, you're dangerous."

Magnus stuck out his chest, furious at the label. "But I'm not a spirit guide!"

Lexie repeated his statement while imitating his adamancy.

Magnus hid his snicker at her impression.

"But he's tied to you. He's compelled to be with you. Those traits are the essence of a spirit guide." Aimee reached for another book on the counter. "A spirit guide is your connection to the other side and helps to direct your destiny." She held up a blue leather-bound book with the title *Spirit Guides* embossed in gold on the cover.

Lexie took the book from her. "But a spell must have bound us together. Something was done to him back in his day." She opened the pages. "When I met him, he haunted an old mansion. I believed that house tied us together, but it must have been the voodoo doll I found in the attic."

"What happened to the doll?"

"Burned in a fire, along with the mansion. We think a man named Remi Glapion caused the blaze." Lexie waited for Aimee's reaction, but the woman showed no interest in the name. "Ever since the fire, Magnus has been attached to me."

"A spell is what binds a soul to a person. If no spell exists, then you should read the book in your hands. Whatever has joined the two of you, there's a reason."

Lexie's jaw slackened. "Are you saying I'm stuck with him?"

The throaty laugh Aimee uttered took Magnus by surprise. It reminded him of the time he spent in Madam Simone's cozy sitting room, listening to the same deep chortle.

"You must begin to ask yourself, not if you are stuck with him but why?" Aimee said once her laughter subsided. "The universe always has a purpose. You just have to figure out what it is."

Something about the comment did not sit well with Magnus. He'd fretted for decades if his penance for his crimes had been his attachment to Altmover Manor. But with his house destroyed, he found himself bound to the kind of woman he'd lusted after. Smart, sexy, determined, and with a face like his Frannie, Lexie Arden would have ended up in his bed—if he'd been alive. Magnus decided the universe had a twisted sense of humor. Or perhaps he'd stumbled into Hell and Lexie Arden was the personification of all his sins.

# Chapter Thirty

Settled in their open white carriage, Curtis drove Lexie and Magnus to the edge of the French Quarter.

"Where are we going?" Lexie asked.

Magnus glimpsed the white shopping bag in her lap, stuffed with books on voodoo from Aimee's shop. He had a feeling she liked to read. Such women his father had referred to as *dangerous*.

"I want to see what's become of the place where Simone Glapion had her Mahogany House."

"What was she like?"

"Madam Simone?" He shrugged, not sure of how to describe her. "Pretty and a shrewd businesswoman."

"How did she get into being a madam?"

Magnus struggled to recall the conversation in Simone's sitting room. "Born to a local businessman and the granddaughter of a plantation owner, she possessed the sight, like you. We never talked about how she fell into the business, but I got the impression she'd been raised in it. Most quadroon women were in those days."

"I remember reading about quadroon and octoroon women in a book in high school."

The carriage came to a stop at a long track of muddied land enclosed by a wire mesh fence. The empty area went on for several blocks. The tall buildings surrounding the site cast long shadows on the ground in front of their carriage.

Magnus grieved at the emptiness before him. There had been so much life here before.

"There used to be rows of beautiful homes. Houses of sin, yes, but they were so magnificent. I can't believe they're gone."

He climbed from the carriage and headed to the fence.

Lexie followed. "What did the Mahogany House look like?"

"It was made of white marble with long stained-glass windows that rose all the way to the fourth floor. I remember the terra cotta roof shimmered in the evening sun. And there were white marble steps that led to a porch, and brass lanterns. At night, they shown so brightly the marble gleamed like glass."

"Sounds like a hell of a place."

He waved to the barren land before him. "There were streets lined with houses, packed with carriages, music filled the air. Lively music, not unlike the jazz you spoke of. It was an elegant world."

"Yeah, a real Disney World for men," Lexie said. "I bet the women working there hated it."

He'd never considered the plight of the women in those houses. To him, it had been business.

"What made you so fond of the Mahogany House anyway?"

"It gave us anything we wanted," he told her, attempting to be discreet.

"After what you made my fiancé do, I know you're a man with

certain desires. Otherwise, you wouldn't have such fond memories of Madam Simone's place. She gave you something you couldn't get anywhere else. What was it?"

"I may be your spirit guide, Lexie, but you are not my confessor. Allow me to keep some of my secrets."

"All right." She held up her hands, giving in. "But if you'd confessed your sins to someone, you might not be here with me."

Magnus dipped his head to her, grinning at her wit. "Something else to consider while I await the resurrection."

"You've got to get that horse back to the Quarter, buddy," a man shouted.

"Oh shit." Lexie took off running toward the carriage.

A stocky police officer had taken a determined stance in front of Clarisse. The gun in his holster attracted Magnus. He bet it was stronger than the rifles he'd used for hunting as a child. The shiny badge on his chest read, *NOPD*.

"Is there a problem, officer?" Lexie asked.

"This horse is supposed to stay within the French Quarter limits," the officer said in a gruff voice to Curtis. "Did you hear me?"

Oblivious, Curtis stared straight ahead and held the reins as he sat on his bench.

"It's my fault, sir," Lexie jumped in. "I wanted to see where the Mahogany House had been."

The officer rested one hand on his hip as the other hand pushed back his blue cap. "The what?"

Lexie's gaze veered pleadingly back to Magnus. He should have helped her—stepped in and whispered to the police officer, sending him on his way—but how she fidgeted in her funny white shoes was too good to interfere.

"The Mahogany House was …" Her cheeks took on a rosy tinge. "Ah, houses of ill-repute in this portion of the city."

The police officer mouthed the term *ill-repute.* His face lit up. “Oh, you mean the whorehouses.”

Magnus did his best to contain his laughter. He hadn’t seen anything so entertaining since … He couldn’t remember when.

“Ma’am, Storyville was shut down back in World War I. Those buildings were destroyed in the thirties to make way for the Iberville housing projects.”

Magnus inched closer to the officer as he listened to his distressing tale of progress.

“Then after Katrina, all the projects were torn down. This here’s gonna be a mixed-income development. The city’s already got thirty million set aside to start construction next year.”

Since discovering his connection to Lexie, Magnus had enjoyed learning about computers, the Internet, and the irritating device called a television. Never once in discovering those technological miracles had he felt out of time. But the sadness pervading him reminded him of what he was: a soul witnessing the present through eyes still focused on the past.

“Get that carriage back in the Quarter,” the officer ordered. “City ordinances state they can’t leave the Quarter. These things are a goddamned traffic menace.”

Lexie climbed back into the carriage and urged Magnus to hurry with her eyes.

“I can’t believe he spoke to you in such a manner.” Magnus took his seat. “Curtis, it’s time to return to Jackson Square.”

“He was a cop doing his duty. Don’t be too hard on him, Magnus. They have a tough enough job.”

He got comfortable next to her as Clarisse trotted back toward the French Quarter. “What he said about Storyville, world war, and the rest. Can you explain those things to me?”

“Well, Storyville was the old red-light district in the city,” she told him. “The area was where legal prostitution took place and ended around the First World War."

"A First World War? I cannot fathom it." Magnus shook his head. "What about the other thing he mentioned? The woman's name? Katrina?"

"Over a decade ago, a hurricane named Katrina hit this city. It was the worst disaster anyone in this country had ever seen."

He scanned the street. "You can't tell."

"An army of machines, volunteers, and hard-working residents fought to help the city recover. Took them a while, but they've rebuilt and moved on."

Magnus sat back on his bench. "I'm glad to discover some things haven't changed."

She crinkled her brow. "What things?"

"The human spirit. It still can't be broken."

# Chapter Thirty-One

Curtis guided Clarisse to the back of the carriage line in front of Jackson Square. After collecting her bag, Lexie stepped onto the sidewalk. Within minutes, Curtis reclined back into his napping position.

Lexie slung the plastic bag and her purse over her shoulder as Magnus petted Clarisse's thick neck. The horse turned, attempting to nuzzle him.

*A shame the man didn't apply his skill with horses to people.*

Magnus snapped his fingers at Curtis. The carriage driver startled awake and gaped at Lexie from his bench. "Hey there, you want to go on a French Quarter tour, little lady." He waved to his gray mare. "Clarisse and I are tons of fun."

"No thanks, Curtis."

"Hey? How'd you know my name?"

Inside Jackson Square, Lexie viewed the iconic façade of St. Louis Cathedral. She raised her face to the sun, relishing the tickle of the breeze on her skin.

"Treasure it," Magnus said next to her. "People take being alive for granted. The smell, touch, and taste of it all."

"What do you miss most from your life?"

"That's easy. Coffee." He rubbed his hands together. "I adored coffee."

The cathedral bells rang out, chiming noon.

"It's been a while, but those bells would mean lunch, correct?" he inquired in a playful voice. "I have the perfect place. The best food in the city. Antoine's Restaurant must still be around. The food is divine and—"

"Why would you want to waste time on lunch when there is so much else for us to do?" She took off toward St. Louis Cathedral.

"There's the time issue again," he said, gliding alongside her. "You and the rest of your generation are besotted with the topic."

"And you're obsessed with food." She halted outside the open doors of the church. "This may come as a shock to you, Magnus, but it's good to skip a meal now and then."

"In my day, one avoided skipping meals and too much fresh air. Doctors considered it a surefire way to get sick."

"But people still got sick in your time."

Magnus nodded as he browsed the tall church spires. "I'm sure you have sickness as well."

Lexie shrugged. "The diseases killing us today are much more insidious. Cancer and heart disease are the big ones."

He peered out over the crowds gathered outside of the square. "Typhoid took my mother and brother. Edward went unusually fast."

"What was he like?" She moved away from the cathedral entrance.

"Edward?" Magnus stepped beneath the shadows of The Cabildo. "He was several years younger than me, and a sickly child. He had my mother's quiet temperament and elegant way of moving."

She followed him into the shade. "You must be more like your father."

"I hope not. Reynolds Blackwell tortured his business associates, my mother, and he especially enjoyed hounding me. I had to always do more, be better, set the example because I had the Blackwell name."

"You two never got along, huh?"

"No, never. I went to Harvard because he insisted. I studied architecture because he told me I had talent, which I didn't. And when he died, he left me a small empire to manage, but unfortunately, little instruction on how to handle it."

"I can't believe it." She chuckled under her breath. "You ran the family business into the ground?"

"Don't sound so happy about it," he snapped. "And I didn't run the family business into the ground so much as neglected it. Renovating Altmover Manor took up so much time other areas suffered. Namely the family businesses."

"About damn time you admitted you failed at something. You always come across as so smug."

"That's because I am smug, dear woman. It's part of my charm." He stopped walking and bowed to her.

With a smirk, she stepped onto the cracked sidewalk of Chartres Street. "You don't have any charm, Magnus."

They ambled along Royal Street. Occasionally, Magnus would

comment on artwork in a shop, or Lexie would become distracted by a trinket for sale.

Then, in the shadows of the renovated courthouse in the center of the French Quarter, Lexie stopped.

"What is it?" Magnus followed her line of sight to a pink building on the corner.

"I've got a crazy idea."

They approached a neo-classical building. It had a number of policemen in dark blue uniforms gathered out front. Magnus considered the firepower holstered to their hips.

"Lexie, what are you going to do in a police station?"

"Remi once told me his brother works as a detective with the police and is stationed in the French Quarter. Let's see if he's here."

"But how are you going to explain about Remi and the cane to the police?"

"You'll see." She approached the portico-covered entrance.

Magnus rushed after her, cursing under his breath. The woman's determination flummoxed him.

*How am I to control her?*

At a high front desk with several officers, Magnus waited by her side as Lexie stood on her tiptoes and spoke to the officer behind the desk. Her courage impressed him. He could never envision his Katie being so bold.

"I'd like to file a police report. Something was stolen from my home, and I want it back."

The officer at the desk, a black man with a thick neck and bulging biceps, leaned over the desk to her. "Did you call 911?"

"Ah, no. I thought I'd come down and file myself."

"Lexie." Magnus hovered around her. "They will ask questions you can't answer."

The officer sighed as he reached under his desk. "You're gonna need to have an officer go through this with you and create a case number. You can use that to file with your insurance and—"

"This piece wasn't insured. And I know who stole it."

The officer gawked at Lexie. "Then that would make our job easier, wouldn't it? Got a name, sweetheart?"

Magnus didn't care for the condescending tone of his voice. She was a lady and deserved better.

"His name is Remi Glapion. He has a brother who—"

"Remi Glapion?" another dark-skinned officer to the side of the desk inched up to Lexie.

Lexie had too many men around her. It didn't matter if they were police officers—in Magnus's experience, a man's profession never trumped sex.

"Yeah, he worked for the coroner's office as a lab technician," she said to the police officer.

"Care to give me any specifics?" the officer asked. "Height, weight, race, for instance."

"He's a big guy, and black. Knows a lot about fixing up old houses. Said he grew up fixing them."

The men gave each other a knowing glance. "You need to come with me, ma'am," the officer to her side directed. "I've got someone who will want to talk to you."

She took a step away from the high desk. "Is there a problem?"

The officer came alongside her and took her elbow. "Not at all. I'll bring you to an officer who can help you. But first, he'll need to ask you some questions."

"I don't like this," Magnus whispered to her. "We should leave."

Lexie ignored him.

*Stubborn woman!*

After passing a glass enclosure, they were shown to a secured area behind the front desk. The large room was packed with desks along with plain-clothed and uniformed officers darting about.

Magnus inspected the shiny badges on the chest or belt buckle of every man he passed. When he encountered a woman wearing a blue uniform and badge, he froze.

"A woman? How can this be?"

Lexie's scowl told him the middle of the police station was not the time to discuss it. He made a mental note to grill her about the woman later.

At an all-glass corner office, a man rose from his desk and came toward them. The officer's wide face and bright white smile elicited a shiver of familiarity in Magnus. He was impressive in height, and his gray shirt and black slacks hugged his muscular frame. On his belt, the same silver badge.

"Detective Emile Glapion is gonna help you, ma'am."

*Emile Glapion?* The reason for escorting Lexie to his office became clear.

Magnus's worry escalated when the door closed behind them.

"Lexie Arden." Lexie extended her hand over the desk to the detective.

Emile Glapion came around his desk. "Have a seat, Ms. Arden. The officer at the front desk said you wanted to file a stolen property report."

After setting her shopping bag next to her chair, Lexie sat in front of the desk. "Ah yes. But I know the man who did it, and I want to find him."

"Yeah, so I heard." He let go a soft chuckle and rubbed his eye, giving Magnus the distinct impression he didn't believe Lexie.

Magnus hovered close to a file cabinet by the doorway. "Stick to the facts, Lexie. And I would skip the bits about me."

Lexie cleared her throat and gave a curt nod, letting him know she understood. "Remi Glapion stole a valuable piece of property from me, and I want it back."

"Remi Glapion?" Emile sat on the corner of his desk. "Tell me what do you know of the man?"

Lexie sat back in her chair, eyeing the detective. Magnus didn't like the stubborn look on her face—trouble was on the way.

"He was a caretaker for an old manor house my fiancé purchased on Mount Desert Island in Maine. He worked for us for a brief time and then disappeared."

"Maine?" Emile Glapion jumped up from the desk and then calmed and sat back down. "This is New Orleans, Ms. Arden. You should be speaking with the police at … wherever it is you came from."

"But Remi's here. He was from here, and he stole my cane and came back to New Orleans."

"How do you know that? Do you have any information about him? Have his whereabouts?" Emile raised his voice. "Are you involved with him? Did you have any dealing with him? Talk to me, and I will help you, Ms. Arden."

Lexie slammed her mouth closed, and Magnus sensed her fear. She was second-guessing her plan to come here, and the detective's rude behavior wasn't helping.

"I can't tell you how I know, I just do. I feel it." She placed her hand over her chest. "In here."

"Okay, I get it." Emile wiped his hand over his face with a *why me?* look in his eyes. "I need to set you up with one of the officers outside who can take your report and give you—"

Magnus rushed up to Emile and whispered in his ear, "You know who Remi is, don't you?"

"I know who Remi is," Emile replied. Dazed, he shook his head. "Why did I say that?"

"Who is he?" Lexie pressed.

Emile stood from the desk. "I'm sorry. I shouldn't have said that."

"But you did say it. Something compelled you." Lexie

grinned. "Or someone."

Emile stepped back from her. "Who are you, Ms. Arden?"

Lexie's eyes got smaller and colder, her carefree smile slipped away and the nervous energy she gave off evaporated. Bewitched by her metamorphosis from a vibrant woman to calculating vixen, Magnus speculated Lexie was about to turn the tables on the detective.

"Glapion is a name associated with Marie Laveau and voodoo. She related to you, Detective?" Lexie grilled in a decisive manner.

The veins in Emile's neck pulsated. "Any tour guide can take you to the Glapion tomb, Ms. Arden. Why don't you tell me why you're in my city and what you know about Remi Glapion?"

Infuriated, Magnus shouted, "Tell her the truth, man."

"The truth?" Emile took on a befuddled expression. "About my brother, Remi?"

Smug satisfaction coursed through Magnus. "See? I got the job done, dear girl."

Emile went back to his desk and plopped into his chair. "Please tell me I didn't just say that."

"You did." Lexie scooted closer. "You couldn't help it."

Emile glowered at her, his tense cheek muscles twitching. "What are you? A juju woman? A witch?"

Lexie bit her lower lip. "No, I'm a tourist."

Emile's deep laughter resonated throughout the glass room. "I must be losing it. So much for sticking with police procedure. When you walked in here after mentioning my brother at the desk, I thought you might know what happened to him and be a suspect in his case. Now I'm more curious about you than suspicious." He rested his hands on the desk, studying her. "What do you know of Remi?"

Magnus floated back to the file cabinet, pleased with his efforts. He got the impression the man had some ability, but he denied it, making him all the more pliable for Magnus.

"Mind what you say, Lexie. He's testing your sincerity."

Lexie folded her hands in her lap. "Remi came with our house in Maine, or we thought he did. He told us he traveled up the east coast doing construction work after Katrina and then happened on the caretaker position for the property we bought and had been there for a few years. He often spoke about New Orleans. I could tell it meant something to him. After the fire, we found out the bank never hired Remi Glapion. I assumed once he had what he was after, my cane, he would return home."

Emile unfolded his hands and reached for a pen. "How long ago was this fire?"

"Five weeks."

The detective jotted down some notes. "And the name and address of this house of yours?"

"Altmover Manor on Mount Desert Island, Maine. Lieutenant Hartwell was handling the case. You can check with him about the fire."

"I plan to." Emile wrote down the details. "How long had you lived at this house before the fire occurred?"

"Not long. Less than a month."

Emile kept taking notes. "Where did you live before Maine?"

"Boston with my fiancé, Will Bennett. I'm an interior designer. Will's an architect."

Emile stopped writing and tossed his pen aside. "Why don't you start at the beginning? Tell me how you got here from Boston."

Lexie recounted her tale, about the house, her research and she included the parts about the cane, skipping over the mention of ghosts.

After she had finished, the lines in Emile's brow deepened. He ran his hand over his mouth and leaned back in his chair.

"Hell of a story."

"And do you believe my Remi Glapion is your brother?"

"Sounds like it." He opened a desk drawer, removed a manila folder, and set it in front of Lexie. "After I couldn't track him down a couple months back, I filed a missing person's report. I'd about given up hope getting any word on him." He opened the folder and pulled out a photo. "We were never close, but he always checked in with me."

"Losing track of a brother must be tough."

"Remi and I fought like cats and dogs most of our lives. Since our mother passed away several years ago, our relationship deteriorated to the occasional phone call. He lost his home in Katrina and fell on hard times. I wanted to help, but he refused. Then I got wind he'd joined a voodoo cult in the city. Most of these cults are a cover for drug trafficking. When Remi stopped showing up at his job in the coroner's office, I suspected drugs. The last time I spoke with him, he called me in the middle of the night. He kept talking about someone being after him." Emile pushed the picture toward her.

The lack of grief in Emile's voice bothered Magnus. The loss of his younger brother, Edward, had crippled him. Why wasn't Emile more distressed?

Lexie inspected the photo. "That's the man I knew, but he never struck me as paranoid or afraid. He was levelheaded."

Emile dropped his head and took a moment. Magnus suspected the gesture was genuine, but the man was holding something back.

"Remi was solid as a rock until he got involved with that cult." Emile Glapion sat back. "What makes you so convinced my brother took this dragon cane?"

Magnus moved away from the metal filing cabinet. "Careful, Lexie. You don't want to say too much."

"He seemed obsessed with it," Lexie reported. "He pushed me

to find it. The day the house caught fire, he asked me where the cane was and ran back inside."

"How do you know he didn't perish in the fire?"

Magnus scowl at her. "Don't tell him about the woman in the car, Lexie. Keep your secrets hidden."

"No body was found," Lexie told the detective. "Remi also mentioned he was aware of the cane's former owner. A Storyville madam named Simone Glapion. Said he was related to her."

"We are." Emile stood from his chair. "Simone Glapion died in a fire in her famous Mahogany House. Her daughter, Estelle, rebuilt the establishment and called it Mahogany Hall. She carried on the family business until Storyville was shut down in 1917. Everyone, including Simone's daughter, assumed her famous dragon cane burned to ash in the fire. If the cane you found is indeed the same one, how did it get to Maine?" He walked around his desk.

"A man named Magnus Blackwell claimed Simone Glapion gave him the cane."

Magnus groaned. "Lexie!"

Emile had a seat on the corner of his desk. "Simone would've never given her cane to anyone other than her heir—the one to inherit her power. The cane acted as a sort of crown in voodoo families. It was reputed to have once belonged to Marie Laveau. Simone Glapion would have died before parting with her cane."

"Forgive me, Detective, but you sound like you believe in voodoo." Lexie stood. "I thought cops were skeptical and I was a suspect."

"We grow up with the mystical and supernatural in New Orleans, Ms. Arden. Voodoo, ghosts, magic—it's a way of life to us. I believe in it, and so did my brother. And you're still a suspect until I can prove your story."

"Do you have any other suspects?"

Emile went to the file cabinet where Magnus stood. "There's something you should see." He stopped in his tracks, his countenance troubled.

"Is something wrong, Detective?"

He shook his head and opened the cabinet. "No, for a moment I swore …"

Hope glistened in Lexie's eyes. Magnus needed to stifle her before she said something she shouldn't.

"Don't pry, my dear. You can't trust him."

Emile Glapion searched through some folders as Magnus peeked over his shoulder. He selected a thick file and then slammed the cabinet door closed.

"Be prepared," Magnus warned, coming up to her. "It's a file on the woman, Bloody Mary."

Detective Glapion laid out the file on the desk and opened it for Lexie. He retrieved a photo of a heavyset older blonde woman with a round face and set it in front of Lexie.

"Do you know this woman? Have you ever seen her before?"

Magnus kept his sights on Emile and not Lexie. The detective was pumping her for information, testing her credibility. Magnus wanted to whisper to him again to convince him of her sincerity but changed his mind. Lexie could handle the police officer like she'd handled his brother.

"I have no idea who she is," Lexie said.

Emile's tempered sigh floated around the office.

"Her name is Helen Shaver," Emile explained. "She runs a voodoo cult out of her home in the Garden District. She's known around town as mambo or voodoo high priestess." He tapped the woman's picture. "Her devotees also happen to be big time drug dealers. We got tips on her in the past. The information led to a couple of drug busts, most happened at her rituals on Bayou St. John. We've arrested her twice, but each time the charges got dropped."

"How can she get away with being a drug dealer?"

"It's easy enough to do in New Orleans when you have money and connections." Emile went to the window behind his desk. "The last time Remi called me, he warned me about Helen Shaver. He feared she was going to hurt him and make him get something. Something related to voodoo. Nothing he said made any sense until you walked in here and told me about your cane."

Lexie fingered Helen Shaver's picture. "My dragon cane is in New Orleans, Detective. I have to find it."

He came around to the front of the desk and slammed the file closed on Bloody Mary. "You need to be careful down here, Ms. Arden. Voodoo is dangerous. I've seen enough bodies cut up by rituals to understand the dark side of voodoo is alive and well and living in this city. Don't go asking for trouble."

"I don't want any trouble, Detective, just my cane."

"Liar," Magnus edged in. "You've been searching for trouble since we got here."

"Ms. Arden, if your cane is in this city, someone went to a lot of trouble to get it. They're not going to hand it back to you. Not without a fight."

Lexie retrieved her bag of books from the floor. "I don't scare easily, Detective."

Emile Glapion plucked a white business card from the gold card holder on his desk.

"Take this. My cell is on there in case you need it."

Lexie gripped the card. "Thank you for your time."

He escorted her to the office entrance. "Thank you for telling me about my brother."

She was about to walk through the glass doorway when Emile Glapion blocked her way.

"Ms. Arden, I meant what I said. You call me if you see

anything you can't explain."

Lexie nodded as the man removed his arm. "I'll keep that in mind, Detective."

Back out on the street, Magnus waited until the pink police station was far behind him before he spoke to Lexie.

"You're mad! Do you know that?" He refrained from using the assorted expletives running through his mind. "What was the point of notifying the police?"

"I took a gamble, and it paid off. His brother working in this precinct was pure coincidence."

"There is no such thing as coincidence. If you ask me there have been far too many since we arrived in New Orleans. You need to be careful. You shouldn't tell a total stranger your story."

"He's a cop, Magnus."

"Keep your voice down." Wary of the people on the street, Magnus drifted closer to her. "Perhaps it's time to go home."

She came to an abrupt halt. "Go home? Are you kidding me?"

Motivated by her outburst, Magnus encouraged her to move along the sidewalk. "You've seen New Orleans and toured the places I visited. What else is there for you here?"

"My cane!" She struggled to keep up with his stride. "Don't you want your cane back? You were so hot for it back in Maine."

"I should never have brought you into this." Magnus hung his head as O'Connor's warning about staying away from Lexie repeated in his head. *Damn, the man.* "Lexie, you must be reasonable. You held the cane. You know what it can do."

She maneuvered in front of him and forced him to stop. "What can it do?"

Several tourists passed them, but Magnus paid them no heed. "Madam Simone told me the cane has the power to read the heart of the bearer and bring forth those emotions into their life. When I held the cane, the stones were red. Hate was what filled my world.

For you, the dragon's eyes changed to rose."

"Which means what?"

"Love, Lexie." His genuine smile brought a hint of warmth to his sharp features. "The love you and Will share ignited the cane. Your passion blossomed in its presence. I bet you could do so much more with the dragon cane than I ever did."

"Does that mean you still want to help me find it?"

"The cane is gone." His smile faded as the white stone of the Hotel Monteleone came into view. "You need to put an end to this before you get in trouble."

"An end? I'm just getting started." She stomped away.

Magnus couldn't help noticing her slender curves, bouncing honey-blonde hair, and the way she rolled her hips as she walked. His attraction to her was a nagging concern. If he'd been alive, he would have long ago satisfied his lust for her and walked away. Why had fate bound him to such a tempestuous creature? And how was he going to protect her?

With a newfound resolve, Magnus vowed to do everything in his power to make sure Lexie Arden didn't end up like him.

# Chapter Thirty-Two

Once Lexie reached the shade of the white canopy at the hotel entrance, her cell rang. She paused on the steps, put down the heavy bag, and reached inside her purse for the phone.

"Hey there. You miss me yet?"

Will's throaty chuckle was exactly what she needed at that moment. "I miss you, baby. How's New Orleans?"

She scoured the tourists strolling along Royal Street for Magnus. "Good."

"Good? You're in New Orleans. Shouldn't it be fantastic?"

"If I were getting drunk on Bourbon Street and dining my way across the city, it would be fantastic." She picked up her shopping bag and climbed the last steps to the glass doors. "If you were here, it would be perfect."

"I wish." His friendly tone became a shade darker. "Is Magnus still with you?"

The menacing way Will growled Magnus's name made Lexie smile. "He disappeared on me." She searched the hotel lobby. "We were walking from the police station—"

"The police station?" Will shouted.

"It's not what you think, Will. I went there to find information on Remi."

"Involving the police is not a good idea. They might suspect you of doing something to Remi."

"The detective I spoke with did suspect me initially." She shrugged off the alarm in Will's voice. "But he believed me in the end. So it all worked out."

"Damn it. Did he go with you to the police station?"

"Yes, he was there." Lexie proceeded toward a white sofa in the lobby. "But I met Remi's brother. He's the detective I spoke with. His name's Emile Glapion. He said Remi got involved with some local voodoo cult years back. Emile suspected drugs were involved."

"Drugs?" Will's voice cracked—not a good sign. "You'd better come home before you get in trouble down there."

She plopped her bag on the sofa. "What is it with men thinking a woman can't handle trouble?"

"Lexie, you're in a strange city with no one to take care of you but a ghost." He was back to shouting. "You can't go barreling into dangerous situations by yourself. What if something happens? I'm not there to protect you."

"I can take care of myself."

"Can you?" Will blew out a feverish breath, sounding like a deflating tire. "I wish you would listen to me when I advise caution. I'm trying to accept your ability, and the ghost that goes along with it, but you have to stop running after trouble like a bulldozer."

"Don't you dare call me a bulldozer!"

"You were the same way when you went on the hunt for

Magnus's cane. You never considered the risks. You brought the cursed thing into our lives and ended up blowing up our house."

How could he say such a thing? "The fire wasn't my fault, and you know it!"

"I didn't mean it was." Another long, pensive sigh rang in her ears. "Look, we've got our money back. We can replace what we lost in the fire and move on with our lives. Don't you want to get married, find a new house, and settle down?"

The question hit Lexie like a hammer blow to the center of her chest. "You know I do."

"Then why are you in New Orleans, baby?"

Lexie couldn't give him an explanation. Her rational mind urged her to get back to the man she loved, but her heart begged her to stay.

"I guess that answers my question," he said after her brief silence.

"Will, let me finish what I came to do. When I get home, we can plan our wedding and buy any house you want. I have to stay and see where this goes. If I don't, I'll always wonder."

"And if I demand you come home?" he grumbled.

"Are you serious?" She released a nervous snicker. "You can't tell me what to do."

"No, I can't. But I am asking you to consider what you're doing. Use your head and stop being so damned stubborn."

The comment made something inside her snap. "I'm stubborn? You know what, Will, you're an asshole." She promptly hung up the phone.

"That didn't sound good." Magnus materialized, seated next to her.

"What is it with men? Why do you bastards all think you run the world and women are here for your amusement?"

Magnus reclined on the sofa. "Sounds about right to me."

"You're impossible." She picked up her bag and headed across the lobby.

"Where are you going?" Magnus asked, keeping pace with her.

*Where am I going?* Lexie had no idea. She needed to hit someone, preferably someone made of flesh and bone.

"You're angry," Magnus surmised.

She came to a grinding halt. "Ya think?"

"All right." He raised his hands. "We need to be rational about this. You can't fly off the handle because of one fight with your fiancé."

She saw the sign for the Carousel Bar while gazing through Magnus's translucent form. "Get out of my way."

"Where are you going?"

"Screw it." Lexie stormed through his ghostly presence and made a beeline to the bar.

Strings of white lights lit the entrance. The bar was a revolving merry-go-round decorated with a roof of mirrors framed in gold and surrounded by bright lights. Several guests took up the high bar chairs, forcing Lexie to move to the neighboring Carousel Lounge. She searched for a quiet place to drink and found a leather chair by a window overlooking the foot traffic on Royal Street.

She had not yet made herself comfortable when Magnus manifested in the chair across from her.

"This is what always bothered me about women. Your kind is so emotional. It's difficult for men to understand."

"Well, you guys are no walk in the park, either." She set her purse and shopping bag on the chair next to her. "I'm getting sick and tired of hearing how I can't take care of myself." Lexie sunk lower into her seat.

"Will is worried you're getting in over your head and so am I."

"You're worried?" She snorted. "I didn't think you gave a shit about anyone."

His green eyes narrowed. "You're cursing again."

She leaned across the table to him. "How many people did you care about when you were alive?"

"I beg your pardon?"

Magnus's rigid posture made Lexie grin. Her question had struck a nerve.

"Come on, Magnus. How many? Ten, one, no one, anyone? Tell me."

He relaxed and traced his fingers on the wooden table between them. "I cared, Lexie. I might have been considered a heartless bastard by many, but there were some I did care for."

"Like who?"

Magnus raised his chin and browsed the bar. "They had no turning carousel in my day, only the gold framed mirrors and such." A wistful grin curled his lips. "I first met Oscar in here. He wasn't stuffy or pretentious. With Oscar, everything became fun."

"Did you ever read the book he wrote about you?"

Magnus gave a curt nod. "I remember I thought he had hated me and …" He stopped himself. "The story hit a little too close to home. I decided I needed to change my ways and I made an effort with people after reading his book." He patted the table with his hand. "In time, I met Katie. With her, I hoped to be better. I'm not sure whether I succeeded."

"Welcome to the Carousel Bar." A willowy brunette with doll-like features placed a drink napkin in front of Lexie. "What can I get you, hun?"

"A Sazerac," Magnus said to the server. "And keep them coming."

Two drinks later, a tipsy Lexie entertained Magnus. She wasn't slurring her words or yelling like most inebriated people. She had, however, opened up about her father.

"I used to talk to him after he died. For some crazy reason, I believed he listened to me."

"He did," Magnus affirmed. "We can hear the living, especially the ones we love."

"Who talked to you after you died?" She pushed her empty glass away.

"Emily Mann, my secretary."

Lexie laughed a little too loudly and sat back in her chair. "She was in love with you."

"I never suspected when I was alive. All those years and I never noticed."

"Boy, are you dense."

Her funny, scrunched up smile made him chuckle.

"Why else would a woman spend nearly fifty years taking care of someone else's house?" She pointed a wobbly finger at him. "She did it for you."

Their waitress returned to the table. "Would you like another Sazerac, sweetie?"

"She's had enough," Magnus said.

The waitress bobbed her head. "You've had enough."

"You need the tab," he added. "Bill room 1407."

"I'll get the tab," the brunette parroted, picking up Lexie's empty glass. "I'll charge the drinks to room 1407."

Lexie glared at him. "You need to stop doing that."

"Do you want to pay for your drinks?" He glimpsed the retreating waitress. "I can call her back."

"What's going to happen if you do your little trick one day to someone who can see you?"

He stood. "It will prove to be interesting. Now, my dear, you need to stand up and collect your things. It's time to get back to your room."

Outside the window to Royal Street, night blanketed the city and the bright neon lights from the shop windows glowed in the darkness. Her boisterous manner dissolved and she drooped in her chair like a wilting flower.

"Why are we here? You ever think about that, Magnus? Why us?"

"More and more with every passing hour." He scanned the bar.

"What Aimee said to us today? Do you think it's true? Are you my spirit guide?"

"I'm sure you can discover the answer to your question in your bag of books. We need to go."

Lexie collected her things, swaying as she stood. Magnus reached for her arm to prevent her from toppling over. His hand went straight through.

*Damnit.*

He had to get her back to her room before she fell over. He should have known better than to let her drink too much.

*Women and alcohol don't mix.*

After she had righted herself, he helped her to the entrance. There were more people in the establishment than when she'd first come in. He hoped no one would comment on her unsteady gait.

"What I don't get is why you?" She passed through a small group of men in business suits.

The men ogled her slim figure.

"Where ya goin', darlin'? Come back." One man reached out to put an arm around her, but she was too fast for him.

Magnus cursed under his breath. He didn't possess the power to move the smallest chair, so how would he protect her?

In the lobby, Lexie made an awkward gesture back to the bar

entrance. "That's what I'm talking about. Men. You're all a bunch of assholes."

He hurried her to the silver elevator doors across the lobby. "Lexie, please. We need to get you to your room."

She tripped on her way to the elevators. Once inside the car, Magnus relaxed, believing they were home free. Then a young couple caught the elevator right before the doors closed.

They groped each other and giggled in the corner of the car. Magnus detested such a public show of affection.

"You two visiting the city?" Lexie asked the couple.

The redhead beamed while her lanky escort hugged her close. Magnus's patience waned.

"We're here on our honeymoon," the man told her.

The snug fit of his jeans around his crotch hinted at his excitement to get his bride back to bed.

Lexie clenched the elevator railing as the car rose. "Congratulations."

Magnus swore he caught a glimmer of sadness in her voice. Funny how he detected the slightest changes in her moods.

"Yeah, we have three days before Buddy has to get back to his platoon," the bride added. "He deploys overseas in two weeks."

Lexie struggled to stop swaying and smiled at the groom. "Thank you for serving our country."

A swell of pride bloomed inside Magnus. Old soldiers on the streets of Boston had been ugly reminders of the War Between the States. Though his side had won, many remained reluctant to mention what had happened. With his perspective rooted in the aftermath of ignorance, Magnus comprehended the cost of such indifference to the soldiers and the country's future.

"You here with anyone?" the bride softly inquired.

"Yes, we came to find—"

"Lexie," Magnus cut in.

She tucked a loose blonde strand behind her right ear. "I, ah, came with a friend. She's still shopping."

The elevator stopped on Lexie's floor. After giving the couple a friendly nod, she darted from the car.

In the hallway, she weaved as Magnus encouraged her on.

"I can't carry you so you'd better keep moving."

She tugged her heavy bag over her shoulder, but never argued with him or chastised his impatience. In the bar, she'd been so loquacious. Here, she was as silent as a church mouse. The change puzzled him.

"You're upset. Was it those newlyweds?"

She attempted to stand up straight, but the motion made her dip to one side. "They seemed happy."

"All newlyweds are happy, Lexie. Give it a few months. The shine wears off when real life returns."

"Is that what happened to you and Katie?"

The question sent a ribbon of regret scurrying through him. "What makes you ask such a question?"

She struggled, going through her purse while they moved along the hallway. "The way you talk about her. It's more like you tolerated her, not loved her."

Dismayed by her insight, he hovered in the middle of the hall. "I loved Katie. I would not have married her otherwise."

Lexie made it to her door, still rummaging through her purse. "If you loved her, why aren't you with her? For a man who claims to have loved the woman, you rarely mention her."

Magnus came up to the door and touched the lock, making the light flash green. The door popped open.

"It's not polite to bore people with your tragedies."

"Magnus, when love comes to an end, it isn't a tragedy—it's a warm remembrance meant to soothe the soul."

Lexie kicked the door open and tumbled into the room.

Magnus questioned if she was right. His muddled feelings for Katie those last days before their deaths he'd attributed to his growing suspicion of O'Connor. Magnus thought of her daily but never allowed himself to hope she'd forgiven him for their ending. He had yet to forgive himself.

"Whoops," Lexie blurted as she fell close to the bed.

He wanted to reach for her, to help her, but he couldn't.

"Lexie, get up!" He thundered around the room.

She rolled over to her side and wrinkled her nose at him. "You're no fun."

"I'm dead. We don't have fun."

She slowly sat up. "My head is spinning."

"You have to get yourself into bed. I can't do it for you."

Her purse and shopping bag left on the floor, she crawled on her hands and knees into the bed.

Magnus imagined her bent over in such a way beneath him, but he quickly shut down the lecherous visions.

When she finally made it into the bed, she flopped onto her back and slapped her hand over her face. "What in the hell was in those drinks?"

He stood over her. "Sleep it off until I return in the morning."

Before he slipped away, he heard her mumble, "You're a good man, Magnus Blackwell."

"A good man wouldn't still be here as a ghost."

She rolled over on her side, somewhere between sleep and wakefulness. "Bad men don't get a second chance." She tucked her hands under her chin.

As he stood by the bed, taking in her darling face, a measure of hope came to life within him—a hope for something better for his soul and for hers.

He touched the hair that had fallen across her face, and to his amazement, it moved.

Magnus examined his fingers, dumbfounded. To control the thoughts of the unenlightened, manipulate electronics, and create cold drafts, had been the extent of his abilities. He'd never moved anything with his hands before.

When he left her, the mist outside the world of the living embraced him, creating a sense of nothingness. Instead of dreading another day among the living, he longed to return to their world. There was more to this ghost business than he'd initially surmised.

# Chapter Thirty-Three

Her feet pounded on the courtyard as she ran from a red-eyed beast. The monster chased her through misty corridors filled with shadows. The abomination changed into the homely face of the woman known as Bloody Mary. She wanted Lexie to give up her powers and submit to her will. As Bloody Mary closed in, Lexie screamed …

She sat up, wide awake in bed. Safe in her hotel room, she realized she'd been dreaming.

"How weird," she mumbled, wiping her face.

Someone pounded on the door.

Snapshots of the Carousel Bar, the drinks Magnus had ordered for her, and falling on her room floor burst into her head.

"I'm going to kill him."

"That would be quite a feat, considering I'm already dead."

In the plush white chair in the corner, Magnus adjusted the sleeves on his black coat. Lexie wasn't sure if it was her blurry vision, but his clothes had changed. They didn't appear as dull and dingy as they had yesterday.

"I must still be drunk."

"At the door is your strong black coffee and breakfast." He stood from the chair. "I took the liberty."

Lexie stood, a wave of nausea came over her. She then stumbled for the door.

On the other side, a short man in a white tunic and black pants greeted her with a cordial smile.

"Good morning, Mrs. Arden. Here's your complimentary breakfast."

He wheeled a white linen-covered cart in through the door. As soon as he passed Lexie, the aroma of coffee called to her.

"Did you say complimentary?"

The stout man wheeled the cart into the room. "Yes, ma'am. The computer said breakfast was on the hotel."

Lexie shot Magnus a scolding glance. "How did that happen?"

The slight man chuckled. "It's part of our honeymoon package." He dipped his head to Magnus. "Mr. Arden."

Astonished, Lexie padded to the server's side. "You can see him?"

The hotel employee took a guarded step back. "Why? Is he supposed to be invisible?"

"Thank you, my good man," Magnus said, getting out of his chair.

"Enjoy your breakfast, Mr. and Mrs. Arden, and congratulations."

After the waiter had closed the room door, Lexie stared at Magnus. "I can't believe he didn't notice you were … a bit out of style."

"He didn't perceive me as a ghost. He assumed I was human."

"How could he not see the difference?"

Magnus considered the question as he moved toward the service tray. "Unless he's never accepted his gift."

"A person would catch on to something like that, right?" Lexie lifted the silver lid off a plate of waffles. "I've seen strange things all my life." She snatched up a piece of bacon.

"Everyone handles their gifts in different ways. Some ignore it, others fear it. You had your grandmother to help you. Maybe he has no one. Might explain why he identified me as normal."

Lexie chewed on her bacon. "I guess that makes sense."

"You need to call Will. He's worried. He rang you five times on your phone."

Lexie went to her purse still on the floor. "How do you know it's him?"

"While you were sleeping, I've been sitting here listening to your phone make several infuriating noises. Guessing it is Will isn't difficult."

She cringed as she scrolled through the numerous voicemails and text messages from Will. Lexie considered calling him, and then put the phone aside.

"To hell with him. We've got nothing to say to each other."

After two strong cups of coffee, waffles, and a long hot shower, Lexie descended the hotel steps to Royal Street.

"Any suggestions?"

Magnus shrugged as he scrutinized the shadowy street. "Let's take a walk and see where we end up."

"Spontaneous? You?" She chuckled.

He trotted down the steps. “I have my moments.”

“You’re an odd man.”

He waited for her to catch up to him. “I’m a ghost, not a man.”

The morning sunlight peeked through the angled rooftops gleaming on her hair. “You don’t feel like a ghost. Not anymore.”

“I’m glad,” he told her and meant it.

They strolled along regarding the quaint, old structures. Lexie asked him several questions about the romantic wrought-iron balconies and gabled roofs. Magnus answered, amazed his fondness for the topic had not dimmed with time.

“You know a lot about the architecture here,” she said.

Magnus eased into the shade of a townhouse balcony next to them. “It was a passion, or became a passion once I visited this city.”

She followed him into the shadows. “Is that why you changed Altmover Manor?”

He nodded, noting a passing couple with a small child to his left. “I wanted the house to reflect me, my personality, and not my father’s. The house was so cold and lifeless before the renovations by O’Connor.” He left the shade from the balcony and strolled back into the morning sunlight.

“Why did you hire him? Of all the architects in the world, wasn’t he the worst choice?”

Magnus glided next to her. “In retrospect, yes. But at the time I wanted to have Frances close to me. If I hadn’t hired him, made my obsession with her worse, I would not be what I am.”

“You’d still be here. Your anger determined your fate. If it hadn’t been Jacob O’Connor, you would have found someone else to destroy.”

He bunched his brow. “Destroy? Rather a harsh assessment, wouldn’t you say?”

"Is it? You were out to destroy him, and yourself."

While Lexie perused a store window filled with colorful teacups and saucers, he mulled over her words. He'd never considered the ramifications before engaging O'Connor. It had always been his goal to seek revenge for losing his Frannie. But destroy? Had he meant to do that?

When Magnus observed her reading a sidewalk sign outside of a pair of open french doors, her wispy smile enthralled him.

"What is it?"

"A cooking school." Lexie peeked inside the doors. "Will always wanted me to take lessons."

"Call him, Lexie. One argument is no reason to avoid talking to him."

She hugged herself, and he sensed her sadness. "I'll think about it."

Magnus decided she needed a distraction to lift her spirits. He encouraged her inside the doors. "Why not take a class and surprise him with your newfound skills?"

Lexie shook her head, refusing to budge. "Because one class won't help me. I'm a terrible cook. My father was awful, too. My mother always said I'm a lot like him."

Magnus remembered the uppity older blonde who had visited their apartment soon after the fire. He'd found her overbearing and rude. "What did you get from your mother?"

"From Angela?" Lexie snorted. "Not a damned thing. She's one of those proper women. The kind you like. Always well-dressed, says the right things, knows the right people. I'm her greatest disappointment."

"I can't believe that." He inched closer to the open french doors. "You can do anything you set your mind to. Including cooking."

Lexie stood, deliberating the prospect. Tired of waiting on her,

Magnus floated inside.

The first room was a compact office with one woman behind a small desk. She wore glasses as she read from a pile of paperwork.

When Lexie approached the desk, Magnus was already whispering to her.

"Ah, Ms. Longennecker," the woman said, standing up. "We were wondering when you would arrive." She moved to a doorway behind her desk. "The class just started, but if you go on in, there should be room at one of the cooking tables in the back."

Lexie apprehensively stepped through the doorway.

"What did you do?" she muttered.

"Announced your arrival, Ms. Longennecker. I got the name from a list on her desk."

Lexie hesitated before entering the room beyond. "What do I do if Ms. Longennecker shows up?"

Magnus raised his eyebrows. "Run."

They progressed through a short passageway and arrived in a large kitchen. There were six work tables arranged in two rows on each side. Magnus flinched when he noticed the woman standing at the front—she had a black soul. He had not sensed anything like it since his dealings with Remi.

In a long red skirt and loose-fitting white top, she had a yellow turban on her head. She stirred a soup pot on a black, commercial stove, her deep brown eyes spotted Lexie.

"There's room at the back table for you. Go on ahead. We're learning how to make shrimp Creole."

At the back table—Lexie had it all to herself—she pulled out a wooden stool and sat. Before her, a green pepper, a red onion, some cooked shrimp, a chopping block, and one small metal pot sat on top of a single burner.

"Turn on your burner and pick up your wooden spoon," the instructor said. "Stir the oil and flour already in your pots. Watch for the mixture to turn brown and mind your heat. Too much and it will burn."

Lexie retrieved her spoon.

"You need to turn on the gas, my dear." Magnus pointed to the controls for the burner below the table top.

"Once you have a good brown roux, prepare your ingredients. Collect your vegetables and chop them into small pieces."

Lexie attempted to chop a green pepper, stir the pot, and check her flame like the instructor had demonstrated. Magnus thought he might never stop laughing.

It reminded him of the first dinner he'd shared with Frannie. When he had arrived at her home, a horrible odor wafted through the front door. He'd found Frannie sitting on a back porch, her oven mitts around the remains of a charred pot roast. It was the night he'd fallen in love with her. But he had never told her.

The memory was promptly interrupted by Frannie pleading with him as he'd thrown her over the cliff.

*I am a monster.*

"Before you add your shrimp, you want to make sure they have been deveined," the instructor said, calling Magnus back from the past.

"Shit, I still haven't chopped my onion."

The panic in her voice made him yearn to help her. "Concentrate on one thing at a time."

She regarded the other students. "They're already working on the shrimp."

"It's not a competition, Lexie."

"The hell it isn't. You ever put ten women in a room and not have it turn into a competition."

The hard edge to her voice disturbed him. "Where is this fierce determination coming from? It's unseemly for a woman."

She whacked at the onion with her knife—making more mess

than necessary. Her tears building, she kept a wary eye on the other tables.

"Unseemly?" She chucked handfuls of green pepper and onion into her pot. "Magnus, it's the twenty-first century. Women do everything men do: vote, go to war, and hold political office. Nothing is unseemly for a woman anymore."

"But women are still wives and mothers. Those callings can't have changed."

She picked a large shrimp and examined it. "They still are wives and mothers. They juggle those things with their careers." She dropped the shrimp on the cutting board. "Do you see a vein in this thing?"

Magnus was about to tell her to examine the back when Lexie reached for her knife and stabbed her hand.

"Fuck!" she shouted.

The room went quiet.

Magnus rolled his eyes as her expletive vibrated through him.

She reached for a nearby towel, blood pouring from her hand.

"What's all the ruckus?" the instructor asked, hurrying toward Lexie's table.

While Magnus remained on his stool, the instructor removed the towel around Lexie's hand, but then she turned to Magnus and stared right at him.

The chill he got unnerved him.

"Let's take you into the back room and look at your hand." The teacher raised her head to her students. "Class, continue stirring those pots."

She escorted Lexie to a pair of double doors. The swinging doors pushed open, and before they whooshed closed, Magnus stepped through.

On the other side, he discovered a storage room. Large metal shelves held everything from paper towels to cans of tomato sauce.

The instructor lifted a wooden chair out from a round table and set it in the middle of the room.

"Sit here. I'll get the First-Aid kit." She went to the sink. "Then you can tell me about your darkness."

Lexie refrained from sitting down. "What darkness?"

The woman opened a cabinet above the sink and pulled out a First-Aid kit. "It follows you. During the class, you were talking to it."

"I wasn't talking to anyone." Lexie had a seat. "That would be crazy."

"It's not crazy to talk to those that have passed on. When I'm not teaching Creole cooking, I'm reading spirits next door. My name is Renee Batiste." She set the First-Aid kit in Lexie's lap. "What's your name?"

"Lexie. Lexie Arden."

She removed the towel wrapped around Lexie's hand. "And where are you from, Lexie Arden?"

"Boston."

Renee examined the stab wound and clucked. "Not too bad. Just a superficial cut. We'll bandage you up and you'll be as right as rain."

Lexie inspected the woman's wrinkle-free, light brown skin. "What do you mean you read spirits, Ms. Batiste?"

The cackle Renee Batiste unleashed made Magnus uncomfortable. He didn't trust her.

Renee flipped up the lid on the First-Aid kit. "It's just Renee, and I was born with the gift, like you. You can interact with the dead better than me I'd bet. You have a strong *pourvoir*, or power. It's why the dark man is attached to you. You must learn to harness it. Then you can become like me and dance with the dead."

"What do you mean by 'dance with the dead'?"

"It's a ritual I perform on the banks of Bayou St. John when the moon is full, like it will be tonight. I help the spirits stuck in this world pass on to the next. For a fee, I can help you get clear of your dark man over there." She waved to where Magnus waited inside the storeroom doors.

"How can you be so sure it's a man?"

"His arrogance." Renee took a bandage from the box. "He tries to assert his will over you. Probably lived his life playing games with people and believing he was better than everyone else." She snorted and ripped the package open.

She gave Magnus the impression they had met before.

*How can that be?*

"This ritual?" Lexie asked, cutting into his thoughts. "Is it a voodoo ritual?"

Renee set the bandage over her wound. "You interested in voodoo?"

"Yes, I've been learning more about it since I arrived in the city. I've read some books and been to Marie Laveau's tomb."

"If you want to learn about voodoo, you can't read about it in books." Renee reached for the white tape. "You need to experience it. You must take part in a ritual to appreciate the power." She removed a long piece from the spool and ripped it with her teeth. "How long have you been able to communicate with the dead?"

"All my life, but it didn't get insistent until a few weeks ago with Ma—"

"Don't tell her my name," Magus interrupted.

"I mean my dark man," Lexie said.

Renee secured the bandage with the tape. "Does he talk to you?"

Lexie nodded.

"What does he say?"

"What *doesn't* he say? He tells me I'm not ladylike enough."

"Lexie," Magnus grumbled. "Careful." He didn't like this.

The woman wanted information from her for a reason.

"Is he old dead or new dead?" Renee asked.

The edges of Lexie's mouth crept downward. "I don't understand the difference."

Renee ripped off another long strip of tape. "The longer a person has been dead, the more power they have. They're harder to remove. It takes strong voodoo to get them to move on."

Lexie went over Magnus's long black jacket and high black boots. "He's definitely old dead."

She patted down the tape on Lexie's hand. "How did you come by him?"

Lexie hesitated. "Ah, I stayed at his house not long ago, and it caught on fire. After the home had burned to the ground, he attached to me."

"He wants something from you," Renee warned, her voice deep and gravelly.

"This is ridiculous," Magnus snapped, growing impatient. "You can't believe a word out of this woman's mouth."

Renee held onto Lexie's hand. "Do you want to make this spirit go away?"

Lexie's apprehension cut through Magnus like a knife. Her emotions, at times, were as transparent as glass. It was as if she existed inside him, and Magnus didn't want to lose her.

"My dark man can be separated from me with your ritual?"

Renee lifted the First-Aid kit from Lexie's lap. "We start at eight at Bayou Bridge. All the cab drivers in the city know where it is. Come before the festivities begin."

Lexie grinned at Magnus. "He's asking me, how much will this cost?"

Magnus frowned, showing his irritation at how well she knew him. "Nothing will happen tonight. She's a charlatan."

Renee returned the First-Aid kit to the cabinet. "I don't want your money, child. But I would like for you to show me your gift. Are you willing to find out what you can do?"

She pretended to consider the proposition. Magnus decided her performance was a bit too convincing.

"Okay. I'm game."

Lexie's exuberance perturbed him. When they arrived in New Orleans, he'd hoped some sightseeing and window shopping would be enough to quell her desire for the dragon cane. This was not what he'd expected.

Renee's dark eyes twinkled as she sized up Lexie. "There are some things you must do before you come tonight. Bathe in cold salt water before sundown. Eat no food and drink only water from this point forward. It will help prepare you."

Lexie flexed her hand against the bandage. "Anything else?"

"Come alone. You and your ghost will be welcome. No one else."

"Lexie, you can't be serious?" Magnus badgered. "You have no idea what you're getting into."

"I'll be there." With an impertinent smirk at Magnus, Lexie got up from her chair. "Me and my ghost wouldn't miss it for the world."

# Chapter Thirty-Four

A white minivan parked along the water's edge of Bayou St. John. Magnus lingered in his misty world as Lexie stared out the passenger window at the lights from the homes surrounding the bayou.

"Miss, you're sure you want me to drop you off here?" the cabbie asked. "It's not safe for a pretty girl like you. These ceremonies can get wild."

Lexie handed him his fare. "I'm meeting a friend, but thank you for your concern."

The weight of what they were about to do pressed down on Magnus as his ever-determined Lexie got out of the cab. Small and vulnerable, she stood beneath the beam from a bright street lamp. The cabbie shook his head, then drove away.

Magnus waited as she shoved her cash into her front pocket

and her cell phone into the back pocket of her jeans. He sensed the butterflies in her stomach and wished she'd come across as more terrified than excited. Might be easier to talk her out of it if she was scared to death.

"How did you enjoy your frigid bath in salt water?" Magnus inquired, taking shape next to her. "All ready to be rid of me?"

She placed her hand over her nervous stomach. "I'm doing this to get a lead on my cane, not to get rid of you. Besides, it's a chance to witness a voodoo ritual in action."

"I've been to one of these rituals at this same spot on Bayou St. John. I, at least, had Oscar with me. Who do you have?"

Lexie worked her injured hand. "I don't need anyone. I've got my superpowers, a cell phone, a nasty right hook, and you."

"What if I can't help you, Lexie? You heard what Emile Glapion said about voodoo in this city. It's dangerous."

"What other choice do we have?" She gazed out over the black water of the bayou. "Magnus? What if tonight does work and you leave me? Where will you go?"

"Dancing beneath the full moon is not going to get rid of me." He tipped his head to the side, eyeing the ringing cell phone in her back pocket. "Will's calling you."

She retrieved her phone. "One day, you have to tell me how you do that."

"You should talk to him. He's worried."

"Let him suffer a little longer." She turned off her phone.

With a curt humph, Magnus explored the newer homes built along the bayou's edge. Several of the classic double-gallery residences he remembered from his last visit remained. The moon came out from behind a cloud, and a structure previously cloaked in darkness came to light.

"I can't believe it. The house is still here."

Lexie turned away from the water. "What house?"

The green and white Creole Colonial country house appeared run-down against the newer homes around it, but to Magnus, it retained its majestic appeal.

"The house I wanted O'Connor to recreate." He motioned to the residence. "Much of the area was undeveloped then, but that house made a deep impression on me."

Lexie took a moment to examine the building. "The more I'm here, the more I can understand why you changed Altmover Manor. The homes here are so welcoming."

Pleased with her answer, he realized it was the first time anyone had understood his vision. Everyone, including O'Connor, had believed him mad for altering his family home. None of them had grasped the reason for his rebuild—he wasn't destroying the house but erasing the painful memories associated with it.

The pound of drums broke through the quiet night. Next to the bridge, someone lit torches set in a circle not far from the water's edge.

"You'd better stay close to me," she muttered.

Other drums joined in, adding to the electricity in the air.

"Not to worry, my dear." An uneasy cloud settled over Magnus. "I'll stick to you like glue."

They drew closer to the torches, and the number of people gathered along the shore surprised Magnus. Tourists in T-shirts took pictures with their phones while members dressed all in white swayed to the drumbeat. Some sang in an unknown language, and off to the side, away from the torchlight, another group wearing tattered clothes lit small pipes while others pressed syringes into their arms.

"What are they doing?" Magnus questioned.

Lexie shrugged. "That's the drugs the detective spoke of."

"This isn't at all like my experience."

The drums picked up their tempo. Magnus detected a shift in

the air and then spied a mist gathering in the middle of the bayou.

"There's an uncanny feeling here. I had it the night I came with Oscar."

Lexie waved her hand in front of her nose. "All I can smell is pot."

"What's pot?"

From the other side of the bridge, a woman in a flowing white dress and white turban cried out in a shrill voice. She held up a lit torch and waved it in the air as she came toward their group.

"Dramatic," Lexie remarked. "Must be our hostess."

Renee Batiste called out, "Tonight, we dance the *lune hantée*, my children."

She half-danced and half-strutted her way across the bridge until she joined them. Renee planted her torch in the ground and stepped off the bridge.

"The guest of honor is here," she said, coming up to Lexie.

Renee took Lexie's hand, and immediately Magnus grew anxious. She led her into the circle of torches near the water's edge. Magnus went to follow her, but as soon as he reached the outside of the circle, an unseen force prevented him from taking another step.

"Lexie!" he shouted. "Something's wrong."

The drums grew louder as the water lapped at Lexie's toes.

"You have a sacred task, child." Renee clamped a hand on her forearm. "We will set free your dark spirit and allow you to open up to others who need your help."

Lexie tried to shake off her tight grip. "I don't want any others."

"Come, my children," Renee called out to the water. The mist gathered like a rising fog. "You must accept what you are, Lexie Arden. Stand before the water and wait. Let's find out if the spirits bend to you."

Renee let her go and then clapped her hands. The mist reacted to the noise by briefly retreating, but then it blossomed, spreading out over the water.

The dancers twisted and rocked to the drums as they ran into the circle of torches. Their chants of, "Mambo," wafted through the air, cutting off the other sounds from the revelers.

The drumbeat sped up, thundering around Lexie. Her gut tingled, and her hands itched. Something wasn't right. She searched for Magnus in the crowd outside the circle, but couldn't find him. Lexie wished he'd manifest by her side. She'd feel safe knowing he was close.

The drums continued their relentless pounding, and the faces in the crowd blurred. She located Magnus behind a short black man with a red handkerchief around his neck. Then she lost him again.

*Damn!*

The drumbeat grew even louder, roaring in her head like a speeding freight train. The dancers inside the circle swayed one second and then crawled on the ground, resembling insects the next. Renee's movements became erratic as if she were handing her body over to the rhythm. In her hand, a cane magically stretched to life.

*Where did that come from?*

The head of the cane resembled a hissing snake. It wasn't as beautiful as the dragon cane, but Lexie found it mesmerizing. The way Renee tossed it into the air made Lexie believe the snake wiggled in her hands.

Overwhelmed, Lexie put her hand to her head. The heavy

amount of pot in the air was the reason for her hallucinations. She needed fresh air and turned from the firelight to the black water.

The slight breeze cooled her skin and the fuzzy feeling in her head faded. She peered out over the water, and the swirling mist mesmerized her. It moved like one of the dancers. The longer Lexie observed the odd fog, the closer it got to shore.

A heaviness in the air settled around Lexie, and her senses came alive. She could taste, touch, smell, and feel everything around her. Lexie's heart raced, and despite the cool breeze from the water, a light sweat covered her arms and face. She wiped the perspiration from her forehead when a terrible wave of nausea followed by extreme dizziness came over her.

Something shimmered within the mist. Lexie swore it was the moonlight glistening on the water, but then the unusual light morphed into a shape.

As if sucked into a vacuum, all noise around Lexie stopped, and a woman stood before her. Her dark hair hung around her face, blocking her features, and her wet nightdress clung to her figure. A sudden breeze whipped up her hair to reveal her luminescent skin and black eyes.

The woman was not of this earth. While the apparition came forward, Lexie discovered she could not move.

Forced to view the woman's haunting features, Lexie contemplated the ugly scar above her right lip. Her nightdress torn, she had dark splotches on her neck and chin. The eerie form stopped at the water's edge, her feet hidden below the surface.

Petrified, Lexie was like a statue as the spirit raised her hand and pointed at the bayou.

"They've been waiting for you," the woman whispered in a voice like wind against Lexie's ear.

Behind the spirit, other misty figures rose from the water. Lexie shut her eyes and prepared for the horror to come.

A voice from deep inside her cried out, *"Move, Lexie!"*

Her eyes flew open, and she heard it again. She found Magnus next to her at the water's edge.

"Move away from the water, Lexie."

He held out his hand to her. She wanted to reach for it but wasn't sure if she should.

"Do it!" he shouted.

In the water, spirits set out in her direction: a man carrying furs to trade over his shoulder, a Native American with a loin cloth and a bow, and a woman in a hooped dress who was the epitome of a Southern belle. A sad little girl, maybe five or six, held a blue teddy bear to her chest and wore a blue gingham jumper with her long blonde hair braided to the side. Others—men and women—had collars around their necks, shackles about their wrists and ankles with chains dragging on the water's surface behind them.

Lexie shuddered. She couldn't bear any more. It was as if all the dead lost to the water rose up and set their sights on her. She had to do something.

With a newfound strength in her legs, Lexie stepped back from the shoreline.

"No, you mustn't move," Renee ordered. "You're their light. Control them. You are their master."

Lexie ignored her and backed away from the water. She spun around, and someone big stepped in front of her.

She gazed up from the imposing chest of a man blocking her way.

Two black sockets had replaced Remi Glapion's eyes. Weird symbols covered his bare chest as if carved into his skin. She stepped to the side to go around him when Remi reached for her.

"I should have stayed away from her, Lexie. Tell my brother, I should have listened to him."

The deep voice was Remi's, but the bloody and beaten face

looked nothing like him. She recoiled from his icy hand.

Lexie had known Remi—heard his deep laughter, and felt his warmth. The bitter taste of fear climbed the back of her throat. The second she opened her mouth to release an ear-piercing scream, he vanished.

"Lexie!" Magnus rushed up to her. "Get out of the circle."

Stunned, she hobbled toward the edge of the torchlight when Renee came up to her, waving her snakelike cane. "You cannot go. The dead are yours to command."

Lexie glanced over her shoulder, horrified to discover more spirits rising from the water—dozens more.

Suddenly, blinding bright white lights shone into the circle. She covered her face, not sure what to do or where to go.

"Nobody move," a man's voice blared through a bullhorn. "Everyone stay where you are. This is the NOPD."

# Chapter Thirty-Five

The holding cell was nothing like she had imagined. The many television shows and movies she'd seen did not convey the horrible stench of urine and body odor, or the constant noise of the other prisoners moving around. No actor had portrayed the complete hopelessness Lexie experienced. Alone in her cell, she was thankful she didn't have to suffer any company—any human company, that is.

"I told you not to go," Magnus said from the cement bench in her cell.

She paced in front of the door. "Don't remind me. I'm stubborn and too determined for my own good."

"I like determined people, Lexie. I admire determined and talented people even more. But what you did tonight ..."

She stopped pacing. "What did I do? I didn't make all those

dead people rise out of the water."

"Who else would you suggest?" He leaned back, wrapping his hands around his right knee. "Those spirits were coming to you. They sensed the same thing I did when I first met you—your power."

"What power?" She rocked back against the bars to her cell. "What happened tonight had nothing to do with me. It was the ceremony."

"All right." He stood from the bench. "Think what you like. Your rescuer is on the way here."

"What rescuer? What are you talking about?"

The outer doors opened to her section of the holding area.

Magnus eased alongside her. "When they were loading you into the wagon with the rest of the rabble from the raid, I put into the police officer's mind who handcuffed you to contact—"

"Well, well, Ms. Arden." Emile Glapion stood before her holding cell. "Why am I not surprised to find you here?"

He wore a casual black jacket and a white T-shirt. The only thing official about him was the badge clipped to the waistband of his blue jeans.

"Detective Glapion." Lexie sagged against her cell door. "I'm so glad to see you."

The detective waved to the female guard. "You can let her out now." He stood to the side as the guard unlocked her cell door. "I got a call from one of the arresting officers. He said you mentioned my name."

"Yeah, I told him I knew you."

"You said you were working with him to find his brother," Magnus whispered.

"I mean, working with you to find Remi," Lexie corrected.

"Why would you go and say such a thing, Ms. Arden?"

Lexie debated how much to say. "I know where Remi is."

"You do?" Magnus leaned in closer to her. "Since when?"

Emile stood in front of the open cell door. "And where is he?"

Lexie wasn't about to tell him what she'd discovered. "Am I free to go?"

Emile stepped aside. "I explained to the sergeant on duty you're a tourist and not a drug dealer."

"Me, a drug dealer?" She walked through the door. "My mother would crucify me."

"Several people arrested at that little party of yours are well-known distributors." Emile clasped her arm and steered her out of the holding area. "After we collect your things. I'll take you back to your hotel."

She wanted to ask after Renee Batiste, but Magnus's scowl told her not to. Maybe he had a point. Get out of jail first, ask questions later.

It took another fifteen minutes to collect the contents of her pockets and sign her release form. When Emile accompanied her through the back doors of the Orleans Parish Prison Central Lockup Unit, Lexie wanted to shout with joy.

"My car is over here." Emile stepped into the parking lot reserved for police officers and hit the remote on his keychain.

The lights on a black Toyota Forerunner flashed. Lexie peered over her shoulder for Magnus, but he'd disappeared.

She climbed into the front seat of Emile's car and let out a long breath. Her ordeal was over.

"Do you want to tell me about my brother?"

At a loss for words, Lexie struggled to come up with something. How could she tell him?

"I think Remi is dead," she managed to say, buckling her seat belt.

Emile put the key in the ignition and asked, "How do you know?"

"He was at the ritual on Bayou St. John."

"How can he be dead if you saw him there?" He turned the key, and the engine hummed to life.

"Because it was his ghost."

She waited for the cool detective to give her a verbal lashing or at least a lecture about how ghosts didn't exist, but he remained quiet. He drove the car out of the parking lot and turned left.

They traveled in silence. Lexie kept peeking at him, but Emile ignored her and fixed his eyes on the road. She wondered if he planned on taking her from prison to the psychiatric hospital, which after what she'd encountered on the bayou, might be a good thing.

Emile coasted to a stop at a red light. "At the ritual, what did Remi have on? How did he act? Did he say anything?"

Lexie shifted in her seat, formulating her answer. "He was different. Not like how he was in Maine."

Emile turned to her. "Different? How?"

Lexie scratched her head, agonizing over how to make what she encountered not sound too horrible. "He didn't have a shirt on, and there were … marks on his chest."

"Are you talking about tattoos?"

She shook her head. "No, carvings. He had symbols carved into his chest." The light turned green, but Emile didn't hit the gas.

"His eyes …" His voice cracked. "How did they appear?"

The car behind them flashed their headlights.

"Shouldn't you go? The light's green."

He didn't make a move. "His eyes, Lexie. Tell me, what were they like?"

The car honked behind them.

"He didn't have any eyes, Detective. They'd been cut out."

Emile stomped on the accelerator, and the car lurched

forward. Lexie grabbed at the door handle as the speedometer climbed. He passed car after car, racing down the road. When he came to another red light, he slammed on the brakes.

"Hey, what are you doing?"

He slapped the car into park. "Remi's body was found five weeks ago. Right around the time of your fire in Maine. He'd been sliced up, his chest covered with strange symbols, and his eyes cut out." He lunged across the console at her, getting right up in her face. "I had you checked out, confirmed your story with the sheriff on Mount Desert Island, talked to the bank who sold the house, and ran background checks on you and your fiancé. I believed your story, but then you sit here and tell me details locked away in a police report. How did you know about Remi?"

Lexie recoiled, pressing her back against the car door. "The same way I know about your famous ancestor and her cane. I can talk to the dead."

He returned to his seat, laughing, but it wasn't a jovial sound. It was cold and deadly. "You talk to the dead?" The light turned green, and he shifted the car into drive. "Did my dead brother say anything to you at this ritual?"

Sickened by the image of Remi in her head, she nodded. "'I should have stayed away from her. Tell my brother, I should have listened to him.'"

Emile tightened his grip on the steering wheel. "I could use a drink. How 'bout you?"

She let out a long breath. "After the night I've had, absolutely."

Located on the other side of Canal Street in the Warehouse

District, Carmine's Bar wasn't much on the outside. On the first floor of a renovated warehouse, neon signs glowed in the four wide windows facing the street. Inside, the bland interior boasted a few tables, one long wooden bar, and a single standing jukebox right next to the restrooms. All the tables were empty, and the three men at the bar glued to the football game on a flat screen TV didn't notice them walking in.

After showing Lexie to a table, Emile went to the bar and ordered two neat bourbons.

The burn of the alcohol down Lexie's throat soothed her frayed nerves. Her life had been one disaster after another since moving to Maine. When was it going to end?

Emile held his empty glass, examining it for the longest time. Lexie wanted to offer him some encouraging words to ease his obvious pain, but how did one make death sound comforting? Until Magnus, she'd believed it to be so final. Since then, she'd learned there was a hell of a lot more to the afterlife.

"Remi was my younger brother, so I always looked out for him," Emile said in a low voice. "In high school, when he got a lot bigger than me, I still felt like I had to stick up for him, which always made him laugh."

"I liked your brother's laugh," she offered, hoping it helped.

"Yeah, he had a memorable one." He banged his glass on the rickety wooden table. "What he told you, the last phone conversation we had he said he was sorry he hadn't listened to me. I begged him to get out of that cult. But …" He sat back in his chair. "Remi being Remi, he didn't listen. He was always pigheaded."

"Pigheaded people are tough to deal with. I should know." She shot back the rest of the bourbon.

"As a cop, I must advise you to go home, Lexie. Get on the first plane out of here and never come back."

Lexie set her glass on the table. "But you don't want that, do you?"

"No. I have a feeling you can help me find who killed my brother."

"A feeling? Yeah, I know what you mean." Lexie pondered the tense man next to her. "You should tell me what you know, Emile. Might make it easier for both of us."

He rubbed his hands together. "They found Remi along Chef Menteur Highway. It's a long stretch of highway running down to the bayous. Same place we find all the victims of ritual killings. What did him in wasn't the carvings on his chest or what they did to his eyes—it was the bullet in his head."

"How many others have you found like your brother?"

Emile rested his arms on the table as he watched the men at the bar. "This shit has been going on for years in this city. We've got unsolved murders going all the way back to the fifties. Every one of them was sliced up, some had their eyes cut out, some their tongues, but they all died from a bullet to the head."

"What else can you tell me?"

"The symbols on his chest came from voodoo. We had an anthropologist at Tulane confirm it. They're used in a ceremony. Something about allowing a person to possess another. It all sounded way out there to me." He paused and tapped the tabletop. "When you met him in Maine, did he act funny, say the wrong things, or seem afraid of anyone?"

Remi had always made Lexie uneasy during their time together, but he'd also helped her. Or had he? Had he been using her to find the dragon cane all along?

"The first time you laughed, you reminded me of Remi. He was friendly and cordial but also secretive. I got the impression he was hiding something."

"Did anything else happen at the ceremony tonight? Any clue

to help me locate his killer?"

She took a moment to find a way to explain her gift.

"All my life I've received impressions of others around me, but they were fleeting images." She summoned the courage to go on. "Tonight, I encountered souls coming out of the bayou. Dozens of them, and they were so clear. I saw their clothes, their faces, everything. A fur trapper carrying pelts on his back, a Native American in a loin cloth with a bow in his hand. And slaves—so many of them—wearing their shackles around their wrist, necks, and ankles. And this little girl, in a blue gingham jumper. She couldn't have been more than five or six, and she held a blue Teddy bear to her chest. She had her blonde hair braided to the side."

She flinched when Emile stood and backed away from her. She guessed by the open-mouthed look on his face, what she'd described shocked him. And why not? Lexie had experienced the event, and she still had a hard time believing it happened.

Emile wiped his hand over his face, collected himself, and resumed his seat. "Many people have died in those waters. The bayou goes back to when Native Americans lived around it. What you saw was history coming to life through the souls still buried there."

"You almost sound like you believe me."

"I do believe you, Lexie. You want to know why? The little girl you mentioned in the gingham jumper, her name was Ginny Lovell. She disappeared next to the bayou a little over a year ago. Divers combed those waters for days. All they found was her stuffed blue teddy bear. I remember the case because her uncle worked in my department. You just confirmed what we all suspected. She drowned in the bayou."

Lexie fingered her empty glass, wishing she had another drink. "I'm not sure if I should be relieved or terrified by what you told me. I've never experienced anything like this before."

"I want you to come to my place in the French Quarter for breakfast tomorrow. I live at the end of Burgundy Street close to Esplanade." He pushed his glass away. "There's someone you need to meet."

"Who? A shrink?"

He stood from his chair. "No, my Aunt Titu." He pulled his car keys from his pocket. "She's like you; she can talk to the dead."

# Chapter Thirty-Six

"About time you called me back!" Will shouted. "Where in the fuck have you been?"

She settled on the comfy white bedspread and kicked off her muddy tennis shoes. "You said you never used that word." Lexie admired the full moon through her balcony doors glad to hear his voice.

"I've called. I've texted. I've left a dozen messages at the hotel."

She glimpsed the blinking red light on the hotel phone next to her bed. "Yeah, I noticed."

"Where have you been?" His voice was stern.

At a crossroads, Lexie reasoned if she was going to have any life with Will, she needed to be honest with him.

"I went to a voodoo ceremony on Bayou St. John and spirits came out of the water. Dozens of them. And then I got confirmation later from Emile Glapion, Remi's brother, that one of the spirits drowned in the bayou a year ago."

Silence. It went on for several seconds. Lexie checked her phone to make sure the call hadn't dropped.

"Lexie, I'm trying to stay calm, but you're scaring the shit out of me."

"I can communicate with the dead, Will. Not just Magnus, all the dead. At the ceremony, I had this—"

"What were you doing at a voodoo ceremony on a bayou?" The fury in his voice returned. "Was this part of a tour? Where in the hell is your ghost while this is going on? When are you coming home?"

Lexie slapped her hand on the bedspread. "Remi is dead. His brother told me they found his body and—"

"That's it! I'm coming to get you."

"No. I have Magnus and Emile to keep me out of trouble."

"They're not me. And as for Magnus, he is—"

"Magnus has been good to me," she cut in. "Don't be angry with him."

"You're defending him?" he shouted. "He killed a woman, Lexie. You said he tossed her over the edge of the courtyard."

"Yeah, he did shitty things during his life." The image repeated in her head, but somehow she couldn't reconcile the ghost she knew with the man who had committed the heinous crime. "He's different. He's not the same man."

"Because he's a ghost. He's still the same conniving asshole he was in life."

She shook her head. "I can't believe that. We always have the opportunity to change, alive or dead; it's up to us. Magnus is changing. If you talked to him, you'd understand."

"You're not making sense."

She longed to lie down and close her eyes. "Can we do this

later? I'm exhausted."

"No. I need answers. You're hanging out with ghosts, cops, seeing dead people. I'm losing it here!"

Lexie reclined on the bedspread. "Call me in the morning. We can straighten out everything after I've gotten some sleep. You wouldn't believe the night I've had." She yawned into the phone. "I promise we can have a long talk in the morning."

"All right." His heavy sigh sounded laden with emotion; it tugged at her heart. "Go to sleep, baby. Call me first thing in the morning." He hung up.

She dropped the phone right as Magnus showed up next to the bed.

"Where have you been?" Maybe her eyes were playing tricks on her due to fatigue, but he shone brighter, and his clothes were less shabby. "What did you do? Haunt a dry cleaner or something?"

"What are you talking about?" He tilted forward, inspecting her features. "Have you been drinking?"

"After the night I've had, I'm entitled."

He scowled down at her. "What did you learn from the detective?"

"Remi is dead. They found his body."

"And the cane?"

Lexie yanked a pillow out from under the bedspread. "Emile never mentioned it."

"You need to ask. If not on his person, then someone either stole the cane from him, or he stole it *for* them."

She rested her head on the pillow. "You think whoever wanted the cane used him to get it and then killed him."

"That's what I would do."

Another yawn snuck up on Lexie. "I'm so sleepy."

"You've had a long day, an eventful night, and too much alcohol." He reached out, and a gentle breeze removed a wisp of hair from her face. "Sleep, dear girl."

Her mind flooded with images of the ghosts she had seen on the black water.

"Can those spirits come into my room, Magnus?" She pulled the white bedspread around her shoulder, disturbed by her visions. "Are they going to hang around me like you?"

Magnus went to a white plush chair and had a seat. "No one will bother you, I promise. I will stay here all night to watch over you."

Through her foggy gaze, she found comfort in his presence. "Thank you."

"Sleep, my dear." His voice grew fainter as she closed her eyes. "No one is going to hurt you. I'm here to protect you."

The room was dark when she woke with a start. The chair by the balcony was empty. *Where did Magnus go?* She sat up and kicked away the bedspread, unable to go back to sleep.

She went to the bathroom and flipped on the light. When Lexie caught her reflection in the mirror, she jumped back.

"Never wear mascara to bed, Lex."

She turned a pearl handle on the sink and ran her fingers through the water. A rush of cool air enveloped her.

Lexie searched the bathroom for an open window or an air-conditioning vent, but none existed. Something brushed along her right arm. She turned to the mirror and froze.

There, staring back at her, the face of the beautiful woman she'd seen standing at the edge of Bayou St. John. The woman's flowing dark hair fluttered around her face as if teased by a soft breeze. Her snowy white skin accentuated the fire in her black eyes.

"Come back," she whispered to Lexie. "I'm not done with you."

She held up her hand, forcing the image away as a scream escaped from her lips.

"Wake up," a voice called from the darkness clouding her mind. "You're dreaming."

She awoke in her hotel room. The lights were as she had left them.

"It was a dream, dear girl." Magnus hovered over her. "You had a bad dream."

She felt for her phone on the bed. "I saw the woman from the bayou."

"What did she look like?"

Lexie wiped her hand over her brow. "She had this pasty white skin, long black hair, and was covered in dark blotches. She glowed like nothing I've seen before."

Magnus stood back from the bed, his jaw clenched. "I saw her, too. The soul you described." He pressed his hand to his ascot tie. "When I attended a ritual at Bayou St. John with Madam Simone, a woman rose out of the water and floated to the shore. I became entranced by her. But then Madam Simone pulled me away and saved me from the spirit's grip. I learned later seeing the spirit was a harbinger of death. Not long after, I received news my father had died. The next day, I left New Orleans."

"Did she speak to you?"

Magnus shook his head. "No."

"She spoke to me during the ceremony. She said, 'They are waiting for you.' Do you think she's telling me someone's about to die?"

"Of course not. She spoke to you because she recognized your ability. Put it out of your head and go back to sleep."

Magnus went back to his chair and waited as she got comfortable under her covers. He observed the rise and fall of her chest as her breathing slowed. He relaxed into his chair when certain she was fast asleep.

Moments later, the spirit of the woman from the bayou swept out of the bathroom toward the balcony door. Her wet, white gown clung to her curves. Her skin shimmered in the light and her black hair wafted behind.

When the spirit reached his chair, she turned to him. "She is not yours anymore," she said in a breathless voice. "She belongs to all of us."

Unhinged by her black eyes, Magnus remained silent. She glided through the glass doors to the balcony.

Magnus rushed to the balcony, searching for the ghost, but she wasn't there.

At the rail, he viewed the rooftops of a sleeping city and was afraid for Lexie. Magnus had detected the change in the air at the bayou and sensed a door opening during the ceremony. Whatever fate had in mind for Lexie Arden, he vowed to stay right by her side for as long as spiritually possible.

# Chapter Thirty-Seven

Up with the sun, Lexie was refreshed and eager to get to Emile's house on Burgundy Street.

"If he knows you can speak with the dead, Lexie, he may have ulterior motives," Magnus protested as they made the long walk to Emile's home.

Lexie laughed while ducking tourists on the French Quarter sidewalk. "What ulterior motives? What's he going to do? Have me channel dead relatives to find the family jewels?"

Magnus maneuvered in front of her, halting her progress. "You might help him discover secrets, Lexie. The secrets the dead take with them are always valuable to the living."

"Exactly what I would expect from a man who kept plenty of secrets when he was alive. And even more, after he's dead."

Magnus had no witty reply, no cutting remark.

"One day you're going to have to talk to me, Magnus." Lexie stepped around him. "Alive or dead, we all have issues."

"Have you told me your secrets?" he asked as she walked away.

She stopped but did not turn to him, but raised her head to the balcony above. "When I was seven I stole my best friend's rhinestone barrette because I considered it too pretty for her. At sixteen, I cheated on a geometry test, but then found out everyone cheats on geometry tests. At seventeen, I snuck out of my stepfather's house to go out on a date with a boy my mother hated. Hence, the reason I went out with him. At eighteen, I told my two best friends that I'd done it with Fred Hughen when I didn't have sex until I was twenty-one. Short of extra exemptions on my taxes, lying about my weight on my driver's license and wishing I cooked like Martha Stewart, that's about it for me."

He floated up to her. "Why did you lie about having sex with Fred Hughen?"

She bit her lower lip, not sure about sharing something so private with him. *He's dead, who's he gonna tell?* "I lied because everyone was having sex and I wanted to fit in." Lexie waited for him to say something, and when he didn't, she moved in closer. "There's a reason they say confession is good for the soul, Magnus."

"Religion is not reality."

She set out over the cracked and broken pavement, making her way to Burgundy Street.

Lexie checked the address Emile had written on his business card as she stood in front of a three-story, red-brick townhome with black shutters, iron balconies, and a white front door.

"Not what I expected on a cop's salary," Lexie muttered. "I bet this place costs a fortune to keep up. The taxes alone must be—"

"Perhaps you can understand why I told you not to share too much information with him," Magnus edged in. "We don't know enough about his activities to trust him yet."

She pressed the doorbell. "You need to have a little more faith in mankind, Magnus."

He joined her at the door. "Wouldn't dream of it."

The door swung open, and Emile Glapion came forward. His pressed button-down shirt, polished black loafers, and shiny silver watch reminded Magnus of O'Connor's first days at Harvard. But O'Connor never put on airs and hid behind a fake persona. Emile Glapion's pretentiousness irked the hell out of Magnus.

"Come in, Lexie. My aunt has been waiting for you to arrive."

Emile ushered Lexie into an entryway with shiny pine floors and exposed red-brick walls. Above, a brass chandelier hung from a wooden beam.

"Titu is finishing up our breakfast in the kitchen."

"Does your aunt live with you?" Lexie asked.

The entryway opened into a formal living room. With plush yellow velvet furniture and polished oak floors, the room reminded Magnus of his former home. Paintings highlighting the city decorated the walls. The artistry was superb. Magnus slipped closer, wanting to get a peek at the artist's name.

"I live with her," Emile admitted as he guided her toward an alcove dining room off to the side. "This is my aunt's home. It's been in the family for over a hundred years."

Magnus caught the smirk Lexie gave him over her shoulder as she exited the room. He left the paintings and tagged along.

He found Lexie in a modern kitchen with shiny stainless appliances and dark cherry cabinets. She and Emile were chatting with an older woman.

"Lexie Arden," Emile said, turning to a woman with lovely mahogany skin. "This is my aunt, Titu Hebert."

After removing her apron, Titu shuffled across the floor in golden slippers. Her shoes matched her baggy, gold dress and gold turban. She took Lexie's hand, pivoting to face Magnus.

"Are you going to introduce me to your ghost?"

"Auntie Titu, please," Emile begged. "Can we at least have our coffee before we get into the mumbo jumbo?"

"Mumbo jumbo, is it?" His aunt shook her bony finger at him. "Better not mock the power, Emile."

"Can you see Magnus, Mrs. Hebert?" Lexie questioned.

Titu went around Lexie and came right up to Magnus. "You must call me, Titu, Lexie." The older woman nodded at Magnus. "Welcome to my home, Mr. Blackwell."

Magnus graciously dipped his head but did not speak.

Titu's devious smile accentuated her delicate, high cheekbones. "My gift isn't as strong as yours. I can visualize the dead, but I can't hear them. Such ability takes a much greater power than I possess." She returned to a pot on the kitchen stove. "Emile told me what Remi said to you." She lifted the lid of the pot and checked inside. "Your ghost speaks to you as well, doesn't he?"

"Yes, we talk all the time."

The older woman turned off the burner. "You're what they call a *Purs de Coeur* in voodoo. It means pure of heart. There are no impediments to your gift. The dead are as the living to you." She wiped her hands and stepped away from the stove. "There was another like you a long time ago. She reigned as the premier voodoo priestess in this city. Her name was Simone Glapion." Titu headed for the kitchen entrance. "Come, I will show you her portrait."

"You show her, Auntie." Emile went to a cabinet. "I'll take

our breakfast to the courtyard."

Magnus trailed behind as Titu led Lexie down a yellow-painted hallway. They came to a bright room. Along the back wall, a row of windows overlooked a large courtyard.

"We give her the place of honor," Titu announced, making her way to the fireplace.

Magnus took a wary step back when he spied Madam Simone's green eyes. It was the same portrait he had seen in her Mahogany House sitting room. The one of her in the white-beaded gown with her hand gripping the dragon cane.

"It's a beautiful portrait," Lexie said as she stood beneath the painting.

"It hung in her brothel and was rescued from the fire by her daughter, Estelle." Titu found Magnus in the room. "The dragon cane she holds was important to her."

"The cane seems to be important to a lot of people lately." The sarcasm in Lexie's voice was not lost on Magnus.

"And do you know why?" Titu challenged. "Fashioned from a branch of the Sang Noir tree in Holt Cemetery, the cane belonged to the chosen high priestess of the city."

"Holt Cemetery? Is that near St. Louis Number One Cemetery?"

Titu's brief chortle cut through the air. "Holt is the black cemetery outside of the old town and dates back to 1879. Civic leaders wanted to have a place where funerals of the poor proceeded around the city and not through it."

Lexie's attention returned to the portrait. "What about the stones in the eyes of the dragon?"

"Changeling stones," Titu said. "The stones change to represent the heart of the person who possesses the cane. They are pearl in this portrait because the heart of the chosen high priestess for the city is filled with peace."

"In a painting in Magnus's home, he was holding the same cane, but the stones were red. I was told red means hate. Is it true?"

"It is," Titu confirmed. "Mr. Blackwell's an angry man. And angry men do desperate things."

"Are you still an angry man, Magnus?" Lexie asked.

"Not yet, but the day is still young." He gave her a curt dip of his head.

Titu crept closer. "What did he say?"

"He's not an angry man anymore," Lexie told her.

"But his soul is still tainted." Titu examined his black hands and the condition of his clothes. "He must have committed many sins in his life. Why has he not confessed them to you?"

"Me?" Lexie snorted. "Magnus confesses to no one."

Titu's soft *tsk-tsk* grated Magnus's soul. He'd hated the sound in life—his father had used it repeatedly. But in death, it jarred more than ever.

"Your Mr. Blackwell must confess his sins to clear his soul. If he does not, he will remain the tattered and stained creature he is."

"Are you saying Magnus's appearance can change?"

Titu nodded, and her gold turban bobbed. "It's his choice."

"If I hear his confession, will he be free?" There was a hopeful lilt in Lexie's voice; he didn't like it.

Titu held up a weathered hand, curbing Lexie's enthusiasm. "His stain may go away, but free, I don't have the answer. Fate has brought you two together for a reason."

"What reason?" Lexie asked. "We have nothing in common. I find him cocky, arrogant and he's—"

"Here for you, child." Titu cupped Lexie's left cheek. "You have been given a gift. You must use it to help others."

"But I never communicated with ghosts like this before. And last night, at the ritual, when I saw those spirits in the water, I wanted to run—"

"What ritual?" Titu interrupted in a raspy voice.

"At Bayou St. John. A woman named Renee Batiste invited me. She said the ritual would free me of Magnus, but—"

Titu's high-pitched cackle shocked Magnus. Her diminutive exterior belayed the power inside her.

"Renee Batiste was testing you," Titu affirmed. "She summoned the spirits at the bayou to gauge your power. She will spread the word a *Purs de Coeur* is in the city. News will spread quickly. We don't have much time."

"Time for what? I don't understand." Lexie's voice rose, and Magnus sensed her anxiety.

Magnus went to her, hoping to assuage her when Emile entered the living room, clapping his hands.

"Everyone hungry?"

Titu gave her nephew a cutting gaze. "You never told me about the ritual, Emile."

"Auntie, please. I knew it would upset you. Remember what your doctor said—no excitement. It's bad for your heart."

"My doctor be damned. She'll find out about her powers and come after her."

"Who will find out?" Magnus snapped his fingers at Lexie. "Ask them?"

"Who will find out?" Lexie repeated.

"Bloody Mary," Emile replied.

"She will not be happy to learn a challenger to her position as high priestess is in town," Titu added.

Lexie's features sank. "What challenger?" She slapped her hand against her chest. "I'm not challenging anyone to anything. I came here to get my cane back."

"The dragon cane?" Titu confirmed, sporting the victorious half grin of a seasoned soldier about to set off for battle.

Emile waved his hands in the air. "Enough of this. Auntie,

you're upsetting our guest."

Titu's grandmotherly smile returned. "Forgive me, child. My nephew is right. Let us enjoy a nice breakfast, and then we'll talk some more."

"I won't be able to eat a thing," Lexie mumbled to Magnus as they strolled out of the room.

"Stick with the coffee and then press them for answers," he advised.

"What's going on here?"

"I wish I knew," he whispered as his agitation rose. "But I have a feeling it isn't good."

Green ferns in giant red terra cotta pots lined the patio while the gentle gurgling of a waterfall flowing from an open lion's mouth added a soothing atmosphere to the breakfast party. The air felt crisp, the coffee hot, but the french toast on Lexie's plate remained untouched. The mention of Bloody Mary's name, and her possible interest in her abilities, had killed Lexie's appetite.

"Why would Bloody Mary view me as a threat?" Lexie asked while Emile refilled her coffee cup.

Titu put down her fork and sat back in her chair. "Renee Batiste works for Bloody Mary. She needs her. Renee can speak with the dead and has considerable power."

"My sources haven't confirmed any link between the two women, Auntie," Emile countered.

"Your sources aren't my nose." Titu tapped her finger against the side of her nose. "For years, Bloody Mary has had spies all over the city ferreting out any hint of a challenger to her position. Now she's arrived."

Lexie banged her hand on the black iron table. "I'm not a challenger."

"Child, I told you, your gift isn't meant for you, but for everyone." Titu lifted her coffee cup. "The spirits have determined the time has come for you to use it."

Lexie searched for Magnus. Against the wall to her right, he listened in on their conversation. He arched a blond eyebrow at her and shrugged with a causal nonchalance.

Lexie slumped in her chair. "I came to New Orleans to get my cane back, not fight in a duel."

Titu observed Lexie over the rim of her coffee cup. "But what made you decide your cane was in New Orleans?"

"Remi told me he was from here. I assumed he would come back."

"What else? There's more, is there not?"

Lexie fidgeted in her chair. "Well, there was one other thing."

"Lexie, be careful what you tell them," Magnus advised.

"Back off, Magnus," Lexie mumbled. "Who in the hell else are we going to trust around here?"

Titu set her coffee on the table. "Oh, she's feisty. She will make a fine mambo."

Lexie recalled the term. "Mambo? I remember reading something about that."

"Mambo is a high priestess in voodoo," Emile explained.

"Me? A high priestess?" Lexie scoffed at the idea. "But I'm a Presbyterian from Boston. I can't—"

"You can and you will, child." Titu patted Lexie's hand. "I will help you. I will train you. Then you will be ready to face Bloody Mary."

"Are you insane?" Lexie shrieked. "I can't get mixed up with a drug dealer parading around as a voodoo priestess wannabe. I like my life. I want to keep it for as long as possible."

Magnus rushed to her side. "Lexie, calm down. I'm sure there is something we can do."

"Your life isn't yours anymore, Lexie Arden." Titu dismissed Lexie's reservations with a casual wave. "You said something else brought you to New Orleans besides the cane. What is it?"

Lexie clasped her hands under the table, squeezing them together with all her might. She fought to keep her panic in check by concentrating on Titu's question.

"After Altmover Manor burned to the ground, my fiancé, Will, received a check for the entire amount he'd paid for the house. It was delivered to our apartment door by a chauffeur. He told us the check was a gift from a friend." She bit her lower lip, hesitating. "But when the limo pulled away from our apartment building, we got a glimpse of someone in the back. It was a woman, and she had the dragon cane."

Emile wiped his hand over his mouth. "Why didn't you tell me this the first day you came to my office?"

"I didn't trust you."

"She tempted you with the cane," Titu said. "Bloody Mary must have known about your powers all along."

"But how? I didn't have any gift or power or anything until I moved to Maine and met Magnus."

Titu smiled at her. "Destiny has a funny way of pointing us in the right direction."

Magnus leaned over the table next to Lexie. "We were told this Bloody Mary had no gift. How could she have known about you?"

Lexie nodded as she listened to him and then repeated his question.

"Your Mr. Blackwell is sharp. His cunning will serve you both well." Titu stood. "From what Emile told me of the marks on my poor Remi, I suspect he worked for Bloody Mary. She used him to be what we in voodoo call a *sentinelle* or soldier. Like ants send out scouts to survey the terrain, some priestesses will send out those under their spell to gather information. Bloody Mary sent him to find the cane for her. He must have told her about you. Then, after he had served his purpose, she did away with him."

"Titu, this must be a mistake." Lexie rose from the table; her legs wobbled. "It doesn't make any sense. How would she know I would come here or want to get involved? I could have stayed in Boston and forgotten about the stupid cane."

"Bloody Mary couldn't chance letting you slip away. She doesn't have your gift and has been paranoid about losing her grip on the city. Once she learned you existed and had the power to challenge her, she had to seek you out. The reason why she delivered the check in person. Perhaps she hoped to have more time before you arrived in New Orleans, but your coming here was inevitable."

"Titu, I'm no high priestess. I'm a lousy cook. I'm clumsy—I couldn't make the high school volleyball team—and I'm not any good at being an interior designer. I studied it so I wouldn't have to do math."

Titu patted her hand. "We never choose, child. We are chosen. Once the die is cast, all we can do is allow the tide of fate to carry us on our journey." She tipped her head to the side. "And I promise you will have a magical journey, Lexie. A remarkable journey many would envy." Titu gripped her hand. "Come."

She combed the patio for Magnus, but he'd vanished. "Where are we going?"

"To begin your training."

# Chapter Thirty-Eight

Lexie was shown to a windowless room in the rear of the home. Unfinished floors and wood beams in the ceiling gave the room a rustic vibe. Shelves crammed with an assortment of jars and pots lined the walls. Drying herbs draped across long poles scented the air while tulip-shaped sconces on the walls held melted white candles.

"This is my *atelier* or workshop." Titu shuffled to a wooden table in the middle of the compact room. "I mix potions and perform spells here. Rituals are conducted out in the open so all the spirits can attend."

Lexie ran her hand over the table top, caressing the rough wood. "Are you sure this is what I'm meant to do? You might be mistaken."

Titu stretched for a jar filled with white powder on a shelf. She sprinkled some powder on the work table and then turned to Lexie.

"Place your right hand in the center."

Lexie recoiled from the table and frowned. "What is it?"

"Put your hand in the powder and find out."

She spotted Magnus hovering around the closed door. He motioned for her to do as told.

"Ah, you trust him." Titu nodded her approval. "Good. It will make things much easier. If there's no trust, there can be no union between the physical and spiritual world."

She positioned her hand over the powder. "What union?"

"Like with people, a priestess must be bonded to her spirit. Magnus is your spirit but the bond is not yet secured." She tutted at Lexie's hand hovering above the powder. "You must not show any fear in voodoo, Lexie. The spirits will know, and they will not obey you. Open your mind and put your hand in the powder. We haven't got all day."

Fed up, Lexie slapped her hand on the table. A magnetic jolt traveled up her arm as soon as her hand touched the powder. Flashes of light danced before her. She saw things in her mind: the people on the street outside, traffic in the French Quarter. She caught a fleeting conversation between a husband and wife walking along the river; she even heard the Mississippi River churning.

All she had to do was concentrate on an area, and she traveled there. It was as if every sight and sound beyond the house were at her fingertips.

Lexie yanked her hand from the table.

"What did you see?"

"Everything. It was like flying, but so much faster."

"You weren't flying." Titu wiped her hand with a towel. "You were out of your body. A spirit, like your friend over there." She nodded to Magnus.

Lexie eyed the remnants of powder. "What is that?"

"Nothing but baby powder. I had to get you to loosen up and open your mind." Titu tossed the towel to the table. "See what you can do when you let go?"

"Baby powder?" Lexie smelled the talc on her hand. "But I was so free. How did I tap into everything around me? I overheard a couple talking by the river. How is something like this possible?"

Titu took a seat on the bench next to the table. "Lexie, voodoo isn't about magical potions or spells. None of magic is. It's about belief. If you believe you can, then you can. The one thing limiting us in life is our misconceptions. If others tell us something cannot be done … Well, we believe them. But then there are people like you and me. We don't listen to what the others say. We listen to our hearts. That's where magic lives."

"How can this help me with Bloody Mary?"

Titu rocked forward, her smile that of an eager schoolteacher. "She has no heart. Therefore, she has no power over the spirits. Everything she'll do will be nothing but hocus pocus. Spells and ritual anyone skilled in magic can do, but she can't hurt you—not unless you believe she can."

"So what? I'm to keep believing and everything will be all right."

Titu rose to her feet. "It's a start, but I'm going to teach you some things to help you along the way. I'm going to give you a crash course on how to be a high priestess. And we begin with an altar."

Magnus groaned like a child bored with his lessons. His impatient grimace made Lexie giggle.

"Your altar is where your power finds a home. A place to focus your spirit, like a power center. It doesn't have to be anything elaborate: a glass of distilled water—not tap—two candles, preferably white, and some herbs. Basil is best, and flowers to purify your energy." She reached for a bunch of basil hanging from the ceiling. "You will use your altar to purify yourself before any ritual or spell. This helps keep you focused and banishes all evil influences. You will eventually need to make one at your hotel and spend some time with it every day to stay grounded. I will build one for you here, and then you can see how it's done." She handed the basil to Lexie.

She smelled the sweetness of the herb.

"We will work on building up your powers, which I believe are considerable. There are spells we can try to strengthen your ability." Titu returned to the shelves along the wall. "After you have a feel for your gift, we will need to conduct an initiation to join you and your spirit guide. To make you a team." She reached for a book on a shelf filled with jars.

Lexie stole a peek at Magnus. "Since he's my spirit guide, aren't we a team already?"

"You're compelled to each other, but not joined." Titu opened the book and came toward her. "You've not opened up to each other completely. There are no secrets between a spirit and the person he or she follows."

"Yeah, we might have a problem there," Lexie muttered.

Titu dropped the book on the work bench. "I would suggest you two resolve these differences before the initiation. Might not be a pleasant event for either of you if you don't have absolute trust."

Lexie gleaned the open page in the book. "What's this?"

"A simple spell you can try with your spirit." Titu ran her fingers along the words. "I want to see if you can change him."

"Change Magnus? How?"

Titu turned to face Magnus. "Empower him. He's your spirit guide after all. His power flows through you. I want to discover if you can make him stronger."

Magnus stood upright, his face a mask of trepidation. "Lexie, what's she talking about?"

"Stronger to do what?" Lexie asked.

"To move things," Titu answered. "I want you to imagine a ribbon flowing between you. An energy ribbon where you give to him, and he gives to you. Picture him lifting objects, moving things without a body. As you hold the image in your head, raise your arms and call to the spirits to help you."

"What spirits do I call on?"

Titu shrugged. "What spirits have always brought you comfort? What spirits have you turned to for strength?"

"My grandmother. When anything went bad, or when it went well, I talked to my Nana."

Titu patted her shoulder. "Then talk to her, child. She'll hear you."

Lexie took a cleansing breath, rubbed her hands together, and leveled her gaze on Magnus. A black cloud of doubt enveloped her, but she pushed through it.

*I've got to try.*

"You do realize this may all be nothing more than a fool's errand," Magnus asserted.

"Go along with it, all right?"

"As you wish, my dear."

Lexie concentrated on forming a ribbon in her head. She made it white and observed the energy flowing back and forth. The image firmly planted, she called to her grandmother.

"Nana, can you help me?"

A tingle sprouted in her gut, grew into a burning, and then spread outward to her limbs. The white energy ribbon transformed, turning into a blinding white light. She felt it pulsating, building in her body.

Magnus glowed—brighter and sharper than he had ever been. He raised his right hand and inspected it.

"Go ahead," Titu said to him. "Try to pick something up."

Magnus looked to a small jar at the end of the shelf closest to him. He wrapped his hand around the glass. Then he picked it up.

Excitement washed over his features as he held the jar in his hand. "Well done, dear girl."

"He'll be able to move on to bigger things soon enough," Titu explained. "After your initiation, he will be energized by your power."

Lexie let out a long breath and relaxed as Magnus set the jar down. "And then we'll be a team, right?"

Titu went back to her book. "No, becoming a team takes time. Joining is just the first step in your journey together."

Dusk had descended when Magnus and Lexie walked back to the Hotel Monteleone. Tourists crammed the streets. Music blared from the open doors of the bars they passed along the way. In a hurry to get back to her room, Lexie weaved around the slower moving people as Magnus floated beside her.

"You're angry."

"I don't like crowds," she told him. "Especially unruly, drunk crowds."

"You're keeping something from me, dear girl. What is it?"

A group of men holding plastic cups tripped out an open doorway and ran into Lexie.

"Oh, shit, I'm sorry." One young man stumbled back from her. "Let me help you."

She backed away from his extended hand. Magnus rushed up to the drunk.

"No, leave him alone," Lexie shouted, stopping him. "I'm

fine."

Lexie headed down the street again, leaving the incident behind her when Magnus popped up at her side.

"Are you all right?"

She waved behind her to the group of men. "What were you going to do back there? Punch him?"

"Forgive me, but for an instant, I forgot what I am."

"Was that your typical reaction as a man, to lash out at people?" she roared.

"Why are you yelling at me?"

Lexie came to an abrupt halt. "Because I don't know anything about you, Magnus. You still haven't opened up to me. It's like you don't trust me."

He tapped his foot on the sidewalk. "What are you asking, Lexie?"

She stepped closer, detecting the cool indifference he so often showed, but Lexie needed to go beyond his surface to find the deepest reaches of his soul. "How did you get the cane, Magnus?"

"It was a gift," he affirmed in a testy voice.

"A gift?" Lexie stood back, shaking her head at his stubbornness. "Did you lie to your wife the same way you lie to me?"

"I never lied to Katie."

"Did you tell Katie what you did to Frances?"

Silence.

"That's what I suspected." She was about to dart away when he spoke.

"Katie wasn't like most women I associated with. When we met, I believed her to be pure. I was mistaken."

She leaned against an old hitching post on the street. "How did you meet her?"

His tense shoulders relaxed and the ever-present frost in his features slipped away. "We met on the steps of my hotel in Charleston. I had just come from a meeting with some stuffy banker and was angry." A smile crossed his lips. "I rushed outside and bumped into her, stepping on her foot."

The brash, haughty man dissolved as he spoke of Katie. The change in him touched her.

"Was it love at first sight?"

"Not on my part," he admitted. "She intrigued me, but then I never had respected women much before Katie. Except for Frances." Magnus sighed. "I ended up extending my visit to Charleston. We attended parties and took in plays, and when I returned to Boston, I missed her. So I asked her to be my wife. I grew to love her during our marriage."

"Do you miss her?"

"I miss …" He scanned the crowds. "There are still instances when I miss her, but with time I find I think of her less and less."

Lexie sauntered up to him. "How did that feel, Magnus?"

His brow crinkled. "What are you talking about?"

"Being honest. This is the first honest conversation you've shared with me."

He waved ahead to the sidewalk. "We should get back to the hotel. It's getting late."

Lexie didn't bother to pester him for more. The hopes she had cast aside for a stronger relationship with her ghost quickly returned. Perhaps they were a team after all.

# Chapter Thirty-Nine

Lexie and Magnus entered the Hotel Monteleone, arguing about her wanting to skip dinner when a familiar man came across the lobby. Her heart doing cartwheels, Lexie took off running and, after ducking a couple on their way to the check-in desk, ran right into Will's open arms.

"You're here," she said, hugging him close.

Will held her to him. "I didn't want to argue anymore on the phone."

She eased back from his embrace. "What about your job?"

"I told my boss I had an emergency and had to fly to New Orleans right away." Will scoured the hotel lobby. "Is he around?"

Magnus cruised up to them. "This should be amusing. Any idea how you're going to tell him what you're up to?"

"When did you arrive?" Lexie asked, ignoring Magnus.

Will picked his overnight bag off the floor. "I got here about an hour ago, but they wouldn't give me a key to your room."

"What was it you were saying about honesty?" Magnus harassed.

"Never mind." Lexie hooked her arm around Will. "I'll get you a key later."

On the way to the elevators, she listened to him talk about his flight and his first impressions of New Orleans. Magnus remained in the lobby. She was thankful he understood they needed time alone. Or he knew how Will would react when she told him about her plans. Maybe Magnus wanted to stay out of the line of fire.

"Where is he?" Will asked after Lexie opened her room door.

"He's down in the lobby. He came in with me." She dropped her purse and key card on the dresser across from the bed.

"You haven't found a way to get rid of him yet?"

She took a seat on the bed and patted a spot on the bedspread, encouraging him to sit. "Things are a little more complicated between us."

"Don't tell me he'll be joining us on our honeymoon." Will sat beside her. "This trip was supposed to help you get him out of our lives."

She rubbed her hand along his thigh. "It may take more time for us to separate."

Will lifted her chin, forcing her eyes to meet his. "I thought you wanted to get rid of him."

"I want to, but I'm discovering what I have with him is unusual. He's not the only ghost I've communicated with since I've been here."

He dropped his hand. "Please tell me O'Connor isn't back."

"No, he's not here, but other spirits are. I can see them, Will, and talk to them."

"What are you telling me? There will be more like Magnus

hanging around us?"

"No, Will. I'm ..." Lexie lost her nerve. *How can I tell him what I'm involved with? He'll have a stroke.* "I'm working hard to get him out of our lives," she said, sounding upbeat.

His hearty smile returned. "That's what I was hoping for." Will's arms went around her. "How about a proper welcome?" He kissed her hard on the lips.

With all the things she had to tell him, Lexie should have pushed him away and cleared the air before they went one step further, but his kiss erased all her good intentions. The world she'd been living in, the fantasy she'd been enduring, was erased by the reality of his embrace.

She tugged at his white, long-sleeved T-shirt, eager to get it over his head. They laughed as they stripped away their clothes. Once naked, they luxuriated in each other's skin.

The moment Lexie squeezed his butt, he pushed her knees apart and, without hesitation, thrust into her.

Wrapping her legs around his waist, she urged him deeper. Her rational mind screamed about the need for a condom, but she ignored it. Will grunted into her hair, whispering her name, and as the tingle at the base of her spine soared upward, Lexie gave in to her hunger.

She arched her back and gasped, quivering with her release. Her small cry must have excited Will. He slammed into her, and when he moaned, Lexie held him as he came.

Spent, they laid on the bed and enjoyed their intertwined bodies. Lexie's mind returned to her plight. She considered ways to tell him about her plans, but every scenario she visualized ended in another argument. Tired of fighting, Lexie reasoned she needed to save her energy for what lay ahead.

"I didn't use a condom," Will murmured against her neck.

"I know." She pulled his arms tighter around her.

"And if we made a junior, then what?"

She snickered. "Then my mother will be mortified."

He joined her laughter. Lexie relished their glimmer of happiness.

Will trailed tender kisses down her neck. "Angela would die if we told her she was about to become a grandma."

Lexie rolled over to him. "Her expression would be worth nine months of fat fingers and cankles."

Kissing her lips, Will climbed on top of her. She felt his erection against her thigh. He wasn't through with her yet.

"What do you say we do it this way until Junior shows up?"

She cupped his face. "Are you sure? You said you wanted to wait."

"I want you, the baby, the marriage, the white picket fence. I want our life to be perfect."

When he kissed her again, Lexie's unease about their future didn't disappear as readily as before.

*How can we have a perfect life when everything around me is falling apart?*

With her world changing, one question ate at Lexie. Would Will change, too?

Magnus waited in the hotel lobby, entertaining himself with the idle tourists and hotel staff. Lexie needed to spend time with Will, to ease him into her plans and share a few moments in bed. It was what he would have done with a woman, had he been human.

He sighed as he considered the delectable image of pounding into a woman. He still missed the sensation.

Unable to take the confinement of the lobby any longer,

Magnus slipped out the glass doors and stood on Royal Street, listening to the city. Part of him ached to stay near Lexie, but his more rebellious nature needed space.

Out on the street, he clucked at the lapse of decorum in manners and clothing. Magnus took in the shiny lights blazing from each shop window and became acquainted with the modern world.

Times had changed, but Magnus had not. He wondered if he could ever put his old-world ways behind him. He didn't want to spend eternity as a Victorian man stuck in a modern age.

Magnus strutted along the broken sidewalks, and an uncomfortable gnawing erupted inside him. He made his way down Royal Street, and the feeling took over his limbs, guiding his movements. His abrupt gestures, as if he were a puppet, alarmed Magnus. He didn't like it. Something was wrong.

Magnus stood outside the same cooking school where Lexie had first met Renee Batiste. But he kept moving on until he came to rest next door at the Shop of Divination.

Pulled inside by some unseen force, he moved past the entrance until he came face-to-face with Renee Batiste and another woman.

Round, blonde, and with a heart-shaped mouth, the stranger lingered over a table where Renee sat burning herbs.

"Is he here?" the blonde demanded.

Renee searched the smoky room. "I can't see him."

The surly blonde bellied up to the table. "You said this spell would call him to us. What's wrong, Renee?"

Renee sat back. "Perhaps her power is stronger than mine. The girl does have the gift. I sensed it the first moment I saw her."

"Her gift be damned." The aggravated woman slapped the table. "I'm not giving up being high priestess of this town to some nobody. You know how much money is involved. Keep at the spell."

Renee blew on the herbs, creating more smoke. "I still don't see why you don't banish her from the city. You've done it before with others who craved your position."

"I've tried, but my spells don't work on her. I have to find another way to warn her. She needs to back off from tangling with Bloody Mary."

Yanked backward, whatever held Magnus suddenly let go. After he'd been whooshed out the shop and onto the street, he paused to get his bearings. The magnitude of what Magnus had seen astounded him.

He needed to tell Lexie, but it would have to wait. She had enough to handle for the time being. He didn't want to make things tougher for her, especially with Will in the picture.

Magnus set out at a brisk pace toward the hotel. "Things are getting interesting."

Will insisted on going to the best restaurant in town for dinner. Magnus suggested Antoine's, and Will embraced the idea. The impending evening troubled Lexie because Will had never agreed with Magnus about anything.

They arrived via cab at the two-story Creole townhouse on St. Louis Street—home to a New Orleans icon for over a hundred years. Lexie took in the romantic green wrought iron balcony with its hanging ferns. Along the entrance, gaslights flickered while inside the restaurant's warm yellow glow beckoned to her.

Lexie checked the wrinkle on her black trousers, worried her outfit would be too casual. Will, in his gray suit and black tie, made her feel frumpy.

After the cab sped away, Will took her hand. “Where is he?”

Magnus rested his shoulder against the wall of the restaurant, his scowl leveled at Will. “You do realize this is tantamount to torture for me.”

Lexie gave him an encouraging smile. “How ’bout I order something you would like for dinner? That way you can watch me eat it.”

“You vixen,” he grumbled.

“What’s wrong?” Will asked. “He wanted us to come here.”

Lexie tugged at his hand. “Never mind about him.”

When they walked past Magnus, he groaned with annoyance.

A simple hallway with dark paneling ended at a podium with two potted ferns on either side. A gray-haired gentleman in a tuxedo greeted them with a brief nod.

“Welcome to Antoine’s. Do you have a reservation?”

Will cleared his throat. “Ah, no. The hotel where we’re staying said a table for dinner shouldn’t be a problem.”

Magnus arched over to the podium and checked the reservation book.

“It’s not a problem. We have seating available in our main dining room,” the host told them.

Relieved Magnus had not pulled one of his stunts, Lexie relaxed. She didn’t want to have to explain his abilities to Will.

*I’ll never hear the end of it.*

They were led through a long hallway and past the Hermes Bar, filled with a boisterous evening crowd. Soon they entered the spacious all-white main dining room.

Once shown to a white-linen table in a cozy corner, Will helped Lexie to her seat. Their host placed two menus on their plates.

Once in his chair, Will turned to Lexie. “Where is he now?”

“At the table.” She patted the place setting next to her. “He’s going to help me order."

Will swiped the napkin from his plate and put it in his lap. "Maybe we should get him a bell so I'll know where he is all the time. Like a cat."

Please tell the man I am here for you. And I am not a cat." Magnus rolled his eyes. "I detest cats."

"Don't call him a cat, Will. He's my spirit guide, so please show some respect."

Will snatched his menu. "Respect? How can I respect a man I can't see?" He perused the menu. "And since when has he been your spirit guide?"

Lexie picked up her menu. "It's something I've learned since we've been here."

"Put your menu down," Magnus ordered. "I already have your meal planned."

She obliged him and set her menu aside. "What am I having?"

"The Chateaubriand in a Béarnaise sauce for your entrée. It's done to perfection here."

She gave him an indulgent smile, but Lexie dreaded eating such a rich meal. But if it kept her ghost happy …

"What else have you learned since coming to the city?" Will posed from behind his menu. "You must have discovered something more."

"Now that you mention it. Ah, today we went—"

"Welcome to Antoine's," a waiter in black pants with a white apron sang out. "What can I get you folks to drink?"

"Champagne," Will said, astonishing Lexie.

"Very good, sir." Their waiter cleared the two extra plates from the table. "May I recommend the Krug Grand Cuvée Brut?"

"Sounds wonderful."

"Are we celebrating?" The waiter balanced the plates as a busboy rushed to the table.

"Yes." Will put his menu to the side. "We're getting married."

After congratulations from the waiter, Lexie waited until they'd been left alone before she confronted Will.

"Why did you say we're getting married? We're already engaged."

"We should change our status while we're here in New Orleans. I was thinking a small ceremony. No fancy wedding—none of Angela's nightmarish plans—just you and me. What do you say?"

She sat back in her chair. His statement had knocked the air from her lungs. "When … when did you decide this?"

"You need to tell him, Lexie." Magnus was in her ear. "Before you marry him."

Which calling did she heed? The one of her heart to be with Will or the one in her soul to find her place with Magnus?

*Do I have to choose?*

Will gripped her hand. "After our fight on the phone the other day, I went to my boss and said I needed a week off because I wanted to get married. Jake Forrester told me to take two weeks." He reached into his pocket and pulled out a blue velvet jewelry box. "I got this to seal the deal."

Will pried open the small box. A one-carat, round diamond set in platinum winked back at her.

"I should leave." Magnus got up from the table.

He floated through the window next to them. She wanted to call him back but didn't.

"So, what do you say?" Will slipped the ring on the third finger of her left hand.

The ring sparkled in the light and Lexie's stomach locked up. Frozen tentacles of dread seized her heart. She might lose him, but what choice did she have?

"Will, I need to tell you something."

He set the box on the table. "What? You don't like the ring?"

"No, I love the ring, I do." She sucked in a torturous breath. "Things have happened to me since coming to this city. You need to hear everything and then if you still want me ..."

She didn't have the strength to utter those words. Instead, she went into a detailed account of her adventures: her night on Bayou St. John, her brief incarceration, her meeting with Titu, and her upcoming initiation into the voodoo religion.

Her confession garnered only a smattering of disapproval from Will. Lexie expected a sterner reaction when she mentioned her time in the Orleans Parish Lock-Up, but he remained calm, much to her relief. When she came to an end, highlighting her yearning to pursue strengthening her abilities, Will remained silent—too silent.

"Aren't you going to say anything?"

With his lips pressed together, Will let go of her hand. His head lowered, he played with the ring box.

"If you become this voodoo priestess, will it make you a better cook?"

The breath Lexie had been holding rushed out of her lungs in happy laughter.

"Baby, if you want to become a voodoo priestess and talk to ghosts, I'm with you." He took her left hand and kissed the ring. "I love you, Lexie. No amount of voodoo or ghosts is going to change us."

Her tears gathered, and her heart lifted. She vowed to find a way to make both her worlds exist together. "When I'm done, we'll get married. Okay?"

"Sure, but are you going to be able to practice voodoo in Boston, or are you going to have to stay here?"

"I never considered if—"

The *pop* of a champagne cork interrupted them.

"Compliments of the management," their waiter announced, flourishing a Dom Pérignon bottle.

A busboy placed two long crystal flutes on the table. Lexie combed the dining room for Magnus, but he never returned. The idea of him not sharing in their celebration choked her happiness. Magnus had become so ingrained in her life; she wanted him to share in all her experiences—like family.

"To us," Will toasted, holding up his flute to her.

Lexie snapped up her glass. "To our new life." Before she raised the glass to her lips, she mumbled, "And to my new beginning."

# Chapter Forty

The following morning, Lexie walked hand in hand with Will to Titu's house on Burgundy Street. She remained painfully aware of how Magnus stayed away. He had not returned to the restaurant after she'd ordered Chateaubriand with Béarnaise sauce to please him. And as the sun rose the following morning, he still had not returned.

"You say this woman, Titu, is helping you?" Will asked as they neared her townhome.

"She's a priestess—or was, years ago. I'm sort of like her apprentice. She's going to show me how to develop my power."

"Are you sure you want this, Lexie?"

She stopped before Titu's door. "Don't ask me to explain why. This feels right to me. I was unsure at first, but then Titu told me about the people she used to help—the people I could help—and it made sense. Shouldn't I use what I have to help others?"

He stood by as she rang the doorbell. "Of course. I'm just wondering how—"

The door opened. Titu held a mug of strong smelling coffee in her hand. She wore a bright yellow muumuu with matching slippers and turban.

"Ah, Titu, this is my fiancé, Will Bennett. He came down from Boston yesterday and—"

"Your Mr. Blackwell showed up here earlier." She sipped her coffee. "He's been pacing my living room floor."

"Magnus is here?" Lexie bounded in the door. "Why is he here?"

"Probably wanted to give you and your fiancé time alone."

Will extended his hand as he entered the home. "Pleasure to meet you, Titu. Lexie has told me so many things about you."

Titu ignored his outstretched hand. "I don't need you hanging around while I work with Lexie and her spirit."

Will dropped his hand. "Do you want me to leave?"

"Emile!" Titu hollered.

Her nephew showed up at the door, dressed for a day at the precinct and with a slice of toast in his hand.

"Emile, this is Lexie's fiancé. Will Bennett." Titu gave Will a dismissive wave. "He needs a tour of the city. A long one."

"Auntie, are you asking me to—?"

Titu shoved Emile out the door. "Don't come back until sunset."

"I have to work today," Emile argued from the sidewalk still holding his toast. "I'm sure Will can stay with you—"

"I need time alone with Lexie and her ghost." Titu pointed to the street. "Go. Both of you."

Will kissed Lexie on the cheek and then stepped back out the front door. "I'll, ah, take a walk."

"Emile," Titu called. "Take him to work with you. Keep an eye on him." She shut the door on both men.

"Titu, you can't expect Emile to keep Will company all day," Lexie argued. "And Will came to New Orleans to be with—"

"You need to concentrate," Titu interrupted. "He will be a distraction."

Lexie gathered there was no point in fighting with her and headed for the entryway. When she arrived in the living room, she saw Magnus standing beneath Simone Glapion's portrait.

"Why did you leave last night?"

He kept his distance from her. "Did you have a pleasant evening?"

"You'll have problems if the two men in your life are at odds," Titu asserted. "You must make them learn to live together."

Lexie's apprehension, like a belt around her chest, ratcheted up another notch.

Titu marched to the doorway. "We have lots to do."

She scurried behind her, still gripping her purse. "Is there any way I can get some coffee before we start?"

Titu kept going. "No coffee before a spell. The caffeine interferes with your clarity."

"I'm not sure how much clarity I'm going to have without it," Lexie complained.

"At least you can drink coffee," Magnus added while floating next to her. His trademark grin returned. "Try getting through a morning of Titu without it."

After gathering at the work table in the atelier, Lexie and Titu hovered over an open book while Magnus waited by the door.

"I don't get it." Lexie sat back on the bench and folded her arms. "I just say the words on this page, and I will summon a spirit."

"Most spells aren't complicated." Titu went to some potted plants she had lined up in a row along a shelf. "People in this business aren't exactly brain surgeons." She snapped off a twig from a plant and brought it back to the workbench. "Bloody Mary doesn't have your gift, but she can perform powerful spells."

"What's that?" Lexie picked up the sprig Titu put on the table.

"Sage. You usually burn it when dried to clear a space of bad energy, or when doing a spell to summon good powers to you. But when green, sage can be a magnet for spirits." She moved the open book on the table closer to Lexie. "When you speak the words, say them over the sage, but you must feel it here." She placed her hand over the center of Lexie's chest. "This is where your gift comes from. Whenever casting a spell or doing a ritual, always work from here."

Still not sure what to do, Lexie picked up the book and held it as she spoke over the sage. While enunciating the jumble of words, Lexie focused on her center. The entire time she felt silly.

"You'll never get anywhere unless you tap into your ability," Magnus suggested.

Lexie scowled. "Do you mind?"

He came to the table and took a seat on the bench across from her. "Look at me when you speak."

Her scowl deepened. "Why?"

"You're summoning a spirit. I am a spirit. Concentrate on me and visualize what you hope to accomplish."

"Ah, your Mr. Blackwell is coming closer to help you." Titu came around the table to Magnus. "He senses you must work together to be successful."

"I can also sense Ms. Titu has had too much coffee this morning," Magnus declared.

Lexie fought to contain her laughter.

"Pay attention, dear girl. We must please the old bat. Otherwise, you will never get back to Will by sundown."

She fastened her sights on Magnus, but couldn't take his harsh stare and instead concentrated on his white tie.

As she repeated the strange words, Lexie pictured a flow of energy from her chest. Minutes passed, a tickling manifested swelling like a flame exposed to oxygen. The heat took over and devoured all thought. Magnus's tie became a tad bit clearer as the fervor spread to her limbs. His image sharper than before, the light he radiated burned brighter.

"Ah, there in the corner," Titu whispered. "Someone is here."

A stitch of fear caught in Lexie's stomach as mist crept up from the floor. Lexie became transfixed by the apparition forming in the center. A woman with a turban—not unlike the one Titu wore—and dark chocolate eyes beckoned to Lexie. She had a commanding presence and an intoxicating aura.

"Mon Dieu," Titu mumbled.

The ghost smiled, and the burning in Lexie's chest exploded into a thousand rays of light. Lexie gasped and the room flooded with light. Her chest raised up, lifting her off the bench.

Then everything stopped. The light, the ghost, even the sensation vanished.

All three sat around the table, gaping at the small room.

"A successful test, I would wager," Magnus said, breaking the silence.

Lexie shifted around to Titu. "What was that?"

Titu grinned like a proud mother. "A blessing from an extraordinary spirit. She is watching over you."

Lexie examined her hands, still shaking from the after effects. "I'm vibrating. It's like I had the sun inside me."

"You had the light, child. The white light of life. Everything we are, and everything we become, like your Mr. Blackwell, belongs to the light. You tapped into it."

"What do I do now? How do I get it back?"

Titu nodded, considering the question. She maneuvered around the table and went back to the shelf. "We must speed up your training."

"That may not be enough," Magnus murmured.

"What are you talking about?" Lexie whispered.

His gaze went to Titu, rummaging through a shelf behind Lexie. "Yesterday, after Will arrived, I went for a walk. While out among the crowds, I was pulled like a fish on a hook to the cooking school you attended. I couldn't resist. In the shop next door to the school, I discovered Renee Batiste and another woman. It was Bloody Mary. They had summoned me. At least, they attempted to. Bloody Mary wants to send you a warning not to challenge her for control."

Lexie curled her fingers into a fist, her nails digging into her palm.

"Why didn't you tell me this last night?"

"And ruin your dinner with Will? The man hates me enough." Magnus's snort bounced around the room. "I'm dead, Lexie, not insane."

*Bloody Mary? Things are getting out of control.*

Lexie jumped from the bench and paced the floor.

"Magnus told me Bloody Mary knows about me," she announced. "She and Renee Batiste summoned him to Renee's shop. He says they want to send me a warning."

Titu set the jar in her hands on the table. "If she gets to your Mr. Blackwell, she can cut off your link to the spirit world. She believes it will make you weaker, but she's wrong." Titu pressed her finger to her mouth. "We need to move up your initiation ceremony. Tomorrow night you will become a priestess. The next morning, you and I will pay a visit to Bloody Mary."

Lexie stopped pacing. "What? You want to go into the lion's den?"

"This lion has no teeth." Titu sat on the bench. "After what I just saw, I'm certain you're a lioness to be feared."

The new moon rose in the sky as she stood on the balcony of her hotel room. Below, the French Quarter streets teemed with tourists, shouting, dancing, and soaking in the sights.

She enjoyed their energy. There was something magical about New Orleans. Although she'd only seen a small section of the city, Lexie understood why Magnus had been so enamored. She dreaded returning to Boston. Life wouldn't be the same away from the Big Easy.

Lexie moved to go inside, and her foot brushed against the books from Aimee's shop she'd left on the floor. She'd hoped studying the different components of voodoo—like the initiation ritual, and the dreaded *haute défi*—would appease her restlessness. But it only kept her from sleeping. She glimpsed Will, deep in slumber on the king-sized bed and envied him.

"You have a big day ahead of you tomorrow," Magnus said as he cropped up on the balcony. "You need to rest."

Her mind brimmed with questions. She tried to force images of Bloody Mary and her evil intentions from her head, but they returned more terrifying than before. Fed up with fighting demons, she embraced the inevitability of their situation.

"I don't think I'll be able to sleep again."

Magnus observed Will through the glass doors. "Did you tell him your initiation got moved to tomorrow night?"

"Not yet." She shook her head. "I'm not sure he should be

there."

"He'll want to be there for you."

Lexie willed the icy dread numbing her heart to go away. "What if he's so freaked out by what happens, he leaves me, Magnus? I don't know what I'd do if I lost him."

"He loves you. He won't be scared off. Will's a good man. Better than I ever was."

She recalled all she'd uncovered about her ghost. What other secrets hid behind his grin? What would happen when she discovered them?

"Are you ready for tomorrow? We'll be joined, and everything you are will be revealed to me."

Stoic as ever, he faced the French Quarter rooftops. "Whatever you learn, know it's not who I am. I've changed."

"I believe it. I mean if spirits can't change, then what hope do we have for the living?"

"Life isn't about having a heart and lungs, Lexie. It's about having a soul, and as long as you have that, you can change."

Will rolled over in the bed. Her heart broke for the man she loved. What must her decisions be doing to him?

"He spent the evening telling me about all the sites he'd seen in the city. He went on and on about the architecture and how much he loved it. He reminded me of you." She raised her head and faced Magnus. "I want you to promise if anything happens to me, you will watch over Will. Make sure he's okay."

"Nothing will happen to you, dear girl." He winked at her. "You have me and your super powers, remember?"

Still swimming in doubt, she slipped back into her hotel room. She cuddled next to Will, and in a loving reply, he turned over to pull her into his arms. Nestled against him, Lexie enjoyed their last night together as a normal couple. After tomorrow, she wouldn't be the same.

# Chapter Forty-One

With Magnus discreetly behind them, Lexie and Will arrived at Titu's before sunset. They'd spent the day doing touristy things. Riding the streetcar down St. Charles Avenue, dining at a splendid outdoor café in the French Quarter, and visiting museums.

The getaway had helped her. But once inside Titu's home, the prospect of what awaited made Lexie itch to sprint out the door. The thrilling encounter with the powerful spirit the day before kept her doubts from consuming her.

"Lexie and Magnus will come with me," Titu said to Will after they gathered in the living room. "She will remain locked in the atelier from sundown to sunup. You won't be able to have any contact with her during this time. I'll be checking on her to make sure everything is progressing smoothly. In the morning, I will make us all breakfast, but you must not ask her any questions about what happened. She will need time to process the changes within her."

"What changes?" Will frowned.

"She will be a much stronger woman, a mambo. Lexie Arden will die tonight, and another version of her will be born."

She waited for Will to explode. Lexie guessed he had a flurry of questions. She had some of her own, but he didn't need to know that.

"It will be okay." Lexie patted his clenched right fist. "I'll still be the same old me."

He exhaled a ragged breath and then kissed her cheek. "We can still make a run for the airport if you want?" he whispered as his lips grazed her ear.

She shook her head, the inevitability of her fate settling into her bones. "I can't run away from this. No matter where I go, it will be with me."

Titu pried them apart. "The sun is setting. Come. We must prepare you."

As Titu led Lexie and Magnus to her workshop, Lexie caught Magnus giving her a thorough going over.

"What's your problem?"

"The day you walked into my home, I knew you had the gift to work with spirits, but lacked tenacity. I was wrong."

The door of the workshop loomed ahead of her.

"What choice do I have?"

"Not to worry, Lexie. I will be with you. I'll make sure nothing happens to either of us."

"Wow, Magnus." She chuckled, releasing the tension building in her chest. "You almost sounded sincere."

"I told you, I've changed."

Titu waited before the plywood door. "I have lit the candles, sage is burning, and I've made a small altar for you." She moved closer to Lexie, touching her shoulder. "Did you bring the things you want with you?"

Lexie withdrew the picture of her grandmother from her jeans pocket, along with the engagement ring Will had given her.

"I will put the ring and picture on the altar," Titu instructed. "Then you can take your seat on the bench. There's water and lemonade on the table if you're thirsty or get lightheaded. Sleep if you're tired." She rested her hand on the back of a chair set up by the door. "I will be here. If you need me, call."

Lexie twisted her fingers together as her breathing sped up. "What else do I do?"

Titu touched the center of her chest, and as if pressing a button, a pulsation of peace cascaded through Lexie.

"Keep your center open all night," Titu advised. "Allow the light to flow through you, to understand you, to accept you."

"Shouldn't there be more?"

Titu opened the workshop door. "It's enough."

Magnus escorted Lexie into the cramped room.

"Mr. Blackwell, your job is to help her, protect her, and keep the bad spirits away," Titu said. "To do that, you two must become one. Open the ribbon of energy I showed you. Keep it flowing between you all night long."

At the table, Lexie waved her hand in front of her nose. The smoke in the air was thick and made her yearn to sneeze. She waited as Titu placed her engagement ring and the photograph at the altar set up on the tabletop. It consisted of two jars of water surrounded by white candles sprinkled with dried herbs, and in the center, a silver cross. Scattered on the shelves and in the tulip-shaped sconces around her, more white candles flickered.

"Can we talk?" Lexie asked as Titu came up to her.

"Talking is encouraged between a priestess and her spirits."

She brushed Lexie's cheek. "Don't be afraid. Nothing can hurt you. In the morning, you will be different. You will be in tune with all things."

Then she spoke words Lexie did not understand. When she finished, Titu stepped outside and closed the door.

"She said a prayer for you," Magnus told her. "In French. A blessing."

"You speak French?"

He tilted his head while wiping his hands together. "I'm the product of an upper-class Victorian education. French was required."

Lexie rhythmically tapped her fingers on the table as her mouth ran dry. The coming storm registered with her senses like the dropping mercury of a barometer. She wanted to be sure of the man responsible for her spiritual care, but her certainty wavered.

"Anything else you care to tell me before this begins?"

Magnus smirked. "Ah, I love a determined woman."

An ice-cold draft wafted into the room.

"Here it comes," Lexie whispered.

"What is it?"

"The room got colder."

He relaxed his wide shoulders. "The games are about to begin."

The temperature dropped. Lexie shivered as she detected her breath.

"Concentrate on me," Magnus directed. "Remember the ribbon? Let's work on it."

Lexie pictured the white ribbon between them, flowing back and forth, and as she did, the cold around her subsided. A flush of warmth ran from Lexie's cheeks to her toes, helping to relax her.

Some comfort came from having her connection with him. The ribbon grew wider and flow increased between them. The burning in her center took over. Her eyelids drooped as the heat permeated her muscles. The ribbon pulsated, its white light brighter than before. Flashes of people came and went, but she didn't recognize anyone.

A cloud of smoke wafted up from the table. A beautiful woman with honey-blonde hair formed in the smoke. She'd seen this particular woman before—Frances. Lexie assumed she'd intruded on some image of Magnus's past as the snapshots of Frances streamed by.

"My thoughts are yours, Lexie." His deep voice resonated in her head.

Other women materialized in the smoke. A bevy of young, attractive women, naked and helpless, paraded before her. A man's hands caressed their round asses. But the women were not laughing or acting anxious for the encounter. Fear poisoned their beauty. Lexie perceived Magnus's intentions, and a sickening feeling rose up her throat.

When he rammed into them, forcing their flesh apart, she covered her mouth. He hurt them, listened to their screams, and Lexie knew he relished the sound. Every thrust registered with her like movement in a car, rocking her to and fro. The excitement he experienced was hers, and the satisfaction he got when he came snaked through her, making her gag.

"This is what I am," his voice rumbled in her head. "This is what I've been afraid to show you."

A flash of white blinded her and then she stood in a cozy sitting room. A green marble fireplace, oak-paneled walls, and built-in shelves stuffed with leather-bound books helped reassure Lexie. Mahogany furniture upholstered in pale yellow damask graced the room, but what sat above the mantel escalated her anxiety. A woman wearing a white beaded gown with the dragon cane at her side peered down from the painting.

The same painting graced Titu's living room.

Figures materialized all around. Magnus, along with the woman in the portrait, sat in front of a fireplace. The light from the fire highlighted Simone Glapion's café au lait skin and vibrant green eyes. The two chatted, and Lexie gathered from Magnus's hint of a smile he respected the businesswoman's acumen. Their conversation escalated into an ugly row. Their voices rose, and Magnus stood. He threw his drink into the fireplace. The sound of crashing glass echoed throughout the room.

Simone Glapion challenged him; her shoulder's squared, she provoked him with her words, adding to the anger contorting his features. Magnus ripped the dragon cane from her hand. His evil grin as he held the cane terrified Lexie. She knew what he was feeling; the same thing she'd experienced the first time she'd held the cane—its power.

Simone grabbed for the cane, but he was too fast for her. He raised the handle high in the air, and Lexie cringed. When Magnus brought the dragon-head handle down on Simone Glapion's head, Lexie wanted to vomit. The *crack* of the cane connected with the woman's skull reverberated through her bones.

An injured Simone writhed in pain on the floor as blood trickled down her temple. Despite her pleas, Magnus raised the cane once more.

Lexie could not turn away or blot out the image as Magnus hit her again and again. Simone Glapion became an unrecognizable mess. Her long brown hair tinged with bright red blood had come undone from her fancy coif and lay spread out beneath her on the floor.

Panic twisted Magnus's face. He showed no regret over his actions. He put the bloody cane aside and removed books from the shelves around him. He stuffed them into the fireplace and arranged some books in a line from the fire to the lifeless Madam

Simone. Within minutes, the fire had spread. Magnus gathered up more books and flung them about, adding fuel to the flames. Satisfied, he collected the cane and walked out of the room.

The images faded. Lexie wilted, devastated by the vision. "You killed her the same way Jacob O'Connor killed you."

"You have all my secrets, Lexie. You've witnessed my sins. Am I to be damned for all eternity?"

When Lexie's sight returned, what greeted her was not his cruel grin, but something much more horrific. The workshop overflowed with spirits. Men, women, children, all in a variety of period clothing, floated above the table and crowded every nook of the cramped room. The dead were everywhere.

Magnus sat before Lexie, dissecting her every move. "Are you all right?"

She wanted to shout at him to look around, but he couldn't see the dead crammed into the workshop. It was her vision. No one had prepared her for this many. Her grandmother had spoken of a few spirits haunting her, not a whole village.

A rustle arose in the corner of the room. The spirits parted, and Lexie waited as a path opened up. The gathering of souls bowed as another came forward.

The same spirit of the woman she'd summoned the day before slowly approached. Gliding on an unseen wind, she wore a flowing white cotton dress and a red turban.

"You need to let it in, *mon petite*," the spirit told her. "Let it in so you can be strong."

Lexie was dumbstruck. Could she change her mind? This was more than she'd bargained for.

The woman floated up to Lexie and placed her ghostly hand on her chest—the same spot Titu had touched. An intense ray of white light rushed into Lexie. The light took over her body, shooting out her fingers and toes. She rose from her bench carried by invisible hands. The ceiling came rushing toward her, but Lexie was powerless to stop her momentum.

She became inundated with images, sounds, smells, and tastes of the city around her. A dog barked down the block. A couple had sex in their bedroom. A baby cried for more of her mother's milk. She tasted the fried soft shell crab diners ate in a restaurant a few blocks away. Everything came at once, overwhelming her.

A loud *bang* echoed in the room. The light vanished, and Lexie went crashing to the ground. Depleted of her strength, she barely had enough energy to breathe. Every muscle hurt, and she craved water.

Then everything went black.

The sun crept under the flimsy door when Lexie opened her eyes. Still on the floor, she shot up and backed away until the plywood door stopped her. Her eyes wide with fear, she searched the room for spirits. She shook as she remembered the hundreds of faces entreating her for help, their voices swirling in her head.

"You've been out for hours," Magnus said.

The sight of Magnus elicited images of a bloody and beaten Simone Glapion. Her shaking transformed into violent trembling.

"Stay away from me, you son of a bitch!"

Magnus floated toward her. "It's over. You understand me."

"I don't understand you one damned bit! You killed her. You beat her to death with the dragon cane and then left her to burn."

"Your visions were of the man I was. The reason I wear these reminders." Magnus held up his black hands. "But it's not who I am now."

"Bullshit," she hissed through clenched teeth.

The door yanked open. "What's all the screaming about?" Titu demanded.

Lexie got up and barreled out the door.

"Lexie?" Titu called after her. "What happened?"

Lexie kept going until she found the entryway leading to the front door. She heard voices behind her—Will called her name—but she couldn't stop. Lexie had to get away from Magnus. She would never be able to look at him again without thinking of his brutality and the misery he caused.

On the sidewalk, she grimaced against the sun while gulping in fresh air. *What the hell is the universe thinking to attach such a twisted soul to me?* Lexie put her hands on her knees as exhaustion hit her.

How would she be able to regard Magnus as her spirit guide when his soul sickened her?

As her breathing settled, Lexie stood up and surveyed the early morning traffic on Burgundy Street. She couldn't put her finger on it, but something was different. The air, the colors of the buildings, the sounds of the traffic, and people moving about had all changed for her. She'd become attuned to every nuance, every slight whisper in the breeze.

A moth dashed in front of her and she heard its tiny wings flapping. The city noises should have made the moth undetectable, but to Lexie, the sound was like waves crashing against the shore. The colors on its wings seemed so vibrant; she yearned to touch it and discover if the mirage was true.

She raised her hand to the small insect and became cognizant of her movements. She sensed every tendon and muscle flexing in her arm. The fatigue lifted from her body, and as she stretched her limbs, a burst of energy overtook her.

Her head cleared, and an unusual clarity surfaced. The horror of the night before retreated, and a purposeful quiet blanketed her soul. In her heart, she no longer feared the future—she welcomed it.

Like a long runway stretched in front of a plane, her purpose lay before her. Help the lost. Give comfort to the grieving and assurance to the ones plagued by more questions than answers. Her path was clear. She understood why the spirits had chosen her.

*And Magnus?* The nagging voice lingered in the air around her like an unwelcomed fly. Doubt's malicious grip still choked her. Perhaps she needed time to acclimate to her new world. The problem of how to deal with Magnus she could postpone for another day.

# Chapter Forty-Two

"I'm going to take you away from here." Will came up and took her arm. "Let's get some breakfast."

From Burgundy Street, he guided her back toward the river. He didn't speak as they strolled along. Lexie, grateful for the quiet moments, needed to contend with the blitzkrieg of information coming from the other people on the sidewalk, the homes and shops around them, even the dogs on leashes passing by.

They arrived at the green and white canopy of Café Du Monde. Lexie inhaled the aroma of coffee and sweet beignets.

Will found a table toward the back of the patio, facing a quiet alleyway next to the river floodwall. After placing his order with their server, he sat back in his chair.

"Do you want to talk about it?"

She crumpled in her chair. "I have no idea how to begin."

He arched forward, examining her left hand. "Where's your ring?"

"On the altar, back at Titu's house. We can get it later."

He clasped her hand. "Talk to me, baby."

With Will's encouragement, she recounted her initial feelings in the smoky atelier and explained about the white ribbon of energy. But when she came to her visions of what Magnus had inflicted on so many women, her voice failed her.

Their coffee and beignets arrived. Lexie's hands trembled as she reached for her cup. She sipped her coffee, and when the warm liquid hit her stomach, a sense of normality returned.

"He killed Simone Glapion," she divulged after a long silence. "The woman who originally owned the dragon cane. In the sitting room of her house, he bashed her head in with the handle."

Will put his coffee down. "You saw him murder her? How?"

"When we connected through the ribbon I told you about, it showed me his life—every disgusting detail." She slammed the cup on her saucer. "I want nothing more to do with him."

"How are you going to do that?" Will picked up a beignet. "He's your spirit guide."

She reached for a powdered sugar-coated donut. "Maybe I can send him back."

He took a bite of his beignet and returned it to his plate. "Look, I'm not going to sit here and pretend I comprehend a tenth of what's going on, but I do know you're stuck with him. So you'd better figure out a way to deal with it."

Lexie took a bite of her donut. Powdered sugar trickled down her chin.

"What else happened?" Will asked. "Seeing what old Magnus did in his former life couldn't have been enough to flip you out. You're a level-headed woman, Alexis Arden, and you don't go flying off the handle unless you experience something you don't understand."

She gulped down her food. "What makes you think what I saw with Magnus didn't freak me out?"

"Because you've seen worse on the news, on the Internet, and on the streets of Boston. It may have been disturbing to observe him beating a woman to death, but you aren't naive about his past. He wouldn't have been haunting Altmover Manor if he'd been a good man."

She held back a cutting rebuke.

He picked up his half-eaten beignet. "What else happened?"

Lexie told him of the other spirits.

"You feel any different?"

She sat back, checking out the tourists entering the establishment. "Yeah, I do. It's like I'm connected with everything. I'm stronger, smarter, more in tune with the people and things around me."

Will wiped his hands on a paper napkin. "What do you do with this power?"

She detected the humming in her heart. The vibration had been there since the moment she'd opened her eyes on the atelier floor. "I'm supposed to use this to help people. Somehow, I have to give back what I've been given."

He nodded, stretching for his coffee. "How do you do that?"'

"Titu wants me to meet someone. A woman named Bloody Mary who runs the city. I'm sure she has our cane and is the one who killed Remi."

"Emile told me about his brother. We spoke at length about him yesterday when he took me for a ride around the city. I like Emile. He's a good man, like Remi." Will nursed his coffee in his hands. "What are you going to do when you meet this Bloody Mary?"

Lexie shook her head. "I have no idea. Titu does, and she'll tell me what happens next."

"You're the one with these new superpowers, Lexie. What do you feel?"

She ran her finger around the rim of her coffee cup. "Like I'm meant to change things. I was sent here to make things better for the people in this city. Bloody Mary has hurt them, and it's my turn to help."

Will eased back in his chair as the sounds of the French Quarter rose around them. "I like it here. I like the people and their slow Southern style. They don't rush everywhere like everyone in Boston. I used to always be in a hurry. But then I got here, and, even though it's only been a few days, I'm starting to wonder what I was rushing for." He rested his arms on the table. "There's still rebuilding going on. Emile knows several contractors in need of a good architect. He said he'd introduce me around. Help me get some clients."

Lexie beamed and fidgeted in her chair, unable to contain her excitement. "What are you saying? Would you consider staying in New Orleans?"

"Well, if you're to be the new high priestess in town, I figure we're going to have to stick around for a while. Besides, what do we have to keep us in Boston? Your mother can always visit. I know mine would love to come here." He held out his cup to her. "What do you say? You game?"

She lifted her coffee cup in a silent toast. "Absolutely."

"And what about this Bloody Mary? Any idea how you're going to deal with her?"

Lexie's excitement ebbed and her stomach twisted into knots. "I haven't got a clue."

"Well, you need to figure it out, fast. What you're taking on is dangerous as hell. Emile told me about this woman, and if it were up to me, I'd get you on the first flight back to Boston." He sighed.

"But it's not up to me. It's up to you." He leaned in closer to her. "This world is like nothing you've ever known, baby. You need to be sure you want this—absolutely sure. Are you?"

Lexie's mind swam with excuses to flee New Orleans. She could live out her life with Will and have happiness, but she would never be content. The Pandora's box she'd opened had changed her, and the things she once wanted would never soothe the unrelenting drum beating in her soul.

"I have no idea where this road will take me, but I have to see it through." She reached for Will's hand. "Last night I realized this isn't about me. It's about my gift, and all the people, dead and alive, I can help."

After breakfast and a hot shower, Lexie waited on the hotel steps for Titu. She'd left Will napping in their hotel room. Sleep had eluded her. Either the leftover energy from the initiation, or Will's desire to stay in New Orleans had wound her up. She doubted if she would ever be able to sleep again.

Her thoughts drifted to Magnus. He'd been absent the entire morning. She did miss his company but also dreaded seeing him again. Her visions had forever changed her opinion of him.

*Can I work with him, knowing everything I do?*

A black Mercedes-Benz sedan pulled in front of Lexie. She stepped to the side, thinking it for someone else—someone important.

A driver in a black suit got out and opened the back door, motioning to Lexie. Bewildered, Lexie got closer to the car. She discovered Titu sitting in the back seat and laughed.

"When meeting the enemy, arrive in style," Titu said with a

flourish of her hand.

Once seated in the car, Lexie inspected Titu's fitted black designer dress and black heels. "I'm underdressed."

"Your slacks are fine." Titu patted her hand. "The simpler, the better with this woman. She won't consider you a threat."

"Am I a threat?"

Titu nodded as the driver took his place behind the wheel. "There's only one way to settle anything between you two. An *haute défi*. It's when two mambos duel for the right to a territory."

Lexie flopped back onto the leather seat. "I've read about it. Have you ever been to an *haute défi?*"

The car eased away from the curb.

Titu shrugged. "No one has. The last *haute défi* in New Orleans took place during Marie Laveau's time."

She hungered for air, and her hands tingled. "Then how will I know what to do? How do I prepare?"

"There's nothing to do, child." Titu patted her hand. "Queen Marie's spirit chooses the winner of the *haute défi*. Bloody Mary knows she doesn't stand a chance against your power, but once challenged she cannot refuse to take part. She would lose face and others would see her as weak. If we challenge her, she must accept."

"How can you be so positive she will lose?"

Titu smiled as the car waited for a green trolley to cross Canal Street. "I have a feeling. But I may be wrong."

Bloody Mary lived in a white double-gallery house on a quiet block in the Garden District. Nothing about the neighborhood of historic homes struck Lexie as sinister. The beautiful Greek Revival home before her wasn't garish and gave no hint of the evil lurking inside. The black wrought iron fence in front, the landscaping of red azaleas and white gardenia bushes, and the steps to the white front door all came across as warm and inviting.

Before stepping out of the car, Titu turned to Lexie. "Let me do the talking. No matter what she says to you, who she threatens, do not say a word. If you respond to her tricks to draw you out, you will be giving her ammunition to use against you." Titu reached for her black handbag. "When will your ghost be arriving?"

"I'm not sure."

"It may be best if he stays away. Bloody Mary may not be able to see him, but I will, and she will take advantage of it. She may not have your ability, but the woman is shrewd. Keep that in mind."

Lexie's stomach churned as they approached the door. Inundated with dread over coming face to face with Bloody Mary, she debated if she was in over her head.

*What am I doing? Why am I challenging a drug dealer to a half-assed duel?*

"Maybe this is a bad idea. We should go."

"Too late." Titu pressed the doorbell.

Lexie gulped back the lump in her throat. She almost bolted when the door creaked open.

A petite woman in her mid-fifties with a round girth and short cut, brassy blonde hair stood before them. Her skin sagged around her jawline, her mouth had deep furrows on either side, and the only appealing feature on her chubby face was her heart-shaped mouth. But it was her essence Lexie found intolerable. Black as coal and giving off an offensive odor akin to rotten eggs, she got the impression the woman hid a litany of sins behind her disapproving frown.

When Lexie saw the dragon cane in her hand, it took everything she had not to leap across the threshold and tear it from her. Then she noticed the dragon's eyes—they burned bright red.

"Hello, Titu." Helen's craggy voice resonated around the front porch. "My spirits told me you were coming."

"Can the theatrics, Helen. You don't have spirits. You have informants."

"Still the same plucky, Titu." Helen's beady brown eyes swept over Lexie. "So you're what everyone's been buzzing about. The *Purs de Coeur*."

Lexie bit her tongue.

Helen held up the cane. "You're admiring my baton juju."

Titu placed her hand on Lexie's forearm. "The rightful owner of the cane has yet to be determined, Helen."

Helen snickered at the remark. "On the contrary, Titu. This cane belongs to the high priestess of the city, not to a non-believer. Passed down from Marie Laveau, it is a sign of her blessing."

"Which you do not have," Titu said.

"I am the chosen." Helena tapped the cane's tip on the floor. "I have the Queen's baton juju, which proves my right."

"The right you claim to have is why we're here," Titu insisted.

"What? Are you bringing her to declare her oath to me?" Helen studied Lexie. "For me to accept her will cost you, Titu."

Lexie summoned the power awakened by her initiation and blocked the black wave Helen sent in an attempt to read her. The darkness lurking in the woman's soul was strong, but for Lexie keeping Helen out of her head was like swatting at an insect. She decided to turn the tables and delved into Helen's soul. The landscape of her inner being came across as a vast cave without any writing or pictures carved into its walls. She had no spirit guide, no ability to see the dead, and didn't possess any psychic gift. Titu had been right. Helen Shaver was a fraud. Only her mastery of spells, and her ruthless intent had kept her in power throughout the years.

"There will be no oaths, Helen. Not today." Titu stared the

woman down. "I have a proposition for you."

"If this is a formal call, you are to address me as Bloody Mary."

Titu obediently dipped her head. "I come to speak about terms, Bloody Mary. My protégé must practice her skill in the city."

Helen pondered the proposal, but eventually nodded and ushered them in the front door. "We'll talk in the den."

The energy from the entrance hall sent a shockwave through Lexie. Packed with bells, small drums, tambourines, animal skulls, jars of dirt and colored liquid, crucifixes, bunches of dried herbs, voodoo dolls, and even a shrunken head, the room throbbed with negativity.

As Lexie moved deeper into the house, the shelves of voodoo relics turned into Zuber wallpaper with depictions of early American scenes. The menacing atmosphere of the home's entrance was temporarily forgotten as Lexie admire ornate plaster moldings, antique crystal chandeliers, and several original oil paintings by well-known artists.

At the entrance to a paneled den, Helen showed Lexie and Titu to a red velvet loveseat. Lexie pegged it as either an eighteenth-century Empire Style original or an expensive knock off. Behind them, placed above a white marble mantel, was a rendering of Bloody Mary in white voodoo attire and holding a human skull.

Strutting to a settee across from their love seat, Helen made a point of thudding her cane on the floor. She took a seat, and after she had set her cane to the side, Helen raised her head to Titu.

"What terms do you wish to discuss?"

Titu situated her purse in her lap while crossing her ankles, reminding Lexie of a Sunday school teacher. "Before we begin, I want you to tell me what happened to my Remi. You owe me that."

The indignant snort the woman gave infuriated Lexie.

"I have no idea what happened to your nephew," Helen

replied, stroking the cane's handle. "After he gave me this, I never heard from him again. You know as well as I Remi ran with a bad crowd. I'm sorry for your loss, Titu, but I had nothing to do with his death."

"He had *les droits des noirs* carved into him. I saw the police photos. You have any idea who would do such a thing to my boy?"

Helen waved a pale hand. "Many in the swamps work such spells. Taking over another is the black art. I try and stay away from the dark side."

"If you ever hear of anything, I would appreciate if you would let me know."

Lexie became distracted by something rubbing against her pant leg. A spindly black cat wrapped its tail around her.

She went to pet the cat, and as soon as Lexie touched the animal's black fur, her visions stirred. A man—older, feeble with hazel eyes and a smattering of gray hair. She got the impression he'd been important, but now he was relegated to sitting around the house all day in the guise of the cat.

"Lester, leave them be," Helen snapped.

The cat ran out of the room, hissing as it went.

"You must forgive Lester. He's an old stray I took in after my husband returned to our home in Nebraska."

Lexie tipped her head to the side, letting her visions come through. "Lester was also your husband's name, wasn't it?"

She sensed Helen's ire at the question but had to challenge her. She couldn't remain silent any longer.

"Lexie!" Titu scolded with a threatening gaze.

"No, let her speak, Titu." Helen's smug grin lifted her features as she sat back on her settee. "Very good, Lexie Arden. I was told you have the gift and a handsome ghost to go with it. Unfortunately, I wasn't made aware of how Remi got the dragon cane until after I read about your home's fire. I wanted to compensate you and your fiancé for your loss. But I'd hoped you would take the money and stay away. You must understand, my cane needed to be returned to the city it was made to protect. You have no idea the power you're dealing with."

"I'm well aware of the cane's power," Lexie said. "But why do the stones in the dragon glow red for you? When Simone Glapion owned the cane, the stones shone pearl. Why do you think that is?"

"The color of the changeling stones is irrelevant," Helen maintained. "The cane is in the hands of a chosen high priestess."

Titu's loud laughter echoed throughout the room. "There hasn't been a chosen mambo in New Orleans for over a hundred and fifty years."

"And what am I?" Helen's cheeks reddened. "I am the chosen mambo."

Titu shook her head. "You were never chosen. Everyone knows that."

Helen stood, reaching for her cane. "How dare you? I am mambo. I have the baton juju of Marie Laveau."

"Which you stole from the one destined to have it." Titu turned to Lexie. "She's the chosen mambo."

"Careful," Helen warned in a gravelly voice. "I've tolerated you and your family because your bloodline goes back to the Voodoo Queen, but if you anger me, I will make sure you pay for your insubordination."

Titu rose from the loveseat. "Lexie is the true mambo. You either step aside and pass the baton juju to her or she will demand an *haute défi*."

Lexie stood up next to Titu, not sure what to say or do. She defiantly kept her head held high, but on the inside, her resolve shriveled up faster than her stomach.

"An *haute défi*? Are you mad, old woman?" Helen screeched. "There hasn't been an *haute défi* since the time of the Queen."

"Exactly the reason I'm calling for it."

Helen pounded her cane on the floor. "I refuse. I am mambo of New Orleans."

Clutching her purse to her body, Titu moved across the oak floors. "Deny us, and I will spread the word you're *poulet* of facing a *Purs de Coeur*."

"I am not chicken! I can defeat your little girl. I have the power on my side."

"But not the spirit." Titu squared her shoulders, reminding Lexie of Simone Glapion. "Settle the difference once and for all. If you're as powerful as you say, let her spirit decide."

Helen glowered at Lexie over Titu's shoulder. "You are aware what will happen to her if she loses."

"What will happen?" Lexie demanded.

"You will cross the bridge to blackness and be nothing. You will suffer an eternity of consciousness without form, function, or the ability to change your stars."

"Only if she loses." Titu kept her gaze fixed on Bloody Mary. "You say you're innocent of my Remi's death. Prove it. Stand before her tomb and swear your fealty to her memory. Let the Queen decide."

"The Queen will choose me. Make no mistake, Titu. I will turn your little pretender into black dust."

"What makes you think you have the ability to eliminate Lexie? The best you ever managed was turning your husband into a cat."

A strained silence compounded the tension in the room. Lexie could almost make out the waves of the hate radiating from Helen's aura.

"Tomorrow night at the tomb," Helen declared. "Let the *haute défi* begin at midnight."

Satisfied, Titu went around the settee. Lexie hurried to catch up to her, anxious to leave the negative energy in the home.

"When I've erased your apprentice from this earth, I will come for you," Helen called after them. "You will follow Lexie Arden across the dark bridge. I promise I will send you there myself."

"You're always so damned theatrical." Titu headed for the entrance, waving her hand. "See you tomorrow night, Bloody Mary."

Once back in their car, Lexie sighed. "Are you sure about this? It's one thing to put my ass on the line, but what about you and Emile? I can't be responsible—"

"Child, you worry too much." She sat back as the car traversed the bumpy Garden District street. "The Queen will accept you. You're her chosen heir."

"An unemployed interior designer from Boston can't be the chosen heir of Marie Laveau."

Titu patted Lexie's knee. "Who you were is of no consequence. It's who you will become that matters."

"What was the spell you mentioned? *Les droits de* something?"

"*Les droits des noirs,*" she corrected. "It is a takeover spell. You can possess a person with it. They will act normal—walk, talk, and be like everyone else—but underneath, the priestess is dictating their movements, their motives. Sort of like a zombie you can remote control. It's a tedious spell, and you have to maintain a strict diet: food of the earth, they call it. Extended periods of intense meditation are needed to stay connected to your subject. Only those skilled in voodoo dare perform it."

"Remi mentioned the same diet to me. But he said it was for health reasons?"

"Did he disappear at sundown? The spell is good from sunup to sundown."

"Yes, he would always leave the manor before sundown and refused to stay in the house with us. We believed he lived in the caretaker's cottage, but the police found no trace of anyone living there."

"Nor would they. After sunset, the one possessed must sleep in the earth and recharge. Remi had to stay somewhere away from the house to avoid being found."

"Titu, if Bloody Mary can work such a spell… I mean how can I confront her? I'm not anyone of—"

"Bloody Mary could never perform *les droits des noirs.* She doesn't have the gift. Someone else hexed my Remi."

A stranglehold of anguish cinched around Lexie's throat. What kind of depraved world had she entered? Everyone she loved, everything she knew was in jeopardy.

"Never you mind about any of that." Titu placed her hand over Lexie's chest, in the same spot from which all her power flowed. "No matter what happens, listen to this. It will guide you, and so shall the Queen."

# Chapter Forty-Three

They arrived back at the hotel to discover firetrucks and police cars blocking the entrance. Lexie reached out with her newfound ability and didn't like the impressions she picked up about Will.

"Something's wrong."

Titu tapped their driver's shoulder. "We will wait here while she goes inside." She opened the door for Lexie. "Go to your room and get Will."

Lexie bounded up the steps to the hotel entrance. In the elevator, she checked her cell phone, but Will had not contacted her. When the silver doors opened on her floor, the stench of smoke forced her back against the wall, and a sickening fear churned in her belly.

Firemen and policemen crowded the hallway. They stopped

her as she approached her room.

"I'm sorry, ma'am," a police officer said several feet from her door. "You're going to have to go back downstairs."

"But my room is up there. I need to—"

"Lexie?" a deep voice called.

Emile emerged from between two firemen and came toward her.

Horrible images of Will hurt or burned took over her mind. Her legs wobbled, and her chest heaved.

"He's all right," Emile said, patting her back. "There was a fire in your room. The fire chief isn't sure how it started. Luckily, something woke Will from his nap and he called 911."

Lexie remembered Magnus. Had he been keeping an eye on Will?

"Where is he?" A trembling fit overtook her.

"I'm here, baby."

Will's arms went around her and pulled her close. He stunk of smoke, but he was alive. When she stood back from him, she glimpsed his soot-stained jeans and wet shirt through her tears.

"All our stuff is soaked with water," he told her while wiping his hand over his grimy face.

"I don't care about any of that."

"I'm glad you weren't here. I wouldn't have held it together so well if I knew you were in danger."

Emile moved them to the side, out of the firemen's way. "That fire was deliberately set," he whispered.

"But how?" Will asked. "I was alone in the room."

Lexie read the dread in Emile's heart. Her soul connected with his and she knew his thoughts. "You think she did it."

He nodded. "Auntie told me what you two were doing this morning. The fire was a warning."

Will crinkled his soot-smudged brow. "A warning from who?"

Emile guided them to the elevator. "You can't stay here. I'm going to take you two back to Titu's. I can protect you there. I can ask for extra patrols from men I trust to watch the house."

"What a minute?" Will shrugged off his hand. "What's going on?"

Lexie calmed him by putting her hand on his chest. "The woman I went to visit today is a powerful high priestess in the city. I told her … Well, Titu told her … I'm challenging her claim to the city."

"And Bloody Mary sent a message to Lexie by threatening you," Emile added.

"Any idea who woke you?" she asked, already guessing the answer.

"Yeah, it was him." Will slipped his arm around her waist. "I dreamt he yelled at me to wake up."

Emile encouraged them down the busy hall. "Let's get you two out of here before anything else happens."

It was after midnight when Lexie and Will settled beneath the thick comforter on a king-sized bed in Titu's upstairs guest room. But the comfort of Will's arms did nothing to ease Lexie's edginess. The events of the day had been stressful, but the reason for her anxiety didn't relate to Bloody Mary or the fire.

She missed Magnus.

Since the day of the fire at Altmover Manor, they'd never spent so much time apart. Lexie considered him obnoxious, conceited, and utterly bombastic, but she longed to see his handsome face. His presence gave her comfort, and without him, her confidence suffered.

"Are you sure he didn't say anything else to you in your dream?"

"For the last time, no." Will sat up on his elbow. "He shouted 'Wake up, Will!' and that's it. No 'How is Lexie?' or 'Give her my best.'"

"Here I am about to go into the most important confrontation of my life and the one person I need by my side I sent away."

"What about me?" Will scowled.

"You know what I mean. How can I explain it? I miss him, but then again I dread seeing him, especially after everything he did."

"Lexie, it's not your place to judge his crimes. He's paying for them. Instead of joining the people he loves, he's here with you, making amends."

"Would you call our being together *making amends*? Sometimes it feels more like I'm on an ocean liner about to slam right into an iceberg."

Will rolled on his back, blowing out a long breath. "Perhaps this is God's way of giving him a chance at redemption."

"Can God forgive someone like Magnus Blackwell?"

He turned to her, running his finger along the outline of her profile. "Magnus carries around an awful lot of demons. Your job is to help him find a way to let those demons go."

"I can't forget what he did."

Will wrapped her in his arms. "Whatever divine providence brought you two together had a plan. If you ask me, you make each other better."

She curled into his broad chest. "I thought you didn't like him."

"He saved me, Lexie. You may believe he's a monster because of what he did, but he cares. He wouldn't have bothered waking me during the fire if he didn't give a damn."

"What if he's not there for me tomorrow night?"

Will nuzzled her cheek. "You don't need Magnus to wrestle with a voodoo priestess. It's your power, not his. And I'll be with you. So, will Emile. He said he doesn't trust this Bloody Mary, especially after the fire. You'll have plenty of back-up tomorrow night. Not to worry."

All the guns in the world wouldn't help her. From everything she'd read, the *haute défi* wasn't so much a contest, but a choosing. The spirit of the former Voodoo Queen had to decide on her proper successor. But why would the renowned Marie Laveau pick her to carry on her work? Inexperienced, still wavering in her belief, and not at all certain she would help anyone, Lexie considered herself the most unlikely candidate.

Despite her misgivings, she had to do whatever possible to save those she cared about. For Titu, Emile, Will, and even Magnus, Lexie had to try her damnedest.

# Chapter Forty-Four

It was a little past daybreak when Titu knocked on their bedroom door. Will and Lexie roused themselves as she came in and crooked her finger at Lexie.

"Time to get you ready, child."

Titu led her to the workshop. Lexie yawned as Titu sat her down at the workbench. A small pile of flower petals, a folded white dress, and a long strip of red linen were on the table next to her altar. Lexie eyed a metal tub filled with water in the corner.

"You must be cleansed according to ritual," Titu explained. "Bathed in salt water and dried with flower petals. Then your hair must be covered. You will wear a turban of red linen and a white cotton dress. You will stand before the Queen in your bare feet. You cannot put on any deodorant or any lotions or jewelry."

Titu guided her to the tub. "Wash every inch of your body

and your hair. Then dry yourself with the flower petals. After you've put on the dress, I will help you with the turban."

"What happens if I lose?" Lexie shook her head. "I know you think I'm the chosen one, but what if you're wrong? What happens to me?"

"The time for questions has passed. You have charted this course, child. You have to see it through." Titu cupped her cheek. "Stay here and prepare for what is to come."

After Titu had left the room, Lexie muttered, "I'd be better prepared for what is to come with some coffee and a fifth of bourbon."

Lexie browsed the shelves with their assortment of mason jars, herb plants, and the occasional crucifix. She considered the world she was about to enter.

She'd seen many bizarre things since arriving at the steps of Altmover Manor, but this world of voodoo, and the city in which it thrived, was beyond comprehension. The shimmer of her engagement ring still atop the altar pulled her from her worry. Lexie picked up the ring and slipped it on.

*Poor Will.* If anyone had suffered for her choices, it was him. Instead of fleeing, he had stuck by her, making her love him more.

She raised her head and sent out a silent prayer for the other man in her life to stick by her side. She asked for tolerance, clarity, but above all, strength.

"I'm not sure how you feel about this voodoo stuff, God, but I need your help. And I could use Magnus's help, too."

The sun had set when Titu opened the plywood door and stood before her.

"It's time, child. You ready?"

Lexie was far from ready. The turban hurt her head, the cotton dress was too sheer for her liking, and she yearned to put on some deodorant. But Lexie guessed Titu wasn't interested in her bellyaching.

"I'm ready," Lexie announced, attempting to sound upbeat.

On the street, Lexie spotted an unmarked police car. She slid into the back seat with Titu. Emile nodded at her through the rearview mirror.

"How you holdin' up?"

The bulge of his gun showed through his brown jacket. "As good as can be expected. Where's Will?"

"He and my men are meeting us at the cemetery. I'm positioning plain-clothed officers around the cemetery in case she tries to send her thugs to scare you off."

Lexie's heart skipped a beat. "Doesn't she have to go through with this thing, so she doesn't lose face in the voodoo community?"

"She's scared off others who have challenged her authority," Titu said. "She won't do it with you. She fears you, but more than anything she fears what the Queen will do if she harms you. You are the chosen one."

A crushing weight settled over Lexie. "Titu, I'm not sure I can do this."

"Nonsense. This is what you're meant for, Lexie. When the sun rises, and Bloody Mary is no more, you'll feel differently." She touched the center of Lexie's chest. "Remember to concentrate from here. This is where your power flows from. No matter what happens or what you encounter, stay true to this."

"I hope you're right, Titu."

No guard greeted them when they arrived at the cemetery, and there were no lines of tourists waiting to take late-night pictures of the dead. The desolate entrance, and the absence of traffic on the street, added a pall of gloom. As if moved by ghostly hands, the black gates swung open. Seconds later, the sound of drums carried over the cemetery walls.

"Bloody Mary and her people must be inside," Emile said as he exited the car.

"About time you guys showed up," Will griped, coming up to them.

Lexie threw her arms around his neck.

Will unfurled her hands. "What's this?" He clasped her hands. "You're shaking."

"I'm scared shitless."

"Everything's gonna be fine, baby. I'm not going to let anything happen to you." He kissed the engagement ring on her finger.

The drums picked up their tempo.

"It's time," Titu said, handing flashlights to Will and Emile. "We must go."

With Will on one side and Titu on the other, Lexie followed Emile into the cemetery.

They maneuvered the shadowy paths through the tightly packed tombs, and something pulled at the center of Lexie's chest. She stopped and scoured the vaulted crypts surrounding her. In the shadows, next to a domed mausoleum, the outline of a familiar figure stepped into the beam from a nearby streetlight. Lexie rushed toward her ghost.

"Where the hell have you been?"

Magnus shined like a bright penny in the sunlight. "Did you think I would miss this, dear girl?"

Her happiness at seeing him recharged her energy and sparked her hope. With Magnus, she was ready to face any challenge.

"I've missed you."

He gave her a brief smile. "I've never left. I stayed invisible until you needed me."

"You're a good man, Magnus Blackwell, even if you are a ghost. I hope you can forgive me for being such an ass. I had no right to judge you."

He raised his hand to her cheek. Lexie swore his slight caress tickled her skin.

"There's nothing to forgive."

Titu gave Magnus a disgruntled snort. "Took you long enough to show up, Mr. Blackwell."

Magnus dipped his head to her, but muttered, "I didn't miss you either, dear lady."

"Are we ready?" Emile asked.

Their party proceeded deeper into the maze of paths making up St. Louis Number One Cemetery. When they arrived at the final resting place of Marie Laveau, several torches had been set out around the mini-mausoleum. Two men, off to the side, sat on the steps of another crypt and banged out a steady beat on their skin-covered drums. A ring of salt circled the tomb and lit white candles flickered at the four corners. White roses lay at the base, along with a crucifix and two white jars. One jar contained water, and the other held a burgundy liquid resembling wine.

Bloody Mary stepped into the center of the torches. In the same flowing white dress and red turban, she came across as more comical than aristocratic. She held the dragon cane; its stones glowing red in the torchlight.

"Titu, are you ready to begin?"

Titu went to the tomb and inspected the preparations. She lifted the jars of water and wine.

"Everything is as it should be."

Bloody Mary's cackle disturbed the peace of the cemetery. "I have no reason to stack the deck in my favor, Titu. The Queen's spirit is with me." Renee Batiste came alongside Bloody Mary. "Renee will act as my second."

Titu acknowledged the woman next to Bloody Mary. "Renee, good to see you again."

"You and your girl will cross the bridge to blackness tonight, Titu." Renee spat the words like venom from a cobra.

"The Queen will send them on their way soon enough." Bloody Mary proceeded to the Voodoo Queen's tomb, bowed, and laid the dragon cane before it.

"I wouldn't count us out yet," Titu said as she turned away.

Titu took Lexie's right hand and led her to the front of the tomb. "You will stand here and concentrate on your power. That's all you have to do. When the Queen's spirit arrives, she will search your heart. Let her in. She will not hurt you."

"What about you?" Lexie asked, her voice trembling.

"I will be right here, child, calling on the spirit. I will not leave your side." Titu patted her cheek. "All will be well. I promise."

# Chapter Forty-Five

Magnus hovered off to the side, tuned into his surroundings. He'd sensed others lurking in the darkness.

He floated among the graves, listening for the slightest noise. A cough filtered from around the side of a family crypt. He rounded a corner and discovered three dark-skinned men. They had guns tucked into their waistbands and puffed on cigarettes.

"How much is she giving us?"

"A thousand a piece. Another five hundred to dump the bodies in the swamp."

"You said we'd get to keep the girl, right?" the tallest of the three men asked.

The short man nodded. "We can play with her until dawn, but then we have to kill her and get rid of her like the rest."

The tall man chuckled. "I've always wanted to fuck a woman in the ass. Tonight, I'll get my chance." The other men laughed, but the conversation turned Magnus's stomach.

The things he'd done to women came back to him. Had he been so cruel? Blinded by his desires, he'd never comprehended how despicable his sexual escapades had been until witnessing them through Lexie's eyes. But she had forgiven him; Magnus had yet to forgive himself.

Magnus hurried back through the tombs and reached Emile at the edge of the torchlight. He kept watch over Lexie as Titu and Renee Batiste had their arms raised to the sky, entreating the spirit to join them.

Into Emile's ear, Magnus whispered, "There are others here. Three men, about fifty feet away. They mean to kill you all."

Emile's placid countenance fell, his jaw flexed, and he peered around the cemetery. He removed a cell phone from his pocket and turned away. Emile called for help as Magnus stayed with him, listening to the conversation.

"About fifty feet away from Marie Laveau's grave. There are three of them."

Magnus frowned when he took a wrong turn on one path and whispered in his ear for him to go back and take another route. Minutes later, Emile arrived at a tomb right next to the three hidden men.

He pulled the gun from his holster and softly spoke into his phone. "Got 'em. Southwest corner. Get me back-up."

Magnus detected a rustle in the air. He left Emile and floated toward the sound. He found a man, gun in hand, and a shiny police badge on his belt.

"This way," he told the man, leading him toward Emile.

Another man jumped out from behind a square family crypt not too far behind him. Magnus relaxed, certain Lexie had the utmost protection.

A nagging twinge cut across his chest. The discomfort meant one thing—something was amiss with Lexie. He rushed to her side, desperate to check on her safety. As he darted in and out of assorted oven-like tombs, the uncomfortable pressure in his chest blossomed into an unfamiliar sensation. Pain.

He found Lexie in front of Marie Laveau's grave. Her head tilted back, she stood next to a terrified Bloody Mary. A white cloud reached like a hand from the base of the tomb and curled around Lexie's feet. Inside the rise and fall of its waves, he spotted spirits—lots of spirits.

"You care for the girl, don't you?"

Magnus spun around and confronted a woman in a red turban, not unlike the one on Lexie. Her dark chocolate eyes and the smile on her lips confounded him. But her alluring aura drew him in like a lighthouse beacon on a stormy night. His pain lifted, and his curiosity replaced his concern.

"Who are you?"

She floated above the ground, her feet covered in the white cloud connected to Marie Laveau's final resting place. "I'm here to give help when needed, Mr. Blackwell."

*A spirit.* But why here? Why now?

*Perhaps she's a diversion sent by Bloody Mary to keep me from Lexie.*

"I don't know who you are, but I'm here for Lexie Arden." He approached the spirit, showing no fear. "I will protect her at all costs."

"I have no wish to harm such a *Purs de Coeur*," she assured him. "Is she worth giving up all you once were to be what you are now? I can free you of her. You can roam the earth and have no bonds to tie you down."

Magnus gave her his best smug grin. "I have no wish to be free of Lexie Arden. I've been more content as a ghost with her than I ever was as a man."

"Then keep her safe, Mr. Blackwell." The ethereal creature examined his figure. "If you're going to be her spirit guide, you should look the part." With a smirk, she faded from view.

Magnus took a step back, stunned by the encounter. He raised his right hand to his face, his skin was perfect again. White, glowing, and without the ugly blackness. His clothes bright and new like in his painting.

And then his cane returned. The dragon cane, the source of his troubles, was firmly in his grasp.

"What does this mean?"

A *bang* reverberated around the cemetery.

The sound of a gunshot made Lexie open her eyes. Encircled by a white mist, faces crowded her—hundreds of people called to her, asking for help. Lexie wanted to run, but her feet, as if fitted with cement shoes, wouldn't move.

"There is no need to be afraid," a soothing voice said.

The mist retreated, and Lexie recognized Titu and Renee Batiste. Behind them, Will and Magnus hurried toward her, but then another spirit came forth. A woman, in front of Marie Laveau's tomb, beckoned to Lexie.

Lexie inched closer. She recognized the woman's stunning features, café au lait skin, and red turban. The rest of her was hard to make out. "You're from the workshop. You were there."

"I've been observing you, Lexie Arden."

Lexie sensed the woman's kind soul and her desire to do good, but there was a touch of ruthlessness intermingled with her essence.

"Who are you?"

"A friend." The spirit faded in and out as the cloud around her rolled and weaved. "I have something for you."

The cane in front of the tomb rose in the air and flew into Lexie's hands. She gripped the handle, and her engagement ring twinkled. She'd forgotten to remove it before the ceremony. Dread like an Amazonian waterfall flooded her heart. She'd broken the rules Titu had given her.

Certain she would turn to ash, Lexie wanted to beg the spirit's forgiveness, but the woman held up her hand, silencing her.

"True love is stronger than the best gris-gris, *mon petit*. It's a prize longed for by many, but given to a certain few. Treasure what you have." Her translucent hand stretched from the white cloud around her and caressed Lexie's cheek. "You have work to do, Lexie Arden. You and your ghost."

The mist enveloped her. It grew fainter until the last remnants snaked back into the bottom of her tomb.

A frigid blast of air startled Lexie out of her daydream. Stunned, she stood before Marie Laveau's grave, holding the dragon cane.

The power of the cane ripped through her arm and traveled throughout her body like a tornado. She felt invincible once more.

Renee Batiste dashed in front of her and dropped to her knees.

"Mistress, I'm yours to command. You have freed me from Bloody Mary's control." She got to her feet and backed away.

She was about to question the woman's sincerity when a high-pitched scream sliced through the air.

Renee took off running.

Lexie turned toward the source of the shrill sound. She grimaced as Bloody Mary convulsed. Her skin darkened until it became a horrendous shade of black, undulating and pulsing as hairs sprouted into a thick, shiny coat. Bloody Mary shrieked as fur covered her hands and arms. Her screeching changed as her mouth and nose elongated into a snout. Whiskers shot out from her cheeks, and her howls morphed into something that didn't sound human.

The warbled wails of a beast bounced between the mini-mausoleums. Then to Lexie's dismay, Bloody Mary shrank like a deflating balloon. She grew smaller and smaller, dropping onto all fours. A loud *whoosh* blew past Lexie, and then the animal's pitiful cries ceased.

Her attention returned to the spot where Bloody Mary had stood. All that remained was one fat black cat.

Another gunshot rang out. The cat dashed away, hissing as it went.

From out of nowhere, Magnus darted toward her. The image of him rushing toward her played out like slow motion in her head. She could make out every detail of his red vest and black coat. He looked different. This Magnus appeared shiny and clean. The blackness clinging to him was gone. His skin, and clothes were as in the portrait. Then she saw it. In his hand, he gripped the dragon cane—her cane. But the eyes were the color of pearls.

*How can that be?*

A man emerged from the crypts behind Magnus. He was short, stocky, and carried a gun. The brute pushed Will aside and ran toward Lexie. Will crashed into the side of a crypt and then fell to the ground.

"Will!"

She wanted to run to him, but then the gunman set his sights on her. All the strength the cane gave her siphoned out of her system as she peered down the barrel of the gun.

"Lexie!" Magnus yelled.

The gun fired. Lexie grimaced, waiting for the painful rip of flesh and bone. But nothing happened. When she opened her eyes,

Magnus hovered in front of her.

More shots rang out. A blur of activity happened around her. Emile jumped out from behind an oval-shaped tomb and shot her attacker. The short man dropped with a *thud* to the path. His groans of agony were all she could hear. The sickening sound made Lexie turn away.

Will tossed his arms around her.

"Are you hurt?"

She held on to him, fighting back tears. "No, I'm all right."

Magnus drifted to the side. The *clink* of metal hitting the cement resonated throughout the tombs.

She faced Magnus. "What happened?"

"Just keeping you safe, dear girl."

Mystified, Lexie picked up a bullet from the ground. "How did you stop this?"

"I couldn't let anything happen to you. We're a team, remember?" Magnus winked at her.

Men brandishing guns rushed in, the shiny silver badges on their belts shimmering in the torchlight.

Emile came up to them, still holding his weapon. "Everyone okay?"

Will put his arm around Lexie. "We're good."

Emile ran his finger over the handle of her dragon cane. "I guess you got what you came for." He left her side and went to the other officers gathering at the scene.

"Lexie?" Will nudged her. "Weren't the stones in the dragon rose-colored when you touched it before?"

"Yes, why?" Lexie examined the dragon's head. The stones had changed to pearl.

"It means the cane is in the right hands." Titu came forward, carrying the black cat in her arms.

Will grimaced at the cat. "Is that ...?"

"Bloody Mary?" Titu nodded as she scratched the cat's neck. "The Queen showed mercy. Instead of casting her across the bridge to blackness, she gave Helen a taste of her own medicine."

"What about her husband?" Lexie asked. "What happens to him?"

"He and his wife can live with me. I need two good mousers." Titu raised her head to Magnus. "The Queen has given you a gift, don't squander it, Mr. Blackwell."

Magnus brushed his hands down his clean clothes and held up his ghost cane. "I will honor her trust in me."

"Did something happen to Magnus?" Will muttered to Lexie.

She patted Will's arm still around her waist. "I'll explain later."

Emile and the other plain-clothed officers gathered around the tomb. "I doubt any of you want to explain why you're here to the uniformed officers on their way, so I suggest you leave—now."

Titu regarded to the dead man on the ground. "What will you tell them?"

Emile holstered his gun. "A voodoo drug deal gone bad will explain the paraphernalia around the tomb and why there were no guards at the gate. It's the story we've all agreed on."

Will's mouth dropped. "Is that legal?"

Emile chuckled, reminding Lexie of his affable brother. "It's New Orleans. We play by a different set of rules down here." He kissed his aunt's cheek. "I'll meet you back at the house later."

With his arms around Titu and Lexie, Will hurried the women from Marie Laveau's tomb toward the path leading to the front gate.

Once outside the walls surrounding the cemetery, Will took them to a waiting blue Lexus.

"Whose car is this?" Lexie asked.

"Mine," Titu said while stroking the cat in her arms. "I told Emile to give the keys to Will just in case."

"But you didn't know how things would turn out, did you?"

Titu winked at her. "Now get in the car before the police arrive."

About to climb into the car, Lexie spotted Magnus standing by the cemetery wall. His long black coat, black boots, and dragon cane bathed in an unearthly glow.

"You've got your cane back."

He tapped the dragon handle. "Our cane. You possess the real one, and I have this. One power divided between the spirit world and your world."

"What does it mean?"

Magnus smiled. "It means I've finally replaced what I once took away."

"What did you take away?"

"I was referring to Simone Glapion. I have given the city back its true mambo." He fondled the ghost cane in his hand. "Do you feel any different?"

"Yeah, I do." She breathed in the cool night air and appreciated the life flowing in her veins. Her connection with Magnus was also there, rustling deep inside her like a fledgling in the nest. "For the first time in my life, I'm awake."

"I understand. When you arrived at Altmover Manor, it was like being roused from a long sleep."

"Do you miss your home?"

"Not in the least." He haughtily tapped his cane on the sidewalk. "This city appeals to me. Maybe because I sensed I would end up here one day, even if it is as a ghost."

"I want to thank you. Without your encouragement, I would never have come here, and never have found my true gift."

"It was meant to be, dear girl."

What would the future bring for her and her ghost? Somehow, she wasn't worried anymore.

"We should get back to the house."

"I will be there when you arrive." Magnus bowed and faded away.

Will gunned the engine, and the car sped from the curb. They had driven down a side street at the same time flashing red lights arrived at the cemetery entrance.

Finally able to relish her prize, Lexie ran her fingertips lovingly over the cane. The baton juju hummed in her hands. The glorious energy she'd first experienced at Altmover Manor zipped through her. Empowered, she speculated about how everything would change.

"What a night," Will said. "I'm not sure I'll ever wrap my head around what I've seen."

"You'll witness a lot more," Titu confided from the back seat. "You're going to be the husband of a mambo. Your life is about to become extraordinary."

Will reached for Lexie's hand. He kissed the engagement ring on her finger. "Extraordinary, huh?" He flourished a boyish grin. "I can't wait."

# Epilogue

A handyman climbed the ladder leaning against Lexie's Creole townhouse on Royal Street and positioned a business sign under the balcony.

"A little more to the left," she called from the sidewalk.

Lexie held up her hand to block out the morning sun as the handyman secured the red sign with a chain. When the sunlight caught the platinum wedding set on her left hand, Lexie wiggled her fingers.

"How's that, Mrs. Bennett?"

Lexie checked the position of the sign. "Perfect, Ralph."

With a surge of pride, Lexie took in the other shops around her.

"Looks great," Will said, coming out the french doors.

Switching the dragon cane to her left hand, Lexie straightened out the crooked knot in his yellow tie. "It's not too much?"

"Baby, how can a voodoo shop called Mambo Manor be too much?" He kissed her cheek. "I've got to go. I'm meeting new clients at the office in half an hour."

"Third set of new clients this week. Sounds like business is booming."

"I guess word is getting out about Bennett Architecture." He patted the red turban on her head. "I hope you're not getting used to this thing."

"It's for the tourists."

He raised his head to the balcony above. "Are you sure you want to live above your shop? We could get some place in the Warehouse District."

"I like the Quarter. Later on, when we need more room, we can move."

"Whatever you say, Mambo." He winked. "I'll be back at six so don't burn down the house while I'm gone."

"Cute," she mumbled.

"I wish someone would explain to me how you can have these powers, but you still can't scramble eggs."

She pushed him away. "Go to work."

Will set off at a brisk pace, heading toward Canal Street.

Magnus materialized on the sidewalk next to her. His ghost cane in his hand. "You should take Renee up on those free cooking classes."

"She's been kissing my ass for weeks. Since the *haute défi,* Renee keeps swearing she wants to make amends for working with Bloody Mary. All the spells she conjured on Bloody Mary's behalf against me and others will keep her indebted to me for years."

"You should pay her back for what she did to Remi. An eye for an eye."

"What you would do as mambo, Magnus?"

After shoving the ladder into the back of his truck, Ralph waved at Lexie. "Give me a call, Mrs. Bennett, if you want to move the sign."

"I will, Ralph. Thank you."

As the truck drove away, Magnus turned to her. "I wouldn't have let Renee Batiste continue to practice voodoo in this city. She'll turn on you one day."

"She might." Lexie tapped her dragon cane on the sidewalk. "But I have this and the power. If Renee opposes me, she'll have a fight on her hands."

A young woman in a yellow dress jogged across the street toward Lexie. When she stopped before her, she respectfully bowed her head.

"Mambo, can you help me?"

Lexie inspected her bloodshot eyes and puffy face. She felt her distress and directed the woman inside her shop. On the way to the open doors, Lexie gave Magnus an encouraging glance.

A grin lit up his face, and his green eyes danced with mischief. "And so our work begins."

After Lexie and Magnus stepped into the shop, the french doors magically closed behind them. From out of nowhere, a large gray Maine Coon cat trotted up to the building. It took up a position in front of the doors like a lion guarding its territory. The animal's sharp green eyes peered out into the street, keeping watch.

Sounds of the French Quarter coming to life rose around the cat. A gentle breeze tossed the creature's scruffy mane while it tipped the sign above Lexie's shop.

The wind picked up, and as it rolled across sidewalks, carrying away hats and bits of paper, a newfound optimism stirred in the city. Many had no idea where the excited energy had come from, but those sensitive to such occurrences understood what the change meant—the reign of the chosen mambo had begun.

# About the Authors

**Alexandrea Weis** is an award-winning author of twenty novels, a screenwriter, ICU Nurse, and historian who was born and raised in the French Quarter of New Orleans. Having grown up in the motion picture industry as the daughter of a director, she learned to tell stories from a different perspective and began writing at the age of eight. Infusing the rich tapestry of her hometown into her novels, she believes that creating vivid characters makes a story moving and memorable.

A permitted/certified wildlife rehabber with the Louisiana Wildlife and Fisheries, Weis rescues orphaned and injured animals. She resides with her husband and pets in New Orleans. Weis writes paranormal, suspense, thrillers, horror, crime fiction, and romance.

**www.AlexandreaWeis.com**

**Lucas Astor** is from New York, has resided in Central America and the Middle East, and traveled through Europe. He lives a very private, virtually reclusive lifestyle, preferring to spend time with a close-knit group of friends than be in the spotlight.

He is an author and poet with a penchant for telling stories that delve into the dark side of the human psyche. He likes to explore the evil that exists, not just in the world, but right next door behind a smiling face.

Archery, photography, wine making, listening to jazz, blues, and classical music, and helping endangered species are some of his interests.

**www.LucasAstor.com**

"A dark story of passion, revenge, and a Faustian pact ...
a guilty-pleasure read that kept me captivated." ~ New Orleans Magazine
WINNER
FINALIST
FINALIST
INDIES WINNER
HELL HAS A NEW MASTER
BLACKWELL
A MAGNUS BLACKWELL NOVEL: PREQUEL
Alexandrea Weis With Lucas Astor

# BLACKWELL

A MAGNUS BLACKWELL NOVEL: PREQUEL

## HELL HAS A NEW MASTER

In the late 1800s, handsome, wealthy New Englander, Magnus Blackwell, is the envy of all. When Magnus meets Jacob O'Conner–a Harvard student from the working class–an unlikely friendship is forged. But their close bond is soon challenged by a captivating woman; a woman Magnus wants, but Jacob gets.

Devastated, Magnus seeks solace in a trip to New Orleans. After a chance meeting with Oscar Wilde, he becomes immersed in a world of depravity and brutality, inevitably becoming the inspiration for Dorian Gray. Armed with the forbidden magic of voodoo, he sets his sights on winning back the woman Jacob stole from him.

Amid the trappings of Victorian society, two men, bent on revenge, will lay the foundation for a curse that will forever alter their destinies.

YOU CAN'T ESCAPE THE DARKNESS
BOUND
A MAGNUS BLACKWELL NOVEL: BOOK TWO
Alexandrea Weis With Lucas Astor

# BOUND

## A MAGNUS BLACKWELL NOVEL: BOOK II

## YOU CAN'T ESCAPE THE DARKNESS

***Magnus Blackwell's past is about to catch up with him.***

An evil force has seized New Orleans. Pestilence, suffering, and darkness cloak the city. The citizens are scared and need their mambo to guide them, but Lexie Arden can't help anyone. A diabolical presence has taken Lexie's power and severed her ties with the other side.

Magnus Blackwell is fighting demons of his own. Torn between his devotion to Lexie and a spirit from his past, Magnus's loyalty is put to the test. He must revisit his sins to uncover the key to the hatred ripping the city apart.
If he doesn't, Lexie's reign as mambo will end.

Their search for answers leads them deep into the darker realms of voodoo—until a desperate Lexie does the unthinkable, and Magnus can do nothing to spare her from her fate.

AND THE DEAD SHALL RISE
SEIZE
A MAGNUS BLACKWELL NOVEL: BOOK THREE
Alexandrea Weis With Lucas Astor

# SEIZE

A MAGNUS BLACKWELL NOVEL: BOOK III

## AND THE DEAD SHALL RISE

Lexie Arden has a loving husband, a thriving business, and consults with the New Orleans Police Dept on murder cases. Kalfu has given her everything she desires, but challengers to her authority are closing in.

Her dark secret remains hidden from everyone except Magnus. He sees the evil growing stronger, changing her, and hurting her marriage. If Lexie doesn't rid herself of Kalfu's influence soon, the consequences will be irreversible.

When she unexpectedly inherits a cottage in the swamp, she uncovers a library of rare books on voodoo. Their spells can reverse the dark lord's hold and set right the balance between darkness and light. But such magic requires a great sacrifice; one Lexie isn't willing to make.

With the shadow spirits and raging voodoo gods vying for her attention, Lexie is on the verge of losing everything—her husband, her power, Magnus, and possibly, her life.

***The battle for control of the mambo's soul is about to begin.***